The M

D0864706

Gerrard Cowan hails from Derry, in the North West of Ireland. His first known work was a collection of poems on monsters, written for Halloween when he was eight; it is sadly lost to civilisation. He lives in South East London with his wife Sarah, son Finn and daughter Evie. He can be found at gerrardcowan.com, on Twitter @GerrardCowan and at facebook.com/gerrardcowanauthor.

The Machinery

GERRARD COWAN

The Machinery Trilogy

HARPER
Voyager

Harper*Voyager*
An imprint of HarperCollins*Publishers* Ltd
1 London Bridge Street
London SE1 9GF

www.harpervoyagerbooks.co.uk

This Paperback Original 2016

First published in Great Britain in ebook format by Harper*Voyager* 2015

A catalogue record for this book
is available from the British Library

ISBN: 978-0-00-812074-0

Set in Sabon by Born Group using Atomik ePublisher from Easypress

For Sarah, Finn and Evie

Chapter One

I am breaking, the Machinery said.

Alexander had not heard it for days.

I am breaking.

It sounded different tonight: like a child.

'Again,' said Amile. The tutor's voice seemed distant, as if it came from another room. 'Recite it again.'

Alexander looked to the window. His sister was below, playing with marbles in the courtyard. *I'll try to speak to father again tonight.* He knew he would be called a liar. But there was no other choice; he had to make them understand.

The boy turned to face Amile, and started over again.

'On the third day, the tribe gathered on the Primary Hill, to be entertained by the madman.

'"This is when all shall change," the madman said. But the people did not believe him, and laughed in their ignorance.

'"You will be punished," said one.

'"Punished by the Gods," said another.'

I am breaking.

Alexander paused, and looked to the ceiling. There was nothing there.

Ruin will come with the One. You know who it is.

'*Continue.*' Amile's hooked nose twitched. 'And *mean* it; as things stand, you are lying to us both.'

Alexander looked once more to the window. *Clack, clack, clack,* went the marbles.

'The prophet Arandel lifted a stone. He held it before his people and said: "This is matter; it too has energy. It too is understood by the Machinery, which knows the birds in the sky and the fish in the sea, the rocks at the core and the reptiles of the South. These words have been spoken by the Operator."

'The people laughed again. "If he told you all this, Arandel – where is he?" Arandel dropped the stone and looked to the sky.

'"He is here."'

Amile was smiling.

'In the centre of the ground, at the peak of the hill, ten paces from where they sat, a fire had started to burn, as if of its own accord.

'"Arandel, what have you done?"

'"What witchcraft is this?" But their talking ceased, for they had seen something in the fire. A man stepped forth from the blaze, his cloak burning with flames of its own, dark and cold. The people wept, for they saw in this cloak the reflections of their own souls.

'"He has come from the ground itself," said Arandel. "From the ground and into flame, to the salvation of us all."

'This man came amid them and, as the tribe fell back and cowered before him, opened his arms. "It is your first Selection year," he said. "You have been chosen. Nothing will be the same for you now."

'He walked among them.

'"I have come from the Underland. I have come to save the Plateau."'

Amile clapped his hands. 'In seven years, Paprissi, that is the best that you have read.'

Alexander bowed.

'What happened next?'

The boy cleared his throat.

'And so the tribe received the Machinery, the power of the Underland. It would choose the greatest leaders of the Overland, its Tacticians and Strategists, from now until the end of time, be they bakers or butchers, merchants or artists, boys or girls, men or women. And thus, the Overland would grow under their wisdom, to become the envy of all the great Plateau.

'In return for this gift, the Operator asked only one thing; that the people must never question the Selections of the Machinery.'

'And long may it continue,' said Amile. 'The Machinery knows.'

'The Machinery knows,' said Alexander. *And I know the Machinery.*

Before Alexander was a red velvet curtain, fastened by a golden knot. The boy stood still for a moment, wondering if he had been noticed.

'Come.'

Sucking in a breath, Alexander pushed through.

The study was an airy, spherical, stone-walled space, its ceiling formed of thick clear glass that could be winched open at points to allow the entry of cooling airs. It was night, now; starlight illumined everything. This room, unlike its counterparts in other parts of the dreary mansion, was in constant flux. Perhaps it reflected the mind and travels of Jaco Paprissi, Alexander's father, the head of the Paprissi Financial House and lord of the manor.

Jaco and his men were the only Overlanders allowed to sail from the Plateau, and he had just returned from his most recent voyage. Items were still being unpacked from the wooden chests that filled the great courtyard, the most interesting or curious gravitating upwards to this study where they could be examined more closely. Alexander drank it in: on the second shelf to his left, a wooden statue depicted a man and a woman locked in primitive combat; above this, a row of silver instruments, like finely wrought blades; and on the floor to his right, a bronze representation of some kind of war machine, what appeared to be a trebuchet lined with cannon, rolling forward of its own accord.

In the centre of the room was a brass contraption, a long thick tube covered in golden letters in some foreign tongue. At the bottom of the tube was an eyepiece, into which Jaco peered.

'This is new,' the older man said. 'It is … incredible. You can see things … well, it matters not.'

He turned to the boy and grinned.

'It's much better than banks and credit, eh?'

Jaco left his new toy and walked to his son, putting a hand on his shoulder and smiling down at him.

It is coming. The voice had grown weaker.

'How was the lesson, Alexander?'

I'll tell him, thought the boy. *I'll tell him.* But he was afraid. *Why should he believe me this time?*

'It was all right, but Amile made me do—'

'The same thing all over again?'

'Yes!'

'The arrival of the Operator and the Gifting of the Machinery?'

'*Yes!*'

Jaco laughed. 'I hated it too, when I was your age. I wondered why I had to learn this stuff, when there was a whole world out there waiting to be found. But as I grew older, I began to see things differently.'

'How?'

'Well, things change. Your life goes off in different paths. And the Overland changes, too. Even the Plateau changes. The city grows, Tacticians and Strategists come and go. But one thing remains the same: the Machinery. It is the constant. It is important that we remember its birth.'

'The Machinery knows.'

'The Machinery knows,' his father echoed, before leaping to his feet and returning to his lettered tube. Alexander hesitated before taking the plunge.

'Father … I think I have heard it again.'

Jaco stopped dead, his hands falling to his side.

'No, boy. You have not.'

Silence fell on the study.

'It told me again, father. The Machinery told me who it is. I know who will bring Ruin.'

'No.' Jaco turned his eyes upon his son. 'No. This is the madness of old women and Doubters.' He held the boy's gaze for a moment, then turned back to his machine. 'I assume you are going to play in the Great Hall tonight?'

'Yes, father.'

'Good. Take your mind off this foolishness. And don't stay up too long; it is already late.'

The elder Paprissi leaned down and put his eye to the telescope.

'Yes, father.'

The Great Hall covered the entire southern section of the ground floor of Paprissi House. It was one of the oldest surviving parts of the building, its stone walls the remnants of an ancient keep: a place of faded nooks and crannies, dark snugs and cubbyholes. The summer light was fading as Alexander entered, casting shadows that darkened the aspects of the Paprissi forebears staring blankly down at their young descendant.

Alexander sat with his legs crossed in the middle of the cold stone floor, just next to the dining table, swinging a thin piece of white parchment through the air in a kind of sporadic dance. This strange, private little ceremony helped unleash his imagination. He was transported to other realms: to flaming battles on open plains; to dynastic struggles with Doubter kings; to the ruins of ancient cities, heavy with sorcery. Here, he could control events. Here, he did not feel like a plaything of a voice.

The One will come here …

The boy's gaze floated to the Operator shrine, at the back of the hall. It had been there for as long as the hall itself, a grey statue on a black chair, proud and solemn. The sculptors of the Middle Period were renowned for the subtlety of their work, Amile had told Alexander; hence the fine detail of the wrinkled face, the perfect smoothness of the bald head, the laughing wisdom of the eyes. The cloak, though, was the symbol of the Operator; it had been refreshed in more recent years by one of the new artists of the Centre, and the talent of this master shone through, from the strange swirls of purple and black to the hints of faces in the ether.

GET OUT.

Alexander swung round. The voice seemed closer now, more urgent, as if the speaker was behind him. There was no one there. *I can do nothing.*

He turned back to the statue.

There was someone in its place.

'Play, play, playing, like the little child you are.'

6

He – *it* – regarded Alexander thoughtfully, steadily rapping the arm of his dark throne with his sharp fingers. He was filth itself: his mangy skin red with scabs, his grey tongue flickering at the sides of his mouth. A torn gown billowed out onto the floor around him, coating the flagstones like oil on water, its colours in perpetual motion like the sky in a summer thunderstorm. The faces were ghosts in a silken prison.

'Do you know who I am, Alexander?'

The boy was silent.

'I am the Operator.'

The voice echoed of another world. *A time before the Machinery.*

'I have known it for a long time,' the Operator said. 'You here, on your Plateau, you have known only ten millennia of it. But it has been my companion for much, much longer.'

Alexander steeled himself. Somehow, he always had known that this would happen.

'How did you do that? How did you make a statue come to life?'

The Operator seemed surprised by the question. 'I am a child of the Underland, boy. I know all its pathways and byways.'

He leaned forward in his throne, placing his head in his hands.

'You have evaded me for some time, Alexander. I heard the Machinery speaking, you know. Oh yes. I could hear it, in the night, though its words were hidden from me. It took me a long time to find you, such a long time.'

'It does not trust you. It knows you do not believe it.'

The Operator laughed, and the room seemed to darken. 'I like you, Alexander. I like that you think you can talk to me, in such a way, about my own creation.'

'You do not understand it fully, Operator. If you did, you would believe the words. Ruin is coming.'

The Operator slammed his fist on the arm of his chair. 'Tell me what it has told you. Then we will see what I believe.'

Alexander approached the Operator. 'Your enemy has returned, Operator. You thought you had destroyed the One, all those years ago. But you failed. The One has returned, and the One will bring Ruin.'

The Operator was on his feet in an instant, and loomed over Alexander. The faces in his cloak cringed, afraid of their master.

'That is a lie,' the Operator said, his voice trembling. 'You have read a book about the past, I think, one that I overlooked. I have been too lenient with you all. You use these words you do not understand. The One is dead, and the Prophecy is a lie.'

The boy did not answer. He looked hopefully at the door, but no one was coming for him. Was his grandmother outside, sitting in her old chair?

There was a pattering of rain on the windows.

'That is not what the Machinery told you,' the Operator sighed. 'It cannot be. Something is wrong with it, and it has told you, and you will not tell me.'

'I have already told you the truth.'

The Operator shook his head. 'No. No, that is not what it told you. But I will find the truth.' He glided over to Alexander's side and wrapped a long arm around the boy's shoulder.

'We will go to the Underland. You will be happier there. Yes, oh yes. We will be able to study your broken brain.' Alexander snatched a quick look at a jagged smile; he willed himself to resist, but something had encircled and taken power over him, and he could do nothing but follow the strange creature to the window.

The Operator gathered him in his arms, smiled, and leapt into the rain of the night. They seemed to fall slowly, like feathers in the breeze. The authority that had been exerted over the boy allowed no room for fear. There was no need to scream, it assured him, no need to cry out or fight back. *We are floating, not falling.*

As he fell, he looked up and saw a face at the window: a girl gazing down at him; a girl with round black eyes and long black hair; a girl with marbles in her hands.

But then Alexander Paprissi was gone forever: gone below the earth.

Chapter Two

'Could I take part today, Tactician? I believe I am ready.'

'Why do you think you are ready?'

'I have served my time. I have trained now for almost fifteen years.'

'Almost fifteen years, indeed. And you think you are ready. Ready for what?'

'For whatever you need me to do, Tactician. I could go in there now, if you like, and—'

'You are always overreaching, Katrina. You must develop caution.'

Katrina Paprissi nodded. She had heard this a thousand times before. As ever, she smiled at the Tactician, before brushing some sand from her feet.

They were alone on the shore. Behind them loomed the great edifice of Northern Blown, the once dominant fortress that had stood apart from the Overland for longer than any other power. It had managed this through a mix of skilful diplomacy, deference, solid defences and the fact that its desolate lands were the least attractive in the entire Plateau. But now, its day was coming to a close. The castle seemed downcast in the bleached light of the dawn, as if aware that soon, perhaps this very day, its time would end. Even its curtain wall seemed to sag, as if willing itself to collapse before the onslaught of modernity.

'Are you even listening to me, Paprissi? No, I imagine you are off in your world. What's it like there?'

Katrina forced herself to meet Tactician Brightling's gaze. She still found it difficult to look directly at those grey eyes. Brightling was the Watching Tactician of the Overland, her authority reflected in her golden gown and the silver half-moon crown that sat so easily upon her head. She was in her middle years, but her thin frame was hard with muscle. White hair flowed around her like a mane, unruffled even by the wind that whistled in from the sea.

Brightling was a woman of the new era, the progress of which she was hastening through her work. A pair of semicircular spectacles sat on her nose, the frame wrought from ivory. From the Tactician's mouth hung a pipe, an elegant, curling affair of cedar wood. She wore a handcannon on her side, the hilt a twisted swirl of stars, the barrel inlaid with diamonds.

'Katrina, by the Machinery, will you take your turn!'

The wind picked up, then: it tore through Katrina's long black hair and laughed at her white rags, wearing her legs raw.

'Now,' the Tactician said, a new hardness in her voice.

Katrina looked at the board with bleary eyes. She hated Progress. This game was designed for people just like Tactician Brightling: cold souls with no stirring of action. Indeed, Brightling had actually *designed* its latest iteration. The woman had sat on the Progress Council for longer than she had been a Tactician.

They said the Operator himself had invented the First Iteration of Progress. Katrina wondered if that game had borne any resemblance to this version, the Nine Hundredth and Seventy-Fourth Iteration, which had been active for two years. She was just getting used to this one, which usually meant a new Iteration was imminent.

'Tactician, do we really have to play this? Does it not seem strange to you? We're about to conquer the Plateau, and we're sitting here playing a stupid board of Progress.'

Brightling did not respond, but fixed Katrina with a stare. The young woman turned her attention to the board, her courage evaporating into the wind.

Katrina had the East and the South of the board, Brightling the North and the West. Her tiles were white, the Tactician's black. She could see that she was in an impossible position. Over half of Brightling's forces were poised to take the South, and Katrina had just one Watching tile remaining. *How does this thing work again? A Watching tile destroys an Expansion tile, but only if there are no Operator cards left in the opponent's hand. Does Brightling have a card?*

'You should take care what you do with that. I can see a move that would open your options and expose one of my flanks. Remember, I have only two Watching tiles left, while you retain two cards. You are still in this game. *Do not overreach.*'

Katrina studied the board again.

'This game is impossible.'

'This game always evolves, but it is not impossible. Everything evolves, everything changes. We must adapt to that.'

'Except the Machinery.'

'Except the Machinery.'

Katrina looked up to see that Brightling was smiling at her, white hair now blowing in the wind. The last of the Paprissis lifted her Watching tile, and prepared to put it in place.

'Madam.'

Aranfal had appeared from nowhere, as he always did. He had the appearance of some creature of this icy habitat, with his aquamarine cloak and dirty blond hair: a beast that had crawled onto the beach. Amusement played across his thin face, his blue eyes alight with a joke that no one else was ever told.

'Aranfal, welcome. What news?'

'Good news, Madam Tactician.' Aranfal's voice was smooth and deep, his accent hinting at the far North, where they now sat. 'King Seablast has agreed to grant you an audience.'

'Good!' Tactician Brightling clapped her hands. 'How did he seem?'

'Oh, obstreperous, my lady. Most incorrigible. But that could be a good sign. It might be a show.'

'Yes, Aranfal. It might be. How many Watchers in the building?'

'Two, madam, apart from me.'

'And you will join them now?'

'Yes.'

'Where?'

'In the ceiling, madam.'

'Good.'

Aranfal smiled at his superior and bowed. He cast an uneasy glance in Katrina's direction. They had never got on. She suspected he envied her closeness to the Tactician. He seemed on the verge of speaking to her, before something on the ground distracted him.

'What's this?' He lifted a yellow and black object, around a foot in length.

'I think it's a bone,' Katrina whispered.

'Be quiet, Katrina.'

'It is, Tactician. It is an arm bone. There are more, further along the shore.'

'Ridiculous. It is a rock, perhaps. A formation of some kind.'

Aranfal chuckled. 'The northerners call this the Bony Shore, madam. Perhaps it is aptly named?'

'Nonsense. Where would they come from?'

'I don't know. Perhaps they drift here from a darker place. A terrible place, where people are thrown to the sea ...'

Brightling tutted. 'You do not know, Aranfal. Do not talk about this.'

She waved Aranfal away, and turned back to Katrina.

'Your mind is full of nonsense. If your father could see you, plucking rocks from the beach and calling them bones, he would be horrified.' She sighed, gathering her composure. 'We will go in.' She pointed to the fortress. 'You are about to witness history, my girl.'

Katrina sucked in a breath. 'I can come in this time?'

'Yes, yes. But you will *not* do anything, Katrina, do you understand? You are there to observe me, and Aranfal.'

'Yes, madam.'

Brightling turned to leave.

'Madam, the game.'

The Tactician waved at the table.

'It's just a stupid board of Progress.'

'There – that is it, then: the last holdout on the Plateau. Prepare the cannon, men! Prepare the cannon!'

General Charls Brandione reluctantly turned to face his assistant. Farringer was a cringing, scraping man of at least sixty who stared at the enemy position through his weasel eyes and scratched his arse with the hilt of his stumpy sword. He had an unaccountable love of fashion and had come to the field in full, ancient plate armour – heavy, inflexible, and useless in modern warfare. To make matters worse, he had festooned it with ribbons and feathers. The decorations ranged across the full gamut of gaudiness, from the orange of a sunburst to the pinks and greens of some southern bird.

Brandione's armour was less striking, but better placed, allowing for manoeuvrability: a battered steel breastplate, a plate for his back, and a standard steel helmet, worn and rusted through years of use but solid and dependable.

'Farringer, bring me a map of the city.'

The older man hesitated.

'But General, I want to see—'

'Now, Farringer – do it now.'

Prepare the cannon. Brandione smiled at that as he turned back to the great wall of Northern Blown. All around him, men struggled with the new artillery pieces, cursing as they hoisted them awkwardly into position. Soldiers traipsed to the supply lines to collect barrels of precious gunpowder, recently arrived from the West, which they gingerly rolled back to their iron dragons.

It was the smell that got to Brandione, more than anything else: that acrid stench.

But they were powerful, oh yes. Brandione had seen them in action since their first development. Rapid advances over the last two decades meant the largest could fire stones weighing hundreds of pounds, though the damned things seemed to kill more of his own troops than the enemy, when he ever got to use them.

He tapped the weapon at his side. This sort of cannon, he could live with: one that fitted in his hand.

When he looked to the fortress before him, some faith in the old ways returned. The new weapons were powerful, true, when pointed in the right direction and not falling victim to one of their many flaws. But Northern Blown was old, and hardened through constant war. Standing in resplendent isolation, with the Northern Peripheral Sea behind it, it looked like it had been torn from the Plateau itself, a living creature of alleyways and moss-covered towers that had forced its way into the continent. And all around it stood that jagged iron wall, thirty feet thick at its weakest point.

Between Brandione and this armoured metropolis were spread the more conventional forces of the Overland, still active today despite all the changes in the world, a metallic mass of thousands of serrated pikes and halberds that shimmered in the early afternoon light. Dotted among them were the siege machines of old: trebuchets, catapults and battering rams, all standing at the foot of the city. In a way, these reassured him more than the exploding iron pipes.

Is this really the end? Brandione had served the Overland for almost fifteen years, ever since he had left the College and turned his back on a career as an Administrator. He had seen towns razed to the ground and ploughed through corpses. He had struck down rebellion in the West. He had seen cities fall, here in the North. *Is all of that really over, now? Or will we find a new enemy, one worse than all the others?*

He shook himself; there was no time for this, not any more. He eyed the walls for signs of the enemy. *Still nothing.* He shifted on his feet.

'*Surrender?*' King Seablast was red in the face. 'Tactician, know that Overland waves have broken against my wall in the past. Yours will be no different; we will cast you into the Peripheral Sea.'

Seablast is a warrior, thought Katrina. *Even here, in his throne room, with our forces all around, he is prepared to fight.* He was a thickset man, stout without being fat, his belly like a cannonball. He wore a wooden breastplate below a chainmail mesh, his helmet at his feet and his sword at his side. He was standing over Brightling, who sat in a high-backed, silver chair. The King leaned in close, his black beard almost touching her forehead and his bright-blue eyes blazing into her own.

Katrina stood some way behind the Tactician, her attention flickering between the scene before her and the furnishings and trappings of the throne room. Light spilled through four huge, stained-glass windows, bathing everything in a hazy purple and orange glow. At the far end of the hall, beneath a window on which was engraved a flaming sword, sat the throne itself, a large but unadorned iron chair that spoke of older times.

A slight cough from Brightling was enough to refocus Katrina's attention. The Tactician was unruffled, smiling serenely at the King. She had been disarmed of her handcannon and sword upon entering the castle, but seemed utterly at ease.

'You come here,' Seablast continued, beginning to pace his throne room, 'with a handful of troops and fire spouters, and you make the most outrageous demands of me. I know where this comes from. It is that toy of yours, that *machine*; it makes politicians of you all. But our walls will stand against politicians and toys.'

The King's retinue laughed. As Brightling lazily regarded the monarch over the rim of her spectacles, her smile grew thinner.

'What year is this, madam?' asked the King, cocking his head to the side.

'I do not know what the date is in the heathen calendar, but by our reckoning it is the 10,000th year.'

The King whistled between his teeth. 'A bad time for you then, no?'

Brightling was very still as the King spoke.

17

'Did you know, men, that according to the bullshit beliefs these people follow, on the 10,000th year since the Gifting of the Machinery, it will all far apart? It will break!'

The men laughed.

'That is an evil Prophecy,' said Brightling, so quietly that Katrina struggled to hear her.

The King shrugged. 'That may be so, but I know that many of your people believe it.' He turned back to his men, a glint in his eye. 'You won't find that Prophecy in their Book of the Machinery, lads. No one knows where it comes from, they say. It's an old wives' tale. But enough of these bastards believe it. Enough of them think that something really *bad* will happen. Well, I suppose we'll just have to wait and see.' He spat on the ground, inches from Brightling's feet. 'I have sent word to our vassals,' he said, leaning over the Tactician's chair again. 'They will be here within the day. I suggest you and your friends return to your machine, before it dies.'

Tactician Brightling nodded slowly, appearing to think this over. Then she was on her feet, the King and his guards taking an involuntary step backwards.

'Your vassals?'

'Yes!' The King was nervous now; Katrina could feel it. His anger was exaggerated, his confidence feigned. 'The Second City; Anflef; Siren Down. These three and others will come at my command.'

The Tactician cocked her head to the side and smiled again.

'Do you read books, your Majesty?' she asked, her face a picture of wide-eyed innocence.

The King hesitated. 'My kingdom, madam, contains the greatest scholars on all the Plateau.'

'You should know, then, your Majesty, that I have allies of my own.'

There was a flurry of black as three robed figures fell from somewhere in the ceiling to the stone floor. The King's guards leapt into belated action, swinging their swords wildly. They halted as quickly as they had begun when they saw that, in the arms of each of the masked strangers, was one of Seablast's daughters.

The King became very still.

'No doubt you have steeled yourself for such a scenario, King,' the Tactician said. She returned to her seat, patting away the creases in her gown.

Seablast said nothing, but Katrina noticed a slight movement in his sword hand. Brightling turned to one of her Watchers; Katrina saw immediately that it was Aranfal, wearing his raven's mask, a black and twisted thing that still frightened her, even today. The girl in his arms was the youngest, perhaps ten or eleven years old, with long, curly, blonde hair, thin, regal limbs, and fierce blue eyes. Katrina was suddenly seized by the image of her own brother, in the Operator's arms, falling through the earth to the Underland. *Is he afraid, still? Is he even alive?* She had told no one what she had seen, back then, in the Great Hall of Paprissi House. Not even Brightling. What would she tell them, anyway? She had not been able to hear much of what the Operator had said; all she knew was that Alexander had been taken. Perhaps it never actually happened. Perhaps her family was destroyed for another reason.

There is no time for these thoughts. Not now.

'Do you surrender, King?' Brightling asked.

Seablast looked at his daughter; Katrina could not read the expression in his eyes. Was he weighing up his options? His daughter or his kingdom? He nodded at the girl, an almost imperceptible tilt of his head, and turned back to the Tactician.

'No, madam. I do not.'

Brightling sighed and nodded to Aranfal. A slight jerk of a gloved hand and the girl's neck was bleeding. She flinched, but did not cry out.

There were some parts of being a Watcher that Katrina Paprissi did not like.

'The Second City, Anflef and Siren Down,' Tactician Brightling said again. 'Your Majesty, do you have a map?'

'What?' the King stammered, his eyes on his daughter, whose face had grown pale.

'A map, your Majesty. Have you not heard of such things? They are developing so well. Oh, forgive me,' said Tactician Brightling. 'There it is.'

She walked to the southern wall, on which hung a map of the Plateau, if it could be called that; it was an unsophisticated affair, lacking the remotest sense of distance and perspective. Brightling reached into her shoe and withdrew a short, thin blade. The guards had not dared to carry out a thorough search, Katrina realised. It was always the same way.

'The Second City, Anflef and Siren Down,' Brightling said, pointing each out on the map with her blade. 'The Second City,' she said again, before slashing the city away. 'Anflef,' she said, and tore it apart. 'Siren Down,' she concluded, stabbing into its position with her knife, which vibrated as it stuck into the wall.

'Your Majesty, you should pay more attention to your neighbours,' she said, turning to the King. 'These three allies of yours are now part of the Overland and under the beneficence of the Machinery.'

Seablast's face was a pallid grey, his arms limp at his sides.

'That cannot be,' he hissed. 'I would have heard something.'

'Why? Your Majesty, while you slept, I conquered. Some of your allies fell to the General Brandione, a clever man who knows his way around the most terrible weapons you have ever seen. Others fell to me. I won't tell you how I did it.'

Brightling's smile returned.

'If you become part of the Overland, willingly, the Machinery will forgive you. You will have a chance, like every one of its subjects, to rule the greatest nation in the world, if you are Selected.'

'To be one of the politicians,' the King rasped, his eyeballs rolling. 'And if we resist?'

'Then an entire continent will be thrown against the walls of this city.'

Farringer came stumbling back, lifting his visor to expose his sweat-drenched face.

'What happened here, anyway?' he asked, handing Brandione the map. 'Why did they declare war?'

Brandione sensed a new tone in the older man's voice: fear. Farringer was not made for this.

'They have a new leader,' he replied. 'Their last King died a year ago. He was a clever old sod, that particular Seablast. He towed the line, and tugged his forelock, and did whatever Brightling told him to do. The new one is possessed with … something. You know the type.'

'He thought he could lead his people against the Machinery.'

'Yes.' Brandione rolled his eyes and drew a finger across his throat.

Farringer chuckled and spat in the dirt. 'Where's Brightling?'

'She's in the city, talking to the King.'

'He let her in?'

'Yes.'

'Well then, this should not take long.'

As if in response, the great gate of Northern Blown began to open. The troops jolted to life, hoisting their weapons and leaping to attention at their war machines. But only two individuals emerged: Tactician Brightling, admired and distrusted in equal measure by the soldiery of the Overland, and King Seablast, whose very beard looked disconsolate. He lumbered along behind Brightling, a prisoner without chains.

There was someone else there, too: a girl in a state of mourning, to judge by her white rags. She flittered along behind the Tactician and the King, her footfalls swift and light, her black hair gleaming in the cold northern sun. Brandione had not seen her before: some Watcher, no doubt.

How had Brightling managed it? She had been able to enter one of the greatest fortresses in the world and *persuade* it to surrender, and not for the first time. Brandione had served with her before, here in the North and in the Western Rebellion. There had been other times like this one, when his skills were entirely worthless. Even when they did deploy their military might, she was always somewhere nearby, giving him little words of advice, he who had forgotten more about war than anyone else could remember, he who had been hand-picked by the Strategist himself to serve as his most senior adviser. Truly, there was something about the Tactician. She had been a Watcher for twenty years before her Selection, Brandione knew. That was a long time to serve the See House. The troops bowed as she brushed past, lowering their heads and averting their gazes.

The Tactician and her prisoner arrived at Brightling's tent, a modest, green affair, and entered, the girl following in their wake.

'No battle with Northern Blown, then,' Farringer said.

'No.'

'What are your orders, sir?'

'Nothing. We wait on Brightling.'

'Ah! It looks like they're done already.'

Indeed so. Just moments after she had entered the tent, Brightling had reappeared. Brandione could not see the expression on the Tactician's face, but could well imagine her satisfaction.

Brightling crossed the bloodless battlefield to a trebuchet, wind-battered and pockmarked with arrows. Its operators scrambled away as the Tactician scaled the machine, refusing all offers of assistance. The troops crowded around her without prompting, Brandione among them.

Brightling pointed to the defeated city.

'After a journey of almost ten millennia, the process of Expansion is complete.'

The soldiers cheered.

'The city of Northern Blown, which just an hour ago was at war with the Overland, has now realised the truth of the Machinery. This is a great day.'

The cheers of the troops grew louder; they loved her ability to spare them a fight.

'This victory does not belong to us, but to Northern Blown,' Brightling continued. 'Its people will now share in the glory of the world: the Machinery.'

Brandione wondered if the people inside the city knew what their King had done.

'The Machinery knows,' said Brightling.

The cheers became deafening. Brightling closed her eyes, taking it in. She was enjoying this, Brandione knew: the adulation of the crowd. Perhaps she had hated being an ordinary Watcher, skulking in the shadows while others took the glory. Now she was the focus of attention. It was not even her role, by rights: Expansion was the remit of Tactician

Canning. But he would not mind. He had not been one of the Machinery's most successful Selections; he always gave the impression of wanting to be somewhere, anywhere, other than the Fortress of Expansion.

Brightling lowered her eyes and looked back down at the crowd, whose applause was dying. She opened her mouth to continuing speaking, but was unexpectedly interrupted.

A commotion had begun on the edge of the troops. A small, thin man in the coarse goatskin of a peasant was rushing up and down the lines in an agitated state. With his spindly limbs and bulging eyes, he had the look of a panicking insect.

'It is a messenger,' Farringer said, screwing his eyes up tightly. 'He doesn't bring good news, by the look of him.'

Well spotted. Brandione hailed a nearby soldier. 'Bring him here.'

The trooper ran off and cuffed the anxious man around the neck, dragging him to the trebuchet.

'What's the matter with you?' Brandione demanded. 'You're disturbing the Tactician's speech.'

The messenger burst out of the sentry's arms. A cluster of troops immediately made for him, but Brandione stopped them with a raised finger.

'Let him speak.'

The wretch fell to his knees. 'Are you General Brandione, the Strategist's adviser?' he asked.

'Yes. What of it?'

'I bring terrible news, lord; the worst in sixty-two years!'

Farringer stepped forward.

'What do you mean to say? What is wrong?'

But Brandione already knew. *It is sixty-two years since Kane was Selected.*

The man doubled over, his body shaking. After a fit of coughing and shivering, he stood, dragging himself up by grabbing onto Farringer's arm and rising to his full, unimposing height.

'Strategist Kane is dead!'

Chapter Three

Sometimes Katrina felt older than the world itself.

She had first experienced the sensation as a child, before the Operator took her brother, before her mother died and her father sailed away. It was as if part of her was broken, the part that should have governed childhood and put a fire into youth.

No. It wasn't broken. It was there, all right. But it was not alone. By its side was something else entirely, a tired creature that gazed on the world with weary comprehension, unsurprised by anything.

The feeling had grown stronger over the years. When her brother was taken, the old part of her had begun to dominate. *Don't tell anyone what you saw. What would they do, if they knew? How would they treat you, if they thought you were telling lies about the Operator?* And so she had told no one, not even her father or Brightling. Sometimes, though, she wondered if the Tactician knew anyway. Nothing could stay hidden from her for very long.

She had hated it, at first. It conflicted with some of her most cherished beliefs about herself. She saw herself as courageous, perhaps even reckless; the older part restrained her. She saw beauty in the world, in the trees and in the mountains; the older part snorted at such sentimentality. She recoiled at some elements of the Watcher's life, the cruelty and the treachery; the older part reminded her of the practicalities of the world, and of the hard decisions one must make to thrive.

She became aware, as time went by – she never knew how – that other people were not like this. Other people, people like Brightling, were complete. They were whole. She was two jagged halves.

But she had grown to appreciate it. She found herself able to tap into it, when she needed to. It was as if she had a deep and cool reservoir, hidden within her, which she could use to extinguish even the most searing of flames.

It was another mask.

'Where is your mask?'

She jolted.

'I do not have one yet.'

Aranfal frowned. 'Why not?'

'I am still an Apprentice.'

'You are how old?'

Which part? 'I am 21.'

'Hmm. That is old, to still be an Apprentice. And even an Apprentice may wear a mask.'

'Brightling—'

'Tactician Brightling.'

'Tactician Brightling says I can visit the Hall of Masks when we are back from the North.'

Aranfal nodded. 'Well, good for you. I'm sure you'll get the prettiest mask in all the fucking Hall.'

Katrina bit her tongue, though it took all her willpower. Or rather, it took all the power of her older half to beat down the tempestuous girl.

27

'Are you celebrating the end of Expansion then, petal?' Aranfal asked.

'No. There are no celebrations.'

'Why not? I thought you young people would have drunk half of Northern Blown by now.'

'No. The Overland is mourning for the Strategist, Watcher.' *And I am not permitted to fraternise with young people, or with anyone who isn't Brightling.*

Aranfal nodded. 'I know that, girl. Don't take me for a fool.'

The older part once again suppressed her natural instincts, which this time pointed towards violence. 'I am sorry, Watcher Aranfal.'

He nodded. 'Good.'

They remained in silence for a moment.

'Why am I here, Watcher?' She looked around the hall. It was just as she would have expected from a place like this, all stone and straw and fireplaces and wood. Aranfal was sitting at a long, oak table, papers scattered before him. Dozens of candles burned around the hall.

'Why are you here? How should I know?'

'Brightling told me to come. She said you had something to show me.'

'She said that?' He squinted his eyes. 'Was she any more specific?'

'No.'

Aranfal sighed, and pointed at the papers. 'Well, in that case, she must want you to bathe alongside me in the glamour of my life. At the moment I'm cataloguing the sheep and cattle in the surrounding fields. Yes indeed, being a Watcher is truly glorious at all times, as you will find out one day.' He broke into a smile. 'Although perhaps not, now that I think about it. You'll get the plum jobs, I have no doubt.'

Katrina bowed her head, and did not speak. Aranfal had always been this way with her, though she did not know why. No Watcher outranked him, save Brightling herself; he was arguably the most powerful man in the world, now that Kane was dead, or if he was not, only Charls Brandione had more of a claim. But when he looked upon her, he did so with envy. The youthful part of her could not see this; it was her older self that recognised this emotion, and laughed at Aranfal for being so weak.

'I firstly have to be made a Watcher,' said Katrina, 'which is easier said than done.'

There was a knock at the door, and a young Watcher entered, in a bull mask. He approached Aranfal, handed him a piece of parchment, and scuttled away, bowing as he went.

Aranfal scanned the parchment, and smiled.

'Ah, now I understand,' he said with a nod.

'Understand what?'

He lifted the parchment. 'It's from Brightling. There's going to be an interrogation, led by yours truly, and you are to attend. How does that sound?'

'Excellent, Watcher.' *Nightmarish,* said her younger self, and the other half did not disagree.

Seablast was a broken man.

Gone was the proud bearing of the warrior King, that sense of power he had conveyed only the day before. In its place was a downcast creature, his eyes dead, his black hair unkempt, his armour replaced with a dirty and torn white shirt. He even seemed thinner, shrunken, as if the loss of his lands had physically deflated him. He sat on a wooden stool before a stone table, and his legs and arms were shackled, like some kind of Doubter or common criminal.

Katrina stood at the back of the cell, pressed against a clammy wall. She wished she already had a mask of her own, when Seablast looked up at her. But he did not seem to see. His eyes looked through her, into nothing.

Aranfal took a seat opposite the King. He did not wear his raven's mask, but laid it on the table, in front of Seablast. The King seemed to come to life when he noticed this strange object, this black, alien artefact that had made its way into his world, signifying the end of so much he had once held inviolable. Aranfal could have looked into the heart of the King, if he only chose to wear his mask. But it did not work like that. A Watcher only used his mask when he had to. Sometimes, wearing the mask actually *hurt*.

'Do you recognise this?' Aranfal had a certain tone to his voice, sometimes. Katrina pressed herself against the wall, willing it to suck her in.

'That is a mask, Watcher,' said the King. 'I know all about you people. You live in a tower on a hill by the sea, and you run around with little masks on, and you think they are a gateway into people's souls. Sometimes the masks are trees, sometimes they are people, sometimes they are cats, and sometimes they are dogs. Sometimes the masks are even made to look like sweet little birdies.'

He grinned at Aranfal, but Katrina saw through the smiles. He had lost everything, he was a husk of a man, yet still he felt the need to be combative. That wouldn't do much good against Aranfal. That wouldn't do much good at all.

Aranfal nodded, once, short and sharp. 'Very good, King. It is a mask. But that is not what I meant to say. What I meant to say is, do you recognise *this* mask, *in particular*?'

Seablast thought this over for a moment, casting glances at the raven, which stared up at him from the table, waiting and watching. Katrina hated that bird, and feared it too. Seablast seemed unafraid. *That will change.*

'Yes,' the King said. 'It is the raven of Aranfal, the renowned Watcher, Brightling's hand-servant and general dogsbody. It is the mask of a weak man, who torments his victims by hurting their loved ones. It is the mask of a non-person.'

And then Seablast spat at Aranfal. It was a pathetic effort, the detritus of a dried and parched mouth. But it was not the quantity that mattered; it was the act itself.

In one cool, swift movement, Aranfal was on his feet. He leaned over the table and smacked the King with the back of his hand, sending a crack echoing in the cell like a shot from a handcannon. Seablast was knocked back, and would have fallen from his stool had it not been for his chains. He righted himself and glared at Aranfal through watery eyes, the right side of his face blooming red.

'So, this is how the Watchers of the Overland treat kings,' he said, his voice trembling.

'King? You are a king no longer, Seablast. But don't worry about that. You will have a place in history. You will always be remembered as the last independent ruler on the Plateau, who lost his lands through his own idiocy. Your name will echo through the ages. Children will sing songs mocking you, and drunks will lie in the gutter, puke drying on their lips, and thank the Machinery that they are not Seablast, knowing that it could be worse.'

Aranfal shrugged.

'I am still a king,' Seablast said. 'One is born a king, by dint of one's blood, which flows through the ages like a river. One is not Selected to rule by a machine; one is Selected to rule by one's ancestry.'

'Ancestry? Let's look at your ancestry. Your father was a great man. He was respected by everyone in our land. He was a true diplomat, and he would have kept his people free, if he sat on the throne today.'

'He was a weak streak of piss, and he only kept us free by placing us under the boot of the Strategist and your bitch of a superior. That is not being a king.'

'Then what is being a king? Not only have you lost your kingdom, but through your mischief-making you have brought Anflef and Siren Down and all the other little kingdoms up here to their knees, too. All these old countries, gone forever, because of you. Not that it is a bad thing. Your subjects – apologies, our subjects – will now revel in the glory of the world.'

'The Machinery? You don't even know what it is!' Seablast laughed. 'You just trust the Operator, some fucking trickster who lives in another realm and pulls the wool over your eyes. He is a king, Aranfal the raven, just as I am. Except he will never give up his power, not to anyone in the world.'

'And yet you handed your lands over to us, freely.'

'Hardly freely. And it was my worst mistake. I should have kept fighting, without allies. I should have let my daughters die. It would have been better than this life.'

Aranfal sighed, and leaned back in his chair, knitting his hands behind his head.

'I don't think this little philosophical chitchat is getting us anywhere.'

Seablast shook his head. 'No.'

Aranfal turned to Katrina. 'Is this what you imagined an interrogation to be?'

Katrina started, and pushed herself off the wall. 'I don't know. Maybe.'

'Maybe? What does maybe mean?'

'No, it's not what I imagined an interrogation to be.'

'Why not?'

'Because you're not asking him any questions.'

Aranfal snapped his fingers together. 'I knew I'd forgotten something.' He turned to face Seablast again. 'Your Majesty, if I were a Doubter, in the kingdom of Northern Blown, where would I be most likely to hide?'

Seablast laughed. 'Everyone here is a Doubter. You have given them nothing to believe in.'

Aranfal's eyes widened. 'Everyone? You know, we have a prison for Doubters, in the South of our lands, in the heart of the desert of the Wite. It's been there for ten millennia, yet none of us know what's in there, or even who mans it. You know why that is? Because no one ever leaves the Prison of the Doubters. So if all your people are Doubters, do I need to send them all down there?'

Seablast looked away from Aranfal.

'Because I could do that, Seablast. It would be pretty hard work. There would be a lot of carts and carriages and horses and so forth. But we're the masters of a continent, now. There's not much we can't do, when we put our minds to it. So I ask again – should I send everyone down there?'

Seablast did not reply.

Aranfal nodded. 'I'm getting fucking tired of you, and this place. I'm from the North too, Seablast, though it's colder and nastier than anywhere you've been. I don't want to be in the North any more, understood? I want to go home. So let me ask you again – where would I find the Doubters in this fucking dump?'

Seablast met Aranfal's gaze. 'I tell you truthfully, I do not know any Doubters. They could be anywhere.'

'What about your lieutenants? Those pricks in the throne room, back when you were a king? A few of them have gone missing, haven't they? I bet they're out and about now, planning to right your honour and make some trouble for us. Aren't they? What are their names?'

Seablast remained silent, and his eyes focused on the table.

'All I need is their names.'

'I don't know who you're talking about. And I don't see why they'd be Doubters.'

Aranfal turned to Katrina, his eyes blazing, his body shaking with fury. She could not tell if it was real or part of his act, but the older part of her told her to do whatever he asked.

'Paprissi, there's a bag on the floor beside you. Bring it over here.'

Katrina looked to her side, and saw a brown satchel. She instantly snatched it in her hand and walked to Aranfal's side.

'Unfold it on the table.'

She did as she was told. The bag turned into a gleaming array of knives, axes and other tools the Apprentice Watcher had never seen before and had no name for. She knew, however, for a certainty, that she would not like to be on the wrong end of any of them.

'I'll get her to use these,' Aranfal whispered, jabbing a thumb at Katrina. 'The only thing is, this is her first interrogation, so she might be clumsy. Thumbs and things might get lost forever.'

Katrina felt her stomach turn. *You are a Watcher, girl,* said the older part of herself. *You know what this life is.*

But this was never supposed to be my life, the younger side responded, in a rare moment of defiance.

She steeled herself, and smiled at the King, in what she hoped was a sinister manner. But it was evidently unsuccessful. Seablast smiled back at her, and winked. *Winked.*

'Is there something amusing, your Majesty?' Aranfal asked. His tone was smoothing, cool. He knew something the others did not.

'I've been tortured before, by people worse than you,' the King said. 'Once I spent a couple of weeks as the guest of some snow bandits. I was humiliated, to fall into their hands. But I got myself free, pretty quickly.' He grinned.

'I've met snow bandits before, too, your Majesty. I'm from a similar background to them, in point of fact. And they are a nasty bunch. But they are not worse than us. Besides, what makes you think we are going to torture *you*?'

The King's expression flickered from confusion to something else entirely: fear.

'Katrina.' Aranfal looked to Katrina again. 'Gather up this bag of tricks, like a good little Apprentice, and take a walk down the corridor, till you come to the fifth cell from this one. It's a nasty cell, that one, your Majesty, not like your own lovely abode. Once you get there, Katrina, pass on my regards to the King's daughters. Don't tell them he's here. Don't even ask them any questions. Just cut off bits of them. Let's say – one finger each. Or a toe? What do you think, your Majesty – what would they prefer to lose?'

The King's face was grey, his eyes once more on the table. But he did not protest. He did not say a word. *By the Machinery, tell him whatever he wants, you idiot. Don't force me to do this.*

'Seablast, you know I am a bad man,' Aranfal said. 'And you know I am committed to my work, and to the Machinery. Tell me where your missing minions are, or your daughters will suffer for your obstinacy.'

The King sighed, and his very bones seemed to rattle. When he looked at Aranfal, there was something new in his eye: resignation.

No. Please don't do it, Seablast.

'I already told you,' said the King. 'I made a mistake in my throne room. Do what you want. My girls would be better dead, than living under your rule.'

Aranfal lifted a finger. 'Not my rule. The rule of the Selected.'

He packed up the instruments, and handed the bag to Katrina again.

'Well, off you go, then.'

As Katrina walked down the corridor, she knew which part of her personality to turn to.

This is what being a Watcher is.

Get in there, do it quickly, get out again.

Show them no emotion.

Do a good job, and you will be recognised.

The world is a hard and cruel place, Katrina. You know that better than anyone. We do what we must to survive. We do what we must to thrive.

Only once did the other part get in.

What would father think of you now? Is this what he would have wanted for you?

She stood at the cell door, the fifth one along.

If father cared about you, he wouldn't have left you to be raised by Watchers, now would he?

She pushed inside.

There was only one woman in this cell, and she was not a daughter of King Seablast.

'Aleah.'

Thank the Machinery.

The woman sat at a table, a book open before her. Katrina knew her as one of the more ambitious generation of younger Watchers, the ones on the rung below Aranfal. She was unusually chubby for a Watcher, with unkempt blonde hair strewn around her face.

'Has he said anything yet?'

'No, Watcher.'

'He didn't break down again, when Aranfal threatened his daughters?'

'Not this time.'

'But he thinks you are hacking bits off them. He'll be talking now, I bet. If he isn't, we'll try a different tack. Maybe we'll send you in again in a while, with a finger. We'll just take one off a corpse, so don't worry.'

'Where are his daughters?'

'No idea. Maybe they're dead. Or maybe old Aranfal let them go. Sometimes he's soft, you know. I would have put the King in the same room as them, and made him watch what I did. But Aranfal only does that kind of thing when he has to. He's soft.'

The woman seemed to catch herself, and grinned. 'I jest, of course. He's a genius at this type of thing. No one better.'

The door behind them opened, and Aranfal entered. He nodded at Aleah, and pointed to the door, waiting until she had left the room before he spoke.

'The King has told me everything he knows. He reckons there will be some rebels out there, but it doesn't sound to me like we've much to worry about. Only took another five minutes. It's funny how it works, sometimes. I didn't even know what I was looking for. I just placed thoughts in his head, about what we knew and what we were doing. Having relatives is a very dangerous business. You are lucky, to be alone.'

I am?

'So, there you have it, Katrina. The psychological art of the interrogation.' He tapped the side of his head. 'In your next class, we really will chop off someone's finger.' He laughed. 'But it'll have to wait. You're to go back south with Brightling in the morning.'

Katrina bowed. 'Thank you, Watcher. This has been a good education.'

'Hmm. Everything is.'

She left Aranfal alone in the cell, and took herself away from the dungeons of Northern Blown. As she made her way up the stairs, one part of her wept with relief that she had not been forced to torture a girl, just to torment her father.

The other part was disappointed.

Chapter Four

'Is it Aran Fal, two names, or Aranfal, one name?'

'Aranfal, one name.'

'Just Aranfal? No surname?'

'Correct.'

The Administrator raised his eyebrows. He was a stout man, his skin a dark brown, his bald head scrunched into folds of fat. He wore a gown of silver silk, embroidered with flowers; it hung open to expose his flabby flesh, and was tied with only a loose knot to hide his most private of parts.

He made quite the contrast with Aranfal, who was as thin as a rake and as pale as a spectre, his sunken features and grey eyes framed by a curtain of blond hair. He wore his blue cloak over a dark woollen shirt and hempen trousers. The pair of them looked like the build-up to a joke, sitting in the Great Hall of Northern Blown with nothing but a crackling fire for company.

'That is … odd,' the Administrator said. He stared at his papers as if they might offer some explanation. The search appeared to fail. 'Uh, why is it so?'

Aranfal allowed his thin mouth to fall into a grimace. In truth, he did not mind the questions, but he couldn't allow this man to assert himself too boldly.

'Ah, not that it matters, Watcher,' the Administrator said, leaning back in his chair and smiling broadly. He did not want to appear frightened, but Aranfal could see it in him. He had seen it all before. 'I was just interested. I am not used to the ways of the North.' He giggled.

Aranfal stood and threw a log into the flames. They crackled back at him appreciatively.

'It's not a northern thing, Administrator. If you must know, it came about when I was a young man. A boy, really. I lost my name when I went to the See House.'

'You … forgive me, Aranfal, but how can a person lose their name?'

'It was taken from me, by the Tactician.'

There was a moment of silence as Aranfal took his seat again, sighing with pleasure as he unfolded himself into the furs of the furniture. They did not make chairs like this, in the South. They did not make rooms like this in the South, either. There was a fire on each of the four walls. The stony ground was caked in the filth of dogs and the detritus of ten thousand meals, and the room was unadorned with paintings or fresco or any of the other fads of the Centre. The hall was filled with long wooden tables, scattered with brass pots and knives and cracked plates. At the top of the room, on a raised level, was a high table, where once the King had sat with his family and his most senior functionaries. No more. Modernity ruled here now.

Aranfal turned back to the Administrator. The man's eyes were wide discs. He had placed his papers on his lap.

'Tactician Brightling stole your name,' he whispered. 'Is there nothing that woman cannot do?'

Aranfal barked a laugh. 'No, truly there isn't. Here is what happened. I showed up in the Centre, in that black tower, a boy down from the cold North. Brightling took an interest in me. She decided she didn't like Aran Fal, though, and since then I have been Aranfal.'

'She didn't like Aran Fal the name, or Aran Fal the person?'

A pause. 'Both of them are gone now.' The Watcher mocked himself inwardly for his melodrama. 'I have spent almost half my life as a Watcher, now. As Aranfal.'

'And a fine job you have made of it.' The Administrator raised his glass of wine, before remembering that Aranfal was not drinking. He shrugged, and took a long slurp by himself.

They sat in silence for a while, staring into the flames. They used peat as fuel, up here, digging it from the bogs. Sometimes they found bodies there, in the soggy muck, preserved for thousands of years, from before the Machinery, even. The fuel took a while to get going, but when it did, the smell was delicious. It transported him back to older days. He had been happy as a child, hadn't he? He could not remember. That was the world of Aran Fal.

He snapped back to reality, to find that the Administrator was staring at him. The man was making a habit of that. What did he think was going to happen, if he stopped looking?

'Have you completed the inventory?'

The Administrator started, then hurried to gather up his papers. 'Yes, master Watcher, it's all in here. Nothing of any great significance, the usual old weaponry, not much use to us now. We can probably melt it down. Some jewels, though. I think the Tactician would like them. And sundry clothes, dishes, etc.'

'Nothing of any tremendous value.'

'No,' the Administrator said with a slight shrug, before raising a finger. 'Apart from the land itself. This is a good spot to control. From here we can keep watch of the northern waters.'

Aranfal nodded. 'Do you expect some enemy to appear from those waters?'

The Administrator fell silent. *He thinks I'm trying to catch him in a trap. If only he were so important!*

'Administrator, I am not trying to trick you. It is important now to think to the future. You would find that everyone in the See House feels the same way, right to the very top.'

The Administrator smiled nervously. 'Well, you know what people say, other lands across distant seas, and all that. Better to be careful.'

'Indeed.'

Silence reigned again. Eventually the Administrator bent over and lifted a bell, which he raised in the air and vigorously shook, creating a cacophony that made Aranfal want to throw the thing into the flames, along with its bearer. Before long a servant came scampering through the main door of the hall, wineskin in hand, and ran to the Administrator's side, delicately refilling his drink before once again rushing out to some other part of the castle.

The Administrator did not once make eye contact with the servant. Aranfal despised this type of behaviour. It was something he had seen many times, especially among Administrators and other middling sorts. Funny, he spent his days with the most powerful people in the Plateau, but he never saw them act this way. It seemed that those with the real authority never felt the need to put it on display. It was just *there*, for the entire world to see, whether handed to them by the Machinery or not.

Aranfal was growing very tired of this little man.

'Administrator,' he said softly, 'I want to get my work done up here as fast as possible, and go home. Have your men found anything suspicious?'

The Administrator leant forward, glancing theatrically into the shadows.

'Do you mean … *Doubters*?' he whispered.

42

'Yes.'

The Administrator nodded. 'Well, as you know, Watcher Aranfal, we humble servants lack your skills in such matters. Indeed, we do not even possess your beautiful masks, so we must look into people's souls with only our own eyes—'

'Please, just tell me how many.'

'Hmm. Well, we have not yet found the ones the King mentioned, I am afraid. Perhaps you have had better luck on that front?'

'No.' *The King was probably lying. People will say anything, sometimes. Perhaps I should visit him again.*

'But we have found three others.'

'Three? That's quite good, Administrator.'

'Yes, well, you know ...'

Aranfal leaned forward. 'They made themselves quite easy to find, didn't they?'

The Administrator cleared his throat. 'Well, you may say that, but really I think we deserve *some* credit—'

'Where did you find them?'

The Administrator cringed. 'Uh, well, one of my men found them when he was out for a walk, you know, with a lady, as it were. They had just taken themselves up to the Bony Shore, and there they were, as bold as you like, three of them, on the sand, huddled around a little fire, and talking *openly* about the Machinery breaking. Strange-looking creatures, if you don't mind me saying so.'

'And your man and his lady friend, they are certain they heard these people speculate on the Machinery?'

'Oh, worse than that, Watcher Aranfal. These folk were saying that the Machinery was breaking. They were delighted by that, by all accounts. They acted as though it was the best thing they'd ever heard, dancing around the fire.'

43

'And your man can definitely be trusted?'

'Oh yes. Anyway, it doesn't matter. They have already confessed. They are positively joyful about it, you know! They seem to *like* the thought of all the things you folk will do to them in the Bowels of the See House. Some people are like that. I heard there are folk in the West—'

'I will speak to them myself. Where are they being held?'

'In the dungeons, sir. Handy thing about old places like this.' He flicked a hand at the walls. 'They have such lovely dungeons.'

Aranfal stood and bowed to the Administrator.

'If you find any more Doubters, Administrator, do let me know straight away.'

The Administrator seemed taken aback. 'I wasn't hiding anything from you! I just thought you might like to relax first, what with all the exertions of taking this place, you know.'

'Thank you.' Aranfal placed his hand in his cloak and felt it, hanging loosely from his belt: his raven's mask. It always reassured him, knowing it was there. He felt almost naked without it, but had decided the Administrator might feel slightly unnerved, sitting across from a twisted raven that could see into his soul.

He turned to leave, and got halfway to the door before the Administrator started yapping again.

'Oh, Watcher?'

'Yes?'

'I have not told you my name.'

One little scare won't hurt him. It might do him good.

Aranfal flipped the mask into his hand and onto his face in one smooth movement.

'That's all right,' he said, staring at the Administrator through the savage holes of his mask. 'I already know everything I need to about you.'

As the Watcher left the Great Hall it took everything in his power to stifle a laugh at the look in the Administrator's eyes.

In truth, Aranfal was not the same as Aran Fal. Aran Fal was dead, and Brightling killed him.

Aran Fal was murdered early on, when he first joined the Watchers. He was a bright-eyed, bushy-tailed kind of fellow, the honest son of an honest father, a golden stereotype who skipped his way along the road to the Centre. His was a soft kind of worldview, though he considered himself a paragon of courage. He was ambitious, yes, but ambition without an edge leads only in one direction, and that is to the edge of a cliff.

How had this big-hearted dreamer ended up among the black-clad operatives of the See House, with their strange masks and their brutish ways? Well, like many a young man, he thought he could change things. He did not like the world as he found it. He thought it could do with some revisions. There was no power in the world like that of the Watchers, the servants of the great Brightling, who at that stage was just establishing herself as the power of the Overland. To the young Aran Fal, the Watchers were the focus of all excitement, adventure, and potential.

He did not have a plan when he went to the Centre. It took him months to walk along those roads, alone for long periods with only his thoughts. They called the Overland a city, but he never understood why. Parts of it were nothing but vast empty spaces, with not a soul in sight. Aranfal had used the time poorly. He did not consider his options, or analyse the pitfalls that could lie ahead. Oh, how he had changed since then.

Despite everything, the Watchers took him in. He saw it as a just reward for his confidence. Perhaps that was even true. Or perhaps they saw something else, within him. Perhaps they saw Aranfal.

Eventually, *she* saw him, and she liked him, and she took him under her dark wing. She showed him many things, not least her technique for extracting information from recalcitrant Doubters.

'If you do not co-operate with me,' he told the prisoner, 'I will find other ways to take it from you.'

The man before him was unlike anyone Aranfal had seen before. This was not to do with his physical appearance; in that regard, he was like many an inhabitant of the Centre. His skin was olive, and he wore his black hair long, tied back behind his shoulders. He had a sharp kind of face, all angles and edges, like something from a painting of one of the old families; a short beard stabbed out from the bottom of his chin. His dark eyes were constantly on the move, examining and dissecting his surroundings. He was like any wealthy merchant or Administrator, though his clothes were odd: he wore a torn red cloak, like an itinerant.

When the man spoke it was with an utter confidence that suggested he was unaware of the seriousness of his situation.

'There is nothing you can do to me, Watcher of the Overland.' He grinned as he said those last words, as if that exalted title was somehow amusing. He did not seem at all perturbed by the chains that bound him to his chair, or put out by the rough treatment he had already received at the hands of some more thuggish Watchers.

Aranfal was sitting opposite the man. He glanced around the room. It was a place of cold wet stone, of chains and dripping water and flickering candles. It was worse even than the cell they'd used for Seablast. A weaker man would already be spilling out his guts, in a place like this.

'What is your name, Doubter?'

'Gibbet.'

'Do not lie to me.'

'I am not.'

There was a pause.

'Where are you from?' Aranfal narrowed his eyes. 'I hear hints of … what, the North, in your accent?'

'But you hear the North everywhere, Watcher Aranfal, don't you? You can't escape it. No, I am not from your North. No.'

Aranfal smiled at the man, but it was a false thing. *How do you know my name?*

'You have already confessed to your hatred of the Overland and the Machinery, long may it save us. You will tell me your plans now, or you will suffer the consequences.'

'My plans? I have no plan. The plan was put in motion ten millennia ago, when the Promise was made.'

'You will tell me your plan, Doubter.'

'Ruin is coming. You can do what you want to me, but you cannot halt its rise.'

Aranfal rapped his knuckles on the table. 'I will look into you,' he said. He reached down and lifted his raven mask from the floor, slipping it on with a flourish. The subjects of interrogations often melted before the mask, afraid that all their secrets would be exposed. This man did not. He simply leaned forward in his chair, clasped his hands together, and stared at the raven with a dark smile.

Strange. Aranfal had a greater mastery of the mask than any Watcher, save Brightling. He would look through its hollow eyes, and sensations would gather within him, hints of treachery and rebellion; they would form like smoke, and he would inhale them. Sometimes he would be transported to

47

other places, to the memories of the subject, and watch their Doubting take place. But with this man, there was nothing.

He removed his mask.

'How did you do that?' He failed to conceal his disappointment.

The man laughed. 'I know the creature who makes your masks, Aranfal. I *know* him. I have known him from days of old. His tricks will not work with me.'

Aranfal sighed. 'Do you know my mistress?'

'I know of Brightling, if that is who you mean. But she is not your mistress. You will learn who your true mistress is, in time.'

Aranfal slammed a hand down on the table. 'Brightling is my mistress, Doubter. Do you know her?'

'I do.'

'She is clever, you know. She taught me ways to extract information, even from those who are strong.'

'Please, try your damnedest.'

Aranfal whistled, a strange shriek of a sound. The door to the cell opened immediately, and a burly Watcher entered, pushing a woman before him. She was relatively young, perhaps in her mid thirties. She had the same olive skin as Gibbet, but she was plumper. Her head was shaved down to the stubble; on her forehead was a tattoo of an eye, wide and staring.

'This is a friend of yours, is it not?' Aranfal asked.

Gibbet nodded. He grinned at the woman. *Still he smiles.*

'Her name is Hood, as strange a name as your own.'

'Oh, Watcher, I am far stranger than old Gibbet,' said Hood.

Gibbet and Hood laughed in unison.

'Your laughter upsets me,' Aranfal whispered. 'Doubters should not be allowed to laugh.'

He nodded at the other Watcher, who grunted as he threw Hood to the floor.

'You should not have laughed,' Aranfal said again.

The other Watcher raised his leg and stamped on Hood's chest.

'Do not laugh at us again,' Aranfal whispered.

The beating that Hood received at the fists and boots of the Watcher was as savage as any Aranfal had witnessed. The woman's bones cracked like kindling, and her face quickly dissolved into a bloodied pulp, the tattoo now impossible to discern. Aranfal turned away in disgust. He did not care for brutality, especially when his true target was the man, not the woman. But it was as Brightling had always said. *A person will endure much suffering, but they will not stand for so much as a misplaced hair on a loved one's head.* This woman had no hair, but the meaning was the same. It had worked for him more times than he cared to remember. Some subjects, like old Seablast, did not even need to witness the torment of their loved ones, to fall apart. It was almost always a sure route to success.

Except this time, it wasn't.

The woman did not cry out. She did not resist the blows as they rained down on her. She *smiled*. Through it all, she was grinning.

And Gibbet laughed.

Something is very wrong.

Aranfal leaned over Gibbet. 'You laugh, still you laugh. But know that *this treatment*' – he pointed at Hood upon the floor – 'is just the *tiniest taste of what I can do*. I am not an impatient man. I can make things *far* worse, over a *much* longer period of time. Do you follow my meaning?'

But Gibbet kept laughing. He laughed as he looked into Aranfal's eyes. He laughed as he looked at his companion. He laughed as he stood, and he laughed as he cast his chains aside, as if they were formed of butter. He laughed as he picked up Aranfal's mask, and he laughed as he put it on.

'No,' was all Aranfal managed to say.

'Yes,' said the man, removing the mask and tossing it to the ground. 'These things remind me too much of their maker.' He pointed to Hood, and Aranfal glanced in the woman's direction. She was on her feet, her wounds healed, her tattoo staring out, once again pristine. In her right hand she held the severed head of the brutish Watcher; his torso was beneath her left boot.

'Now,' Gibbet said to Aranfal. 'Whatever will we do with you?'

Chapter Five

'You are now the oldest of all our leaders,' said Darrah, leaning back in her chair and staring at the ceiling, eyes wide, as if the thought had just this second occurred to her. 'And by some way, too. How does that feel? It must be bloody awful.'

Annara Rangle, Tactician of the West, placed her book face down on the table. She removed her eyeglasses and lowered her head, fixing Darrah with a stare. It was a look her father had perfected: cold eyes, on the edge between anger and restraint. Not a look you wanted to see, from him. But she couldn't do it. She never could. Not to Darrah, anyway.

The Tactician burst into laughter. Her sparrow chest rattled and one of her remaining curls of grey hair bounced about.

'Although, on second thoughts,' Darrah said, 'those are not the giggles of an old lady. Stop them, please; they are an affront to my ears.' She clasped her hands over the offended organs.

Rangle pouted her dry lips and slapped a hand across her mouth. 'Mng mm shorry.'

'You will be sorry,' Darrah said, lifting a fist, and Rangle laughed again.

How many assistants spoke to their Tactician in this way? She had often wondered. And so she asked.

'How many assistants speak to their Tacticians in this way?' She assumed once again her father's mask of disapproval.

Darrah raised a finger.

'Not many.' She stood, and walked to her Tactician, who remained seated. The assistant reached down with her finger, and stroked Rangle's cheek, just once, lightly. 'But we are more than that, aren't we?'

Rangle brushed the hand away. 'Not here,' she whispered, staring up into the darkened rafters.

Darrah laughed, and took the chair beside the Tactician, burying herself in one of the many texts that lay before them.

Rangle glanced around the room. *I should heed my own words more often, here. It would not do for the Watchers to know too much about my weaknesses. Especially this one.* She squeezed Darrah's knee; the gesture was met with a pout.

The Tactician laughed. She turned to her surroundings, looking again for eyes in the shadows. But there was no one there, or not that she could see. Of course, that didn't mean they weren't observing her and making notes. Brightling's servants would pride themselves on being unobtrusive. That was their job, after all.

But it was worth it. This place was the only thing that brought joy to her life, apart from Darrah. The Watchers' Library was a glory of the world, though the world did not know it. It was a vast space, cluttered with shelves and dust, free of any attempt at organisation or categorization, so totally unlike the plain and insipid collections of the College. And the books here could not be found in the College. These were texts and parchments that the Watchers monitored and controlled, on behalf of the Operator himself. They peered into the dark cracks of the Overland, into parts of history that were hidden from the people as a whole: overly ambitious Tacticians stalked the pages, with aims of tricking the Machinery; reigns of terror and disaster were detailed, their histories too painful to be remembered; and there were other things, too, which made no sense, or at least not at first. Things from before the Machinery itself.

Thank the Machinery for Tactician Brightling. If she hadn't let me use this place, I think I would be dead.

'We should go to Watchfold soon, Tactician. The Administrators will be getting anxious.'

Rangle sighed. 'They are already anxious, Darrah. They have been hounding me.'

'They need your wisdom, my lady.'

'They need my stamp of approval for their little projects. That's all they need.'

Darrah had served Rangle for fifteen years now, though it felt like longer. She had changed little in that time: a round face, plump, turning to fat, but lively and warm; a stout, powerful little body, with arms like axe handles; black hair that she cut herself into savage spikes; skin of a light brown, like Rangle's own. She was from the Middle West, like the Tactician, and had wandered one day into Watchfold, demanding a job. She had come a long way, she had said. Watchfold could not even be classed as the true West, she had said. It was like calling Redbarrel the North, or the Far Below the South; they were all too close to the Centre, founded at a time when the Overland was just a speck on the Plateau.

It was lucky Rangle had spotted her. The Administrators would have thrown her onto the road.

They were in the White Rooms, a suite of apartments in Memory Hall that served as the Tactician's base in the Centre. In truth, this felt more like home than Watchfold Hall, where she was obliged to spend some weeks of the year. It was only a short journey down Greatgift from the See House, home of her beloved library. And the rooms themselves were far more to her taste. A large, central reception room dominated the apartments. It was lavishly appointed, from the lengthy dining table to the furniture that was scattered about the space. The main art feature was a fresco depicting the glorious death of the Third Strategist, who fell fighting in some southern war, arrows honeycombing his torso. His blood sprayed across the wall.

Rangle had even shifted her bed into this room, placing it behind a golden curtain. She liked the air here; it helped her to sleep, something that never came naturally.

The Tactician had been sitting at the dining table now for almost four hours, slowly leafing through the same old text. A lamp sent swirling shadows across the fresco. *How many people have stared at that work of art? Which Tacticians have stayed here, have sat in this very chair?* She had asked questions like these since she was a girl, watching her father hack a vineyard from the wilderness. *Did anyone live here before us? Did savages dance their rituals among those rocks, before the Overland came?*

Where have they gone?

Darrah threw herself into the seat beside Rangle.

'What's this one, then?'

Rangle smiled, and gently touched a page. 'It is a very old one.'

'All the ones you read are very old. Why don't you read anything new?'

'There is no fun in the new. I know about the new. I live the new.'

'You do not.' Darrah stuck out her tongue. 'Garron Grinn is here, by the way. He's shuffling about in the hallway.'

Rangle glared at Darrah. 'And you thought you wouldn't tell me till now?'

'You said you didn't want to speak to any Administrators until at least the 27th day of the 11th Month of the 10,000th year.'

'Shut up. Send him in.'

Darrah pouted, leapt up from her chair, and vanished through the doorway. Rangle heard some murmuring outside, before Administrator Garron Grinn shuffled before her.

He was a tall man, and at least as old as herself, giving him a stooped, crooked posture, like a broken finger. A grey beard fell from his chin in unkempt spikes, mixing freely with the silver mat of hair that hung from his irritating head. His skin was black, as were his morose eyes, with which he cast sad little glances at his surroundings. He had a habit of clucking his tongue lightly when he saw something he didn't like, which was often. He was, as usual, dressed in a heavy brown cloak, underlining his carefully contrived air of austerity.

Rangle had known Garron Grinn since she was sixteen years old, when she had first been whisked away from the vineyard to Watchfold. He had not changed in all that time. *I'm sure that's the same cloak.*

'Garron Grinn,' she said, trying to sound as displeased as possible. 'Did you receive my message?'

'No, my lady,' came the melancholy response.

'Are you sure? Did my servant summon you from your bed in the middle of the night, demanding your presence in the White Rooms of Memory Hall?'

'No.'

'Are you certain, Garron Grinn?' It was always both names with him, never just Garron. 'Ah, then I know. My pigeon flew to you, with a message tied to its little foot. This instructed you to come hither, with all possible haste! That's what happened, is it not?'

'It is not, my lady.'

'Then I came to you, in a vision, surrounded in white—'

'You did not.'

'Did you just interrupt me?'

'No.' He clucked his tongue.

She sighed, not to herself, but *at* Garron Grinn. 'If none of these things happened, Administrator, then why, by the Machinery, are you standing before me now?'

Garron Grinn bowed, and it was a strange thing to witness. His rickety body creaked as he manoeuvred it back to what passed for a standing position.

'We must discuss business, my lady.'

There came a giggle from the hallway.

'Darrah,' Rangle called, 'please could you find something to occupy you elsewhere? Maybe in the People's Level?'

There came a series of theatrical tuts, then the sound of feet tapping away along the corridor.

Garron Grinn clucked his tongue again. 'Business,' he said.

'You can take care of business better than I.' She meant it.

'No. You were Selected. It is your duty.'

She rolled her eyes, as she had a million times before. It was most likely better suited to a teenage girl.

'Very well.' The Tactician of the West waved a hand at Darrah's recently vacated chair.

Garron Grinn sat down, which was a much more complicated process than one could reasonably expect. After much sighing and creaking, he reached into the folds of his cloak and withdrew a sheaf of papers.

'Applications for business licences; harvest figures; petty crimes. For you to review,' he wheezed. 'But there is no rush.'

That surprised her. *No rush?* There was always a rush where business was concerned, or so she had been led to believe.

Rangle flicked through the papers absentmindedly. 'If there is no rush, then why are you here?'

Garron Grinn turned around in his chair, staring out into the shadows.

'It's all right,' said the Tactician. 'There is no one here but ourselves.'

The Administrator nodded, and clucked his tongue yet again. 'It is the Watchers, Tactician.'

'What of them?' She cocked her head and gave Garron Grinn an accusatory look. 'Have you done something wrong? Well, I won't help you. You've always been up to no good. I knew it.'

Garron Grinn squinted. 'No. Of course not. But I fear … that they have become interested in us. In our little capital.'

'Watchfold? Fine. Let them. They are right to be. They are the power of this land, are they not? It would almost be an insult if they *weren't* interested.'

Garron Grinn squinted again. 'Ah, ah, ah, well, I suppose that is true. But don't you …' His eyes fell onto the old book that lay before the Tactician.

'You think they care about my studies?' Rangle asked with a chuckle. 'I assure you, they know all about it, as you well know. Brightling herself gives me access to their library.'

'Hmm.'

He had never liked her studies. Well, it mattered not. The Machinery had Selected her, not him. But he had a point, though he did not realise it. There were some things she did that the Watchers might not like. *My study group.* But Brightling did not know about that. She could not know about it. And Garron Grinn certainly did not know about it.

'Garron Grinn, please. What is this all about?'

The Administrator reached back into his cloak. This time he withdrew a single piece of parchment, on which a series of names had been scrawled in red ink.

'This was given to me by the Watchers in Watchfold. It is a list of suspected Doubters.'

Rangle shrugged. 'The Watchers see Doubters everywhere. That's their job. Let them round up these characters.'

Garron Grinn raised a skeletal finger. 'That is not the point. This is more serious. These people have taken their Doubting to a bad level. They are pamphleteers, playwrights, that type of thing. As you know, the Watchers take a very dim view of unlicensed arts.'

Rangle was beginning to understand. Cultural control was fundamental to the Watchers; they simply would not tolerate anything that took place beyond their sanction. If this was happening in Watchfold, right under the nose of the Tactician of the West, it could look very bad indeed. Especially when said nose rarely made an appearance in its domain.

'How long has all this been going on?'

'It's hard to tell. Some of these people are new to us, some of them we have discussed before. They are all harmless, in my opinion. But my opinion does not matter.'

'What have the Watchers said?'

'They haven't said anything, though they've been seen on the dockside and in the Warrens. They've even turned up in the High Town.'

'But not in the countryside?' *The countryside. A quaint name for half a continent.*

'Not as yet, my lady. But when the rot grips Watchfold, it quickly spreads. At least, that is what the Watchers say. And no one wants another rebellion in the West, madam.'

No. No one wants that. Not ever again.

'Hmm. Then they are concerned,' Rangle said. 'And they think we are doing nothing about it. That is not good.'

Indeed it was not good. They could not attack her directly: not a Tactician, Selected by the Machinery. But they could make life uncomfortable. Did Brightling know about this? If she became irritated, she could close off the library.

She could ban me from it forever.

Garron Grinn sighed. 'The question is, what do we do about it?' His eyes flashed as they met hers.

Rangle thought it over for a moment. 'Well, we cannot fight it, that's for sure. I will go and speak with Brightling. Perhaps she will appreciate it, if we show at least some interest in the affairs of our area.'

'Yes, madam. Perhaps.'

When Garron Grinn left, Rangle thought of summoning Darrah back to the apartments. But it was growing late. *Better to be alone.*

She took herself off to her private room, and reached up to a shelf, from which she removed *it*: the book that mattered most. She had shown it to none of the members of the study group, not even Darrah.

It was an old thing – the very oldest she had found, in fact. But it did not look it; the pages were formed of a tough substance, which had survived the ages, and even the binding was unbroken. But she could feel the millennia on its pages. This was a thing from long ago: from the very beginning of it all. It had no title that she could see. In fact, it was entirely empty, comprising just a single image on a single page, in the very centre of the manuscript. It had been painted in oil, which still shimmered as if it had been created that very morning.

A woman stood alone upon a rock, her shoulders hunched. She had been attacked, or had attacked someone else; her emerald dress was torn, her red hair hung in matted clumps, and her pale skin was bruised and bloodied. But there was a defiant gleam in her green eyes, as she stared from the confines of the page. If she had lost her battle, she knew she would win her war.

In her left hand she held a mask, as white as her skin. It seemed to have a life of its own: from its own eyes poured hatred, and its mouth was a sneer. In her right hand was a silver full-moon crown, the type worn by Strategists. It was stained red.

Below this woman, in a harsh scrawl, someone had written: *Ruin will come with the One.*

Chapter Six

Not even the People's Level of Memory Hall could hold the crowds that came for the wake of Strategist Kane.

The old man lay in state in the centre of the hall, his body resting on a circular grey stone, his hands clasped on his chest and his grey hair flowing around his silver full-moon crown. He wore a silken gown of Strategist purple embroidered with recurring patterns of the number 9938: the year of his Selection. On his feet were slippers of silver satin, and an ivory brooch in the shape of an open hand was pinned to his chest. A forty-strong bodyguard surrounded the deathstone, armed with handcannon and sword and eyeing the hordes suspiciously.

Katrina leaned against the Southern Gate, alone in the crowd, exhausted and bored. It had taken weeks to reach the Centre, travelling in a line of carriages and military para-phernalia. The long journey through the ices of the North had been tense and silent, despite the great bloodless victory that had been achieved over Northern Blown. It was never easy to spend time with the Tactician, and Kane's death hung over everyone like a miserable spectre.

It had been weeks now, months, since the Strategist had died, yet still they had only reached his wake. Nothing ever happened quickly in the Overland. Not quick enough for Katrina, anyway. It was one of her many flaws, according to Brightling. *You must develop caution, Katrina. You are always overreaching.* But Brightling only saw the young part of her. She had observed her Apprentice for years, and was the greatest Watcher of the land, yet still she could not see all of her.

Grief was everywhere: the people mourned for the Strategist. Ahead of Katrina was a knot of old women, their worn hemp shawls marking them out as peasants. To their right a girl clung to her father, staring at Katrina from above his shoulder. She was surely too young to comprehend the day's events, but her eyes were red: perhaps she had been swept along by the emotion around her. Katrina wondered if the source of all this misery was not so much the death of the Strategist, but what it entailed. No one had wanted a Selection in the 10,000th year.

As she looked to the weeping mourners, the Apprentice Watcher wondered how they would behave when they attended the Strategist's actual funeral. This was all for show, was it not? But Katrina could not pretend. Not where Kane was concerned. Neither part of her had ever liked him, and both were glad to see the back of his racking cough and lecherous glances.

It was a rare day that she was allowed to visit Memory Hall, the regal home of the Strategist. Her place was in the See House, the black tower of the Watchers that stood alone and resplendent on the Priador. Memory Hall was a smaller affair, a squat, red marble palace in the centre of Greatgift Avenue. Yet the sense of history here – her history, her country's history – was palpable.

The walls were hung with tapestries, each recording an historical event, from the Gifting of the Machinery onwards.

The greatest individuals were immortalised in statues of bronze and stone and gold, staring blindly down upon their descendants. There was Strategist Arandel, the prophet of the Machinery, standing in gold eighteen feet tall at the Eastern Gate, naked apart from his peasant's smock. Opposite him were the stone figures of the Five Warriors, Tacticians of the Early Period, who glared down at onlookers from their destriers. And there by the staircase, so small he was barely visible, stood Strategist Lalle, who died just two days after his Selection at the age of ninety-six, by falling down that very staircase.

She was about to move forward into the crowd, when all eyes suddenly swung in her direction. Behind her, the gate was opening.

Brightling was dressed to mourn, a robe of white rags partly obscured by a black satin gown trimmed with Tactician gold. Her face wore a look of suffering that was so profound it was almost poised: a single tear glimmered on her right cheek, trailing a path through her blusher. Her white hair flowed freely; this struck Katrina as odd, at first, until she realised that the Tacticians would all have removed their half-moon crowns. The Strategist was dead, meaning that all the Cabinet, including the Tacticians, would now face a new Selection.

Brightling floated forward to the deathstone, the crowd melting before her and Katrina following in her wake. A dense silence breathed through the People's Level as the Tactician came to the body of her late superior. She leaned over the corpse, the tear balancing for a moment on her cheek before falling to the old man's pallid face. She reached a hand out, but seemed to quickly think better of it and pulled back, turning her perfectly miserable countenance to her Apprentice.

'Come, Katrina.'

Together, walking almost in step, Tactician and Apprentice strode forward to the staircase, the eyes of the crowd still upon them. Katrina felt exposed, under their gazes. She was used to being shunted around in the shadows, but lately the Tactician had placed her in the foreground, in preparation for her elevation to a Watcher. *If they actually make you one.*

When they reached the base of the stairs, Brightling stopped and turned to the crowd, pointing a finger to the ground, to the Underland. The people fell to their knees, bowing their heads so low that their lips almost touched the stone floor.

In a short, sharp movement, Brightling pulled her hand back down to her side and turned around. Katrina briefly looked behind as they climbed, and saw that the people remained on their knees, driven to the ground by a woman whose time as a Tactician could be over in a matter of days.

'Ah, good afternoon, Tactician,' came a male voice after they had climbed ten or so steps.

Canning, the Tactician for Expansion, crawled out of a compartment in the side of the wall. The man could not abide crowds. In contrast to Brightling, he appeared to be adapting to life without pomp quite easily, clothed in a hairy woollen smock that was tied at the waist with a length of knotted vine, the uniform of the market trader he had been fourteen years before, when he was Selected. He clambered to his feet, sweat cascading down his fleshy face.

'Good afternoon, Tactician Canning,' Brightling smiled, as the rotund man brushed the dirt from his smock. 'Are you ready?'

'Yes, I suppose. These things have to be done.' He glanced at the black staircase that snaked its way upwards. 'On we go, then. May as well start.' He pushed past them and began to climb, his stout legs struggling up the steps. It was not long before he lagged behind the two women, wheezing in their wake.

Eventually they turned off the stairs. Before them was a wide corridor, the walls and floor formed of silver and interlaid with old stones; there were no paintings, statues or tapestries to obscure their terrible gleam.

At the end of the corridor was a huge, silver door. Four helmeted, armoured guards stood to attention as the Tacticians approached.

'Watching and Expansion!' came a cry from an unseen herald, as the small party swept through the entrance into the sumptuous heart of the Overland.

The first thing Katrina noticed was the chandelier, a vast construct of a thousand candles, overwhelming the room in flickering light and blue smoke. Servants pushed wheeled ladders around it, scrabbling upwards to relight extinguished flames. The room had a heavy, sleepy feel, like some brothel of the Far Below.

An immense fresco covered the walls, telling of the Gifting of the Machinery. The observer's eyes were first drawn to an image of a savage tribe: they wore animal pelts, and some had bones as jewellery. Before them stood Arandel, the prophet of the Machinery and the herald of the Operator. The people looked upon him with loathing.

The events depicted on the next wall took the scene forward, to the moment of the Operator's arrival. Arandel, benign and beatific, stood on the Primary Hill, his arms open as he implored the people to listen to his words. Behind him burned a great fire, from which emerged the Operator, his cloak a living thing of dark flame that swirled with faces.

I know you, thought the younger part of Katrina. *I have seen you.*

Do not think about it, said the older part. *It doesn't help you to think about it.*

Agreed.

One scene stretched out across both the east and south walls: a depiction of the three buildings that were left to the people by the Operator. Straight ahead was the See House, the home of the Watchers, a crooked black tower on the edge of the Priador. Behind it, a night sky was smeared with stars. In the centre, painted over the corner where the east and south walls met, sat the Circus, the great stadium of the Overland, built at the very spot on the Primary Hill where the people had first encountered the Operator and where Selections still occurred today. The sky was lightening at this point, the marble edifice surrounded by dusk. To its right, smaller than the other buildings but somehow more imposing, was Memory Hall, the red palace in which they all now stood, its black windows winking at the viewer.

Katrina turned from the walls. Ahead of her, at the far end of the room, was a golden throne.

'Do you know what that is, Katrina?' Brightling asked.

'Yes, madam.'

'Well, off you go then. Pay your respects.'

Katrina nodded, then hesitantly padded forward.

This chair had hosted the backsides of the greatest men and women of the world: the Strategists, Selected by the Machinery to rule the Overland. As she stared at the seat, a sense of history drew up within her, making her dizzy: somehow, despite everything she knew, she could not convince herself that Arandel, Lalle, Kane, Obland, Syer, Barrio, and all the rest, had sat just five feet from where she now knelt.

'It seems simple at first, doesn't it?'

Katrina looked up with a start to see Tactician Canning at her side.

'Yes. I thought it would be …'

'More grandiose.'

'Yes.'

'You can't see it all in the smoke. Give it a moment – look to the sides.'

Canning backed away as Katrina studied the throne. After a moment, the smoke cleared and it emerged: an almost perfect statue of the Operator, sitting on the edge of the great chair with his legs crossed and his arms folded in his lap. His cloak fell in waves around the base of the throne, strange images of trapped souls painted onto its surface. A hooked nose sat beneath two hollow black eyes, their expression impassive, neutral.

Katrina had hardened over the years, grown accustomed to seeing his image. And yet, there he was, again in the form of a statue – the creature that had taken her brother.

You think that, but do you know? You could be mad.

'Brightling, is your skivvy done with her gawping? Is there not much to be discussed among us?'

The voice came from above.

'Black hair, pale skin, nice girlie, very nice. Regal, I would say. From the Centre, yes. A Balatto, perhaps? No, too pretty, too delectable. A strange appearance. What is she?'

Grotius, the Tactician of the North, leered down at her. He was a huge man, fatter even than Canning. Even here in the Cabinet room, above the Strategist's Throne itself, he gnawed on the fried wing of some massive bird, wiping his hands on the bloodied apron he retained from his pre-Selection career as a butcher. Servants flittered around him, carefully wiping blood and grease from the golden robes that were visible just below the apron. A red cleaver hung ominously at his waist.

'Grotius, be quiet. You northern ape—'

'Western whore.'

67

'Redbarrel rat.'

This new voice came from the western wall. Katrina realised, now, that the room was broken into stepped levels: in the gloom, she could make out three sets of stairs, one leading to Grotius on the northern wall, another to this new speaker, the third to the south, at the door through which they had entered.

'I am ignoring you, now, Grotius.'

Rangle, the Tactician of the West, was old; Katrina judged the woman to be in her eighth decade, to guess from the few wisps of grey hair that clung to her withered scalp. It was said she had wept for days when her Selection was announced: a rare reaction indeed among the ambitious denizens of the Overland. Rangle had only ever had one wish in life, they said: to study at the College. Her Selection put an end to all that.

'No! No, I don't want it! Mummy!'

Katrina turned to the southern wall. Bardon, ruler of the South, was nine years old: the youngest Tactician for fifty years. He was a small thing, even for his age, and looked as if a gust of wind could carry him away. He was a beautiful child, his skin a light brown and his wide eyes a striking blue. He sat atop a heap of silk-covered feather pillows, almost drowning in his golden gown, toying with a wooden doll and glancing nervously around the room. A chubby, harassed-looking woman, who Katrina assumed was the child's mother, stood behind his throne: her efforts to hand him his official papers were not well received.

'Katrina – come here now. That is enough.'

Two silver chairs sat on the lower level, in the centre of the floor: Katrina must have walked through them without realising. Canning and Brightling were sitting on them, side by side. The Watching Tactician motioned to Katrina to join her before turning to her colleague.

'Who is chairing the Cabinet, Canning?'

'Hmm? Oh, Tactician Bardon, I believe. His mother is trying to give him his notes.'

They all glanced up at the southern wall, where Tactician Bardon had finally been persuaded to accept his papers, a sullen expression on his face. Brightling hissed under her breath:

'The boy! On a day like this!'

'Yes.'

'Well,' sighed Brightling, 'there is nothing to be done.'

Bardon suddenly looked at the crowd, head snapping up from the papers like a startled rabbit. He clapped his hands together and the room fell into total silence, bar the slurping of Tactician Grotius's gums on avian bones.

Bardon glanced at his hands, as if shocked by what he had done, then smiled, lifted the papers, and began to read in a high-pitched, faltering voice:

'Almost seven weeks ago, the Strategist of the Overland, Kane, who was Selected by the Machinery, was found dead. You will all be aware of this.'

Tactician Rangle made a little noise.

'We, the Tacticians of the people, were Selected to serve for our lifetimes, or until the death of the Strategist, when all must be cast asunder and made anew. That time has come.'

The boy cast a glance at his mother, who gave him a reassuring smile and stuck two thumbs up.

Bardon turned back to the room. 'We must begin the process of Selection,' he said. 'The Machinery, its messages interpreted and transmitted by the Operator, will bring forth a new Cabinet to replace the old, a new leadership for our people. All, some, or none of us may be Selected again. It matters not: what matters is the glory of the Overland.'

A round of applause erupted from the Tacticians and their assistants. Brightling smiled; Rangle twitched; Canning reached for his wine and Grotius finished his dinner.

Tactician Bardon glanced into the far corners of the room.

'I now call on the Operator of the Machinery to tell us when the Selection will be, so that we may prepare the people for their examination and our minds for judgement.'

Katrina gripped Brightling's throne. *Is he going to come here?* asked the younger part of herself. *If he does, you say nothing, and remain calm.*

'There!'

Katrina was not sure who had spoken, but it did not matter; she had seen it too.

A piece of paper was floating in the air from the ceiling above, dipping and reeling like a feather before landing at Tactician Bardon's feet. Katrina studied the ceiling for any sign of the Operator, but realised it was pointless. It was like trying to catch a sunbeam.

Bardon seemed unsure of himself. He touched the paper, quickly withdrawing his hand as if expecting a shock. When this did not occur, he picked it up.

'Three weeks' time for the Tacticians,' he whispered, 'and five for the Strategist.'

Silence held for a moment, before the room broke into chaos. Some assistants ran from the hall to spread the word; others chattered excitedly in little groups. Grotius ate his chicken; Rangle read her book; Brightling examined her fingernails; Canning looked to the floor; and Bardon beamed with pride. But all of them, Katrina saw, cast jealous looks in their colleagues' directions.

She knew what they were thinking; she had lived with a Tactician long enough to read them. Five weeks for the

Machinery to absorb the will of the people. Five weeks until the current group of Tacticians would gather once again by the Portal, the very place where the prophet Arandel had announced the coming of the Machinery, to receive the information they dreaded and anticipated in equal measure. Five weeks, and they would all find out. But they already knew one thing: the favourite for the role of Strategist, given their talents and experience, had to be one of them.

Had it not?

Chapter Seven

Rangle remained in her apartments after the gathering of the Cabinet, and did not leave for days.

Kane's death had affected her in ways she could never have anticipated. She had not liked the man. There was a cruel streak to him. It was nothing severe, just a low-level meanness. She had known him longer than anyone on the Plateau, and she had seen it on many occasions. When she was first Selected, he had spoken with her, and quickly discovered her ambition to study at the College. He said it would be possible, that he would arrange everything. But when she arrived at the Great Hall, her name was not on the register. They all knew who she was, the students and the Scholars; they knew how she had been humiliated. They would never mock a Tactician of the Overland, not to her face. But she saw it; their eyes smiled at her.

She knew he was old. She wondered at his longevity, if truth were told. That cough of his. Those wasted limbs. But still he continued, pestering females, bringing whores to the Cabinet. She had known he would die before long. She could feel death stalking them both, while Brightling and the others looked to the future and schemed.

But something was wrong, in this death.

'How could he fall from the balcony?' Darrah had asked. 'He must have sat there a hundred thousand times. How could he contrive to fall?'

She had not responded. She could not. She didn't believe it either. But she had to. Brightling said he had fallen, so he had fallen.

Someone knocked at the study door.

'Come in, Darrah.'

The younger woman held a bowl of soup in her hands. By the side was a torn chunk of black bread.

'You should eat.'

Rangle nodded and waved to the table, where Darrah set down the food.

'Are you coming to bed tonight?' Darrah glanced at the corner of the study, where Rangle kept a single bed. The Tactician stayed here sometimes, when she felt the need for solitude. Darrah did not understand, and did not like it.

'I don't know.'

Darrah nodded. Her eyes burned. 'The others have arrived.'

Rangle smiled. 'Good. Tell them I will be there very soon. And get them soup, if they want it.'

Darrah nodded, almost imperceptibly, and stormed out of the room. *That girl would be better off without me. I should end it. But I won't.*

There was one thing in the world that prevented Annara Rangle from following Kane off the balcony of Memory Hall. It was not Darrah, and it certainly wasn't her exalted station. It was her study group.

She started it about three years into her life as a Tactician. There were three members back then; Rangle herself, a curious

Administrator called Eddvard, and Brynn, the Tactician of the North in those faraway days.

It began by accident. She had been to the library of the College – it was the only one she could access, at that time, and she was grateful for it – and had borrowed a Middle Period work of philosophy, *The Halls of the Underland*. She had always been obsessed with the Underland. What was this place? Some of the writings described it as another place of existence, or as a repository of historical memory. Some people had accessed it, the stories said, but only when the Underland wished to be entered. Otherwise, its gateways were always closed. And yet, there were so many strange things in the world that could not have come from the Overland. She had always been certain of it.

This book was a revelation. It argued that there was no Underland or Overland, but one country; the Underland could be seen in our daily lives. It was a strange little text, and its author was unknown, which was perhaps well for him or her; the book was not considered Doubting in these enlightened, modern days, but who knew what they would have thought back then, when things were darker and ignorance reigned. It played an important role in the Tactician's life. One evening she was reading it in her study in the apartments (even then she stayed away from Watchfold), when Brynn had arrived unannounced. She heard him enter too late; he was looking over her shoulder before she even knew he was there.

'I have thought about that book for ten years now,' he whispered. He was very young, just a few years older than her; there was something calming in his brown eyes. He was from the West, too, but there the similarities ended; he came from wealth, far greater than that of her family. He stank of it.

'Sometimes I look around me, and I see things, and I am sure they are not of the Overland.' She remembered his words as clearly as if he had spoken yesterday. 'They cannot be. Do you understand me?'

She was frightened. She could still feel the fear, even now. 'I do understand you.'

He nodded, and left the room, forgetting whatever business he had come to discuss. But two days later he returned, with some manuscripts from his own collection. They met in the evenings, after Cabinet meetings; no one suspected a thing. Why would they? He was a Tactician, and they had business to attend to. One day he had simply shown up with Eddvard, as if the Administrator had always attended their clandestine discussions. No one ever asked why he started coming; it was better that way.

Over the years, the group changed members. Brynn died unexpectedly a few years into their studies, to be replaced as Tactician of the North by Syrrian, who was in turn succeeded by Grotius, the disgusting bastard. Eddvard passed away not much later. But the group carried on. As the years rolled by, Rangle grew better at identifying like-minded individuals. She was proud of her success; they had never been discovered.

She wondered what would happen, if Brightling found out. Would it even be considered a threat, the ramblings of an old lady and her friends? Perhaps it would anger the Watching Tactician. After all, she had allowed Rangle access to the greatest library in the Overland, its shelves stacked with dangerous knowledge. How would she feel, if she knew Rangle was showing these books to other people?

All we do is ask questions. Could that really anger her? The Tactician of the West did not care to find out. *All that any Doubter seems to do is ask questions. It would*

*not matter how important one was, if one was found to be
a Doubter.*

They were all there, seated at the long table, when she
came into the main reception room. Darrah had only lit one
of the tall candles, leaving the main lamps extinguished. A
strange, weak light played across the faces of the members
of Rangle's study group.

There were three members these days, apart from her. They
were clustered together at one end of the table, whispering
among themselves. In the centre, at what he undoubtedly
perceived to be the head of the table, was Lanurus Randalo.
In many ways he was a rather pitiable creature. He was the
head of an illustrious family, whose wealth had originally
been built by some hardy Randalos who cornered an offshoot
of the northern fur trade. From these tough, resourceful
people had descended a line of weaklings and dilettantes,
who spent their days carousing and dipping their toes into
a succession of ill-starred careers and ventures. They never
spoke of the business that had made them rich; there was
no allusion to it in their coat of arms, no hint of it in their
halls. Their snobbery was almost amusing in its crassness,
especially as their share in the original venture was all that
kept them afloat.

Lanurus was the scion of this brood. He was a sharp-
nosed thing, with long chestnut hair that he slathered with
oils and an eclectic array of jewellery that encrusted his ears,
nose and fingers. His pale skin had turned a sickly yellow
over the years, perhaps through his legendarily poor diet,
though it did not manifest itself in any extra weight; on the
contrary, he was a rattling bag of bones. He was older than
he looked; he had to be, for Rangle had known him now for
almost two decades, and his appearance had never changed.

To Lanurus's right sat an entirely contrasting character. Maro Danussa was a short man, but he made up for it in sheer bulk; his chair seemed to warp under his weight. But his girth was of a different order to Grotius's, the hideous wretch, or even to Canning's. It was muscle, not fat; he was a round ball of sinew. He was black, and his eyes were quick and wary. He shaved his head entirely, save for a single band of hair that ran from the middle of his brow to the back of his skull.

Rangle did not know what he did in the real world, and she had never asked. But he had attended her group now for almost ten years, and though his interventions were rare, they were thoughtful when they came.

Finally, there was Darrah. She smiled up at Rangle when the Tactician entered, and rolled her eyes at whatever Lanurus had been saying.

'Tactician,' Lanurus said, getting to his feet and opening his arms. Rangle embraced him, and took a seat by Darrah.

'You should call me Annara, Lanurus.'

'Yes, I know. I will do so from now on, Tactician.'

This had been a little tradition of theirs for almost twenty years.

'So,' Rangle said, taking a seat, 'what should we discuss? I cannot remember where we left off last time. I think we were discussing the proscribed literature of the Middle Period, weren't we?'

There was a pregnant silence. Lanurus and Maro exchanged glances, while Darrah tried to suppress a smile.

'Madam Tactician,' said the scion of the fur trade in his most unctuous tones, 'I wonder if things have not rather changed, and whether we could discuss something else.'

Rangle shifted in her seat and cracked her knuckles. She could crack just about everything these days.

'Oh yes?' She turned her gaze upon Lanurus. 'What would that be?'

'Kane,' spat Maro. The word shot from his mouth like a crossbow bolt. He was in no mood for games.

Rangle sighed. 'I know.'

'It is strange, is it not?' Lanurus asked. There was a patina of sweat on his forehead. 'Given the year.'

Rangle nodded. She thought of the book she had, the book with just one image, of a red-haired woman holding a mask and a crown. 'It is strange, yes,' she said. Her voice was wavering. 'But let us not read too much into it, as yet. Kane was an old man.'

'Old age does not explain why someone would leap off a balcony, if indeed he did jump.' Lanurus was growing agitated.

'Lanurus,' said Darrah, 'we don't know anything about what happened. The Watchers are still investigating.'

Maro grunted. The members of the group were not uniform admirers of the Watchers.

Rangle hunched forward, burying her hands in the dark folds of her scholar's gown. 'Lanurus is right, it pains me to say.'

A hush fell over the group. It was rare for Rangle to speak against Darrah, at least so openly. 'I knew Andus Kane for … well, a long age. Too long, really. He was a truly vicious old goat.'

Lanurus snorted a laugh.

'But I do not believe he would have killed himself. He was a grumpy bastard, but there is no doubt he enjoyed his station, and all the benefits it brought him.'

'Booze, whores and high living,' said Darrah. If she was annoyed with Rangle, she did not show it.

'Yes. And he was in good health, as far as that went with him,' Rangle said. 'He seemed content when I last saw him.'

Lanurus leaned back in his chair, to the point that it seemed he might keel over. 'Then we should be asking a different question,' he said. 'If the Strategist did not jump from the balcony, how did he come to be on the ground, in a crumpled, bloodied mess?'

'Lanurus, you are disrespectful,' said Darrah. *Funny, she treats me with cheerful disdain, but she will defend the institutions of our country to the end.*

Lanurus straightened his chair and spread his palms apologetically. 'I only mean to ask the question. You must all be thinking the same thing.'

'So you think he was murdered?' Rangle spoke just above a whisper, but her words brought them up hard.

Lanurus was about to respond, but Maro beat him to it. 'Yes.'

'Why?' asked Rangle.

'Because it is too much to be a coincidence. We've talked about this for years, Tactician. It is the 10,000th year. If the Prophecy holds, it will break this year and Select the One who will bring Ruin. Someone out there probably just—'

'Sought to speed things up,' Lanurus said. Maro nodded.

'Why would anyone do that, though?' asked Darrah. 'The Machinery Selects who it wants. And there's no reason to believe that old story. It isn't even in the Book of the Machinery.'

'But the Machinery might make a bad Selection, if it's breaking. And there have been stories, right from the very start, Darrah,' said Lanurus. 'Some people kept them alive. I can't believe, after all this time, you don't see some truth to it, or at least the possibility of some truth.'

Darrah shook her head. 'It is too unbelievable. We don't know where those words came from. All we know is that the

Machinery and the Operator exist, and that they've looked after us all this time. I can't see any reason why that would change. It's foolish to speculate.'

Rangle had heard all of this so many times before. *What happens if it's true? Who will it Select? What will they do?*

'It doesn't matter if the Prophecy is true,' said Maro. He'd been unusually talkative. 'All that matters is whether someone out there believed it. They might have thought they could impress the Machinery, by acting so decisively, especially if the Machinery is really broken. They might not even care about the Prophecy.'

There was a sound in the hallway and the group fell into sudden, fearful silence. *Surely it can't be the Watchers? They might be especially vigilant, now, after recent events. But no; they don't make sounds. Unless they want us to know they're there.*

Rangle flicked her eyes at Darrah, and immediately the assistant sprang to her feet and ran to the hall. She returned after a moment.

'There's no one there.'

'No disturbances at the door or the windows?'

'No. Nowhere. It was just a book, in your study.'

'What do you mean? A noisy book, flapping its pages?'

Darrah held up her hand, displaying the book Rangle treasured above all others: the book that contained the red-haired woman and the crown, and *Ruin will come with the One …*

'It fell off the shelf.'

'What book is that?' asked Lanurus. *Trust him to be curious.* He did not recognise it, because she had never shown it to him.

'Nothing. Darrah, please put it back.'

The assistant disappeared from the room, and quickly returned, resuming her seat.

Rangle sighed. 'I think Maro is correct, for what it's worth. It is entirely possible that someone out there thought they could impress the Machinery by carrying out a terrible act like this. We've come across this phenomenon before.'

'The Lonely Strategist,' said Lanurus.

'Yes. A great tragedy of the Early Period.'

'The Lonely Strategist thought he would rule alone, if he killed the competition. His Selection was a cruelty, that ended in perdition.' Darrah grinned.

'Not so much perdition as death,' said Lanurus. 'Stabbed to death in his bed at night. Everyone knows his story. Why would anyone want to emulate it?'

'Maybe they think it will be different for them,' said Maro. 'If the Machinery is breaking, and it's going to Select only one person, then maybe they're trying to impress it with their ruthlessness.'

'But it doesn't make sense,' said Lanurus. 'If the Machinery is breaking, and this has been prophesied for ten thousand years, then it's already going to Select the One who will bring Ruin. It's set in stone. There would be no point in trying to influence it.'

'It might not be related at all,' said Darrah. 'Maybe the One already *knows* they're going to be Selected. The murders might be a way to cause chaos, to distract attention from themselves. Or maybe the murderer might just enjoy that kind of thing.'

'You have a devious mind, Darrah,' said Lanurus. 'Maybe that's what the Tactician sees in you.'

He grinned at Rangle. She didn't respond. She sat in her chair, and listened, as the conversation went round in circles, long into the night.

Sometimes, late in the evening, Rangle liked to drink alone.

She knew it was not a healthy habit. But she had a strange relationship with the bottle. Perhaps it came from her childhood. Her father – a mean man – never touched a drop, and despised those who did, though the vineyard was the family's main business interest. He forced his daughter out there, in the heat, until her hands were red raw, but he did not go there himself. He never went there himself. *And now I drink by myself.*

She was still in the reception room, long after the others had left, though she had moved from the table to a soft chair. Darrah had gone to bed behind the curtain, but Rangle was in no mood for sleep.

She held the wine glass up to the light of a candle, so the purple liquid gave off a dull glow. Did this come from her father's estate? *Who runs that these days, anyway? Some cousin or other?* She hadn't bothered to check. She simply never felt the need.

There was a sound, from the study. *The same sound as before. Did Darrah not put the book back properly in its place?*

Rangle carefully placed her glass on the floor and got to her feet. She felt light-headed, somewhat dizzy. How much had she had to drink? She couldn't be drunk, could she?

The Tactician pushed open the door of the study and entered cautiously. The book was on the floor, opened at an empty page.

Rangle covered her hand with her mouth, as if to stifle a yell, but no sound came.

A woman stood in the study, with her back turned to Rangle. Her head hung low, her red hair glowed in the candle-light, and she held a white mask in her hand. She turned to face the Tactician, and stared with depthless eyes that were as green as her dress. Her face was unlined, as clear and waxy as the mask itself, as if she was formed of unending layers, each one harder and more beautiful than the last. Her mouth broke into a smile, but it was a cruel thing, a half-mad grin that set the eyes alight.

It was the woman from the book.

'Ruin is coming.'

Chapter Eight

'Where was he when you found him?'

'He was on the ground, General. Beneath the Western Window.'

'Was he alone?'

'Of course, my lord.'

Brandione was standing by the deathstone. The People's Level was heavy with silence, dark and vacant since the mourners had been expelled from the wake. The General's only company was Bandles, the ancient servant of the Strategist, a tired little man he had never grown to like.

Kane had been dead for weeks, yet there were no signs of decomposition: no doubt he had been laced and slathered with oils and greases to keep him fresh. He looked peaceful, for the first time that Brandione could remember. He had been an energetic man in life, in a febrile, cantankerous way. Now he was still, his face a wax mask in the candlelight, his eyes closed to the world he had once ruled.

'He was a great man, sir. He never suffered fools gladly.' Bandles gave a weak laugh.

'No, he did not.' *He never suffered anyone gladly.* The General shuffled on his feet; he did not like talking about

Kane with others. 'And he … the Watchers think he fell?'

'Yes, General. He simply fell. Drunk, *they* say. Drunk and wandering around too close to the edge, that's what *they* believe.'

Brandione nodded. 'And he was alone then, was he?'

'Yes, sir. I brought him his dinner to the balcony, and he was quite all right and, ah, very much not on the ground, when I saw him.'

'When will the next Strategist be Selected, Bandles?'

The servant seemed surprised. 'You have not heard, sir? Tactician Brightling has printed papers about it: they are all over the city.'

'I have not seen them.'

'Oh. Well, they are everywhere.'

'Yes, you said. What do they say?'

Bandles cocked his head to the side. 'They are about the Selection, of course. The Tacticians will be Selected in three weeks, the new Strategist in five.'

Brandione nodded. This would be interesting: he had never experienced a full Selection before. He had been in the Circus for Bardon's, of course. But a full Selection occurred only on the death of a Strategist, and Kane had ruled for almost half a century.

'What do we do now?' he asked Bandles. 'Where do we go?'

'Go?' Bandles seemed surprised. 'We don't go anywhere. Not until the Selection, at any rate. No, we stay right where we are, in the apartments. You never know: the new Strategist might want to keep me on. And you, of course. He will need a senior adviser.'

Brandione smiled. Bandles would be kept on, no doubt: he was an institution in Memory Hall. *But they won't want me. A new Strategist will want a new adviser. And even if they did, would I want to stay?*

'Bandles, you may leave now. Return to the apartments and prepare supper.'

The little servant bowed and vanished into the shadows of the hall.

Alone together again. Brandione balled his hand into a fist and rested it on Kane's narrow chest. They had last met in the Strategist's apartments, before the long road to the last battles in the North. They were sitting by the Western Window, Brandione looking out over the rolling gardens, the Strategist nodding and chuckling at some unspoken joke. He had drunk too much, as ever, and was strewn across his chair. It was a cold night, though Kane did not seem to notice or care; his purple robes lay open, exposing the mangled white hair and mottled grey skin of his chest. He balanced a glass of Watchfold on his knee, and sucked occasionally on a pipe.

The Strategist coughed: it seemed to wake him from his reverie, making him sit bolt upright and flick his eyes in Brandione's direction, blinking in red-eyed recognition.

'When are you going north again, then, General? Northern Blown still stands, does it not?' It had been the fifth time he had asked this question in the past hour. His chest rattled when he spoke, but his eyes were bright and vital.

'Tomorrow, Strategist.'

'Tomorrow! By the Machinery! You have only been back for a week. Perhaps I shall forbid it, hmm? Would you like that? Would you prefer to stay here with me, with your old Strategist?'

'I serve at your command, Strategist.'

'Hmm.' Kane drew deeply on the pipe, exhaling a plume of grey smoke that writhed upwards, dissipating quickly into nothing. 'I think you should go. By all accounts, General, you are needed there. You are quite ... what did Brightling say? Ruthless. Yes, you are needed.'

'I am pleased that Tactician Brightling values me, Strategist.' Kane barked a laugh.

'Yes! Yes, values you! I suppose she does. Oh yes, she certainly does. Her type is usually different: not you dark ones. No, she normally prefers a *paler* type. Thin, milky little boys. You should see the pair she has squirreled away over there in the See House! Shameful stuff!'

The General looked at the ground. Only the Strategist dared speak to him in this way. His success as a General of the Overland had inspired Kane to move him into Memory Hall, to serve as his adviser. It was a great privilege, second only to being Selected, but Brandione could not help feeling like he had more honour when he was fighting on a muddy field.

'Oh, come come, General.' The Strategist leered at him, his tongue a dying worm. 'Do not take offence. If I truly disparaged you, you would not be where you are today. You are the most highly respected man on the Plateau outside the Cabinet, given your accomplishments. But perhaps not in the West, after that little uprising of theirs. No, they might not like you too much over there.' The Strategist collapsed once more into convulsions.

Brandione shifted, and looked to the West.

'I can see your brain whirring General, like the Machinery itself. Do not worry about anything that happened there. You did well, oh yes. Brightling told me that you were more than just a soldier back then, you know.'

'I do not understand, Strategist.'

Kane chuckled, that rasping noise that set Brandione's teeth on edge. He had seemed permanently amused in life, as if his Selection to the highest office gave him the right to hold everything else in contempt. They said he had been a vagrant, in his old life: a wanderer, singing for his supper, who was propelled from the gutter to the stars. *The Machinery knows.*

The old man took a drag on his pipe, and blew the smoke into the General's face.

'You were needed over there, General. I know it got rough, but you were needed. Canning, who, by the Machinery, is the Tactician for Expansion, was absent when we were fighting a war! I cannot think why he was Selected, except perhaps to show the rest of us in a better light. But you were there, General. You fulfilled a larger role, Brightling says. The role of an overseer. The role of a *Tactician*. She says you've been the same ever since, up in the North too. It never does to question the Machinery, but I would be very surprised if you were overlooked for Expansion, when that fool dies or when I go myself.'

Brandione looked at the ground. 'Strategist, our only enemies now are Northern Blown and its minor allies. Where would we Expand to?'

Kane hesitated: a rarity for him. 'We will find a place to go. Leave that to the Machinery. And Brightling.' He laughed, and the coughing returned.

Brandione snapped back to the cold reality of the People's Level, and lifted his fist from the Strategist's chest. *How did you die? Did you truly jump?*

He pushed the thought aside. He was a soldier; such considerations were for the Watchers. Now the madness would begin. *A total Selection.* It would come soon, Bandles had said: three weeks for the Tacticians, and five for the Strategist.

I would be very surprised if you were overlooked for the role of Expansion Tactician, when that fool dies or when I go myself. The words made the General shudder. He had no wish to sit in the Fortress of Expansion, or in the See House, or in the palaces of the North or the South or the West, or even Memory Hall. He was a soldier, born to serve. *But who will you be serving, now? Canning? Brightling? And who will the new Strategist be, in this glorious age of Overland domination? Grotius or Rangle, perhaps?*

Brandione sighed. Noticing that Kane's shroud was slightly askew, he lifted it to cover the Strategist's closed eyes. He had a sudden urge to plant a kiss on the old man's cold forehead: perhaps it was just exhaustion getting the better of him. He resisted, turned on his heel and marched to the staircase, to return to the silence of the Strategist's apartments.

'We must almost be there sir, hmm? We are, aren't we?'

Farringer gave Brandione a pleading look, brushing peacock feathers from his face. They were part of his new helm. Today he was garbed in a fiery yellow jacket laced with black silk, its shoulders stuffed with straw. He wore bright red hose on his legs, and on his head, the helm, a riotous mauve and golden nest. 'Why do you think the Tactician wants to see us, sir?'

'Me, Farringer: he wants to see me.'

The General turned his gaze to the view ahead. They were making good time: the carriage rumbled along at a reasonable speed, thanks in no small part to the solid horses he had borrowed from the dead Strategist's train. He watched with satisfaction as the driver whipped the beasts into renewed speed. There were parts of working for Memory Hall that he would miss.

'Ah, look General! It's getting bigger all the time! Only a few hours now, by my reckoning.'

Well, the idiot can see all right. It was true; the Fortress of Expansion was visible, up ahead, though its shape was as yet undefined. It stood on the western end of Greatgift Avenue, so was still technically in the Centre, but truly it was alone.

Memory Hall and the Circus were miles to the East, and the See House was further still. This part of Greatgift was nothing more than a dirt track, with the odd inn or dwelling breaking the monotony. The terrain around was grassland, rolling fields that led inexorably to the vast and luscious West.

'We will be there soon, won't we, sir?'

'Yes, Farringer.' There was a nervous twinge in his assistant's dull grey eyes. 'Have you not been before?'

Farringer laughed. 'Oh, no, no not me! I am more the academic type, sir; not a warrior like yourself, oh no. I wear the armour when I need to, sir, but that's all really. No, I am a servant, a functionary—'

'Have you heard anything about it? Perhaps in some intellectual gathering?'

'Oh yes, General. I've heard things. I did not believe them, being a rational man. But I was told that there are ghosts in there: ghosts in hidden rooms of bones.'

Brandione smiled and patted his assistant on the knee. 'No, Farringer. It's far too dangerous for ghosts. There are bones, though.'

Farringer gave a nervous laugh.

'Some say it has a mind of its own,' the General continued. 'And that it likes to ambush people.' He indicated to the road ahead; Farringer turned to look, and almost jumped out of the carriage as the Fortress, which just moments before had been a blur on the horizon, loomed suddenly overhead.

'By the Machinery!' Farringer cried. 'There it is!'

The Fortress of Expansion was a stepped pyramid, as large as three towns stacked one on top of the other. It was a monstrosity of black marble, rearing up from the grasslands like a giant scab, hard and dark. It was the greatest manmade building in the world, rivalled only by the See House, Memory

Hall and the Circus, all of them Operator creations. The Expansion Tactician Defrane, yearning for a power base of his own to rival the See House, had built it towards the close of the Early Period. Thousands died in its construction, slaves marched down from the newly conquered northeast, dragging their quarried stones behind them. According to legend, the Operator had wept with pride when he first laid eyes upon it, this great shimmering heap of black beauty.

'I love this place,' Brandione whispered.

'*Why?* It is fearful.'

The General cracked his knuckles.

'Look at it. It is the pride of our land, Farringer. It stands alone. It would be quite the invader who could approach it unseen during the day, and at night this road burns with torches. Its very shape makes it almost impenetrable. There is only one gate. And it is hard, Farringer. That northern marble Defrane found: we have never since mined the like of it.'

Farringer whistled through his teeth.

'But breaching its walls is just the start of your worries. The interior is a labyrinth of low, winding corridors and hidden rooms, made more treacherous by mirrored walls and smoke-filled crevices.'

Farringer grunted, unconvinced.

'I don't like it, sir. It seems to speak, somehow. Oh, ignore me.'

Brandione shielded his eyes against the sun and gazed up at the Fortress. The wind howled around its vastness, screaming down at them. *Perhaps Farringer has a point about this place. Being a coward does not necessarily make you wrong.*

Strange green fires seemed to glow from within some of the chambers. Brandione knew he would be recognised, but that did not quell the sense of unease he always felt when entering this place.

It was almost two hours before the carriage reached the end of the road, passing through a series of iron gates until it came up against the base of the building itself. The Fortress was a monster here, dizzying to gaze upon. Brandione had long learned to look straight ahead, and never up: a glance at the quivering wretch by his side suggested Farringer had quickly learned this lesson too.

Before them were two oaken doors, studded with iron, each the height of Memory Hall and almost as wide. They lay open, revealing a black chasm beyond, as if a vast cannon had torn a hole into the side of the pyramid. As with the towers along the road, no guard was visible, but Brandione knew they were being watched.

The driver pulled the horses to a stop. Brandione reached into the folds of his robe and withdrew a sovereign; the driver nodded once in gratitude as he took the money, before flicking his whip at the horses and leaving.

'There's noone here, sir.' Farringer was behind Brandione, pressed up close against him.

'They are here. Come.'

The General strode forward to the entrance, Farringer scuttling along in his wake. As they entered the blackness, the sounds of the outside world vanished completely.

'What is this room, sir?'

Brandione reached out a hand and brushed against Farringer's shirt: it was easy to lose people here. 'It's not a room, Farringer. It's a corridor, designed for defence should the outer gate fall. See how it narrows, as we walk? An enemy could only enter three abreast at most. Their progress would be slow and … distressing.'

'Distressing?'

Brandione smiled, though Farringer could not see. 'There are troops above us.'

'I can't see anyone.'

'Exactly.'

Ahead, a dull green light glowed.

'We are almost there, Farringer.'

They came to the end of the corridor, where a torch hung from an iron gate. 'The last line of defence,' whispered the General.

'The torch?'

Brandione snorted. 'The gate, Farringer.' He reached a hand through one of the gaps in the gate until he felt a rope, which he grasped and firmly pulled. A bell rang in the distance.

'Who is there?' a voice asked after several heartbeats. The tone was neutral, bland, and somehow androgynous. It was impossible to tell if the speaker knew the General: the denizens of the Fortress kept their knowledge, or lack of it, to themselves. They had learned much from their rivalry with the See House.

'General Brandione.'

'And his assistant, Farringer!'

The gate drew upwards into the ceiling. Brandione stepped forward, relieved that, once again, he had been permitted entry to what should have been his second home. Farringer clattered along behind, preening his feathers as he went.

Before them was the Map Room of the Overland. It was a cavernous place: the ceiling disappeared somewhere overhead, and the corners melted into shadow. Torches burned in alcoves along the walls, lending the room that familiar green glow. They were placed above ceremonial swords, pikes and rusting helmets that hung from rusting hooks, hammered into the black marble.

It was the area below the visitor's feet, however, that gave the room its name. The floor was covered in a map of the mighty Plateau, its roads and rivers scored into the surface millennia before, the territories of the Overland shaded in red.

'It's beautiful,' hissed Farringer.

Brandione had to agree, though he knew the feature had a practical purpose: to impress upon the young recruits the extent and majesty of the Overland. This had been a constantly changing task for millennia, as the political influence of the Strategists had waxed and waned. But now, history was almost over, and its progress was coloured in red. The original white marble of the floor had almost entirely disappeared as the Machinery's domain had grown. Brandione noticed a group of men hunched down at the far end of the room, painting in the newly taken lands of Northern Blown. Their faces were wrapt in concentration as they set to their task with long, fine brushes, from which dripped blobs of sanguine ink.

The sides of the hall were lined with wooden desks at which sat new recruits of the Overland military, studying for their promotions and completely ignoring the new arrivals: Brandione wondered if these raw children even knew him. They would occasionally stand from their desks and cross the floor to peer at some point on the map, taking notes. Brandione remembered that well. *But what will they work on now? They should go to the West and farm, or join the Watchers. There will always be Watchers in the world.*

'Wait here,' the General commanded. 'I am going to visit the Tactician.'

Farringer whimpered as Brandione turned and walked away.

A staircase ran through the centre of the Fortress like a black corkscrew. The climb was monotonous, the only light the glow of the ubiquitous dull-green torches. Brandione passed no other person on the way up, and the only sound was the echo of his own steps. He had not lied to Farringer about the strange defences of the labyrinth: his own reflection jumped out at him along the way, leering through smoke-wreathed mirrors. The uninitiated would soon end up leaping at shadows and stabbing at glass.

Eventually he came to a mezzanine level. No light shone here, not even the baleful green. To some, this could have seemed like a dead end; the General, however, had made this journey on many occasions. He leaned against the side of the wall and knocked three times. After a few moments there came a noise from the gloom beyond: the creak of a winch. The noise seemed to grow closer, before a panel on the wall fell away and an elevated platform in the shape of a huge trough appeared, swinging back and forth in the air. Brandione clambered on board.

'To the top.'

The lift creaked upwards through the inky blackness, rolling drowsily back and forth. It would be many hours before he reached the summit of the Fortress; like the good soldier he was, he laid his head on his arm and fell asleep.

He awoke to an anxious assistant shaking his shoulder.

'Sir! You are here, sir!' The assistant was a thin, wide-eyed individual. He bowed to the General, but kept his eyes fixed on him, waving his hands to encourage him down from the platform.

Brandione leapt from the lift into the chambers of Tactician Canning, dusting himself down and wincing as he took in his surroundings. He was still unused to the splendour of this place. The pinnacle of the pyramid it may have been, but space was by no means restricted. From the lobby in which he stood, corridors branched off in all directions, and from them splintered countless receptions, bedrooms, and studies. The décor rivalled that of the Strategist's apartments in Memory Hall: the walls were hung with red velvet drapes and inlaid with gold leaf;

the floor was a patchwork of white and black squares, each emblazoned with the coat of arms of a different Expansion Tactician; and a chandelier of towering candles sent heat and light to every corner. All was richness, glory, and luxury, none of which was easily associated with the current resident.

'Where is the Tactician?'

The assistant rolled his eyes theatrically.

'In the study.'

'He will be pleased to leave this beautiful prison.'

'Aye, sir,' said the unlikely gaoler, with a look that suggested the feeling would be reciprocated. He bowed, and led Brandione down one of the plush corridors.

The study was small and plain, a place of wood and leather. It was a welcome respite for Brandione from the gleaming metal and rich cloth of the other rooms. Tactician Canning sat at a wide, circular oak table, dressed in his coarse canvas smock, his half-moon crown discarded at his side. His head was in his hands, the bald pate gleaming in the light of a torch. He seemed to be deep in thought: before him was a book, a small, hand-painted volume. Brandione wondered if he should announce himself, when the Tactician spoke.

'Take a seat, General.'

'I prefer to stand, Tactician.'

Canning squinted at him, his eyes bleary red balls. 'As you wish. Drink?'

'Perhaps some water, Tactician.'

'Ah! Water: very austere.'

Canning shuffled to the drinks cabinet. He poured a large glass of Redbarrel whiskey and a small cup of water, thrust the clear liquid at Brandione, and returned to his chair.

'I hate this place,' he said, glancing at the walls. 'The Machinery only knows why it Selected me.'

Brandione shifted.

'You will be free again soon, Tactician.'

'Ah yes: luckily for the Overland. But what will I do? They will have sold my stall by now.'

So many years at the pinnacle of the world, and all he wants to do is sell whelks.

'You are studying something, sir?'

'Yes. Getting ready for my successor. Don't know where he or she will Expand *to*, although I'm sure Brightling will have some great idea; perhaps she has found some weak little land across the sea.'

That gave the General a jolt.

'I am sure that is not the case, Tactician. The Machinery is meant for the Plateau alone.'

'Aha. I see.' Canning gave a chuckle. 'Perhaps Tactician Brightling has other ideas. I would not know; she does not share her plans for my Department with me. She runs it, you know: has done for years.' His voice was emotionless. 'I wasn't even invited to Northern Blown: the last piece of Plateau Expansion, and I wasn't there.'

He clenched his fist. Brandione thought he would smash it on the table, but the moment passed. The General looked at the floor.

'Maybe you have some ideas of your own, General. You took Anflef, did you not? And Siren Down?'

Brandione hesitated before nodding.

'We'll have to build a fleet, I suppose, or try to cross the Wite. Otherwise they'll have to tear this whole bloody building down.'

The Tactician's strained mood broke. He flung his glass against a bookshelf, cursing as it exploded into pieces.

'Sit *down*, General. You make me nervous.'

Brandione bowed, and took a leather chair by Canning's side.

'Do you know why I invited you here?'

Brandione had been wondering. 'I am now under your command, following the death of the Strategist. I thought that perhaps you had orders for me.'

Canning grimaced. He was not a man for issuing orders, and perhaps had not even realised his new authority over the General. 'No. That wasn't it at all. Forget all about that, General.' He hesitated, beads of sweat forming on his forehead. He looked at Brandione with apprehension, an almost childlike sense of nervous expectation. 'How did Kane die?'

There was silence for a moment. 'Well, he leapt or fell from his balcony in Memory Hall, Tactician, as you know.'

'Yes, but which was it? Fall or jump? Can we tell?'

'That is a question for the Watchers.' *Not for soldiers like me.*

'They will not tell me,' Canning grunted. He rose, poured himself a fresh whiskey, and took his seat again. 'I saw him, you know, just one day before he died. You were up in the North.'

'Yes, Tactician.'

'I tell you, I could see nothing wrong with him. Mentally, I mean. If someone were planning to jump, there would be some sign beforehand, no? Why take your own life? And what a life it was.'

'I am not sure I follow your meaning, Tactician.' Brandione's voice was a touch more anxious than intended.

Canning shrugged. 'Never mind,' he said, sipping his whiskey. 'Ignore me.'

Brandione had tired of this conversation: there was no good to be had from idle hints and speculation. If the Tactician had something to say to him, he should say it. The General rose from his chair and bowed. 'Thank you, Tactician, but I must retire.'

Canning looked surprised; one did not simply take leave of a Tactician, even one like him.

'Very well, General Brandione, I understand. But do me a favour, will you?'

'Of course, Tactician.'

'If you hear anything about the death, let me know. As I said … the Watchers tell me nothing.'

'Yes, Tactician.'

Brandione stood and turned, leaving the Expansion Tactician of the Overland to his whiskey.

Chapter Nine

In a dungeon of Northern Blown, Watcher Aranfal, second only to Tactician Brightling in prestige and power in the mighty See House, was chained to a desk.

Gibbet sat opposite him, tapping the table with a finger. Hood stood to the side, her arms folded, staring at the floor.

'What are you going to do now, Doubters? I don't know how you pulled that trick, but I hope you've thought this through. We are, after all, in a castle filled with Watchers, who will soon come to find me.'

Gibbet smiled, but it was uncertain. *Good.*

'You should not speak to us like that, Watcher.'

'You should not speak to us at all,' said Hood.

'You have seen our powers,' Gibbet went on. 'Actually, you have seen the merest sliver of them. Imagine what we are capable of.'

'Imagine what we could do to you.'

'Imagine.'

Aranfal sighed. 'I don't imagine anything. I haven't used my imagination since I was a young man. It's a very dangerous tool, you know.'

Gibbet smirked, then turned to Hood.

'What do you think?'

Hood stepped forward, until she stood by Aranfal's side. 'Let's look into him. See what he's hiding. There will be something …'

Gibbet shook his head. 'Time enough for all that. But he is right. The others will soon notice something's wrong. We need to get out of here. It's too early to attract attention.'

'Too early to attract the attention of Jandell, you mean.'

'Yes. He is very strong, very strong. He would punish us. He would try to take information from us.'

'Though we have none.'

'None more than he has himself, if he only had the wit to believe it.'

'But he grows paranoid. We should not provoke him.'

'No.'

'What are you talking about, by the Machinery?' Aranfal interrupted. 'Is Jandell your other friend? He is safely trussed up in another room, believe me. If you hurt me, it will be revisited on him tenfold.'

Hood barked a cold laugh, and leaned into Aranfal's face. 'That is not Jandell, idiot! You people have forgotten everything!'

'Everything!'

Hood turned to Gibbet. 'But what about him, in the other room? We should release him, if he has not already revealed himself.'

'He will not be pleased. He told us to be quiet. And now …' He flicked a finger at Aranfal. 'We have not been quiet.'

There came a knock at the door, and Aranfal smiled.

'They have come for me, my friends. You'll need to pick your next move very carefully. If you surrender, right now,

101

this can all be very painless.' *Oh no, it will be very painful, you fucking conjurers.*

Hood walked to the door, very quietly, and placed her palm against it. She closed her eyes.

'It is not a Watcher.'

'No, it most certainly is not!' came a voice from the other side. 'Let me in this instant!'

Hood hurriedly opened the door, and Aranfal's mouth fell open as the third member of the group of Doubters entered the room.

'Can none of you people stay tied up?' the Watcher asked.

'Oh, very good, very good! Can you stay tied up! Ha ha ha!'

The new arrival was about as innocuous a creature as Aranfal had ever laid eyes upon. He was short and fat, but not in a way that suggested a life of luxury; there was a tautness to him, a wiry strength that pulsed through his round frame. He seemed like an average male of middle years, with a few strands of chestnut hair spread across his wide skull. His skin was paler than Aranfal's own, and the Watcher wondered if he was from the North. But his clothing was strange. He wore a shawl formed of some kind of fur – hareskin, if Aranfal did not know better. The Watcher had seen children in such garments, in the cold North, but never an adult.

The man spoke with an intense warmth and wide-eyed glee that Aranfal would normally have taken for stupidity or naivety. But there was something in the way Gibbet and Hood responded to him that suggested otherwise. They bowed their heads and cringed.

'You must, you simply must, be Watcher Aranfal, of such renown throughout the Plateau,' the man cried, his fat little hands spread open. 'I am Squatstout, at your service, here to help in whatever way I can.'

'Squatstout?' Aranfal snorted. 'Is this a joke? If you're going to make up a name, you should stretch your imagination a little more than that.'

'Oh, yes, I can see why you may think it is so.' The man clapped his hands together. 'But I am afraid it is true, it is as true as anything you've ever heard. I am Squatstout, I have always been Squatstout, and I always will be Squatstout.'

He leapt forward to stand at Hood's side, and placed his hand on her bald head. She seemed to physically revolt, her body straining to be away from him, but she held her place.

'Who am I, child?'

'Squatstout,' she whispered. There was a tremor in her voice.

'Have I not always been Squatstout, since almost the beginning of everything? Since long before you and Gibbet were tossed upon the land, hmm?'

'You have, my lord.'

Squatstout laughed. 'Lord! Ha!'

He turned away from Hood, who visibly deflated with relief. He walked up to the table and placed his fists on the wooden surface, leaning forward until his nose almost touched Aranfal's own.

'These are interesting times, Watcher, are they not?'

Aranfal sighed. 'If by interesting you mean terrible, then yes.'

'Terrible? Oh, you can't mean it! Such things will happen soon that you will never believe! They will be so exciting!'

'That may be so, but it's difficult to get excited about them when you're tied to a table, waiting to be tortured.'

Squatstout's eyes widened. 'Yes, you are in chains! How can this be so?'

He glared up at Gibbet, and the room seemed to darken.

'My lord Squatstout ... he is ... I don't understand. Don't you want ...'

'Do not presume to tell me what I want, Gibbet,' Squatstout hissed. 'This poor man. Do you know who he is? Hmm? He is the eyes of the world, this man. He sits at the right hand of Amyllia Brightling. How could you treat him this way?'

Squatstout raised a hand, and closed his eyes. The air seemed to thicken and the torches in the walls flickered. An immense pressure seemed to weigh on Aranfal, and he closed his eyes involuntarily. He felt, rather than heard, a kind of scream, tearing through him in a pitch of agony. When he opened his eyes again, he saw that Gibbet and Hood were gone, and only Squatstout remained.

Aranfal's chains had vanished.

'I am so sorry,' Squatstout said. 'You must forgive them. Gibbet and Hood are really just children, you know, though they have walked through many ages.'

He smiled and licked at the edges of his mouth nervously. His tongue was a sharp, red thing, like a newt.

'Who are you?' Aranfal asked.

The man shrugged. 'I am Squatstout, Watcher Aranfal. I told you this already.'

'No, really. Who are you?'

Squatstout sighed. He took the chair opposite Aranfal and dragged it to the Watcher's side, then sat down. He looked to the ground, and then grinned with delight.

'May I?'

Aranfal nodded.

The little man lifted Aranfal's raven mask. He handled it with great care, turning it over gently, rubbing a finger along its edges.

'Such craftsmanship.'

'They are made by the Operator himself. There is nothing to match them.'

'Yes, yes, he has always been good with his hands. Oh, what skill he has!'

'How can you know anything about him? He is in the Underland.'

'The Underland? Is that what you call it?' Squatstout coughed. 'Such a strange title for such a beautiful place, as if it were just a lesser version of your own reality! Hmm. But then, he has made you this way. He has shaped you all, like he shapes his masks.'

They sat in silence for a moment, while Squatstout continued toying with the mask. Then the Doubter looked up, and there were tears in his eyes.

'You want to know who I am?'

'Yes.'

Squatstout placed the mask on the table. He folded his hands into a steeple and rested his head against them, his eyes closed.

'The man who made this mask is my brother.'

'You are a liar.'

Squatstout sighed. 'I know you have trouble believing me, Aranfal. So let me show you something.'

He clicked his fingers, and they were somewhere else.

It was a hilltop, cold and frosted with ice: it had to be the North. Before them were two others: the Operator, and Squatstout. The Operator seemed so much younger, though it was certainly him; his hair was long and black, and he seemed somehow fuller, no longer a wasted old man. He was not wearing his cloak, but was clothed in black rags, like a mourner.

Squatstout knelt before him, staring up with fear in his eyes.

'What is this place?' Aranfal asked the real Squatstout.

'You did not believe me, so I have taken you here, to make you believe.'

'And where is here?'

'The far past. That is me, and that is my brother. He has destroyed our family, and is sending me into exile, in this lovely scene.'

The Operator raised his hand and pointed. Below the hill was a shore, and on the water sat a ship, black and still.

'I spent so many days and nights on that ship,' Squatstout sighed, resting a hand on Aranfal's arm. 'So many days and nights.'

The scene changed. They had returned to the cell.

'What are you?'

'Ah, now the question changes. It is no longer "Who are you?" but "What are you?" Well, that is good. That is nearer the mark. Well, I can tell you what I am not, how is that for a start? I am not a Doubter, as you call them.'

'Do you believe the Machinery is breaking?'

'Certainly.'

'That is Doubting.'

Squatstout waved a hand. 'Those are the words of Jandell, the one you call the Operator. He is so powerful, you know, so wondrously talented, and yet so insecure. He builds such things as the Machinery, which no one else could have achieved, yet it is not enough for him. Everyone must bask in its glory forever, and close their eyes to its weaknesses. Well, it *does* have a weakness. It *is* breaking.'

'That Prophecy has been around for millennia,' Aranfal said, 'but there is nothing to support it.'

'Because it is not mentioned in the Book of the Machinery, hmm? Oh, that should make you *more* fearful, my friend. These words are hidden in the shadows, hated by the most powerful being in your world, chased by him and his operatives across the centuries. And yet – they survive! That is power, hmm? Power even beyond Jandell.'

Aranfal studied the man opposite him. He could unmask a liar in so many ways. He could read every flicker of an eye or wrinkle of a nose like they were words upon a page, even without wearing his mask. And here he was, listening to the most outrageous claims he had heard in his career – in perhaps any Watcher's career – and he could see no sign that Squatstout was lying.

'You say he is your brother.'

Squatstout nodded. 'Yes, my older brother. So beautiful, in his prime. So glorious.'

'Why don't you go to him?'

Squatstout inhaled sharply. 'I … he is a … he is sunk in his paranoia, at the moment. Jandell … he knows, I think, that his creation is breaking. And he knows who the One is. But he won't believe it. Ruin is coming. The Machinery is going to Select the One, and invest them with such power. I *know* it is breaking. I was there when the Promise was made – for that is what it is, a Promise, not a Prophecy. I know who made the Promise, and I believe it.'

Squatstout leaned forward, and took Aranfal's hand. 'I have seen into your soul, Aranfal. I know you are one of the great people of this world of yours. I know that you travel among the powerful. Let me stand at your side, or hide in the shadows at your feet. Let me observe the things you observe. The One will be a powerful person, oh yes; they will likely be someone you see every day in your glorious life. If I find them, then who knows? I may be able to stop them, and prevent Ruin from ever coming!'

Aranfal tilted his head to the side. 'Come with me? I don't even know what you are, my friend.'

'I am—'

'You are a creature of power. You have brought something

107

strange before my eyes, and I cannot explain it. But do I believe you are the brother of the Operator? I do not know. Do I believe you can stop Ruin, if Ruin is even coming? I do not know that, either.'

Squatstout nodded. 'That is wise, Aranfal, very wise. But listen to me well. On this night, you have seen two strange beings loosen their bonds and recover from ferocious violence, which you had done to them.'

'How do you know about that?'

The little man smiled. 'You saw me enter this room, having escaped my own cell. You don't know how I managed that. You then watched me make Gibbet and Hood disappear. And finally, I transported you to another world, an ancient place. You may not believe me, my friend. But surely it is worth keeping me by your side? Powers like mine should be kept under close observation.'

Aranfal hesitated, before giving a slight nod.

'Very well then, Squatstout. I must have gone mad, but you may come with me, and see what I see. You will tell me everything you see around us – anyone who may be the One, or whatever you call it. Understood?'

'Understood.'

'And you will not leave my side.'

'Understood.'

Aranfal sighed, repeating, 'I must have gone mad.'

Squatstout grinned. 'Happens to the best of us, my friend. It's best to just go along for the ride.'

Chapter Ten

'The funeral is tomorrow.'

'Yes, Tactician.'

'Who is speaking?'

'Tactician Canning, madam.'

'Good. Then it will be short.'

Tactician Brightling's bedroom was at the very peak of the See House. She had picked it over all the other luxurious rooms that filled the upper apartment of the Watchers' keep. It was small and sparse: a wooden bed, two hard chairs, and a dressing table. Damp climbed the walls, and the wind battered against the wooden shutters. This was the room of a lower-grade Watcher, not the most powerful person on the Plateau.

Brightling sat at the dressing table, staring into the mirror as Katrina ran a comb through her hair.

Their eyes met in the glass.

'What is wrong?' Brightling asked.

'Nothing.'

There was a long moment of silence. Candlelight flickered across the Tactician's unblemished face.

'You are thinking of your family.'

Katrina remained silent.

'I wish you would take off those rags and dress like a normal girl.'

'I am not a normal girl.'

'No. I suppose not.'

The entrance of Tactician Brightling's servants disturbed the conversation. They had been occupants of the See House for as long as Katrina could remember, but never seemed to age. They were identical in every way, from their blond hair to their large, dim eyes. To Katrina, they were dumb, beautiful beasts that never left the interior of the apartment, like domestic pets. They wore the same silver gowns, open at the chest to expose their torsos.

One of the twins – they had no names, as far as Katrina knew – approached the dresser and laid a carafe of heavy Watchfold and a glass before Brightling, who reached out and pinched his cheek. He did not react as he turned to leave.

The Tactician watched the twins disappear down the hallway, sipping at her wine and smiling as Katrina ran the brush through her hair. After a moment she turned back to the mirror.

'Did you like the Strategist well, Katrina?'

No. Who did?

'Yes, madam.'

'Liar. No one liked him. Especially not women.'

That was true. Kane had a way of looking at her that she did not like.

'A strange day for your first Watching, the old bastard's funeral.'

'Yes, Tactician.'

Brightling nodded. 'I was already a Watcher when I was Selected, you know. Did you know that, Katrina?' She took a long sip of Watchfold.

110

'Yes, Tactician.' *How could I not? You never cease to tell me.*

'It is rare that a Tactician is Selected from within a Department. Canning had never even set foot in the Fortress. A sad story, in many ways. He worked on a stall in some market on the coast. He didn't really want to leave, if truth were told.'

'The Machinery knows.'

They sat like that a while longer. The sun was setting, now, and little light came through the shutters.

'Are you nervous, Katrina?'

'What about, Tactician?'

'Tomorrow.'

'No, Tactician.'

'You should be.'

'Yes, Tactician.'

'I remember my first Watching well. I was still in Watchfold. We had received reports of a Doubters' meeting in a house by the river, in the kind of area you wouldn't suspect: a rich place, home to many senior people.'

The Tactician stopped Katrina's hand, took the comb and began to brush her hair by herself.

'There were three of us. We went to the house late at night, and we let ourselves in. We were, of course, unseen.'

'Of course, Tactician.'

'It was a big, timber house. They all are, in that part of the city. We went downstairs, and we found a cellar. There were young people there. About thirteen of them, I'd guess. They were all drunk. I remember thinking, "How can we tell who is the Doubter, and who is not?" So we interviewed them all. And that's when I learned a lesson.'

'What was it, Tactician?'

'These were drunks and poppyists. They were detritus; two of the women were with child, though the father was unknown. The room stank.' The Tactician paused, leaning forward into the mirror. 'Do you know who the Doubters among them were, Katrina?'

'All of them.'

Brightling shook her head. 'None of them. Losing one's way in life, and ending up in a stinkpit on the edge of civilisation, is sad, but not unusual. You really need to watch out for the other sort; the ones who seem *too* normal. You will see them, if you look, even without your mask.'

'How?'

'They go against the flow, Katrina. At some stage, even without realising it, they will go against the flow.'

'How will I know?'

The eyes were on her again.

'Instinct. If you do not know them when you see them, you will never make a Watcher, and no mask will help.' The Tactician handed the comb back to Katrina.

The Apprentice Watcher felt a sudden urge to run to the window and leap from the See House, a giddy jolt within her mind. She resisted.

'Here's one to tax your instincts,' Brightling said. She glanced at the door, making sure that no one was there. 'What happened to the Strategist?'

'He fell from his balcony, madam.'

'Indeed. Did he seem like the type of man who would kill himself?'

'Not in my eyes, Tactician. He seemed to enjoy his life, and its pleasures.'

'Such as they were. Does another explanation seem more likely?'

'Yes, madam. It seems likely that someone may have … well, it is something I should not say.'

Keep your mouth shut, said the older part of herself.

'Oh, come on, Katrina. It seems likely, blah blah. Clearly he was thrown from the balcony. It's the 10,000th year. Someone probably thought, "Well, it may Select me as the Strategist, if I show courage and ruthlessness." It happened before, many years ago, with the Lonely Strategist, though it did not end well for him.'

'Perhaps the killer thought it would be different this time, if the Machinery was broken.'

I thought I told you to shut up?

'Indeed, nonsensical as that sounds. Anyway, it's not our job to pick apart the reasoning behind the act. It's our job to identify the perpetrator. Any thoughts?'

'Someone close to him. Bandles, perhaps.'

'Perhaps.'

'Or ...' *By the Machinery, keep quiet. You don't know what you're talking about, and you can't spit out every accusation that comes into your head.*

'Or?'

'Well, the General was very close to the Strategist, madam. And he's a high-ranking man. It's natural that he would be ambitious.' *You are an idiot.* 'He may have thought—'

'Charls Brandione is a man of honour, if such a thing truly exists. Besides, he was in the North at the time.'

'He may have found a way to come here quickly, madam, without our knowing. It could have provided him with the perfect story, fighting in the North.'

Brightling observed her in silence.

You've done it now, said the older part.

Oh no, oh no, oh no, said her younger side.

'I am certain it was not him,' Brightling said. 'But I like the way you are thinking. I tell you what – at the Watching

113

tomorrow, do not refer to yourself as Apprentice, if anyone asks. Let's just call you a Watcher.'

Katrina froze. *That could have been worse,* said both sides of her.

'Thank you, Tactician. I did not expect—'

'Have you been to the Hall of Masks?'

'No.'

'Well, you need a mask, before a Watching, especially if you're a full Watcher.'

She stood from her desk.

'Let's go.'

The See House was a strange place. Some said that while the gates to the Underland were always closed, aspects of that other realm could be seen in the black tower that stood alone upon the Priador. Sometimes, denizens of the Underland made their way here, it was said, where they donned masks and pretended to live as Watchers of the Overland. Katrina did not know if this was true. But if it was the case that the Underland sometimes leaked into the world in general, and this tower in particular, then she was sure of one thing: the Hall of Masks was the nexus.

The Hall was a vast circle, the walls vanishing into a dark sphere in the distance, the ceiling hidden in shadow. Images of masks covered the walls, painted by the Operator himself at the very beginning of everything. The masks themselves hung from every wall, and were of all shapes and forms, the human and the animal. They dangled from poles and were strewn across shelves; they were neatly lined along racks in the centre of the room and grouped into haphazard piles against the walls. Each was unique: a raised eyebrow here, a twisted snarl there. She had looked upon them many times, on her visits with the Tactician, who loved this room beyond all others in the See House. Katrina had often wondered what type of mask she would take for herself. In her heart, she did not want any. The masks came from the Operator, and she wanted no manufacture of that creature on her person. She glanced to the hole in the centre of the floor, from which he emerged to deliver the masks. It was firmly barred. The younger part of her was suddenly seized with an image of herself falling into that hole, and down into the Underland. It was impossible; even without the bars, the Underland could only be accessed by those it wished to allow inside.

But still she kept far away from the hole.

'Well Katrina, here we are. The great moment has arrived.' Brightling swept her arms into the air in a grandiose fashion, waving at the walls. 'You will become a Watcher of the Overland, and will be masked like a Watcher of the Overland. What type would you like?'

Katrina shrugged. 'I don't mind.'

'Don't mind? Well, I suppose I should be pleased. Your father would be proud. Some people try to become Watchers just to get at the masks. They think they are pretty.' Brightling laughed. 'Needless to say, those people are weeded out early on.'

'I'll take whichever one you think is best.'

'Now, come on, Katrina. That really won't do.' Brightling walked to the side of the wall, and traced her finger across a mask: the image of a lizard. 'You must have a connection with your mask. It's with you always; it's your window into the souls of your enemies. The mask is the essence of the Watcher. You must select the one that matters to you the most.'

'You did not select your own mask, Amyllia.'

And he was there, in the Hall, emerging from the shadows.

'Operator.' Brightling fell to her knees.

He was just the same as the last time Katrina had seen him, all those years before: a bald-headed, pale creature, his body emanating a strange sense of decay. The faces in his cloak burned and twisted, their mouths formed into howls.

The Operator walked to the Tactician, and touched her on the top of her head. 'Please stand, Amyllia.' He turned to Katrina, his eyes wide with surprise. She had often wondered if he had seen her, back then. She had watched him from the doorway, and from the window as he fell, her brother wrapped in his arms. *Did he look at me? Did he know I saw him?*

No matter what happens, said the older Katrina, *do not tell him.*

The Operator smiled at her, and she recoiled.

'Tactician,' he said, turning back to Brightling. 'I am sorry to have surprised you. I should have locked the door.'

'No, Operator. It is always good to see you.'

He laughed. 'You are too kind.'

He turned once more to Katrina. 'The Tactician did not pick her mask. I gave it to her. She was the greatest Watcher I had ever seen. She still is. And so she needed a special mask. Have you seen it?'

Katrina hesitated, before nodding.

'Katrina is like my daughter, Operator, as you know. I show her everything.'

'Yes, yes. Katrina Paprissi.' He addressed Katrina directly. 'I know the name.'

Katrina froze. *Of course he knows who you are, fool. You have lived with the Tactician for years.*

She half-expected the Operator to say something, about that night: about why he had taken her brother. But instead he turned from her, and looked again to Brightling.

'Amyllia's mask is made from a different substance than the others. The others are formed of the Old Place, or the Underland, as you would call it. Her mask is something else entirely.' He walked to the Tactician, and placed an arm on her shoulder. 'I cannot control the Machinery, you must understand. But I know it well. I hope that it Selects this woman as our new Strategist, and I will help where I can.'

'Your advice has been invaluable to me, Operator.'

He smiled like a proud father. 'How is your play coming along? That will impress the Machinery, I assure you.'

'Well, my lord.'

'Good.' The Operator turned to Katrina, and his eyes narrowed. 'You remind me of someone I knew, long ago.'

'My brother.'

Why, oh why, did you say that?

The Operator merely smiled. 'No, not him. Someone else entirely.'

He shook his head, then turned suddenly, and walked to the wall. He lifted down a mask: a white rat.

'Here,' he said, throwing the mask at Katrina's feet. 'You are a survivor. You have lived in the shadows, hmm? This is the mask for you.'

He went to the hole in the floor and snapped his fingers together. The bars groaned open, disappearing into the stone floor, and only reappeared after the Operator had leapt into the void.

They had returned to the mirror.

'Did you know about my brother, Tactician?'

It was the first time she had asked Brightling this question. The older part of her had always prevented it. Now, however, it was strangely quiet.

117

Their eyes met in the glass.

'Yes. The Operator told me about it. He tells me about all these things. I am sorry for what happened to Alexander.'

'Did he tell you why he took him?'

Brightling gave Katrina a hard look. 'Don't ask questions like that of me, Katrina. I cannot tell you about my conversations with the Operator.'

Katrina nodded, but she was not finished.

'What did my father say?'

'Nothing. He handed you to me, and he left without telling me why. I probably should have stopped him.'

The Tactician sighed, and took a sip of wine.

'But we live and learn.'

Chapter Eleven

'There it is!'

Strategist Kane's funeral procession had been marching out from Memory Hall for hours, with no sign of the coffin. All the pomp and ceremony of the Centre was on display, stomping along Greatgift to the applause of the populace: feather-plumed regiments from every corner of the Overland; farmers from the West, scythes raised to the sky; southerners, dancing excitedly in their red robes. On and on they came, a steady display of pomp and power.

Katrina stood pressed into a doorway. She did not feel ready for her first Watching. This day could make her career, or destroy it. She was not a confident Watcher at the best of times. But both sides of her could think of only one thing: the meeting with the Operator. *He always knew about me. Did Brightling talk about me, with him? Or did he just know? Why doesn't he care, that I live?*

Because you are a nobody.

She thumbed at her rat mask, hidden beneath her rags.

'At long bloody last!'

When the man spoke, Katrina snapped up from the doorway. And yes, there it was: a block of wood on a wooden carriage being dragged along by black-clad soldiers without the aid of horses, steel blades hanging from their sides, unsheathed.

Move. Move, now.

Katrina stole through the crowd. A swirl of colour above made her glance at the stone roof of a building opposite, where two other Watchers, clad in red and white, whirled by, leaping from roof to roof. *Aranfal?* She could not tell; they were too fast.

Instinct. What is that, anyway?

She came to the Warded Square, a vine-covered outgrowth of the avenue, filled with statues of ancient leaders. A knot of young, bedraggled men had gathered here. They leaned against an iron representation of Strategist Folie, three of them in total, whispering to one another.

Katrina vanished into the background, and for the first time in her career as a Watcher, became a rat.

On a stage before Memory Hall, Tactician Canning cleared his throat.

'Well, you all know that Strategist Kane was a good man. He was capable of making the hard decisions, and was tough. In short, he had all the usually desirable qualities.'

Brandione winced as he watched this performance from the Tacticians' dais. They should not have put Canning up there: it was a humiliation for the man. The General could see Tactician Brightling's smile in the corner of his eye. *She loves to torment that man. Why?*

Canning's gaze flickered over the crowd. He seemed utterly helpless.

'And uh, now, he is dead.'

He bowed his head, folded his hands, and closed his eyes. He seemed lost in contemplation for a few moments, before finally looking back up at the thousands of subjects who stood before him. He scratched his fat head, and climbed down from the stage.

Behind him, the great iron gate of Memory Hall finally swung closed as the funeral procession made its way up Greatgift Avenue. Dusk was falling.

The men by the statue had gone. Katrina had watched them for twenty minutes from the shadows, reading their lips as they whispered to one another. Their conversation was banal and crude, but could not be called Doubting.

When she wore her mask, she felt no different than before. *I should have felt something.*

She left the square, rejoined Greatgift and looked to the west. The funeral procession had passed by long ago. She walked into the centre of the road and kicked her toe into the ground, angry that she had tarried for so long. People were still there, but it was growing late, and her chances of apprehending a Doubter had now surely disappeared. She cursed her stupidity and kicked the dirt again, a plume of dust encircling her pale rags.

Far ahead she could just make out the outline of the Fortress of Expansion, like a black cloud on the horizon. Most Watchers despised the great pyramid. Brightling's servants detested the massed ranks of the soldiery, those clunking battering rams of the city who had been forced to build their own headquarters. But not Katrina: something about the Fortress filled her with awe, precisely *because* it had been conceived in a human mind and formed from human hands. Was this the future, now that Expansion was finished?

She took one last look at the receding funeral procession, then turned and started back in the direction of the See House. Her instinct had failed her, and she had seen nothing with the mask. She was no better a Watcher than she was an Apprentice. She hoped she would be given another chance.

She came to an iron gate looming to the right of the street, lying open despite the hastening night. Feeling a stir of familiarity, she walked up to it, seeking some sign of its significance. But there was nothing: just rusted metal.

Katrina glanced around the avenue, suppressing a strange sensation of guilt. When she was sure that no one was present, she stole through the gate.

Of course.

She had found her way to Seller's Square, a wide space of cobbled stones and elegant, white marble structures, now glowing in the lamps being lit against the falling night. This was one of the administrative hubs of the Centre, and particularly associated with the financial dealings of the Overland. She was used to accessing it from the rooftops; entering by the gate was an unusual experience.

Before her was the Exchequer, the narrow tower in which the fiscal affairs of the Overland were overseen. It was known among the populace as Taxation Tower, and was not universally loved. The Exchequer was supposed to be independent of the Cabinet, but everyone knew who controlled it, and she lived in the See House.

To its right was the Bright House. This was the newest structure in the square, founded just over twenty years before, when her father, Jaco Paprissi, at the behest of Tactician Brightling, had established the first trade route to the South. For this reason, it carried her name. It was a strange place, a home of fantasy and riches where the wealthy of the Overland could invest in burgeoning explorations in distant lands, places they would never be allowed to see themselves. They would fund her father's expeditions and gain a portion of the treasures uncovered as a reward. But those days had gone: the building was now a husk, as were the financial prospects of the last investors.

On the opposite side of the square was the Printing Hall, where the new machines were kept under Brightling's strict supervision. No guards were visible, but Katrina knew that the building was under constant surveillance: if information was the most powerful weapon in the Watchers' armoury, the presses had introduced a whole new dimension. There were whispers, however, that some were in the hands of the Doubters, hidden away far to the West and the North.

There is another building in this place. You know there is. And yet you pretend you do not, every time you are here.

Katrina turned to her left, and sighed.

The Paprissi Finance House was a grey ruin, crumbling onto the side of the square. Even in its fallen state, however, it stood two stories higher than its neighbours: grand without being overbearing, elegant without ostentation, the embodiment of her family. A small sign hung over the door, black stone on which the single word 'Paprissi' was engraved in spidery silver letters. Once this place had been the source of all their wealth. Once it had funded trade with other states on the Plateau. It had provided the capital for the exploitation of the West. It had been the storehouse of great fortunes. Now all of that was in the hands of the Exchequer, and the Watchers.

Gone.

Katrina turned away from this relic of another world. Her life now was Brightling, studying, and Watching.

'Strange, what happened there.'

Katrina turned, her fists balled.

'You probably don't remember any of it, I imagine.' *You know I do.* 'The disappearances. The old girl's death in madness:

123

killed herself as soon as Jaco left, I heard. I wouldn't want to remember those things either, if I were you.'

He was close to her now, their feet almost touching. He was wearing his mask: dark lacquered wood hewn into the head of a raven, twisted and grotesque. His eyes flickered above the beak, and a dirty blue cloak hung at his sides.

Katrina forced a smile for her superior. 'How goes the night, Watcher Aranfal? Have we apprehended many Doubters?'

Aranfal snorted. 'Many. There are always many, at things like this. It's as if they can't help it. Great events of the Overland draw them like moths to a flame; they must gaze upon the beauty of the world they would destroy, and shudder before its magnificence.'

Katrina shuddered, too. *Does he mean this? It is nothing but doctrine.*

'Tonight has been *particularly* productive, however.' Aranfal leaned towards her. 'I believe it is connected to the date. The 10,000th year, etc.'

Aranfal moved away from Katrina, and she felt able to breath once again.

'What of you, Paprissi? How many have you apprehended?'

Katrina fought off a wave of shame. 'There have been none upon my route so far, Watcher. It has been quiet.'

'Quiet?' Aranfal seemed puzzled. 'But you were on Greatgift, were you not?'

Against her better instincts, Katrina turned her gaze to the ground. 'Yes, Watcher. I have failed. I thought I saw some a while ago, but they were not Doubters. I think.'

'So you studied a handful, and then you gave up?'

Katrina nodded.

Aranfal snorted. 'I understand you are a full Watcher now. Well, a Watcher does not give up so easily. Come.'

He turned quickly, the blue cloak sweeping behind him. Katrina followed, taking a last glance at the Paprissi Finance House as she went. Aranfal was quick, at once silent and muscular in his movements. He reached the Printing Hall and turned to Katrina.

'Can you climb?'

'Yes.'

Aranfal nodded, turned back to the building, and threw himself on the smooth stone, shimmying upwards like a lizard. Katrina watched with reluctant admiration. Aranfal apparently had no need of footholds, though she was not so talented. After a moment she located some cracks in the surface, and used them to claw her way to the top of the building.

Aranfal stood at the far side, arms folded, legs wide apart and tensed: this, combined with his mask, gave the impression of a bird about to leap into flight. This would not have surprised Katrina. She hesitated for a moment, tempted to flee the scene, then caught herself and walked to his side.

Greatgift lay before them, wide and unbending. The cortege had long since passed, but the people remained, a throng of mourners sharing their sorrows. The alehouses had begun to open, overlaying the air with the heavy, pungent smell of hops.

'Do you see any there now, Watcher Paprissi?'

Katrina glanced at the strange raven by her side. 'Any what?'

'Doubters.'

She looked back down at the crowd. *How can I even tell one from the other, let alone Doubters from believers?*

The young Watcher put on her mask and turned her attention to the crowds.

'A rat. I like it.'

'You mock me.'

'No, not at all.'

125

Katrina glanced at Aranfal; he appeared quite sincere. She turned back to the crowds.

Four old women stood in a huddle by a roadside inn, clucking to each other. Young men were everywhere; as if in response, the whores were emerging now from the darker squares, the red circles on their cheeks announcing their profession. A child wandered alone in the centre of the road.

It was a perfectly normal evening.

'There is nothing unusual here, Watcher Aranfal,' Katrina said.

Aranfal sighed. 'Are you certain?' He looked at the scene through his own mask, before raising his arm in a sudden jerk and snapping his fingers.

And then the Watchers were everywhere, shadowy forms swirling across the tops of the buildings. There was no way to establish their numbers: they moved together and separately, all at once, a blur of figures that could be ten strong or fifty deep, sweeping onto the ground. A wave of panic stole through the crowd. An ermine-clad merchant clutched his golden chains and protested his innocence as the grey swirl descended on him; a child wailed as his young mother vanished before his eyes; even the innkeeper was taken, a barrel rolling to the ground as he disappeared.

'How can you tell?' That was a foolish question, Katrina instantly realised, but it was too late.

Aranfal smirked at her, teeth gleaming below the mask. 'How can I tell, she asks.' He chuckled. 'When you put on your mask, what do you feel?'

'Nothing,' Katrina said truthfully.

Aranfal nodded. 'A true Watcher feels the world through their mask. A true Watcher feels *everything*.'

Aranfal turned his back on her and began walking across the roof.

'It is a shame your father is no longer alive. You could go and live with him, and wallow in his money all your life. As things are, you will need to think of something else, my dear, for a Watcher you will never be.'

And he was gone, leaving the ragged girl alone on the rooftop.

Tactician Canning lumbered over to the Tacticians' dais and threw himself into a chair at Brandione's side.

'Thank the Machinery that is over. I am not a great speaker.'

Brandione nodded; he did not want to lie. The Tactician did not seem to mind. He stared into the distance, and fell into a heavy silence.

There was not much conversation to be had here, anyway. Grotius lay back on a chair that looked set to break, throwing great handfuls of grapes into his mouth. Tactician Bardon had somehow got hold of a spinning top, with which he was playing at the side of the platform. Tactician Rangle sat before him, glowering at the boy from across the top of her book. To the other side of Canning sat Tactician Brightling, gazing with weary disdain at the goings-on in the crowd, one finger resting on her chin as she sipped from a glass of dark red wine.

The crowds had begun to thin, the procession disappearing into the distance. It would now make the short journey to the Primary Hill, where all sorts of solemn words would be spoken in the Circus before they tossed the Strategist's corpse into the Portal.

Canning gulped back his wine and poured himself another glass. He regarded his colleague from the corner of his eye.

'It will be a strange world for the new Strategist and Cabinet, will it not, Tactician Brightling?'

She glared at him. Brandione shifted in his chair. 'How so, Tactician Canning?' asked the head of the Watchers.

Canning leant back in his chair. 'Expansion is finished. After we – sorry, after *you* – took Northern Blown, the process was complete. We are done; the new leaders must simply consolidate our gains.'

'No.' Brightling spat the word out, drawing the surprised glances of his colleagues.

'No? Why "No", Tactician?' asked Grotius, crunching on seeds as he spoke. 'What else is there to do?'

Brandione watched Brightling carefully. *Does she want us to leave the Plateau?* The idea was controversial. Most believed the Machinery was only designed for one continent. Everyone knew that other lands existed, since Jaco Paprissi's travels. Most believed another trade expedition would eventually be attempted. But going as conquerors? That was another matter.

'There are other—' started Brightling, before appearing to catch herself. 'There are many other *problems*. The Doubters, for one. There are thousands of them now, mark my words; I guarantee you, Katrina had a good haul on her first day.'

'The Prophecy,' whispered Rangle. 'The Machinery will break in the 10,000th year. Ruin will come with the One.'

'A disgrace,' said Grotius.

'A disgrace,' nodded Bardon in childish imitation.

'Indeed,' said Canning, less convincingly. Silence fell, awkward and prolonged, before Canning punctured it. 'How is your Apprentice?' he asked Brightling.

'Apprentice?'

'The Paprissi.'

'No, not any more. She is now a Watcher, and will have proved her greatness today. I have no doubt.'

Canning looked nonplussed.

'I wonder how she is doing?' Brightling whispered to nobody.

In her quarters at the highest level of the See House, Katrina Paprissi wept.

One of Brightling's servants entered the small room, silent on his feet, bearing a bronze plate of blue cheese, red grapes and pink meat, as well as a glass and a wooden jug of wine. He laid the food on the table by her side, poured the wine, and crept away as quietly as he had come, without glancing at the girl on the bed.

Katrina sat up, pulling a ragged arm across her sodden eyes. Ignoring the food, she drained the glass in one gulp and refilled it. She stood and walked to the window, gazing out at the same, spectacular view of the Centre that had greeted her on every evening since she was six years old.

After a moment she turned back to the room, looking at all her worldly possessions: a desk, a bed, a chair. On the wall was a portrait of her father, the only piece of luxury she was permitted.

What now? asked the young part of herself.

Now? Now we wait.

She returned to bed. As she buried her head into the pillow, however, she realised that something was different: there was a sound below of something shifting. She slipped her hand under the pillow and felt a piece of parchment, which she pulled out and opened.

I can help you find your brother.

There was an address underneath, of a building in the Far Below.

Katrina turned the paper over in her hands. She glanced around the room, in case the messenger was still present.

Strange, she did not feel a sense of trepidation. Anyone else would tell Brightling. She would know what to do.

Brightling's words on the shores of Northern Blown returned to her. *You are always overreaching, Katrina. You must develop caution.*

Don't do anything stupid, Katrina. Strangely, it was her younger self that spoke this time to advise caution.

Stupid? Stupid would be staying here. You know you will never make a Watcher, girl. And someone says they can help you find Alexander. At the very least, you should go and see what type of person leaves a note under your pillow in the middle of the night.

It is dangerous, said the younger Katrina.

So is everything.

Katrina stole away from her room, and she did not take her mask.

Chapter Twelve

The woman in the green dress came again, but she did not speak. Not at first.

She always came at the same time, far into the evening. Rangle waited for her, in the study, pretending to read. It was always the same way: the book would fall from its place on the shelf, and the temperature of the room would seem to drop, as if it had been transported to a colder land. Rangle would turn around, and the woman would be standing there, mask in hand, staring at the Tactician.

Rangle always asked her the same thing.

'Who are you?'

There was never a response.

Rangle searched for any description of this woman in other texts, but could find her nowhere. She had abandoned the study group, spending most of her days in the See House, searching, searching, searching.

Darrah was not pleased.

One night, the woman inclined her head, and spoke.

'You are asking the wrong question, yes, you are asking

the wrong question, you should know that.'

The voice had a sing-song quality, but it held no joy.

'What is the right question?'

'You should not ask *who* I am. No, Rangle the Tactician. That is not the question you should ask.'

Rangle stared at those eyes. They were not human; it was like a pair of green stones had been inserted into that delicate face. Sometimes she wore the mask. Tonight, she did not.

'Then *what* are you?'

The woman smiled, and nodded.

'I am the daughter of betrayed parents and the sister of a treacherous brother. I am a broken-hearted lover and I need a friend.'

She stepped forward in a bold stride, and leaned towards the Tactician.

'I am the Mother of Chaos, and I will prepare the way for Ruin. Nothing will threaten it. Do you understand? Do you understand? Do you *understand me?*'

Rangle breathed a ragged breath. 'No, lady. I do not.'

The woman laughed, and disappeared. Rangle leapt to her feet and scoured the study, but there was no sign of her.

What are you?

'What is this book?' Rangle asked the woman. 'Why are you in this picture?'

The woman picked up the text and looked at her image.

'I made this,' she said, throwing it to the ground. 'At the very beginning. Oh yes, long ago, at the very beginning of everything.'

'The beginning of what?'

'The Machinery.' She spun in a sudden movement and spat on the floor.

Rangle pretended not to notice. 'It contains the Prophecy.'

The woman nodded. 'When Jandell built the Machinery, the Promise came to haunt him, though he does not understand or believe it. *But I do.* I know that the One is coming, for I have served at the pleasure of the One for ten millennia. Oh yes. I have a role to play, Rangle of the Overland. I have been preparing for, oh, for, oh, such a long, long time, far away from my home.'

'Who is Jandell?'

The woman smirked. 'You know him well. He is my brother. He is the one you call *Operator*.'

Rangle had been a student her entire life, though not formally. She had pushed herself to accept the widest possible range of views and beliefs, tugging at them like tight little knots until they unravelled. But the woman's words were a struggle for her.

'Then you are also an Operator?'

The woman laughed. 'That is such a *Jandell* word, truly it is.' She turned her back on Rangle.

'I am Shirkra. The Mother of Chaos.'

During the day, when she was supposed to be presiding over the affairs of Watchfold and her western fiefdom, Rangle would instead visit the library in the See House. She would search for any record of a woman called Shirkra, a sister to the Operator. There was nothing. She half-toyed with asking one of the Watchers to assist her, but knew it was too risky. What would she say? *I've met the Operator's sister. Do you have any files on her?* She would be hauled off to a madhouse, or thrown into the Prison of the Doubters, never to be heard from again. No. *They wouldn't do that to a Tactician. They'd probably just kill me.*

And there was nothing more to gain from questioning Shirkra directly. The woman had not spoken in the last few nights. She had simply stared at that page in that book, at the picture she said she had drawn. Once, she seemed to grow emotional, but she hid it behind her mask.

Finally, she spoke again.

'It hurts me, Tactician Rangle. It hurts me so.'

She was not wearing her mask, so Rangle was able to study her features. The green eyes showed no pain.

The Tactician went to Shirkra's side, and with great caution reached out and stroked the side of her face. She had been through the wars, Rangle. She had seen lovers come and go. But she felt something different for this woman, this woman she hardly knew. She did not feel the same thing for Darrah. It was not a physical thing. It was not even emotional. It was primordial; the love of a lizard for the sun.

'Tell me what hurts you. I will try to make it better.'

Suddenly Shirkra was seized by something. She jerked her head upwards and stared at the ceiling. It was as if she was listening to someone else, someone that Rangle could not hear: another voice. But then the moment passed, and the red-haired woman looked once again at Rangle.

'You cannot help me. No one can help me.'

They were in the reception room. Rangle was sitting on one of her soft chairs, and Shirkra stood below the great fresco. The Operator, as she called herself, had turned her focus to the bloodiest part of this piece of art; the death of Hellendro, the third Strategist of the Overland and the last remaining disciple of Arandel, the first Strategist.

'You celebrate such terrible things, here,' the Operator whispered. 'Oh yes, you do. Look at this poor man, this poor man.'

She reached out and touched the bloodied torso. 'Jandell painted this. I can tell.'

'It has always been here.'

'Yes, I am sure it has, ha ha. Jandell thinks he is an artist, as well as an engineer, though he is not, truly he is not, I could have painted *such* a beautiful thing, truly I could have, if they had let me.'

'Would you like to paint something for me?'

Shirkra threw her head back and laughed. It echoed off the marble walls.

'No, not any more. The art has left me. No, I hurt for another reason. I wonder, why have I been forgotten?' She curled her delicate fingers into a fist, and stared hard at the fresco. 'Why have I been forgotten, in this world that Jandell built? Now I know that he hates me, and can never forgive, never, never, never. Well, he will see what I have wrought, and it will bring such Chaos, and he abhors Chaos, oh yes, that engineer, he does hate Chaos so.'

Shirkra spun on her heel, the green eyes flashing with fury. 'He *never* believed the Promise. *Never.* He still does not! But *I* believe it. Oh yes. I am the storm that clears the dirt and the leaves and the tangled briars from the path.'

And she clapped her hands, as if she had just witnessed a wonderful performance.

Say something. Ask her a question. Don't let her finish!

'Operator … what is it like, to live forever?'

Shirkra laughed. 'We have not lived forever. Not even the Old Place has lived forever. One day, we may die. Sometimes, I wish it would come to me, soon. Oh yes.'

Shirkra turned back to the fresco, and pointed to Hellendro, smiling at that old man's death. 'I knew him, you know. He was one of the worst enemies of my people. Jandell gave him the world, though he did not know what he was doing, or how it could be controlled. Oh no, he did not.' She spat again on the floor. 'But he is long gone, and Arandel, and Jammes, and all the rest of them. They are gone to the dirt, and their children will suffer for what they did.'

She was then by Rangle's side, squeezed into the chair beside her, the mask in her lap. 'I will be gone for a while, Rangle. I must help in another way. But I will return to you, if you would like that.'

Rangle nodded. 'I would like that very much, my lady.'

And then the Tactician was alone, and a window was open, and the night blew into the White Rooms of Memory Hall.

Chapter Thirteen

'*What happened to him?*'

The woman was holding Brandione by the arm. There was something wild about her, with her mottled brown hair sticking up in spikes and spittle gathering in the corners of her mouth. She could have been twenty years old, or she could have been sixty.

Brandione had seen many like her, that day.

'*What happened to Kane?*'

The General shrugged, and freed himself from the woman's grip. She watched him for a moment, confused, and turned into the crowd.

The General smiled grimly as he made his way along Greatgift. He pushed the question from his mind. *Kane fell off a balcony. That's what happened. Anything else is up to the Watchers to find out.*

It was the first time Brandione had experienced the death of a Strategist. The avenue was in chaos. People wailed, some kneeling on the ground and pounding the dirt, bloodying their fists and glancing suspiciously at those nearest to ensure everyone was doing their part. Bandles had assured him it would be like this. 'The people will be very sad, master

General, very sad. You'll see. There won't be a dry eye in the Overland.' The General had smirked at Bandles at the time. Not now.

Brandione saw a group of boys, watching the spectacle with confusion; realising eventually what was expected of them, they too fell to the ground, adding their laments to the cacophony.

Watchers overlooked it all, grey figures in the background, the guardians of social behaviour. Brandione nodded at one as he passed, a thick-framed woman with empty eyes; she observed him with suspicion, as Watchers always did. But Brandione was unafraid. As a General of the Overland and adviser to the late Strategist, he was above contempt.

The General rounded a corner into another boulevard, narrower than Greatgift, but somehow grander, too, its marble buildings gleaming and its pavestones smooth and clean: the Duskway. At the end of the boulevard stood a huge gate of black iron enlaced with gold. It stretched right across the avenue, so tall that it blocked all view of what lay beyond.

Brandione approached the barrier, to be greeted by a pair of chainmail-clad guards brandishing halberds. They wore handcannons at their sides, red barrels shaped into the heads of lizards.

The nearest guard eyed the General warily.

'Name?'

'General Charls Brandione, commander of the armies of the Overland and former adviser to the Strategist.'

The guards huddled together, whispering to each other. Brandione stared at them impassively. 'I served with you in Anflef, did I not?' he asked one, a thin boy.

The guard nodded. 'Yes, sir. I am sorry about the Strategist.'

The General nodded.

'Recognised,' the guards said together. They bowed and pulled the gate open.

The Circus loomed before Brandione. It was a mass of dirty marble, fifteen or twenty storeys high, hewn into a rough circle as if carved from a mountainside by the wind itself. This was the centre of spectacle in the Overland, as important as the See House or the Memory Hall or indeed the man-made Fortress of Expansion. The four tenets of the state's survival were encapsulated in these four buildings: surveillance, power, strength, and amusement. This last necessity was not to be underestimated.

The Circus was unusual for a state building, for the simple fact that it was ugly, a filthy lump that crawled with lizards in the heat. It always made the General think of a great toad, squatting on a rock, waiting to catch a fly.

Far above each gate was a statue of the Operator. His expression changed in each representation, so that he stared at the approaching revellers with anger, amusement, sadness and joy. That was what the scholars claimed, at any rate: to Brandione, the depictions of the Operator never changed. He always seemed tired.

Brandione joined a queue behind the Western Gate. The crowd was a throbbing mass, packed with representatives of every strata of Overland life. Immediately before the General stood a portly, black-clad man, wealthy to judge by the golden rings that dripped from his fingers and the silver chain around his neck. *Perhaps a merchant or a high-ranking Administrator.* Beside him was an equally stocky woman wearing a mink-lined velvet cloak.

'… about Kane alone, I should imagine,' the woman said.

The man shook his thick head. 'No,' he intoned in a voice of deep gravel. 'No.'

'Then what will it be about?'

'Not that. You are usually wrong.'

'Thank you, Limian.'

The man grunted.

Brandione had heard much speculation regarding today's play; it was all that Farringer and Bandles had been able to talk about. There were always performances at the Circus, but this one was deemed to be special, coming so soon after Kane's death. Plays were sanctioned by the Watchers, and often written and performed by them, too. Whatever this was, it was something Tactician Brightling wanted the world to see.

They reached the doorway and began to file inside. The Circus was already almost full, thousands squeezed together on row after row of stone pews. Although he was accustomed to armies, the General hated crowds. The walls reverberated with the laughter and febrile chatter of what seemed like half the world. The wind added to the cacophony, creating a peculiar sound when it whipped through the Circus: an undulating whine, as if the structure was crying for help.

In the basin of this stinking, screaming bowl stood a vast wooden stage, so wide that it entirely covered the Portal to the Machinery, that hole through which the Operator dispensed the names of new Cabinet members, and into which the corpses of deceased Strategists were thrown. Usually the Portal was left uncovered, tempting some maniacs to try and leap into the Underland. But as any child could have told them, that was impossible. The Underland only admitted those it wanted to enter its realm.

At the side of the stage was a doorway, hidden by a curtain of mauve satin that twitched occasionally; Brandione imagined a group of players standing behind it, peering out at the mighty crowd and wondering what they had got themselves into.

The Cabinet of Tacticians sat at the highest point of the stadium upon a row of silver thrones, slurping at wine, gnawing on meat, glancing at books and playing with toys.

It took Brandione almost thirty minutes to make his way there, threading along the pews and up the rickety staircases, identifying himself to the many guards in his path. He eventually found his way to a bench beside Canning's throne, on the very left of his colleagues. The Tactician for Expansion, looking as uncomfortable as ever in his elevated position, gave a wan smile.

'Do you know what the play's about, General Brandione? Brightling won't tell me anything.'

'I don't know, Tactician. I'm sure it will be related to the Selection.'

Canning nodded. He twisted his head around to gaze at Brightling, who sat two seats away, then leaned back down to Brandione.

'Notice anything, General?'

'Tactician Brightling sits alone.'

'Quite so. Strange that, is it not?'

Brandione shrugged. 'Who does she normally sit with?'

Canning gave him a surprised look. 'The Paprissi girl. You do not know her?'

'No, Tactician. I thought the Paprissis were all gone – father, mother, son, bank, dogs, cats, everything.'

'Yes, yes, all those things are gone. The Machinery only knows what happened to them. But the girl survived. She's lived with Brightling for years now. A nice thing, quite hard-working, nervous really, not that I can criticise anyone for that. But I fear she's become too much like Brightling,

141

now. Anyway, never mind. You must know her – always in mourning, white rags and the rest of it.'

Brandione suddenly remembered a girl in a ragged white dress, running along behind the Tactician at the fall of Northern Blown.

'Yes, Tactician. I think I have seen her.'

'Not lately, you haven't. She's vanished, like her brother and her father. Brightling isn't happy. Can't blame her, really; it's quite a feat, losing the last of the Paprissis.'

Brandione looked up at the Queen of the Watchers, who sat two seats away, to the right of Grotius and in the very centre of the Tacticians. She glared down at the stage, her face taut. She barely touched her wine.

'Hmm.' Canning sloshed his Watchfold around in a goblet. 'Assistants should not just disappear like that. Not now, at any rate. Not before a Selection.'

Brightling shot a look at the Expansion Tactician and raised a finger to her lips.

'Shh,' she said, with a thin smile. 'The play is beginning.'

The crowd fell into a heavy silence. All eyes were on the wooden stage below, where a woman had appeared. She was entirely dressed in red, from the scarf that held her hair to the slippers on her feet. Even her skin was the colour of blood, lending a startling ferocity to the golden lenses of her eyes.

This woman was instantly recognisable to the crowd as Fate, a character from the literature of old whose legend had survived the Gifting of the Machinery; it was said that she pleased the Operator. She raised her arms high into the air and stared straight up into the sky, her red robes falling from her arms like the wings of some foreign beast.

'Sixty-two years,' Fate intoned in a strangely masculine voice. 'It has been sixty-two years since a Strategist was Selected.'

142

She lowered herself to her knees and put an ear to the floor. 'What will it do now? What is it thinking?'

Brandione looked around at the concentrated faces; thousands of eyes drinking in the spectacle of tradition.

The red woman stood again.

'Sixty-two years. It has been a time of highs … and lows.'

The curtain at the back of the stage was pulled open. Fate bowed to the audience and withdrew, sparking a wave of applause. As she left, five new characters appeared. A ripple of laughter ran through the crowd as they recognised the people before them: the Cabinet of Tacticians.

At the front was the stage version of Tactician Brightling. The woman did not share the Tactician's angled features, but had the same air of casual domination, a sense of power that could not even be obscured by her coarse white wig and excessive rouge. She stalked around the stage, cat-like in her movements. Brandione glanced at the real Tactician, whose slight smile betrayed her satisfaction.

Fading into the background like a forgotten chorus were the actors playing Tacticians Bardon, Grotius and Rangle. These were likenesses in only the loosest sense of the word. Bardon was, indeed, played by a child – a chubby, precocious creature, slightly older than the Tactician himself. The crowds held no fear for this boy, who stared out into the masses with pride, apparently searching for someone. At last his eyes widened and he furiously waved his arms, mouthing the word 'Mummy'.

Behind the boy stood the stage likeness of Rangle, an imperious old woman with a thick book in her hand. She had captured the bored gloom of the ancient student, though whether that was by accident or design was impossible to tell.

Standing to her right, like a sweating boulder, was the approximation of Grotius. This was a poor imitation; the man was almost as massive as the genuine version, but that was where the likeness stopped. He even had a moustache and hair. Perhaps that was to be expected; it would be difficult to find more than a handful of people, let alone players, with the same ample proportions as the Tactician for the North.

The true Tactician Bardon leapt to his feet somewhere off to Brandione's right.

'Ahaahahahaha! Mummy, look at me! Look at how they've done me!'

'Very nice, darling.'

The General turned to see that the boy had climbed up on his seat to improve his view while his mother tried to restrain him. To his left sat Tactician Rangle, ignoring everything below. She seemed utterly vacant, totally unaware of her surroundings. Brandione noticed that the Tactician did not even hold a book.

A bellow drew his attention. Tactician Grotius leaned forward in his chair, his great head turned to Brightling.

'Watching Tactician – am I really so fat as that?'

But Brightling did not respond. Her attention was absorbed with the final character on the wooden stage.

Lying prostrate on the stage floor was the very image of Tactician Canning. The cringing face, the darting eyes, the ample belly: it was hard to tell him apart from the real version, who watched the spectacle through his fingers. To the great hilarity of the audience, the stage version of Tactician Brightling approached this miserable figure, winked at the crowd, and placed her right foot upon his chest.

'Oh, mistress!' the Canning actor whimpered. 'Could you answer a question for me?'

The laughter increased. The stage versions of Bardon, Grotius and Rangle slapped their legs and clutched their chests, convulsed with mirth.

'Yes,' said the stage Brightling. 'But do not take long. It is late and I am busy.'

'Thank you, mistress! That is most generous!'

The fake Brightling kicked Canning out from under foot; he rolled across the stage, then leapt to his feet and dusted himself down. 'You are most kind!' he cried. 'My first question, mistress, is this: why *was* I Selected?'

Stage Brightling made a drama of looking confused, raising a finger to her lips and squinting at the sky.

'Why, Tactician, it is not for me to know! The Machinery chose you because you were the best person to serve the people's will.'

'But madam, I am a humble market trader. All I want is to sell whelks and eat pies! Why was I Selected as Tactician for Expansion?'

The laughter in the Circus grew louder.

Brandione glimpsed across at the real Canning. The Tactician was slumped back in his chair, his face as red as Fate's robes. The General had never witnessed such public humiliation heaped upon a Tactician of the Overland. He looked to Brightling. *Why is she doing this? Just cruelty? Or to impress the Machinery with her own popularity, and destroy that of a possible rival?*

He would never understand the Watchers of the Overland. He decided not to try.

'It is not for us to judge the decisions of the Machinery,' the stage Brightling continued. 'It Selected you because it believed you would fill the role successfully and, indeed, under your management of Expansion, the Overland now covers the whole of the Plateau.' At that, the crowd cheered.

'But madam,' said the stage Canning. 'That was all down to *you*! You have led both Watching *and* Expansion, for I am too tired and stupid.'

145

'Yes,' said Brightling when the latest cheers subsided. 'I *have*, haven't I?'

The stage door opened again; Bardon, Grotius and Rangle scampered away as a new character emerged. The player was so tall that Brandione wondered if he was on stilts. His thin face was painted white, with black circles around the eyes. A cloak fell away behind him, its purple hue signalling that it could belong to only one man.

The stage Tacticians fell to their knees before the stage Strategist Kane.

'And now,' boomed the great man, unfurling a yellowing scroll he had removed from a pocket of the gown, 'a history of the final years of my administration. Our first act covered health. We built new camps for the blighted …'

The actors began to list the achievements of the Cabinets over the past sixty-two years, taking turns to read from their scrolls. The majority of the play was now taken up by the stage Brightling, who read from a lengthy list, with her every achievement receiving a cheer from the crowd. *Is this really just to impress the Machinery? Can it work?*

Brandione felt a gentle nudge at the small of his back. He looked up to find one of Tactician Brightling's aides – a thin man with drooping eyes – staring down at him.

'The Tactician would like to see you.'

What now? 'Very well.'

Brandione shuffled along to sit beneath Brightling's feet. She leaned down so that their heads almost touched, and whispered softly into his ear.

'Do you know Katrina Paprissi, General?' There was a strange tremor in the Tactician's voice.

'I know of her, Tactician, but that is all. I saw her once, from a distance, at Northern Blown.'

146

'She is the last of a great family, and she has just become a Watcher. She has lived with me for fifteen years, and I have guarded her as a promise to her father. She is never far from my side. But General, she is gone.'

Brightling was smiling, but her eyes were hard.

'I do not know anything about this, Tactician. I do not know her.'

The Tactician's smile widened. 'I know you do not, General. That is precisely why I believe you can help.'

'Madam, may I—'

'Come to my apartments later this evening.' She pushed the General away with the tips of her fingernails.

Brandione returned to his place by Canning. The Expansion Tactician had not moved an inch. His eyes were wide as he watched the performance below. On the stage, his shadow was laughing and whooping as the fake Brightling chased him around like a goose.

It was not difficult to find one's way to the See House. It sat proudly on the Priador, hanging over the city and the sea like a black claw, trying to scratch the sky.

The tower loomed ever larger as Brandione made his way east on horseback along Greatgift. It seemed to shift in hue and shape as one approached, like a shadow that was slowly suffering the encroachment of the dawn. It had grown dark since he had set off on his journey from the Circus. The home of the Watchers was only visible thanks to the lights that shone all along its thick frame, candles and lamps that twinkled and glimmered from rooms and chambers and halls.

His horse came to a sudden halt.

'Come on now,' the General whispered into the animal's ear. 'It's only the See House.'

The horse snorted, and began to move forward again.

Brandione could understand the beast's feelings. There was a strange atmosphere in the part of Greatgift that approached the Priador. The low marble buildings appeared to be abandoned, their entrances covered in black cloth, their surfaces in dust. The occasional sound came from the darkness within, as of the movement of feet.

He had never visited this place: the military and the Watchers tended to keep well apart from one another. This had led to bad blood between the two groups in recent years, with the soldiers convinced their weak Tactician was being dominated by his Watching counterpart, to their disadvantage. From Brandione's experience, this was undeniably true.

The General and his horse pushed ahead.

At the foot of the hill was a black house by a black gate.

'Do you wish entry?' a voice asked without prompting.

'I do. My name is Brandione, Gener—'

The gate opened.

The climb was steep, but not arduous. The land seemed to slope away, as if the Priador was urging him on. The Overland opened out before him, the halls and towers and shacks of the city.

To his right was the Eastern Peripheral Sea, an implacable sheet of iron grey in the moonlight.

At last Brandione reached the See House. As he approached, he saw that the surface of the tower was completely smooth, as if it had been formed from a single marble block of vast proportions. It seemed thinner up close than it did from the city.

All was silent, bar the whining of the wind. There was no one here to greet him.

Before him he saw a rope attached to a stump of wood. He tied his horse to it, and approached what he took to be the entrance; it was nothing more than a hole in the side of the marble, with no covering of any kind.

He found himself in a small hallway. A candle burned on a tall iron stand in the centre of the floor. Beside it were two simple wooden chairs. A Watcher sat in each, their faces obscured by masks: a wolf and a dog, Brandione believed, though it was difficult to be sure in the hazy light.

'I am here to see Tactician Brightling. I am here by invitation.'

'We know that,' said the wolf.

'You would not have made it up the Priador if we did not know that,' said the dog.

Brandione hesitated for a moment.

'Where do I go?' His voice was a shade stronger than he felt.

The wolf pointed to the western side of the hall, where a stairwell was just visible.

'Keep climbing until you reach the red door.'

The General nodded and made for the stairs.

'Oh, General.' This time the dog.

'Yes?'

'Do not turn off before the red door, and do not enter any other chamber. It would not be in your interest.'

The climb lasted no more than an hour at a guess, but felt longer: a silent journey into darkness.

Brandione wiped the sweat from his brow, stiffened his resolve, and knocked on the red door. A moment passed in which he could make out a shuffling noise on the other side and what he took to be hushed whispers.

The door opened, and before him were two guards, identical twins to look at them. Their long blond hair, high cheekbones and delicate frames gave them a feminine presence, an impression heightened by the thin, silk gowns that hung from their bony frames.

'Are you General Brandione?' asked one, in a monotone.

'Is it General Brandione that you are?' asked the other.

'Yes – I think that Tactician Brightling is expecting me.'

'She is expecting you.'

'Yes; it is you that is expected.'

One of the twins pushed the door fully open to allow Brandione entry; the other pointed down the corridor.

'It is down there that she is.'

'Yes, that is where.'

Brandione pushed his way past the strange sentries, who watched him dumbly as he passed.

It was a kind of reception room, dominated by shades of red, from the silk drapes to the gold-leafed walls. A long, cedar bench lay against the western wall. Four sofas filled the space, blood-red explosions of feathered pillows and throw-overs. The room was cluttered with statues, dozens of representations of the Operator: they sat on the mantelpiece, they stood in the corners, they lounged jauntily by the sofas. A stuffed eagle clasping a copy of the Book of the Machinery regarded Brandione with a dead expression from the ceiling. A great chandelier scorched the room with burning candle-light, giving it an almost whitewashed, bleached appearance.

A door lay open at the other side of the room.

'Come in, General.'

Gritting his teeth, Brandione pushed forward.

This room was larger than the last, and strewn with similar furnishings. It was designed for luxury: soft red sofas and feather duvets, bowls of fruit on golden tables, a faint smell of musk in the warm air. The walls were lined with portraits of ancient men and women. Brandione presumed they were Watching Tacticians.

The splendour of the room was ignored by Brightling, who stood in the centre with her head in the bowels of a tall pendulum clock, a blade clasped in her right hand.

'Ah,' she spat, 'I should just have bought a new one.'

She moved around to the front of the clock and glared at it. As if in response, the timepiece whirred into life, ticking loudly.

'This is quite literally a grandfather clock,' Brightling said. 'Or rather, it is a *grandfather's* clock. It was given to me by my father's father, when I first became a Watcher. It's one of the first of its type – I like that. I have to fix the damned thing at least once a week, though – I do *not* like that.'

The Tactician made for the far side of the room, indicating to Brandione to follow.

'His name was Simon Brightling,' she said as she stalked across the floor. 'He was a wonderful man: chairman of the Circle Club, you know, although we all know what sort of people frequent that place these days. He built our family's estate in the West. He was the greatest of the Brightlings.'

Brandione's eyes widened. 'But madam,' he started, 'you are—'

'A Tactician? Well, yes. But how did I earn that? What was it about me that led to my Selection? It could have been as much for my weaknesses, as my strengths. Who can tell? At any rate – here we are.'

They had come to a wide balcony that snaked its way around the side of the See House. The city – the *world* – stretched out before them, a panorama of light and smoke, shade and movement. Their position was too elevated to make out the people below, and even the palaces and mansions of the Centre were an amorphous mass.

'Quite a view, isn't it, General? Memory Hall is a pretty little place, no doubt, and the Fortress has its charms, but there is nothing to quite compare with the See House. Sometimes I think that's where the name came from. Because you can see everything. Ha!'

Brightling sat at a simple wooden table by the balcony's edge and indicated for Brandione to join her. The table was covered in books on a range of subjects, from science to the relations between the city-states in the days before Overland domination of the Plateau.

'I read a great deal,' Brightling said. 'I am an academic at heart, I sometimes think. I often wish I had gone to the College. That said, I have learned a great deal here, too.' She waved a breezy hand at the world below. 'You attended the College, didn't you?'

Brandione gave a curt nod.

'Then you are an academic General. Or a General academic.' She chuckled.

'No, madam. I am a soldier.'

'Oh, yes. But an educated one. A clever one.'

Brandione bowed his thanks.

'What is next for you, then, General? Do you hope to become Expansion Tactician? You would be good at it. I would enjoy serving beside you in the Cabinet, I think. If I am Selected again, that is.'

Brandione was taken aback by the manner in which she spoke, as if the workings of the Machinery could possibly be predicted by the human mind. It surprised him, too, that she seemed so keen on discussing his career. She had an ability to switch from indifference to interest, from apparent ignorance to striking knowledge. At best it made him doubt her sincerity; at worst, her honesty.

'There is no future there now, Tactician. Expansion is over.'

'What makes you say that?'

'Because we have taken the entire Plateau; what else is there?'

'You don't believe in other lands?'

'Well … we never talk about them, madam.' That was not strictly true, he thought, remembering Canning's words. *Perhaps she has found some weak little land across the sea.*

Brightling looked out over the city. 'No,' she sighed. 'Well, we shall see that change, I imagine. The Machinery will always seek growth. There is nothing else that is quite so … satisfying.' The Tactician turned her head and looked into the distance. She pointed a finger to the northeast, up along the rugged coastline of the Eastern Peripheral Sea.

'Have you ever been there?' she asked.

'To the Peripheral Sea, madam?'

'No: to the hills by the Upper Shores. To the mansions there.'

'No, Tactician.'

'The Paprissis once lived there.'

'I did not know the family.'

'It is a ruin now,' Brightling sighed, 'but it was once the greatest private residence in the Overland. Katrina's father, Jaco, was a great man. He was the first to go beyond the Plateau, as you know. You will have been to the Bright House. He started all that trade.' She kicked the table leg. 'It is lucky we have learned to develop some of the things he brought, here on our Plateau. The Operator put a stop to all our travels, after Jaco disappeared. Well, it is all in the past, now.'

The General cleared his throat and looked away from Brightling. He was used to private discussions with the most powerful individuals of the Overland: indeed, he had spent many hours whiling away his time with *the* most powerful individual of the Overland, at least officially. But something about this was different. There was something hidden, here.

Brandione was distracted by a sound of music. In the living quarters, one of the twins was sitting on the floor in the corner by a bookshelf and playing a flute, staring ahead as blankly as ever.

'Others will want to go again, now. To look and to Expand,' Brightling whispered. 'But will the Operator allow them? He is a sensitive soul, really. I know him better than anyone alive, yet still ... I do not know him.'

A twin appeared at Brandione's side. He placed a silver tea set on the table, filled two cups, and returned inside, all in total silence.

'But anyway, the Paprissis have gone now. It happened after the boy disappeared. Katrina's mother killed herself, a terrible waste of such beauty. And her father ... well, he let us all down when he left. Katrina is the only one, now. I think she is brilliant, you know. I always did, even when she was a child. I was glad to take her into my care. She is an ambitious little thing. But she is too ... *nice*, I think. I tell her so, I tell her often, but it makes little difference.'

The music inside faded to silence.

Brightling sighed. 'Do you know what happens to Watchers when they betray us, General? When they desert the See House without permission?'

'They die, madam.'

The Tactician gave a curt nod. 'Yes. They die in the Bowels of this very tower, with one of my lieutenants watching over their final moments. I will not allow that to happen to Katrina, General. She is too ... she is the last of the Paprissis, and I will not see her languish down there. Things are particularly sensitive now, with all this talk of ten thousand years.' Brightling removed her pipe from some hidden pocket, lighting it with a flame from a candle. 'Most of the others don't know she's missing, so all is by no means lost. If we can get her back soon, it will be as if it never happened.'

'I am sorry, Tactician, but I fail to see what I have to do with this.'

Brightling arched her eyebrows. 'Then you have failed to listen, General. As I cannot involve the Watchers in this little activity, someone else will have to seek out my assistant. I have heard good things about you. And no one will suspect you; no, not the hero of the age.'

Brandione sighed.

'You will be rewarded, of course.' Brightling smiled. 'Who knows what positions we will all be in after the next Selection? If I am … raised, I would be able to grant you handsome rewards.'

Even if you become the Strategist, there is nothing you could give me. But Brandione had little choice; this was nothing short of an order from the most powerful living being on the Overland, and if Charls Brandione knew how to do anything, he knew how to take orders.

'As you command, Tactician. But where will I look for her?'

Brightling barked a laugh. 'Oh, I know where she went, General. She was observed for her entire journey. I just can't *go*.'

Chapter Fourteen

Everything fascinated Squatstout.

He had bombarded Aranfal with questions since their return to the Centre. He had travelled up and down Greatgift, sometimes with Aranfal, and sometimes alone, examining every rock like it was a precious relic. He had attended Kane's funeral and followed the cortege right to the doors of the Circus; he told Aranfal all about it later that evening. Most of all, he studied every representation of the Operator that he came across, absorbing each detail and telling Aranfal when they were incorrect.

Watchers shunned the company of others, even those in the same profession. It was particularly strange for Aranfal to spend all his time with an insatiably curious, endlessly talkative being in a hareskin shawl, who claimed to be related to the Operator and appeared to hold terrible powers at the tips of his fingers.

That, however, was how the cards had been dealt. The Watcher felt compelled now to keep Squatstout at his side. If the little man could truly find the One, and if he could prevent Ruin, then Aranfal had little choice.

But it was not easy. On their journey back from Northern Blown Squatstout had pointed to every farmhouse, every river and every tree, peppering Aranfal with questions and rocking the carriage with his tremulous enthusiasm. But none of this compared to his unfettered joy when he first laid eyes upon the See House.

They had joined Greatgift at its far eastern point, so they did not have to travel for long before it first became visible in the distance, a dark and crooked blade emerging from the Priador Hill, the Eastern Peripheral Sea grey and unyielding in the background. Aranfal knew that something was wrong with his new assistant when the building first came into view; the small man fell into a trancelike silence, his eyes wide and glistening as he gazed upon the seat of the Watchers.

Aranfal, who was now accustomed to incessant babble, grew oddly uncomfortable as the silence lingered.

'Impressive, isn't it?' he asked, and cursed himself for the swell of pride he experienced.

Squatstout did not respond.

'Are you all right?'

The small man shook his head and chuckled. 'Oh, forgive me, Watcher Aranfal. I have never seen this, you know. He built it after I departed, all those years ago. What a thing he has created! When you look upon it, it is as if he made it from … absence. You know? As if he formed it from the darkness, from the stuff of nothingness itself! But surely that cannot be. It is simply a trick of his skill.'

Aranfal gave a slight nod.

'Yes, it is a great work. The Operator is talented.'

Squatstout nodded vigorously. 'Talented, yes, talented. In ways you can't even begin to imagine, Watcher! How far have we travelled on his roads?'

'What?'

'The roads, the roads, he built them too! Could you not feel it? I bet he built these roads at the beginning, even in lands that did not bow to him, so generous he is! We travelled on them for such a distance, Watcher, such a distance, from the very North of your Plateau to this balmy place. And the journey went by quickly, didn't it? Sometimes it felt like the world itself was moving, and not we. That is because Jandell built those roads.'

Squatstout tapped his nose conspiratorially.

It was the same when they had climbed the Priador and reached the tower itself. Squatstout gazed upon it with undisguised fascination, ignoring the hard glances he received from the Watchers at the gates. But Aranfal did not ignore them. He knew what the Watchers were thinking, and he feared meeting Brightling. How would she react to Squatstout's presence? He could not tell her the truth, that Squatstout claimed he could prevent Ruin; that would be an admission that he, the great Aranfal, saw the potential for truth in the Prophecy. And that was Doubting.

So he decided to do something utterly out of character. He decided to take a risk, and simply wait for events to pan out.

They entered the tower through the main doors, and even the hallway seemed to captivate Squatstout.

'Such a small room!' he cried. 'Small, yet perfectly formed! It is strange to enter a large building, such as this, and find such a room, but that is Jandell all over! He glories in such surprises!'

'This way,' said Aranfal, steering Squatstout to the small staircase on the western side of the hall. As they climbed, Squatstout reached out and touched the walls, gasping with each discovery of some new delight.

'And here, too, Aranfal!'

'What have you seen?'

'Can't you feel it?' Squatstout turned back, facing down the stairs. He quickly spun around and looked up into the darkness. 'This building is tall, so tall, and yet we climb so quickly! It does not obey the laws it should, does it?'

That was true; it was something many had observed before. 'I have often noticed that same phenomenon, Squatstout.'

'Because the building *wants* you here, hmm? If you were an enemy of Jandell, oh, it would be different, I am sure. You would not climb so quickly then, oh no.' He had a sudden realisation, his eyes widening. 'I wonder if it will all change, when the One is Selected? I mean, if we cannot prevent their rise? I wonder, will Jandell's laws become *their* laws?'

And on it went for endless days.

Aranfal's rooms were high in the tower, just below those of Brightling herself; in this building, proximity to the sky was a mark of great importance. They were ordinary rooms, lacking grandeur. But Aranfal's did contain something of note: his collection.

The entire back wall of the reception was lined with shelves, from the ceiling to the floor, all of them filled with curiosities. There were statuettes of naked men and women. There were books, ancient yellow things turning to dust. There were metallic objects, tools of some kind, covered in strange lettering and dials and spokes. Every part of every shelf was filled with some mystery, none of which Aranfal could explain. Sometimes he wondered if he had picked Squatstout up in Northern Blown as simply another curio, one that he couldn't place on a shelf.

These trinkets fascinated Squatstout, who ran straight to them whenever they entered Aranfal's rooms.

'These are old beauties, Aranfal, are they not? Where *did* you find them?'

Aranfal smiled. 'There are all sorts of things like this, hidden around the Plateau. I think they are from a time before the Machinery.'

'They are indeed.'

'I pick them up when I come across them. Often you find … well, Doubters tend to have things like this. They think there was a better world, once. They think such things prove it. But we don't understand what they are, by and large, so I don't see how anyone can claim anything about them.'

Squatstout nodded, and turned back to the shelves. He took an object in his hand, lifting it delicately and placing it in his palm. It was a wooden statue of a chair, perhaps ten inches high. It was a beautiful thing, in Aranfal's eyes. It seemed to have grown from the branch of a tree, in a place of endless forests.

'Do you like that one?'

Squatstout did not reply. He held the chair at eye level, studying it, his tongue flickering delicately at the corners of his mouth.

Aranfal approached Squatstout and lightly touched the man's shoulder. 'Do you recognise it?'

'Hmm,' Squatstout hummed, as if asleep. 'Once there was a great empire, whose emperor ruled from a seat far, far to the south of this place. His throne was made of oak, and it was a beautiful thing to behold. But then the world burned, oh, it burned and it burned. When the flames died down, this chair was warped into something new, a blackened stump. Jandell took it, and he turned it into his own seat. They say he sits on it even now.'

'He has a black throne, in the paintings and statues.'

Squatstout nodded. 'It was not always his throne. He keeps it to remember, I think. All those terrible things we did. He does not want to forget.'

One night there came a knock at the door.

Aranfal sighed, and stole into the hallway. He opened the outer door to find himself staring into the visage of a cat, its fangs bared.

'Hello, Aleah.'

Aleah was young, but there was no doubt in Aranfal's mind that she aimed to take his place at the right hand of Tactician Brightling. That kind of ambition was a good thing in a Watcher of the Overland, and Aranfal approved. But Aleah did not truly believe she could do it – not yet. Aranfal was one of the few Watchers skilled enough to read others of his profession, with or without a mask, and he could sense the nagging doubt that held her back from undermining him before the Tactician or framing him for some crime or stabbing him in his bed at night. A good thing for her, too; the day he sensed her crossing that invisible line would not end well for her.

'Pardon me for being abrupt, Aleah, but what do you want?'

Aleah bowed. She was smart enough to sense the edge to his voice.

'The Tactician wants to see you both.'

Aranfal nodded, and closed the door in Aleah's face. *Wants to see you both.* Brightling had not mentioned Squatstout, since his arrival. But of course she knew he was there. She always knew. *And now I face the consequences.*

Aranfal returned to the interior of his apartment, where Squatstout was still examining the objects on the shelves.

'You know who Tactician Brightling is, don't you?' Aranfal asked his guest.

'Of course, of course!'

'Then you will know that you should keep quiet when we meet her, and allow me to do all the talking.'

Brightling was working on her clock when they arrived. It stood in the centre of one of her reception rooms, refusing to tick or tock while the most powerful person in the world fussed and prodded at it. Sometimes it sprang into life, but the success never lasted long. Aranfal had seen her work on this thing many times before, right back to when he first entered her service. She always seemed to turn to it at times of strain; perhaps it took her mind off things. If she ever managed to finally fix it she would have to break the thing and start putting it together again.

Squatstout adopted his usual role of enthusiastic tourist, gawping at their plush surroundings. The portraits of old Watching Tacticians fascinated him, and he squinted at them as if he could unravel history itself from the paintwork.

Aranfal coughed gently. It did not do to take the Tactician by surprise, though he had no doubt she was well aware of their presence.

She looked up instantly, white hair hanging around her head in an unusually wild fashion.

'I am working on my clock, and I have lost track of time. Ironic.'

'Yes, madam.'

She threw a tool to the ground and approached Aranfal, embracing him warmly.

'That is a strange curiosity,' said Squatstout.

The Tactician and her subordinate parted, and looked to Squatstout, who was now standing beside the clock and staring into its inner workings. *By the Machinery, that creature moves surprisingly quickly.*

'It is a broken curiosity,' said Brightling, her voice impassive. If she was angry with him, he could not tell. But Aranfal could never read her.

'Yes, it is broken,' said Squatstout. 'But still, how advanced your society has become, to have unravelled such secrets!'

There was silence for a few heartbeats, during which Brightling studied Squatstout, and Aranfal studied Brightling.

'Squatstout,' said Aranfal, 'I thought we had discussed the merits of silence.'

'No, no,' said Brightling, raising a finger. 'Please, feel free to speak as you wish. You can begin by telling me who you are.'

Squatstout bowed. 'I am the servant of your fine Watcher Aranfal, madam. I am his assistant. He found me a prisoner in the North, and he freed me, so that I may help him in his efforts.'

'How can you help him?'

'Through my knowledge, oh mighty Tactician. It is such an underrated quality these days, don't you think? I know things that can help him in his work, I most certainly do. I will make a fine assistant, and if I do not, I will return to the road, or to prison, whichever the See House prefers.'

Brightling raised an eyebrow. She pointed at Aranfal. 'Is this true?'

He nodded. *Probably best to keep quiet about magical powers and ancient prophecies and things of that nature.*

The Tactician nodded. 'I trust you, Aranfal. And as your new assistant says, if he fails us, we can deal with him.'

Squatstout bowed once more.

Brightling lifted a cloth from the floor and wiped grease from her fingers. She indicated to a pair of sofas at the side of the room. 'Please, take a seat. There is much to discuss.'

They did as instructed, Aranfal assuming a place directly opposite the Tactician, who unfurled herself like a reposing cat across the entirety of her sofa. Squatstout took a seat beside Aranfal, his smiling gaze flickering between his two companions.

Brightling stared at the golden ceiling and sighed.

'Katrina Paprissi,' she said.

Aranfal winced inwardly. He never knew why he hated the girl as he did. Perhaps there was no single reason. Perhaps it was a combination of things: her ineptitude, her sense of entitlement, the way the world bowed to her and lifted her to the heights. She was the only real threat to his position in the See House, the only one Brightling held in equal esteem to himself, perhaps even higher. But that did not upset him. There were always rivals in the world of the Watchers, always someone with their eye on his back. No, it was the *way* she had emerged as a threat. The girl could not use a mask; they simply did not submit to her. That much was plain at the funeral. She could not analyse a situation with her own eyes, or interrogate a problem until it screamed for mercy. She was here for one reason only; her name was *Paprissi*, and her father had been friends with the Tactician.

That was no way to climb to the top of the tree.

'What has happened to her?' he asked, careful to hide his feelings from his voice. Brightling knew his opinions on Katrina. There was no sense in poking that particular hornet's nest.

'She is gone.'

Brightling sat up on the sofa. Somehow her pipe had found its way into her hand, and soon circles of pale smoke floated through the room.

'Do you know where she has gone?'

Brightling nodded. 'Yes, I believe we have that fairly well established. She was watched all the way.'

'They didn't stop her?'

The Tactician grimaced. 'No. That would have saved a great deal of trouble, but they did not. I suppose I cannot blame them. It is not usual practice to intervene in such circumstances.'

'When Watching alone could bring greater rewards.'

Brightling nodded. 'Precisely. But it matters not. She is gone. They watched her enter a building, from which she never emerged. The question is *why*.'

Aranfal glanced at Squatstout, who was strangely quiet. He stared at the Tactician with wide eyes, fiddling absent-mindedly with his hareskin shawl.

'When Kane died,' Brightling continued, 'there were two theories about his death. One was that he leapt or fell to his doom. That is the officially approved narrative, and long may it live on the tongues of commoners. But we know it is unlikely, don't we, Aranfal?'

The Watcher nodded, and was surprised to see Squatstout do the same.

'Ruin will come with the One,' Brightling whispered. 'I suppose if you were mad enough to believe that one Strategist is set to rule us all, you would think, "Perhaps it could be me. Perhaps I could impress the Machinery, now that it is breaking. Perhaps I will sit in Memory Hall, and I will even be able pick my successors, now the Machinery is no longer working. Perhaps I *am* the One!" We have long feared the emergence of such thoughts, illogical as they are. You know this well, Aranfal.'

'Yes, madam.'

'Well, we failed.' She spat out the word like poison. 'I am certain he was murdered. There is no way a foul old bastard like that killed himself, not with wine to drink and women to paw.'

165

She chuckled without humour.

'Anyway, before his funeral I had a conversation with Katrina. She had an interesting theory about who could have been behind it. Who do we know that might realistically expect preferment by the Machinery? Who was the only person that spent time alone with the Strategist, excepting other Tacticians and his servants and his whores?'

We are ruling out Tacticians and servants and whores? 'I suppose ... but no, he is not ambitious like that, madam,' said Aranfal.

'I thought so too. But now ...'

Squatstout was tapping his feet nervously. 'Who? Who?'

Aranfal raised his eyebrows at Brightling, and she nodded. *Proceed.*

'Charls Brandione,' said Aranfal. 'He is the General of the Overland's armies, and an adviser to the Strategist. At least, he was.'

'The Strategist loved the man,' said Brightling. 'There is a certain poetry to it.'

'And Katrina thought – thinks – that Brandione did it?' Aranfal asked. *Then it just can't be true. We should rule it out immediately.*

'She brought it up as a theory, that's all. And now I have a theory of my own. Katrina has had a hard time in her training. She is not a natural Watcher. Perhaps she sought to impress me. Perhaps at some point she confronted Brandione – say, at the funeral – and accused him. And perhaps she was right.'

'A lot of perhapses, madam,' said Aranfal, who instantly chided himself for his impertinence. But the Tactician did not seem to mind.

'Indeed. But still – I am intrigued by the theory, and I want to test it. So you will test if for me.'

Aranfal's heart sank. 'Yes, Tactician. Tell me what you need.'

Brightling smiled. 'Katrina was last seen going into a building in the Far Below. She did not emerge. I wager that Brandione tricked her into going there, perhaps to … well, I won't say it. I want you to take Brandione there, see if you can read anything on him. Wear your mask if you must.'

'And what do we tell the General?'

'Oh, he knows he is going. I met with him. But he thinks he is going to investigate on my behalf, because I can't trust my Watchers. The poor fool.'

'How did he seem, when you spoke with him?'

'He gave nothing away, but then he is an intelligent man. Perhaps a trip to the scene of the crime will stir his conscience.'

She reached forward and handed Aranfal a slip of paper, on which was scrawled an address in the Far Below.

'Just go to Memory Hall. That's where he's staying. Tell him that you're to accompany him on his journey, keep him safe, all that nonsense.'

'He doesn't know we're coming?'

Brightling laughed.

'Of course not. We want to unsettle him, Aranfal. And you are just the man for the job.'

Chapter Fifteen

The Far Below was known as the worst part of the Centre. Katrina felt the reputation was well deserved.

She was in what was once perhaps a town square, in the middle of four rows of rotten wooden shacks. The cobblestones below her feet were cracked and broken, black weeds sprouting from the gaps. A decaying fountain stood alone, shaped into the likeness of the Operator, crude faces etched into his cape. Brown water spluttered from the index finger of his right hand, which pointed to the Underland. There was a heavy, pungent odour, like rotten spices.

Katrina had seen no one else since she came here, save for the occasional drunk lying against a wall. That did not mean the area was empty, however. She had spotted guarded entranceways to the underground drinking pits and brothels that made the place famous. The people were not absent: they were hidden.

She glanced once again at the note she had found in her room. *This is it.* Before her was a ramshackle structure, substantially larger than the other buildings in the square. It was several storeys high, built from bleached wood, with white paint flaking from the walls. A weathervane of some strange creature hung from the roof, threatening to collapse onto the wide patio below.

Katrina approached in silence, climbing the creaking porch and approaching the door, where a sign hung.

Museum of Older Times.

So this is what you do now? asked her younger half. *Visit strange buildings in the slums, because of a note left in your bed?*

Yes, was all the old part said.

The Watcher looked over her shoulder, confirmed she had not been followed, and entered the building.

It was dark inside, just a shade above total blackness. Katrina closed her eyes for a moment to adjust to the gloom. When she opened them, she could just make out the dim outline of a long, narrow hallway with a winding staircase in the corner. The floors and walls were covered in illustrated tiles, though she could not make out the images. By her side was a coat-stand in the shape of a bird, its wings outstretched and its beak open.

There was a movement in the shadows.

'Come forward.'

Steeling herself, Katrina did as she was told. She came to a black wooden desk, plain and unadorned, behind which sat a woman. Even as Katrina drew closer, the woman remained in shadow, like she had been carved from fog. A pale face with a beak of a nose was just visible behind a heavy veil. Only the woman's hands were exposed, small white things that poked out from the wide sleeves of an intricately embroidered gown of dark lace. Black hair fell in ringlets from below the veil, tumbling upon her narrow shoulders.

'You are not a member of this institution,' she said with slow, melancholic certainty. The voice was impossible to pin down: it had a hard edge that was unusual for the Centre, but was too light and cultured to be provincial. It swam with an easy authority that made Katrina hesitate.

'No. But I have permission.'

A long moment passed. The woman made a slight head movement.

'From whom?'

Katrina reached into her jacket and removed the note. The woman lifted her veil ever so slightly to read the card; Katrina caught a brief glimpse of a scarred, burned neck.

'Take the door at the top of the stairs, on the right.'

The receptionist slipped the card into a drawer and a white finger shot out from the black sleeve.

'There.'

Katrina bowed, walked up the stairs, and found herself in a small hallway. Before her was a door with a frosted-glass frontage, from behind which came a muffled hum of conversation.

She took a deep breath and entered.

It was a large, wood-panelled lounge. The central area was laid out like a restaurant. A few lonely looking figures occupied the tables, hunched over bowls of soup and plates of meat and eating quietly by themselves. In the corner, an old man lay back on a leather chair, cradling a tumbler of whiskey and surveying the room with a bored air. A black horned lizard lay at his feet. It lolled its head around, fixed its eyes on Katrina, and licked its lips.

A strange museum.

She walked inside, feeling her feet sink into the deep, wine-coloured rug. Three doors led off to other chambers. To her left was what seemed to be a games room, in which four hooded figures huddled around a Progress board, only moving to shift the pieces with long, pale fingers.

The young Watcher looked to her right. Beyond was a reading room, its shelves groaning under the weight of worthy tomes. The only occupant was a boy of twelve or thirteen, a spindly creature with thick black hair who sat reading in a leather chair. He momentarily caught Katrina's eye and smiled; she instantly turned back to the main lounge.

There was another room, on the other side, its entrance discreetly veiled behind a covering of red silk.

There, her gut told her. She padded swiftly across the lounge and lifted the covering an inch.

A mahogany bar stretched along the back wall. Chairs were clustered around tables, and an oversized portrait of the Operator hung behind the bar. He seemed to be sitting on a tree stump in a forest at night, staring at his feet as creatures of the woodland bowed down before him, the colours of his cloak and its faces matching the sylvan hues of the scene around him. Katrina, who knew the Book of the Machinery as well as anyone, did not recognise this imagery; it was likely the work of some new artist. It was well Brightling was not here. She did not like this type of thing.

The only people in the room were two shabby old men, sitting together on high stools and glancing around with some confusion.

'Where's he gone then? Actually, what was his name again?' said one, a filthy creature whose corpulence and baldness gave him the look of a large rock.

'I didn't ever find out,' said his companion. This was a thinner character, dressed in a tailored suit that had seen better days. A surprisingly thick thatch of greying brown hair sprouted from his scalp.

The fat one leaned over the bar and filled both their glasses with whiskey.

171

'Let's look at it plainly and from a great height,' he said, stroking his stubble. 'This is the fourth night of the week. We were last here – when?'

'The sixth night of last week, I think.'

'All right then. We were here on the sixth night of last week, and he was here then,' the rock said, glancing at an old clock that sat on the bar. 'So in the past five days, he has gone. Disappeared and left everything open, even took the iron bars down from the door.'

'Yes.'

'Strange for a landlord to do that.'

'Indeed it is.'

They laughed and clinked their glasses together.

The clock on the bar struck.

'I have not yet grown used to those,' said the tall man.

'No. Everything's changed. I always thought this place wouldn't, but then the young lad—'

'Went and bought this clock.'

'Yes.'

They regarded it warily: a black pyramid of stone, its yellow face a scrawl of red numbers overseen by two ornate figures who slouched across the top of the timepiece.

Katrina stepped into the room.

'That is an old clock indeed,' she said. 'My guardian is interested in clocks.'

The two men turned ever so slightly on their seats to acknowledge their new arrival. She smiled at them, but it was not in friendship; she was sure they recognised that.

'Who were you talking about, gentlemen? Who has gone missing? I am a Watcher of the Overland, and I can help you.'

The more refined gentleman cocked his head to the side and eyeballed her. 'As you were spying on us, miss, you should already know who we were talking about. The *landlord*. We haven't seen him for a while.'

'Which isn't like him,' said the fat one. 'Oh no, he normally likes to make his presence felt, I must say.'

'He does indeed,' agreed his companion. 'But we forget ourselves. My name is Sharper, and this gentleman here is Sprig.' He bowed. 'What takes you here, anyway? You are not native, I can see.'

'No. I am not from the Far Below.'

The man appeared briefly confused. 'Far Below ... I suppose it is, really. Aha. Well, if you're not *from* here, what are you *doing* here?'

'And would you like a drink?' Sprig held the bottle before her and grinned.

'No thank you. I was invited here. It's embarrassing, really.'

'Who invited you?' asked Sharper.

Katrina removed the parchment and handed it to Sharper. The confusion reappeared on his face, then became something else: a kind of concern. 'Ah, I see. You want the museum.'

'She wants the museum?'

'Yes, she wants the museum.' Sharper seemed irritated with Sprig. He turned back to Katrina and smiled. 'You want the museum. Well, it's being made up at the minute; they're giving it a nice clean. You'll want to wait here until that clock strikes again, then walk up those stairs.' He pointed to a doorway behind the bar. 'Now come, Sprig. Let us leave her to it.'

'Yes, let us leave her to it.'

The two men drained their glasses, stood from the bar, and walked into the main lounge, bowing as they went.

Katrina sat by the bar for more than an hour, alone. It grew quiet in the lounge beyond as the few occupants dispersed.

173

The candles were blown out, until the only light was a torch on the wall of the bar.

She examined the clock, and saw now for the first time that one of the figures was the Operator himself. Katrina hated looking upon this creature, even in this artificial form. *That was how he appeared to Alexander. He came through our old statue.* But there was more to this small sculpture. To the Operator's left lay a female, a woman in a long green dress, her face concealed by a white mask. That was strange; in all the other art, the Operator was alone, save perhaps for Arandel.

Turning away from the odd clock, Katrina poured a glass of wine and sipped it, drumming her fingers on the mahogany. It was getting early, now, the first grey light of dawn seeping into the bar from some window she could not locate. She wondered if Brightling had discovered her disappearance. It was inevitable. It would be several hours before she made it back to Greatgift Avenue, let alone her bed in the See House.

She hoped this excursion would be worth the trouble. What had taken her to this place? Instinct? No. There was nothing else to lose. *Someone either knows where my brother is, or they are toying with me. Either way, I want to know who they are, and what they want from me.*

The clock struck, a low ring.

Katrina slipped behind the bar.

It was as if a scholarly bird had built a nest by raiding the archives of an academy.

The walls were lined with wooden shelves, each weighed down with books of the old type, bound in ancient leather and formed from milky vellum. There were great encyclopaedic tomes, volumes of history and science, interspersed with thin books of poetry or art. Katrina drew one down from a shelf nearby: a series of delicately drawn images of ancient cities, of white towers and hanging gardens, of places long gone or alive only in the artist's imagination. Instruments of science were scattered around: a telescope pointing at a pane of glass set into the ceiling; navigation instruments, like her father once owned; on the wall, a chart of the stars.

This was not what she expected to find in a rotten bar in the Far Below.

Tack, tack, tack.

Katrina spun around. At the back of the room was a door, swinging open and closed in the night air. Beyond was another staircase.

And so it was that she once again found herself ascending a flight of stairs, narrow wooden slats that protruded from the exterior of the building. She paused briefly when she reached the top, wondering if she was walking into a trap, before stepping out onto the roof.

A wide expanse of the Far Below could be seen from here, a brown sprawl that stretched out like a puddle of vomit. In the corner of the roof was a knot of five trees. They were dark, their thick leaves utterly still, even in the night breeze. They were almost contrived, as if brought to life by a sculptor.

There.

Katrina made her way to the copse and pushed her way through the branches.

A woman sat among the trees, her face concealed by a white mask. She was crouched over, her head leaning against her arm; tears shone on her thin white fingers. Her shoulders shook, sending ripples down through the green dress. Curls of red hair framed her face.

It is the woman from the clock. Has another statue come to life?

The woman's head snapped up like a startled beast. Holes in the mask revealed lively eyes that were as green as the dress; a pair of red lips surrounded a mouth of sharp, yellowing teeth. At first she seemed confused, surprised that her strange rooftop glade had been disturbed. But that soon hardened into something else: a strange look of recognition.

She indicated to a branch by her side, and Katrina sat down slowly. The eyes peered at her, twitching between emotions. The mask itself seemed alive, like a second skin; its expression seemed to change with every glance. The woman raised a finger to her chin, as if lost in philosophic contemplation. She swivelled her head around nervously like a southern lizard.

'It is too bright for me, which is why I wear the mask you see.' She quivered like a leaf on a branch. 'I hope you don't mind.'

Katrina shook her head. How else should she respond? 'Madam, I am here because someone left a note for me, in my chambers,' she said in the masterful tone of a Watcher. 'Was it you, or do you know who was responsible? I'd like to speak with them. This is an urgent matter for the Overland.'

The woman's lips trembled before she burst into laughter. 'An urgent matter for the Overland! Indeed! Very urgent!'

'Madam—'

'Ah, yes it was me, I am afraid.' The woman gave a bow. 'Did you like the note?' There was a new earnestness in the voice; the humour was gone. 'I worked hard on it.'

'It was … a lovely note.'

'Good.' The mask nodded sagely. 'I am glad of it. I will say, though, that it is not easy entering the See House undetected. It is a well-constructed edifice. But then, of course it is.' She smiled. 'I have not written a note in … have I ever written a note? I do not know.'

'Why did you wish to see me, madam? I have come all the way from the Centre.' No response. 'Madam, what is your name?'

The woman turned her back on Katrina and laid her head in her hands. 'My name is Shirkra. Shirkra the old, Shirkra from the beginning.' She glanced at Katrina, as if surprised the young Watcher did not recognise these titles, and then sighed. 'None know of me now. Not here, anyway. Do you like the museum?'

Suddenly Shirkra looked up, as if another voice had spoken. 'Yes … yes … I will.'

She turned back to Katrina. 'I am sorry. Do you like the museum?'

'Certainly, Madam Shirkra, it is very pretty. I would like to spend more time there.'

'Pretty? Oh. I'd have thought it would mean more to you than that. Some of those things are as old as the Machinery itself. It matters not.' She gave Katrina a sweet smile, and said, as if it was nothing: 'I know your brother.'

'You mean you knew my brother, madam,' Katrina said, careful not to betray any emotion. 'He is gone now.'

'No, I know him. And I know where he has gone. He was taken, was he not? By the one you call the Operator.'

It was as if somewhere, in the darkness of a void, a torch had been lit. 'Yes.'

'Your brother is … special. He can communicate with the Machinery.'

I remember him, standing alone, eyes closed and lips twitching.

'He knows what is coming,' Shirkra continued. 'The Machinery spoke to him. That is why the Operator took him.'

Katrina nodded. *Finally. A reason.*

'Why him? Why Alexander?'

Shirkra gave her a sceptical glance. 'You still do not know? Because only he could have stopped the One. That's what the Machinery thought. But nothing could stop the One, not ever.'

'Why did you leave me that note, madam? Why do you want to help me?'

Shirkra laughed. 'I cannot *but* help you. He took my family, too. He took our mother from us.' Shirkra nodded. 'He sent me into exile, far away. But I am free now, though he does not know it. I am free, and I will see that the Prophecy is fulfilled.'

'What is the Prophecy, madam? What will come when the Machinery breaks?'

The woman sat in silence for a moment. 'Ruin will come, and the One will bring it.' She laughed. 'Jandell does not believe it, but I do.' Shirkra smacked a small hand down on a branch. 'Do you wish to help your brother?'

'Yes.'

'Then you must find him, in the Old Place. You have heard of this place, I believe, though you call it something else. The Underland.'

Land of the Operator, Home of the Machinery, Forbidden, Forbidden, Forbidden.

'Madam, I cannot go there. No one can go there.'

'Go there? You are there already, my girl.'

She saw the fear in Katrina's eyes, and she laughed.

'Do not worry. You will be safe from Jandell. The Old Place permitted you entry, did it not? It likes you.'

Shirkra stood from the branch and motioned to Katrina to follow her.

'Madam, who are you?'

'I told you,' said the masked woman. 'I am Shirkra. Sister to Jandell, the one you call Operator. I am an Operator myself.'

Chapter Sixteen

'You have been gone for some time, General. I was worried for you, very worried.'

Bandles did not seem worried.

'There was no need for concern.' Bandles had been mooning around the apartments of late, peering at Brandione from shadowy corners. Was he monitoring the General? No: that was beyond reason. *You are paranoid. You've spent too much time in the See House.*

'Would you like some Redbarrel, sir?'

The General nodded. Bandles vanished for a moment, returning with a glass of whiskey and a half-empty bottle that he left at Brandione's feet.

It was well past midnight. Greatgift was darkened, bar the occasional torch that glowed in the window of a marble palace. Few would be awake in the Centre at this time, and the night owls would be drinking in the Far Below or some other benighted place.

'A great time to be alive, isn't it?' asked Bandles, standing awkwardly at Brandione's side. 'A whole new Cabinet on its way, and us having conquered all of the Plateau! Ah, to be young again!' A thought clouded his eyes. 'I wonder what sort of people it wants now?'

'There is no way of knowing.'

Bandles chuckled. 'I don't mean, *what people* – I mean, *what sort* of people? You can always have a good guess at that. Take Brightling. Before she was Selected, the Watchers were a shambles. The Doubters could get away with whatever they wanted, you'd see them out openly in the streets and everything. I remember those days. Well, everyone was crying out for someone strong in the See House, someone who knew the ways of the place and could sort it out once and for all. And then what happens? The Machinery Selects the greatest Watcher of the Overland to rule the Watchers. Well, I don't mind telling you, it didn't surprise any of us that she was Selected, not at all.'

'And what about now, Bandles?' Brandione doubted very much that Bandles had predicted the coming of Brightling.

'Well, who knows sir? Let's see. We're at a new point in history. It just cannot be denied. Expansion is over. It's kept us all going ten thousand years, but it's over. So we'll need to consolidate. We'll need someone who knows about peaceful things, about science and suchlike, about developing all the breakthroughs of recent times. And we'll need to address the problems we have at home.'

'Domestic enemies.'

Bandles nodded. 'Yes sir, exactly. We'll need someone that can root out the Doubters. That won't be too hard, though. There's a lot of them around now, crowing about their Prophecy, but you wait: once the 10,000th year passes and we're all safe and sound and the Machinery is carrying on as usual, well, a lot of the sting will be taken from the Doubters' tails.'

Brandione sighed. 'Thank you, Bandles. You may leave now.'

The little servant did not seem surprised by this dismissal. He filled the General's glass, bowed, and slipped away into the apartments.

Brandione gazed out at the Centre and sipped from his drink. Out there, millions would be playing the same game as Bandles, trying to second-guess the Machinery. As the good book said, there would be butchers, merchants and artists, men and women, boys and girls, wondering if their time had come. That was what he loved most about the Machinery. It made a mockery of ambition, of social airs and graces and so-called superior bloodlines, exalting only the most worthy and raising only the most competent. As he looked around his surroundings, he wondered who would sit here in a few days.

The General, exhausted from the travails of the past few days, drifted off to sleep. But even there, his thoughts pursued him. He dreamed he was in the inner sanctum of the apartments, in the study. It was late, the candles on the great oak desk and the torches on the marble walls casting a flickering glow across the book-lined space. He saw himself approach the desk, and lean across to look into the seat beyond. A snake was coiled there, red and yellow, eyes glinting amid the dancing flame; it flicked its head at his approach, and seemed to somehow smile.

He awoke to voices, coming from the reception room.

'No, don't do it, Squatstout. Let him wake in his own time.'

'I apologise, Watcher, but we do not have all the time in the world. If the time in the world was a beach, we would have merely the fewest grains. But ah! He awakes!'

Brandione leapt from his seat. Before him, sitting side by side on one of the Strategist's sofas, were two men. They were quite a contrast. One was small and round, an odd creature with thinning chestnut hair, and garbed in a peasant's shawl of hareskin. He hummed with nervous excitement, rubbing his hands together and licking his lips with a sharp red tongue, eyes flickering between the General and his companion.

His companion was tall, his thin body wrapped in an aquamarine cloak that billowed out across the sofa. His hair was dirty blond, his features sharp and delicate, his eyes quick and intelligent. At his side hung a mask: the image of a raven.

The General entered the reception room.

'Who are you, and how did you get in here?' He kept his voice low and steady.

The tall one spread his palms open in a gesture of submission. 'We apologise for disturbing you, General Brandione, truly we do. We didn't mean to surprise you.'

'We did not,' said the small one. This was the one called Squatstout. 'That was last in the long list of our intentions.'

The thin one gave Squatstout a weary glance, then turned back to Brandione. 'You asked two questions, General, which I will answer in reverse order. We were allowed in here by the servant of the Strategist, an excellent man who has served for many long years, as he told me.'

'We are *honoured* to be here, truly we are!' said Squatstout. 'Never did I think I would lay eyes upon the apartments of the Strategist, the great centre of the Centre!'

'Squatstout, please. This, General, as you may have gathered, is Squatstout, an assistant to the Watchers of the Overland. I am Aranfal, a Watcher.'

'I have heard of you.'

'All good, I hope?'

'No.'

'Ha! That is good, too. Well, we have been sent here by Tactician Brightling, to assist you in the task you have been given.'

'That, General, is first in our list of intentions,' smiled Squatstout.

This is turning into a children's story. 'Very well.' Brandione sat in a high-backed chair by the sofa. 'This is a job for Watchers.

In fact, I'm not sure why the Tactician asked me to get involved; surely you gentlemen would be able to deal with this matter alone, without me getting in the way?'

'It is not for us to decide that, General,' said Aranfal. 'It is for our mistress. We were told to be here, so we are here. You should be pleased. The Tactician has obviously seen something in you.'

'Aye – or a lack of something,' said Brandione. 'Maybe she doesn't care what becomes of me.'

'Oh, you are a shrewd man, General.' Aranfal's voice was hard and low, a voice from the North. 'But she trusts you, too. Katrina Paprissi is … special, to her.' Something flashed in the Watcher's eyes, but only for the briefest of moments. 'Tactician Brightling would not send just anyone off to find her little darling, no matter what treachery the girl has committed.'

Squatstout shifted uneasily. 'Watcher Aranfal—'

Aranfal laughed. 'I jest, of course.'

Brandione was growing annoyed. 'Gentlemen, why are you here? You are Watchers of the Overland, are you not?'

'No,' said Squatstout. 'Only him.'

'Very well, but you both serve the See House. Why have you been sent here to help me? I thought the Watchers weren't supposed to be involved.'

Aranfal nodded. 'Indeed not. If we could be involved, Tactician Brightling would have slipped off on this mission by herself, I believe. She does love that girl, and she does love a mission. But there is a bad taste to this one, you see. For all we know, Paprissi has become a Doubter; it wouldn't do for the Watchers of the Overland to be running off in search of a Doubter, would it?'

'That is precisely what you are doing by being here,' said Brandione.

'Oh, no. We won't be involved, General. We are very good at being discreet, you see. When we reach our destination, Squatstout and I will melt away into the air.'

'Like smoke.' Squatstout grinned.

'But until then, we will help you. Now come; we should gather ourselves.'

The Watcher and his servant stood.

'Where are we going?'

'South,' said Aranfal.

'Is that all you will tell me?'

Squatstout laughed. 'What more do you need to know? You know we are going to the South. You can rule out so much already, like the colds of the North or the green fields of the West, or the beautiful coasts of the Peripheral Sea, in the North and the East and the West.'

'Squatstout, please. General, you will need to get yourself ready; we could be gone for a while.'

The two men turned to leave the reception room. The General sighed and followed.

Chapter Seventeen

'What is that?'

'A map of the world. A very *old* map of the world.'

Katrina and Shirkra were in the cellar of the museum. The Operator, as she styled herself, beckoned the Watcher to the far side of the chamber, to stand beside a large, round, painted ball. Katrina had seen such things before – she was the offspring of the world's greatest explorer – but never anything like this. It was *old*, its colours faded and worn, its surface carved with strange characters. The globe was covered in lands that could not possibly have been mapped in the Paprissi voyages. Strange place names stared back at her, in a script she did not recognise, and the outlines of unknown continents were etched into the wood.

'Do you notice anything strange about this map, my love?' A smile seemed to play across the mask. 'There is no Overland on this map. But here is the Plateau.' She pointed to one of the painted patches. Katrina quickly recognised the continent where the Overland had its home. A yellow band cut through the middle: this must be the Wite. But below, the land stretched onwards. If this was accurate, it meant the Plateau was just one small part of a hulking mass, a giant rock covered in forests and lakes and mountain ranges.

'It is smaller than many of the others.'

'Yes.'

'Who lives in the other places?'

Shirkra giggled. 'As I say, it is an old map. Some of those places are uninhabited, now. Others are the same. Some are newly populated, with my people and your own. I understand that some from this Overland of yours have already made contact with other places.'

Katrina nodded. 'My father has been abroad. No one knows where he went, except Brightling. There was trade, of a kind, for a while. But that has ceased.'

'Yes, I know of your father. Oh yes.' There was a smile, beneath the mask, that somehow played across its surface, too.

The globe seized Katrina's attention again. She could make out a black smudge, north of the Plateau, so small she initially took it for dirt.

'Does anyone live there? It is close to us.'

Shirkra blinked three times in quick succession. 'Do not worry about that place.' She turned away from the globe suddenly, like a child losing interest in a toy. 'Anyway, we are not here to look at trinkets, beautiful though they may be. Come.'

The Operator led Katrina to a door on the back wall and pulled it open. Stairs disappeared below, barely visible in the dying light from a torch on the wall.

'What is down there?'

'This is a path to the deepest Old Place, Katrina. I think I know this way, but they have a habit of changing.'

Shirkra vanished. After a moment's hesitation, Katrina followed.

The descent took hours, or at least it seemed to. It felt to Katrina that they made little progress. The light from the torch never changed, as if they were walking on the spot.

Eventually the Operator stopped. Squinting into the darkness, Katrina could just make out a door of solid wood. Shirkra studied it for a moment, laying her hand on the frame.

'Do not touch anything, and do not speak too loudly. Do you understand me?'

'Yes … Operator.'

The mask nodded, turned back to the door, and entered, Katrina following closely behind.

They were in a vast cave. Black rocks tore up from the earth and hung from the ceiling, their surfaces gleaming with moisture. Algae-covered ponds were dotted around, writhing with animal movements. The roof above was a mile away, a rocky outcrop of dark vegetation; the ground below was hard and treacherous. White-eyed lizards emerged from fissures, sticking their tongues out at Katrina before vanishing back into the earth.

Shirkra pushed forward, indicating to Katrina to follow. The Watcher's footsteps echoed like cannon fire in the cave, though Shirkra was utterly silent.

The Operator came to a halt after a few minutes of walking.

'We are at the gate,' she whispered.

Katrina squinted ahead. At first she could see nothing in the gloom. After a while, however, shapes began to emerge in the darkness. Before them was a curtain, a black veil that fell from the ceiling to the roof, miles in length and width. Katrina stepped forward and squinted her eyes. *Could it be?*

Human hands surrounded the curtain.

They were at its sides, its base, and above: pale hands, open as if ready to grasp at anyone who approached. They were a sickly colour, a colour that reminded Katrina of the skin of a drowned man she had once seen in the Bowels. They were utterly motionless.

'What is behind the veil?'

The Operator hesitated. 'This is the gatekeeper. It knows me, so do not be afraid. You have my protection here.'

She reached out and grasped Katrina's arm; her fingernails dug into the Watcher's skin.

'Come.'

They walked forward, towards the curtain. At the side was a gap in the rock, just wide enough to enter in single file. As they squeezed through, Katrina felt a finger gently tracing its way across her shoulder.

She did not look up.

'Where are we?'

Where are we? Where are we where are we where are we, where are we where are we where are we …

The voice echoed, growing softer until it petered out to nothing.

Katrina sat up. Her arms ached from Shirkra's grip. How far had they travelled? The journey came back to her in snatched shards. They had walked under the veil and through a door; the Operator had grabbed her, and they had leapt. Katrina had felt lightness then weight, shallowness then depth. Had they fallen? She could not tell. She remembered little: just flashes of lights, of red stars and black suns, and then darkness. And falling: always falling.

Then there was the Portal to the Machinery, that pit in the middle of the Circus. She had seen it, its gate unbarred; a black tunnel worming its way into the ground. *The way to the Machinery*. In they went. But it could not be so. They had been in the Far Below, nowhere near the Circus.

She could see nothing now. This was a kind of darkness she had never experienced, even in the Bowels. It smothered her.

Paprissi.

The word echoed in her mind. Why? As a tether to the Plateau, perhaps? *Paprissi.* Why now? *I am a Brightling, now, more than anything else.* There are no Paprissis left.

Paprissi. Was she speaking, or was it someone else? There was another Paprissi down here, she remembered: Alexander. Did the Underland recognise her?

Where are we where are we where are we …

The room filled with light.

She was in the lounge of a stately home, so vast that the corners were formed of an almost tactile, malleable shadow. The white walls were cracked and crumbling, their monotony broken by paintings of black chairs. The ceiling was a patchwork of plaster and wood through which came glimpses of a strange exterior: flashes of light and darkness.

The room reminded her of Paprissi House. But it was old, older than any mansion she knew: she could *sense* it. All her doubts about Shirkra melted away. The woman was truly an Operator, and she had taken the Watcher into the very heart of the Underland.

Shirkra herself was sitting at a long, black desk in the very centre of this room, gazing quizzically at Katrina. The Operator had cast off one skin to assume another. Her mask had gone. Curls of dark red hair fell to the side of a face as white as the mask in which it had once been enmeshed, and the green eyes stared blankly at the Watcher. She reached a long white hand out from the folds of her dress, lifted a bell that sat next to her, and shook it violently.

It did not make a sound.

'Next!'

Katrina was tugged to her feet, lifted into the air by an unseen force and dragged before the desk. Operator Shirkra picked up a sheaf of papers, straightened them and placed them in front of her eyes.

'Now then, now then, now then, who have we here and why have they come to our Old Place?'

Has she forgotten?

'Operator, you took me here,' Katrina said, her voice shaking. She tried to edge away from the desk, but found she was held in place.

The green eyes creased in confusion. *She is not lying.* Had Shirkra changed on their journey? But then Katrina detected a flicker of recognition, and the Operator nodded.

'Oh yes,' she said. 'Well, it's still forbidden, you know. I can't think why it let you in.'

'I know. I didn't want to come. You took me here from the museum, Operator. Have you already forgotten?'

Shirkra clicked her tongue. 'Well,' she said, leaning back in her chair and throwing the papers into the air, 'you're here now! I've taken you here. How dangerous! He probably knows you are here, but there's not much he can do about it.'

'Where, Operator?'

Shirkra leaned forward. 'We are where the Machinery lives.' She leapt to her feet in a burst of green and ran to a corner of the room. Katrina tried to follow, but found she was still locked in place.

'He will find me,' Shirkra whispered from the corner. 'He will try and find out what I know. He does not love me any more. He will not want me here.'

'Who?'

'*Him*, you fool. It is always *him*.'

A weight lifted. Katrina ran to the corner, where Shirkra grasped her in her arms.

'I am sorry, my child.' The febrile energy seemed to fade. 'I cannot go any further, today. But you must. You must *go there*. There you will find your brother, and save us all.'

She pointed to the far side of the room, where a door had opened.

Chapter Eighteen

Darrah was unhappy.

She hadn't complained. There were no huffs and puffs. But something had changed. It was in the way she held herself; the way she cast glances into corners, the way she read a book, the way she drank her tea, the way she ate, the way she undressed, the way she slept. Rangle could just see it.

They were in Darrah's favourite part of Memory Hall: the Arboretum. It was only a thousand years old, built by some southern Strategist who was nostalgic for the swaying trees of his youth. He had requisitioned some land behind Memory Hall, and torn down the houses that were there, constructing in their place a palace of glass and iron where foliage from the entire Plateau flourished. The whole place stank of beasts and mud and echoed with chirps and chirrups. It all reminded Rangle too much of her childhood, picking through vine roots in the unceasing rain.

They had a table in a corner of the Arboretum, below a tree that was pregnant with glaring orange fruit. There was no one else there. There never was. Only Strategists, Tacticians and their guests were permitted entry, and none of the other members of the Cabinet ever came, probably because there was no wine. Rangle only ever came because of Darrah.

A servant hung nervously behind them, nipping forward every few minutes to pour their tea and bother them with helpfulness. *You will get no Sovereigns from me. Not today. Not even a clinking handful of Citizens.*

'Bring us some more of this,' the Tactician told the servant, waving at the pot of tea, 'and then disappear.'

The servant did as he was told.

Rangle watched Darrah with open fascination. The woman was the best thing in her life; that was the simple truth of the matter. She was not beautiful, in any conventional sense, but she was entertaining, and there wasn't much that kept Rangle entertained. Darrah didn't meet her eye, but stared at her tea, adding too much milk to the mix and stirring it too slowly.

'We live in an abundant world.'

That was another thing about her: she always surprised Rangle with the strange things that tumbled out of her pretty little mouth.

'What do you mean by that?'

Darrah pointed at her tea. 'This stuff grows in a warm, wet clime. It comes from the southern part of our Plateau: near the Wite, in fact, but not of the Wite.'

'Yes. It is still a part of the West.'

Darrah nodded. 'Yes. The bountiful West. It goes so far from north to south, that everything that can be imagined grows there. But then in the North there is ice and wind. Here in the Centre we have cool breezes and balmy days. And the Wite is a desert.'

'The Plateau is a good land.'

Darrah smiled. 'Parts of it are, yes. I wonder though, do other lands have all that we have? Or do they have just one little piece?'

Rangle shrugged. 'There may be no other lands.'

Darrah snorted. 'You are joking. How can a world exist with just one rock upon it? And you know better than me about the tales in that library of Brightling's. You only have to look. And where did Jaco Paprissi go? Where did he find the things he brought?'

Rangle smiled. 'Perhaps there is one other land, then. A good place, where the Operator has friends.'

'But not any more. He won't let anyone go any more.'

Rangle had heard enough. She leaned forward and grasped Darrah's wrist, as tight as her old hand would allow, and stared her in the eye. 'I know you are annoyed about something, but do not say anything about the Operator here. Do you understand me?'

Darrah narrowed her eyes. 'Don't you fucking tell me what to do. You've given me up; I can *feel* it.'

She stood, raised her fist in the air, and in one movement smashed the tea set to the ground. Rangle sighed, and turned away, which only served to infuriate Darrah more. The younger woman stomped out of the Arboretum.

As Rangle watched her leave, she thought about her situation. Darrah felt ignored, and she was right to; she had been ignored. But there was nothing the Tactician could do about it. How often did someone from a book appear in your study, claiming to be the Operator's sister? She couldn't tell Darrah about it. So she would make it up to her, somehow. Yes, she would find a way.

She raised a bony hand and clicked her fingers, bringing the servant clattering out from whatever leafy hole he had been hiding in.

'Clear up this mess. Send the bill for any damages to the White Rooms.'

The servant fell to his knees and started gathering up the crockery.

'And one more thing,' Rangle said.

The servant looked up. Rangle waved a hand around the room.

'Send my assistant some flowers. Nice ones.'

The servant stood, bowed, and fell to his knees once more.

Garron Grinn was in the White Rooms when Rangle returned, which was just what she did not need. He was standing in a corner of the reception room, peeling an orange and staring at the fresco with undisguised reverence. By the Machinery, he was an irritant.

'Garron Grinn, how many times have I told you – take a seat. You don't have to wait for my permission.'

He made a short bow, which for him was actually quite a long bow, and unfolded his weary bones into a hard chair at the table. No luxury for the Senior Administrator of the West.

'I haven't seen you for a while,' Rangle said. She wasn't sure why she said that. She certainly didn't care that he hadn't been around. *By the Operator's black chair, he's not going to think this upsets me, is he? He's not going to show up more often?*

But if Garron Grinn was worried about her words, he did not show it. He seemed far more absorbed by his orange. It had finally been peeled; he popped the entire thing into his mouth, and seemed to swallow without chewing.

Something was the matter with him. Rangle could tell. And she was sure it wouldn't be long until she found out.

'We must discuss Watchfold, Tactician.'

Ah. Here it comes.

'What is there to discuss? Didn't we talk about our business not long ago?'

'We did. But business never ends.'

'And you wouldn't have it any other way. Why would you want me back there? I'd only get in the way of your management of affairs, which has always been first rate.' She actually meant the last bit.

'Thank you.' There was no joy in Garron Grinn's voice. That wasn't unusual, but normally a good compliment about his abilities was enough to extract a thin smile. 'But I do not think I have managed things well lately, my lady.'

It was very unusual for him to talk himself down. He wasn't one of life's boasters – by the Machinery, there were enough of those in the Centre – but he had a quiet confidence in his own capacities. Something cold and unwelcome reached its tendrils from Rangle's stomach and snaked its way up her back.

'What's the matter with you?'

Garron Grinn sighed. He glanced into the shadows, and spoke in a whisper. 'It's the Watchers.'

I should have known.

'What have they done this time?'

She had completely forgotten their previous conversation about the Watchers. She had promised to speak to Brightling, hadn't she? She couldn't remember. She had been so distracted. So very, very distracted.

The Administrator was literally shaken; he was trembling. 'They haven't *done* anything, not yet. But there has been a change. I met with one of them, the other day. I wanted to find out what they were doing in Watchfold. He was sent to Watchfold directly from the See House, he says.'

The See House? The cold thing slithered off Rangle's back and settled behind her eyeballs.

196

Rangle whistled through her teeth. She and the Administrator didn't always see eye to eye. But they had built an alliance over the decades, an understanding of one another, and their interests were identical. Garron Grinn wanted to sit behind his desk and tick through the affairs of the vast West, uninterrupted, using Rangle's title as his shield and his seal of approval. Rangle wanted exactly the same thing.

'I should have seen this coming,' said the Administrator.

'There's no way that's true. This has come from nowhere; if there had been even an inkling of the Watchers encroaching on the West, you would have seen it.'

She meant every word, but it made no difference to Garron Grinn, who absent-mindedly plucked another orange from somewhere on his person and started picking at the skin.

'So,' Rangle said, 'Brightling is moving on the West.'

'It would appear so.'

'It stands to reason.' The Tactician sounded more nonchalant than she felt. 'She already runs the rest of the continent. Now that the far North is totally fallen, she only lacks the West among her domains.'

'Have you spoken to her yet, Tactician? I think I did mention something to you about this, ah, problem, before.'

'No.' Rangle shook her head. 'I am sorry. I should have.' *I've been rather busy growing infatuated with an immortal being from a book.*

'I cannot see her interest in the West, Tactician. We have run our region well; revenues have increased every year, and we have had a lower level of Doubting than every other part of the Overland for almost the entire time you have ruled.'

Rangle chewed this over. 'I'm not sure what she's up to,' she said. 'But I'm sure we'll find out. I will speak to her.'

This time, she meant it.

As the night wore on, she sat by herself in the reception room, waiting for Shirkra to come. But the woman stayed away, doing whatever it was that Operators did.

She may never return. She may never have been here. You are old. Your mind is a fragile thing. Perhaps ...

The Tactician's doubts were hushed by the sudden appearance of Darrah. Rangle saw her, standing at the doorway, holding a limp bunch of roses in her pretty little hand. *How long has she been there?*

'I've been standing here for ten minutes.'

Ah.

'And you didn't even look up at me.'

Rangle sighed, a deep, raggedy thing that rattled her ribcage like some old instrument. 'You are being a child.'

'You don't really mean that,' said Darrah, accurately.

'No,' Rangle agreed. 'I'm sorry I said it. Please, sit down.' She indicated to another of her soft chairs, pulled close beside her own.

Darrah sat down, still holding the flowers. They looked cheap. Rangle decided to speak to the servant about this later.

'You received the flowers, then?'

Darrah said nothing, but allowed the roses to fall to her feet.

Rangle sighed again, and the instrument in her chest cranked out a few more disjointed notes. 'If you want to leave me, you can. I understand completely.'

The younger woman lifted her head a fraction, and smiled. 'You have a way of deceiving yourself, you know. You don't understand at all.'

'Then tell me.'

Darrah stood and walked over to the fresco. *Some day I'm going to have that fucking thing painted over.* 'You are not really here, Annara.' The utterance of her first name jarred.

'You're in your head. That's where you live. And it's got worse, lately.'

'It is difficult for anyone to escape their own head, darling.'

Darrah laughed, but there was no humour to the sound. 'You aren't here for anyone else. You recognise your needs, it's true. You have me to lie beside at night—'

'Really? I hardly remember those nights.' *Petulant.*

'And you like that. Every now and then you shine your light on me, and all is well. That's always been enough for me. Just every now and then.'

'I don't think that's true, but even if it is, why do you suddenly object? Nothing's changed, that I can tell.'

'And it's not just me. You whinge all the time about being a Tactician, as if it's a curse, when anyone in the country would kill to take your place. But you don't really mean it. You're not stupid. You like the status it gives you. You like the trappings.'

Darrah flicked a hand at the fresco and all the luxury of the White Rooms.

'But by the Machinery, you won't work for it.' She spat out her words like poisoned darts. 'Garron Grinn is there for that, isn't he? He's like me. He just floats in and out of your life, when you need him—'

'That's enough.' Rangle raised a hand, her eyes closed. She didn't really get angry. Ever. But now she was ... irritated. 'Just tell me what you want, Darrah, and I'll see if it can be arranged. Just stop complaining about me. I'm sick of being complained about.'

Darrah returned to her chair, and surprised the Tactician by reaching out and grasping her hand. Her skin was cool; had she been walking about in the night?

'Something has happened to you, recently,' the younger woman said in a hushed tone, staring directly at Rangle's eyes. 'I can just … *feel* it. I've felt this way before.'

'Before?'

'With other people.' Darrah focused on the floor, on the rug torn from the carcass of a golden, exotic beast. 'When they have left me, and gone to another.'

Rangle almost laughed. Was that what this was about? Did Darrah know about Shirkra's midnight visits? *No, she would have said something before now.* So she just believed there was another woman, hidden away somewhere. Rangle had to give it to her – she wasn't far wrong.

'There is no other in my life.' She reached out and touched Darrah's cheek. 'How could I find the time?'

That was technically true. She and the Operator were far from lovers. She wondered what Shirkra would make of the suggestion.

But Darrah turned away from her, and got to her feet.

'I don't know if it's another person, but something has changed,' she said, a tremor in her voice. 'Everyone sees it – the study group hasn't met, because you've been engrossed elsewhere. You haven't even thought about that, have you? If you're going to lead a secret life, you should try and convince the people in your old life that everything is the same as before.'

Good point. Damn.

'I'm leaving,' she said, without emotion. 'I'm going back to Watchfold. Don't follow me there.'

Rangle's eyes narrowed. 'Don't tell me what to do.'

Darrah's smile was a harsh little thing. 'No. You don't like that, do you?'

She turned her back on the Tactician and left the White Rooms. As Rangle watched her depart, this companion of many years, the only one she could turn to through the dark times of the recent past, just one thought occupied her mind.

When will Shirkra return?

Chapter Nineteen

Brandione had tired very quickly of serving the Watchers.

It was almost noon. He had been in a carriage with Squatstout and Aranfal since just after dawn, when they had turned up in Memory Hall to aid him on this unwanted mission. Now they sat opposite him, the two Watchers side by side. *No: one Watcher. The other is just an assistant, whatever that means in the See House.*

The General turned his attention to the world outside. They were still on Southfair, a cobbled tributary of Greatgift. But the road had many aspects, and this was not the brightest. The marble palaces of the Centre had now gone, melting into an anonymous spread of ramshackle hovels and low, dirty inns. The great crowds of the inner city had thinned out, too, replaced with lone drinkers and small, whispering groups. Even the *type* of person here was different, with the furs and silks of the Centre now ragged skins and the brash discourse of wealth and success now hushed despair and sly winks.

The General had been here a few times, as a student in the College and later as a young officer. Such visits were confined to certain days, when the entire world knew that a celebration was coming: the end of a term, the promotion of new recruits. On those days, the Far Below was covered in garlands, like a whore and her paint.

It was all very different on a random day in the middle of the week; the veil had been pulled aside, or never drawn to begin with.

'This is a strange place, I believe.' Squatstout's eyes were wide as he stared at the street outside, licking his lips.

Aranfal turned his attention to Brandione. 'Have you been here before, General?'

'Yes. As a younger man.'

'Ah – enough said.' Aranfal leaned forward. 'Driver, are we almost there?'

There was a grunt from the front of the carriage.

Aranfal leaned back into this seat. 'I think that was a yes. It's difficult to tell, sometimes. Our assistants are often dumb creatures. Why else would one serve in the See House, without the glories of being a Watcher?'

Squatstout appeared not to notice this insult, engrossed as he was. There was something otherworldly about him. He was like no one the General had met before.

'Where do you come from?' Both Squatstout and Aranfal looked surprised that Brandione had asked a question. Squatstout pointed to himself, a puzzled look on his face. The General nodded.

'Where do I come from? That's an interesting one. There are several places, really, depending on what you mean. And I have such a terrible memory, truly I do, cruel and forgetful my parents used to call me, cruel and forgetful. The place I was born was a warm place. So that's where my blood is from. But I left there, and I went somewhere else, and that's where I grew up, with others of my relations. It was damp there, cold and damp, you know. So I am from two places, then: one in the warmth, and one in the cold. It was—'

'Squatstout, please. The General was being polite.'

'I am sure that is correct, Watcher. It is a very boring story.'

Brandione turned his attention once again to the outside world, resolving to keep his questions to himself in future.

After some hours the carriage came to a halt, and the driver grunted again.

'We are here,' said Aranfal. 'General, you must go in alone. We will watch you, in the background.'

'That is what we like to do. It is the thing at which we are best.' Squatstout smiled, lips stretching across yellowing teeth.

Brandione nodded. 'Make sure you stay well behind me, as the Tactician wanted.'

'To stay out of your mission, General?' asked Aranfal.

'No. I don't want to be associated with a Watcher.'

Brandione was in a decrepit town square, empty apart from a broken statue of the Operator that served as the centrepiece of a grotesque fountain. This place had seen better days. It was in a poor state even for the Far Below, with weeds crawling from the broken ground and the buildings shuttered and darkened. The only sounds came from the hooves of the horses and the wheels of the carriage as it creaked its way into the shadows.

Brandione was glad he had brought his weapons.

Before him was a ramshackle building, its door hanging open to the elements. A sign hung by the door. *Museum of Older Times*. When Aranfal had said they were going to the Far Below, a museum was not what Brandione had expected.

He entered the building, taking a last glance back to locate the carriage. It was nowhere in sight.

The General found himself in a gloomy hallway. To his side was a statue of a bird, from which hung three cloaks.

Strangely, his attention was drawn to the tiles below his feet, which were alternately painted with a black chair and a white mask. At the back of the room, in the corner, he could just make out the outline of a staircase. By its side was a wooden desk, where a woman sat, her outline only just visible in the darkness.

'Is there a torch? I can't see anything.' The General hoped his voice was steady.

'No,' the woman said. 'It is too bright in here already. Come forward.'

Brandione hesitated. He felt as if a line was before him, and was not sure he should cross it. Still, he had little choice.

He walked to the desk.

'Strange, to wear a veil indoors.' He wondered about the face beneath.

The woman ignored this. 'Why are you here?'

'On behalf of Tactician Brightling.' The General had expected the name to have an impact. It did not.

'I knew a Tactician once, a long time ago. But he was not named Brightling. I do not know that man.'

'Brightling is ... do you mean to tell me you do not know Tactician Brightling? You are joking.'

There was the slightest movement below the veil. Brandione noticed the perfect whiteness of the woman's hands.

'Why are you here?'

'Where is "here"?'

'The Museum of Older Times. Though not always. They keep changing the name, every century or so.'

This was surely a joke, though there was no humour in the voice.

'I am looking for a girl.'

The woman remained silent.

'She could be in trouble. She ran away from her home.'

The woman shook her head, and Brandione caught a glimpse of scars, running along her neck. 'I do not have the authority.'

'Allow him in.'

At the top of the stairs were two men, barely visible in the glow of light from a room beyond. They were a study in contrasts: one was tall, thin, elegantly proportioned, while the other was a stump of a man with a large, bald head.

'Allow him in,' the tall man repeated. 'I would like to meet him.'

'Yes, allow him in, it is good that you should.'

The veiled woman sighed: even her beaked nose seemed to disapprove. 'Very well. But he is your responsibility, if the masters find out. We can't just start letting uninvited people in off the street.'

The tall man bowed in agreement, and turned his focus on Brandione. 'Come. Let's have a drink.'

'Is it closed?'

'No. But we haven't been able to find the landlord,' said the small man. 'It's been a shame of all shames.'

'Indeed. It has been terrible,' agreed his companion. They laughed and clinked their glasses together.

Brandione had suspected he would end up in a bar, down here in the Far Below. But he did not think it would be like this. It reminded him of the Centre, with that air of established wealth, from the mahogany to the soft red leather of the chairs. A portrait of the Operator stared down at the General from the wall, the great being sitting in some kind of forest glade. Brandione could not recall seeing this use of imagery before.

'You are a military man, I would guess.' This was the tall one.

You do not know me? 'I am a General of the Overland.'

'A noble profession,' said the fat one. 'My name is Sprig, sir. This is Sharper. You may have heard of us before in your travels, it seems possible. Would you like a drink?'

'No.'

'Are you certain?'

'Yes.'

Sprig seemed confused. 'The landlord is not here.' He cocked his head to one side. 'And you are a military man. I am telling you the whiskey is free.'

'Sprig, he said he did not want any.' Sharper rolled his eyes. 'Not all soldiers are like you, you bumbling fool.'

These are no soldiers. 'Where did you gentlemen serve?'

'Serve?' asked Sprig. 'We serve ourselves, it seems, for the landlord is away.'

'I mean, in the army. Were you in the North? At Anflef, or Siren Down, or Northern Blown?'

Sprig seemed confused. 'Those names are … they cannot be …'

'We served a very long time ago,' interrupted Sharper. 'Now we are old, so we spend our time here, drinking and reminiscing.'

'I think we may have bored the landlord, you see. With our stories.' Sprig sighed. 'I am sorry if that is true. I liked him. He was the owner.'

Enough. 'Gentlemen, I need your help. I am looking for a young woman.'

'Oh,' said Sprig. 'This is not that kind of place.'

'That is not what the General means, Sprig.' Sharper laughed. 'Is it, General?'

'No.'

'You mean a girl with pale skin and black hair, dressed in rags of mourning.'

'Yes.'

'She was here. She went to the museum.'

'That was a while ago, now,' said Sprig. Sharper shot him an angry glance.

'That signifies nothing, Sprig.'

Sprig shrugged.

'Where is the museum?'

Sharper pointed behind the bar, where there was a door. 'Up those stairs, General.'

Brandione bowed, and went behind the bar.

Brandione had always enjoyed libraries. It was the scholar in him. There was something in books that he loved: the promise of a journey, perhaps.

These books were very old indeed, hand bound and painted on vellum. He lifted one from the nearest shelf, handling it delicately through fear he would cause it damage. He need not have worried, he quickly realised; the vellum was tough, the book itself well designed. *The Days Before the Fall.* A strange title. The fall of what? He opened it, rubbed the pages between thumb and forefinger. There was little text; it seemed to be some kind of picturebook, though not the kind for children: more a series of portraits. A host of characters played across the pages, sometimes together, sometimes alone. One looked like the Operator, though without the cloak. And this man was much younger, with long, dark hair. The other people were unknown to the General: a pair of small children, a boy and a girl, who leaped across the pages hand in hand; a small man, swathed in animal skins, who looked amusingly like Squatstout, the Watcher's assistant; and a grown man and woman, who spent their time apart from the others. Strange, but Brandione could not look at these two for long without flinching.

Finally, there was the woman in a white mask, ringlets of red hair falling to the side of her face. She was depicted either alone or with the one that looked like Squatstout.

Brandione was half-tempted to slip the book into his pocket. But he thought better of it. The objects here were too strange to simply carry away at will.

Clack, clack, clack.

The General turned and saw a door at the far side of the room, blowing open and closed in the night air. That was unsafe, in a place like this. He crossed the room and closed it. As he turned back he saw a mirror, hanging on the wall to his side. For half a heartbeat Brandione was sure he saw a reflection there, a glimpse of the woman in the white mask. But it was gone as quickly as it had appeared. The General laughed at himself. He truly was becoming a Watcher, paranoid and fretful.

He left the library behind, without leafing through another book.

'How many of them were there?'

Aranfal and Squatstout were watching Brandione very carefully. They sat together on one side of the carriage, staring at him like he was the King of the Doubters.

'Three. A female in the hallway, and two men drinking upstairs.'

'And no sign of the girl?' Aranfal again. Squatstout was silent.

'No. Just those three. The old men said they saw her, but I couldn't find her anywhere.'

209

'Describe the museum one more time.'

Brandione was growing irritated with this interrogation, but he knew he must play along. 'It was full of old things, Watcher Aranfal. Old, museum-type things.'

'Very funny, General, but we do not have time for your jokes. There could be Doubters here as we speak. *What type of old things?*'

Brandione shrugged. 'Books, mainly. I think I saw some navigation equipment, too, though I don't understand that much. They are in a room at the back of the bar. You have to go up some stairs.'

Aranfal's eyes widened.

'Old books usually mean Doubters,' he sighed. 'Squatstout, let's pay these three Doubters a visit.'

'Indeed! You may even find some new additions for your collection there, Watcher Aranfal, by the sound of things!'

'Yes, thank you, Squatstout.' Aranfal turned to the General. 'Stay here.' He took his raven mask from his belt, put it on, and slipped out from the carriage into the night. Squatstout hopped out after the Watcher.

Brandione watched from the carriage window as the two strange creatures slipped around the side of the building, searching for some hidden entrance into the museum. Something told him that would not be possible. Sure enough, the dark figures quickly reappeared and went through the main door.

The General decided to take the opportunity for rest. He closed his eyes and fell promptly asleep.

Brandione did not know how long it had been before the Watcher and his assistant returned to the carriage, though it was now fully dark. He could immediately tell that their mission had not been a success.

'Move, now,' Aranfal spat at the driver, tearing off his mask and letting it fall to the floor. The carriage rolled forward through the darkened streets of the Far Below. 'There are two possibilities we are presented with,' he said, turning back to Brandione. 'Either you have lied to us, which I highly doubt from a General of the Overland and an intelligent man like yourself, or your friends in the museum are very quick.'

'The place was empty,' Squatstout said. His voice lacked Aranfal's passion, but he held the General with a steady, unrelenting gaze that was somehow worse.

'That is not possible,' Brandione said. 'I was there minutes before you. What about the woman in the veil?'

'No.' Aranfal shook his head. 'She was not there. There was nothing but an empty hallway.'

'We went up the stairs,' said Squatstout. 'And we found your bar. But it was rotten, General, rotten to the core and falling apart. No one has drunk in there for a very long time. There were certainly no old men present.'

'Impossible. I was there. There was a tall man and a fat one: they were drinking whiskey and talking about a missing landlord.'

'They are not there now,' said Squatstout.

'An utter waste of our time,' said Aranfal. 'I don't believe you are a liar, General. But this is the Far Below, and there are strange illusions here, and stranger people. We have all been the victims of some trick, and it has brought us no closer to Katrina Paprissi. I fear she has been caught up in some nest of Doubters, I truly do.'

'What about the museum? There's no way it could have just disappeared.'

Aranfal shrugged. 'I'm not sure what to tell you, General. We found the stairs at the back of the bar – we could barely walk on them, truth be told, they were so rotten – and we went up to your museum.'

'There was nothing there but moths, General. We were lucky not to fall through.'

'Stop the carriage,' said Brandione. 'I will go back, to see this for myself. I'll make my own way back to the Centre.'

'Certainly not,' said Aranfal. 'There are numerous possibilities for what happened tonight, General. None of them suggest it would be wise to return to that place.'

Brandione shot him a hard glance, and the Watcher laughed.

'There is no going back there. I will speak to my mistress about what has happened. She will know what to do.'

The carriage rolled on through the night, eventually leaving the broken cobbles of the Far Below for the smoother pavestones of the Centre. Brandione watched the world from his window, as lanterns and candles were lit in the marble enclosures of the Overland.

He wished he had taken that book with him.

Chapter Twenty

'Do you think he did it?'

It was the first time Aranfal had asked Squatstout about Charls Brandione. He waited until they were back in the See House, ensconced in his own apartments, before raising the subject. He did not want to air his opinions out on the road, where all sorts of things were listening.

Squatstout started, as if from a dream. He was sitting on the floor, leaning against the wall by a fireplace, with the flames dancing across his skin.

'Did *it*?'

Aranfal was sitting in a hard-backed chair by a small wooden table, playing with one of his knives.

'Brandione. Do you think he did something to Katrina Paprissi?'

Squatstout summoned a ghost of a smile. 'You mean, is he guilty of murder and ambition? Hmm. Well, not of murder, anyway, I feel. I could not sense it upon him. Nor of ambition, I am afraid. I have seen people like him before. They do not scheme or plot, yet somehow they make it to the top of the pile, just through talent and a sense of duty.'

Aranfal nodded. 'I agree with you. He didn't behave like a

guilty man. Why would he have made up that story though, about the museum?'

'You think he invented that? Hmm. I do not know.'

Aranfal stabbed the blade into the table.

'Squatstout, I don't understand. Why are you here?'

'I am irritating you. I irritate everyone, eventually. My family always said so, the cruel bunch.'

'No, you are not irritating me. But I have the feeling you could figure this whole thing out if you wanted, with the click of a finger.' Aranfal clicked his finger.

'You think highly of my powers, now, when once you thought I was a trickster.'

'Squatstout, please—'

Squatstout's eyes widened. He stood up and seemed larger than before, and somehow harder than the creature Aranfal had grown accustomed to, a thing of threatened violence. 'I am here to find the One, Aranfal, and to stop the One before they release Ruin. I have not succeeded yet. This Brandione is not the One. That is all that matters about this Brandione.'

He seemed to shrink again, and the warmth returned to his eyes.

'I thought the One would be hidden here, in your See House, among the most powerful of the world. But now I do not know. I do not know anything any more.'

There came a knock at the door.

'That will be Aleah,' Aranfal said. 'The Tactician will want to see us.'

Sure enough, the blonde-haired woman was waiting, cat mask held in her hand. But something was wrong.

'We must all go to Memory Hall. The Tactician is waiting for us.'

The boy was lying in his bed, amid the silken opulence of his apartment. His head was to the side, and a pool of saliva had gathered beneath his lolling tongue. By his bedside was a table, and on it stood a glass of water, hardly touched.

The door to the outer balcony was open, and it banged in the wind.

'Leave,' Brightling said to Aleah. The girl bowed, and disappeared. Normally this would have given Aranfal a sense of petty satisfaction. But not tonight.

Tactician Bardon was dead.

The three of them stood around the body in silence, Brightling on one side and Aranfal and Squatstout on the other.

'Who found him?' Aranfal asked. He had to say something.

'Bandles.'

'The servant.'

'Yes.'

'And he is—'

'Utterly trustworthy.'

Aranfal nodded.

'It was this,' Brightling said, waving a hand at the glass of water. 'Someone put something in the child's drink.'

'So two deaths,' said Squatstout, his voice barely above a whisper.

Brightling looked up at the assistant, as if noticing him for the first time. 'Two deaths, yes. Two murders.'

She turned to Aranfal.

'Let us speak alone.'

They went through the open door on to the balcony. The view was nothing compared to the See House, but still they could bask in the glory of the Centre, of torches and marble.

'He has been useful?' asked Brightling, jabbing a thumb back at the bedroom, where Squatstout still stood in silence over the body of the boy Tactician.

'He has, madam. He sees things I could not.'

'I very much doubt that. But if you trust him, then good enough.'

She placed her hands on the edge of the balcony and stared out at the city, her white hair lightly shifting in the breeze.

'How was the trip to the Far Below?'

Aranfal shrugged. 'Very strange, to be honest. I could read no guilt on Brandione. He went into the building alone, and when he returned he said he had met three people, a woman and two men. And these people were in possession of old materials, from before the Machinery.'

'Doubters?'

'That is what we thought. But when we went in there, we found nothing. It was utterly desolate.'

'Then he lied to you. A fantastic story to cover his fantastic lies.'

'I'm not sure that's the case, madam.'

'You believe him?'

'I think I do.'

'Then you are a fool.'

Aranfal winced. She had never before spoken to him in this way.

'Madam, I think it is a neat theory, but I do not see why it trumps all others. You may as well pick Bandles as your chief suspect. He had greater access to the Strategist than Charls Brandione.'

Brightling snorted. 'Imagine. Bandles! Selected by the Machinery to rule alone. Ha!' Aranfal sighed with relief; some warmth had returned to her, the warmth she had favoured him with for so many years. Was her earlier coldness just some aberration? He hoped so.

Brightling looked back to the city. 'Aranfal, you are the greatest Watcher I know. If the Machinery should Select me again, in whatever role, I want to keep you by my side. I would give you more power, if I could. If it does not Select me, then I truly hope it looks to you as my successor in the See House.'

Aranfal bowed slightly. She had said such things to him before.

'But I am better than you, Aranfal. I do not say this to be cruel; it is simply a fact.'

'Yes, Tactician.' It was indeed a fact.

Brightling turned quickly and came in close to her subordinate, taking his cloak in her hands and leaning into him, until their lips almost touched.

'And I am telling you this,' she whispered. 'Every part of my being screams that Charls Brandione murdered Kane, and that he killed this boy too. He wants to be another Lonely Strategist. He thinks it will be as it was before; the Machinery will Select him to rule alone, impressed with his martial valour and his ruthlessness in killing old men and little boys. He is mad with a lust for power.'

She pushed him sharply and he staggered away from her.

'He couldn't have killed this boy, madam. I was with him only—'

'He could have accomplices, Aranfal. He could have placed a slow-working poison in the boy's water, before he left. He could have slipped away from you, when you thought he was in that building, and come here through secret byways. It is not so far from here to there, and some of our roads are strange. There are all *sorts* of ways he could have done it.'

'Yes, madam.'

Brightling took him by the throat, gently, using only the tips of her fingernails.

'This act must not become public knowledge,' she whispered. 'No one must know the boy was murdered, not even his parents. It would not be wise to create a panic. We will say that he died in his sleep, and no one knows why.'

'Yes, Tactician.'

'Leave, now. Take your assistant with you.'

As he left the balcony, he turned to her, and found she was staring at him, a hard look he had seen before in grimy cells in the Bowels.

She saw into him. She knew he believed Brandione. She knew he doubted her suspicions.

And then something moved, within him. He had felt this before, so many times. It was a stirring, and it meant only one thing. He was looking into the eyes of the guilty. *But what is she guilty of?*

He quickly moved inside.

They returned to the See House in silence. When they got to his apartments Aranfal ordered a meal to be sent up, a roasted chicken and root vegetables that Squatstout devoured with gusto while Aranfal picked at his own. They did not speak throughout dinner.

When the meal was finished they retired to the reception room, where Squatstout immediately turned to the shelves and their strange old contents.

'Squatstout,' Aranfal said, lying back on a sofa, 'have you ever heard the tale of the Lonely Strategist? He murdered the Tacticians and the Strategist, thinking it would impress the Machinery. He thought he would be Selected to rule alone, so impressed would the Machinery be by his ruthless ambition.'

Squatstout turned to Aranfal, a small book in his hand. 'Oh, I remember when it happened, Watcher. I watched it from afar. Such ambition that man had, ruthless ambition, as you say. For a while, it made me wonder about the Machinery itself.'

'What do you mean?'

Squatstout cast glances at the walls. 'Is it permitted to discuss such things in this place?'

Aranfal nodded.

'If you are certain,' Squatstout said, but he did not speak above a whisper. He was growing accustomed to the treachery of Watchers, it seemed. 'When my brother built the Machinery, he placed such powers into it, things that you would never be able to look upon or even understand.'

'I do not doubt it.'

Squatstout gave a grim smile. 'We all knew what went into it. We could all *see* what went into it. But even so, it was supposed to have a certain … independence. It was supposed to be immune to all outside influence, Selecting only those who would further the glory of the Overland, according to its own superior judgment.'

'The Machinery knows.'

'The Machinery knows, indeed. But then this man came along, this ambitious little man. Arkus. You won't find his name anywhere; Jandell would like him to remain unknown, a fragment of history. I knew what Arkus was up to, you know, me on the outside. I am sure that Jandell knew, too. It was amusing to me. I watched him carry out his little plans, his murders, and I waited for the Machinery to pick a whole new Cabinet of vengeful people who would string him up by his toes and let the crows peck his life away. But that is not what happened. His plan worked, and the Machinery Selected him alone!'

Squatstout turned back to the shelves and placed the book back in its place. He whistled through his teeth.

'Well, this surprised me. It meant that the Machinery could indeed be influenced. Not only that, but it seemed to reward those who carried out the most terrible acts. This was not what Jandell had in mind when he created the thing, oh no.'

'But it was just a lesson, wasn't it? He was killed in his bed. The Machinery set it all up, as a warning to others who might have similar ambitions.'

'Hmm. He was murdered in his bed, indeed, and all the world carried on as before. But who killed him? Perhaps Jandell murdered him himself, so angry was he with his skill in influencing his creation. Ha ha! Imagine that. But perhaps not.'

Squatstout sighed.

'Arkus was a beautiful man. I think he would have been Selected anyway, you know, without the need for all the things he did.'

'One thing I have never understood,' said Aranfal, 'is how he got away with it. Surely the Watchers would have apprehended him? How could you murder the entire Cabinet, without running into a guard or two along the way?'

Squatstout turned to Aranfal and smiled. 'Why, that is simple. The Watchers could not stop Arkus because he *was* the Watchers.'

'Squatstout—'

'Yes indeed, Aranfal.' Squatstout looked up to the ceiling. 'Arkus was the Watching Tactician.'

Chapter Twenty-one

The path through the Underland went down, down, down.

It felt like hours had passed since Katrina had left Shirkra, although she could not be sure. The light of the reception room had gradually faded until she was in blackness so complete that she lost track of her progress. The narrow corridor wound down into the earth, becoming so steep at points that the Watcher had to reach out to the walls for balance, recoiling from the clammy black stone.

There were noises, too, in the dark: the thud of metal on metal, as of something being shaped.

'You are a Watcher of the Overland. You will not fear this,' she whispered to herself. But despair curled its way through her. She should not be here. The Machinery must know she had come, and it would be displeased.

And what of the Operator? The *real* Operator, who had taken Alexander away? Shirkra had vouched for her safety, had she not? Would that be enough?

The corridor came to an abrupt end. Before Katrina was a hole cut into the rock, dimly lit by a grey light from beyond. She hesitated, feeling around the edges for a sign of a trap. Nothing, but that did not mean she was safe.

She carefully stepped through to the room beyond.

It was as large as the main courtyard of Paprissi House, its three long walls lending it the shape of a tortuous triangle. Peering upwards, Katrina saw that it stretched away into darkness. The walls were covered in black and white tiles, like a Progress table that had been folded inwards. The image of the black chair was everywhere, laid into the black tiles in white and the white tiles in black.

On the wall to her right were three doors: one red, one black and one blue.

The Watcher assessed her options. She had no knowledge of what lay beyond any door; the only way to know for certain would be to walk through. This, however, would arouse the attention of whoever or whatever lay beyond.

It would be better to listen first, said the younger part of herself.

The older part agreed.

Katrina selected the blue door and placed her ear against it. A sound of chattering voices came from beyond, a cacophony of hundreds of people talking all at once. She could not discern the patterns of conversation; even the tone of the voices was confused, lurching off in a hundred directions. She stepped away.

The black door must have led outside; when she pressed her ear against it she could hear rainfall, falling in great waves. It reminded her of an occasion years before when she had travelled to the West with Brightling, where the coast was wild. Yet surely there was something wrong here: Shirkra had led her below the earth.

You are not in a hidden cave below the ground, you stupid girl, said the older part. *This is the Underland. Things are not the same here.*

She sighed, and pushed on.

The red door was perhaps strangest of all. From behind came a grinding noise, like the movements of a great engine: perhaps the sound she had heard earlier, as she walked along the corridor.

'Well,' she whispered to herself, 'I am in the home of a machine, after all.'

She opened the door.

The first thing she noticed was the steam.

Sweating clouds hissed from fissures in the floor, filling the room with a scalding heat. It came in waves; as each burst faded, she was able to snatch a glimpse of the room beyond. It appeared to be a foundry. She had seen such places in the great yards of the Fortress of Expansion, yet it differed substantially from that birthplace of cannon. It was far larger, to start with, a cavern that could easily have swallowed the great pyramid in its entirety. While the foundry was a world of cold, grey iron, this place was dominated by burning red metal. It had a fierce glow, as if a light was hidden behind the walls.

Machines were all around. A long line of steel hammers stretched along the left-hand wall, driving rhythmically into anvils and ringing as they hit their targets. She could not see what was moving them, as the handles disappeared into the wall.

A great wheel dominated the right-hand side of the room, as tall as Memory Hall. It was made of a solid, dark wood, with nails formed of the red metal driven into its length. It turned slowly, emitting a mournful creak as it went. Boiling water fell from hanging buckets, sending fresh plumes of steam into the air.

Is this the Machinery?

Something felt wrong, as it had since she first entered the Underland. The room seemed unreal, like it had been drawn by the hand of a lunatic artist.

But then she saw them, and she knew what this room was for.

In the centre of the ceiling was a long, black tube, which reached down almost to the floor. Every few moments the tube would screech and vibrate, before something fell from it and joined a huge pile of its companions.

They were Watchers' masks.

Near her position, in the centre of the room, was a raised platform, a tower of the red metal topped with what appeared to be a circular desk. A man sat there, an outsized figure in a dirty grey tunic. He wore a mask like Shirkra's, though his was red and not even his eyes were visible. He sat in the centre of a nest of levers, which he pulled in a sequence, starting with two at the left then moving around in a circle.

Katrina steeled herself, and crept up to the platform.

'Can you help me?'

There was no response.

'Hello?' she shouted. Still he ignored her.

Katrina felt no threat from this man: more a dumbness, a total ignorance of her presence. *I must get closer.*

At the base of the platform was a rugged step, from which led a series of hand- and footholds, up to the summit of the tower. Sucking in a breath, she closed her eyes and climbed. Before long she reached the top; she swung her legs over the side and quietly landed at the man's side.

'Who are you?'

He ignored her still, focusing his attention on the swift, almost independent movement of the levers.

'Do you make our masks?'

Again, no response. She reached out a finger and tapped him on the shoulder. He paid her no heed.

Katrina came closer. She saw that his mask was fashioned from a thick, heavy material, perhaps leather: holes on the underside revealed glimpses of skin. It was possible that the mask maker could not hear or even feel her through the material, she realised; it was certain he could see nothing. But this was the first person she had seen in the Underland since Operator Shirkra; she *had* to speak to him.

She noticed that his mask was held in place by a wooden clip, hanging at the base of the neck. Without thinking, she reached out a hand and undid the clasp. It fell to the floor with a thud.

The man turned slowly to face Katrina. The Watcher fell backwards, clutching the side of the platform for support.

It was her father.

How long since I saw this face? A port, somewhere in the North. A ship with red sails. Tactician Brightling gathering her up and instructing her to be quiet.

But as with everything she had encountered in the Underland, something was amiss. He looked *longer*, somehow. It was as if Jaco Paprissi's face had been torn off and stretched over the head of a larger creature, as if his limbs had spent weeks on a Watcher's rack. Her thoughts turned to the Bowels, and she trembled.

'What do you want?' he snapped, the voice familiar but strained. 'I am working!'

Katrina stepped forward to face her father, her composure returning. *This is nothing but some Underland trick*, said the old part.

'Who are you?' she asked, her voice breaking.

The machinist turned back to his levers.

'Why do you look like my father?'

He turned to her again, incredulous.

'How am *I* supposed to know?' he asked. 'You're the one looking at me! You tell me!'

'But I ...'

'It's quite simple. While it is indeed true that I am being looked at, it is equally the case that you are looking at me. In that way, we are both responsible for my appearance. No? Talk about shirking responsibility, girl.'

He turned back to his levers, shaking his head.

Katrina mulled this over. Her fear had gone, replaced by an intense curiosity. She wondered if the creature had a point. She was no longer in the Overland; the world of the Machinery might have a different logic, a set of rules she would have to learn.

She changed tack.

'May I ask you a question?'

The man sighed, regarding her warily from the corner of his eye. She knew that expression well; it made her catch her breath.

'I suppose.'

'Are you an Operator, too?'

The man became still; he seemed to be thinking this over.

'Well, as you can see, I *operate* things. But that does not, I think, make me an *Operator* in the way that you regard them.'

Katrina nodded. From outside the room came a sound of hushed conversation, like the whispering of ghosts. She could not make out what they said, but something about it made her shiver. *The Machinery knows.*

'May I ask you another question?'

The machinist sighed and nodded. He seemed weary; she suppressed an urge to reach out to him.

'I believe a friend of mine is here. His name is Alexander. Have you seen him?'

'No.'

Katrina nodded. *This cannot be my father.* 'Where is the Operator? Will he come here to collect the masks?'

The Machinist abruptly stopped working, his arms falling to his sides. The whirr of activity in the hall screeched to a halt. He slowly turned to face her.

'Who brought you here? Who took you to this place?' He leaned in towards her. 'Was it an Operator?'

Katrina hesitated. Shirkra had claimed to be an Operator, but could she be trusted? 'It was Shirkra.'

The man nodded. 'Lucky. Then he will not be able to find you. I hope.'

The machinist stooped down, lifted his mask from the ground, and once again the face of Jaco Paprissi disappeared. He took the levers in his hands, and his work resumed.

Chapter Twenty-two

There was only one problem with the See House library: it was full of Watchers.

That was to be expected, of course, in the beating black heart of Watcherdom. But it still made Rangle uneasy. When she was forced to stay in the building for long periods, usually when a text was too old or valuable to remove, she tried to find some darkened corner, free of inquisitive glances. The darkened corners were easy to find: the whole place was just one giant darkened corner, as far as Rangle was concerned. But the inquisitive glances were not so easy to avoid.

She had been searching for a trace of Shirkra, beyond the ancient drawing. But it was hopeless. There was no real filing system in the Watchers' collection, and even if one existed, she doubted that 'Masked Redheads' would class as a category. At any rate, she wasn't really here for the books, on this occasion. She just wanted to be away from the White Rooms, from Watchfold Hall, from Garron Grinn and administration and the memory of Darrah.

And so as she sat, examining some dusty piece of detritus from the Early Period, she lost herself in thoughts of nothing, pleasant daydreams she would forget as soon as her mind

lighted upon something else. Images played before her, vine-
yards and Darrah and masked women.

There came a tap at her shoulder, and she almost fell out
of her chair.

The person behind her wore a Watcher's mask, a cat of
some kind. Cold eyes stared out from underneath, hard things,
scanning her. She could feel the power of the mask worm its
way through her. *Confess!*

'Tactician, I apologise.' A woman. She removed the mask to
reveal a fat face and greasy blonde hair. 'I wear this so much I
forget when I have it on.' She gave her mask a look of mock anger
and wagged a finger at it. 'Bad mask! Making me wear you!'

Rangle was a Tactician of the Overland, yet this young
woman unnerved her. She scrabbled around the depths of
her stomach and found the strength to speak. 'Can I help
you with something, Watcher?'

The woman shook her head. 'No, not at all, not at all. I'm
just a messenger. My name is Aleah.'

Rangle smiled. 'If someone like you is the messenger, then
the message can only come from one person. Where is she?'

Aleah bowed. 'I will take you to her quarters.'

'No need. I know where they are.'

'Begging your pardon, my lady, but I will take you nonetheless. There have been strange happenings of late. Tactician
Brightling will tell you more, I am sure, but for now it is
best that I keep you company, if you can only stand me for
a little longer.'

The blonde-haired woman smiled.

'Lead the way.' Rangle closed her book and creaked to her feet.

The See House was a nightmarish place to get around, especially if you were in your eighth decade and had never been

in the best shape to begin with. It was a tower, for a start, giving it an instant disadvantage to Memory Hall. And even for a tower it suffered from fairly ridiculous design flaws. In Watchfold, Rangle could call on a team of burly oiks to hoist her up the stairs. The Fortress of Expansion had that wonderful lift contraption, which had somehow survived all these years of hoisting Canning's tremendous arse into the heights of the pyramid. But the See House was just stairs, stairs, stairs, hard and cold, climbing upwards forever.

Or so it seemed. But nothing lasts forever, and eventually Aleah came to a stop. Rangle had been here many times, since before anyone had even heard of Amyllia Brightling. But that red door always came as a surprise, like it was hidden by some trick of the Operator. It leapt out at her now, suddenly appearing where once there had only been black wall. Aleah turned, bowed, and retraced her steps down the stairs. She put her mask back on as soon as she turned around, Rangle noted.

The Tactician turned back to the door, to find it was already open, and those damnable strange twins were staring at her. She had never liked this pair. They had been around forever, and never seemed to age, damn them. Tonight they both had their blond hair tied back, allowing the strange light of the See House to play across their cheekbones. Their golden gowns were only just closed around their waists, protecting their modesty, if they had any.

'It is Tactician Rangle, of the West,' said one.

'Yes, it is no other but Tactician Rangle of the West.'

'Tactician Rangle, of the West, would you come in?'

'You should come in, Tactician—'

'Shut up.' She barged past the idiot boys. She knew where the Tactician would be.

The view from the balcony of the See House was better than anywhere else in the Plateau. That's what they said, anyway. Rangle could neither agree nor disagree, as she had visited precious few parts of the continent. But it was certainly impressive. On one side was the Eastern Peripheral Sea, a black expanse that crashed and wailed and always seemed to hold a promise. On the other, the Centre, a sea of its own, marble fading into wood, privilege into poverty, and all of it flickering with lights.

Brightling was at her table, the same place she always sat. It was a balmy night, but the Watching Tactician wore a heavy black cloak. Her beautiful white hair hung loose over her shoulders, and she sucked absent-mindedly on a thin pipe, blowing smoke into the ether. On the table were a handful of open books. Rangle scanned them quickly. *Just some science.*

Rangle approached carefully. When she came to the table, she remained on her feet. She was technically Brightling's equal, but technically didn't count for much when it bumped up against reality.

It was a while before Brightling noticed her presence. Rangle, who had known the Watcher for as long as anyone, understood that this was not some show of superiority: Brightling was genuinely absorbed in whatever she was studying. Perhaps it was more interesting than it looked.

The Tactician of the West gave a little cough.

Brightling's head snapped up, and in an instant she was on her feet, her hand diving into some recess of her cloak, about to pull out the-Machinery-knew-what until she recognised the woman standing before her. It was probably something of the pointy variety. *The Watcher in her never went away. She's always there, protecting the Tactician.*

'Annara!' Brightling relaxed, removing the hand from its pocket and opening her arms. 'It's good to see you. Thank you for coming.'

The two women embraced. Rangle had seen Tacticians come and go, but Amyllia Brightling was the one she liked the most. She knew what they said about her, in hushed tones when no one could hear them talking. Yes, the woman was ambitious, ruthless, calculating, and had begun to encroach on the West itself. But Rangle admired her nonetheless. Brightling was from the West, too. She had grown up in its echoing voids and weary expanses; she knew that life was not just cushions and goblets. And she had allowed Rangle access to the greatest library in the Overland. She would have to do a lot of things before Rangle would ever forget that kindness.

'Take a seat,' Brightling smiled, waving a hand at a soft chair by the table. 'Bring the Tactician a drink,' she called to the interior. A twin emerged and handed Rangle a cupful of something that smelled delicious. *Cushions and goblets are definitely not to be sniffed at.*

'What are you reading, Amyllia?' Rangle lifted the book. It was very new. It had in fact come from one of the presses, so had been approved for printing by the Watching Tactician herself. It was a textbook of some kind, filled with diagrams of cannon: their usage, their inner workings, gunpowder, the ranges they could reach, the destruction they could wreak.

'It's a book about cannon,' Brightling said, smiling over her goblet.

'That I can see.'

'You're wondering why I'm reading it.'

'I'm wondering why it exists.'

Brightling nodded. 'You do well to wonder. Well, have you seen these things in action? In the hands of the army?'

Rangle shook her head. 'No. You know I detest war. I would never venture near a battlefield. Not even during the Rebellion.'

The insurrection in the West. A time of sorrow, and pain, and death, for some, but not for me. I stayed in the White Rooms, far from Brightling and Brandione and all the trouble they caused.

'Well, they are strange things. So powerful, when they work. But temperamental. And powerful, temperamental things are deserving of close study. Otherwise they might explode in the user's face. I have literally seen that happen.'

'I agree it is a wise object of study, but it is surely something for the scholars of the Fortress.'

Brightling snorted. 'The Fortress is an empty box, with an emptier head perched at the top.'

'But it may not always be so. There will be a Selection soon. Anyone could take Canning's place.'

The Watching Tactician smiled. 'Exactly. Canning is a weak fool beyond description. The only benefit of his Selection is that his weakness allowed the strong and the clever to control the final days of Expansion. By strong and clever, I am of course referring to myself.'

The two women laughed, but it wasn't really a joke.

'But he will be gone soon. The Machinery knows who his successor will be. It could be someone with a brain. And that might be very dangerous.'

Rangle smiled. Brightling had a good heart, buried underneath that muscle. But to her, anything that tipped the balance of power in the Overland away from the Watchers should be strangled at birth. Wasn't this what the Operator himself wanted? Why else would he imbue the See House with such power, why else would he give them those terrible masks, why else would he visit Watching Tacticians in the dead of night, whispering instructions?

'But we also don't know who will head the Watchers,' Rangle said.

'No. But if our Department gets a head start on these things,' she waved at the book, 'it can only be for the good.'

Rangle leaned back in her chair. A twin emerged from the shadows and refilled her drink. She was growing light-headed. It didn't take much, these days.

'Why do we need them, anyway?' asked the Tactician of the West. 'We are finished Expanding. The Plateau is ours, thanks to you.'

Brightling flashed a look her way. It did something strange to Rangle's crooked spine, something tingly and not entirely unwelcome.

'It is ours,' the Watching Tactician whispered. 'But you know as well as I that this technology, the wit to build it, was gifted to Jaco Paprissi on his travels.'

'The Overland's successes are its own.'

Brightling smiled. 'Perhaps. But anyway, the place that Jaco visited is still out there, maybe more than one place, where they know all about these weapons.' She blew a ring of smoke. 'And they know about tobacco, and all the other glories of recent times.'

'They could be sitting there now, smoking and plotting our downfall.'

The two women laughed. 'They really could,' Brightling said. 'And if they ever come, we should be ready for them.' The Watching Tactician sighed. 'You know about the recent events in Watchfold, then.'

'Yes. Garron Grinn is very concerned.'

Brightling nodded. 'I understand. He is a territorial creature.'

'I must admit, Amyllia, that it also struck me as strange.'

The Watching Tactician raised an eyebrow. 'Really? I thought you would have understood.'

'I understand the need to keep a leash on the Doubters, of course. But I don't see why you didn't check with me first. We could have worked on this together, like—'

'In the old days.'

'Yes.'

'I understand you feel put out. But the old days are gone. And you are reading too much into this.'

Rangle felt a swell of anger. *Careful, now. Remember who this is.* 'Forgive me, Amyllia, but I'm not sure I am. I'm a terrible Tactician. I know I am. But you can't just send your people into Watchfold without telling me first. It's an insult.'

Brightling laughed. 'A terrible Tactician! You are very far from terrible. For a start, you actually care about your region, unlike that animal Grotius. All he cares about is his stomach and whatever else it is he does. I pretend not to know. I wish I didn't know.'

The Watching Tactician gave Rangle a significant look, daring her to ask what else Grotius got up to. The Tactician of the West decided she didn't want to know, either.

Brightling grinned. 'As for Canning, well, he is not an animal. But he is a weakling. You know, when I first looked into helping his Department, there were some others who thought me greedy, or power hungry, or whatever. I don't think anyone would call it a bad idea now, though. Not after all I have achieved.'

Rangle had to suppress a smile. *Helping his Department, indeed.*

'I am not greedy, and I am not weak,' Rangle said. 'So why do you treat me this way?' There was an unexpected edge to her voice that surprised even herself.

'You are the best of them,' Brightling said after a pause. 'And for years I have kept my Watchers in the West under tight control, out of respect for you. But they cannot be tied forever. I am not disrespecting you; I was far too careful before. We are in the 10,000th year, Annara.'

'I didn't take you for someone who believed all that.'

'I'm not. But even the Operator is concerned. He doesn't tell me everything, but I gather there have been stirrings in his world, in the Underland itself, perhaps.' She looked at her pipe. 'It all started with this.'

'With your pipe?'

Brightling chuckled. She only ever chuckled in front of Rangle. 'No. With tobacco, and the cannon, and the place they came from. The Operator was reluctant to allow us to start our explorations in the first place, but I persuaded him. Around that time, something happened to the Machinery. The Operator became … distressed. He tried to find the source of its problems. He has been trying ever since.'

She leaned forward, so close she could whisper directly into Rangle's ear.

'He fears the 10,000th year as much as anyone. I don't know why. I don't think he knows why, either. He certainly does not believe the Prophecy. But there is something wrong with the Machinery, and he does not understand what it is. And his fear is *real*. He wants me to be on my guard, more than ever. And so I have to be everywhere, Rangle. My little eyes must look into every dark corner, with no one to answer to but me. Do you understand?'

Rangle nodded. Suddenly she felt small, her concerns petty and unjustified. There was no arguing with Tactician Brightling of the See House. There never had been.

Brightling leaned back in her chair. 'At any rate, the West is the *most* important place to monitor.'

'Why?' Rangle could not keep the concern from her voice. Had she missed something, over the years? Or more accurately, had Garron Grinn missed something?

'Because *we* are westerners, Tactician Rangle!' Brightling slapped the older woman's leg, and it screamed with pain. She didn't mind. 'How bad would it be if some nest of Doubters emerged in the very place that produced the two greatest Tacticians of this Cabinet?'

Rangle laughed. 'Of any Cabinet, Amyllia.'

'Indeed! Any Cabinet in the history of the Overland!'

They clinked glasses.

'But very soon we will be gone,' said Rangle. 'I can't see me being Selected again. The Machinery will go for someone young. Unless it really is broken. Then maybe I have a chance.'

Brightling shook her head. 'I think we will both remain in the Cabinet.'

The Western Tactician hid a smile. The role Brightling eyed was not hard to guess. But what was wrong with that? The Machinery could Select a worse Strategist. In fact, it had done so quite recently.

'Yes, perhaps,' Rangle said with a shrug. 'And Bardon, too. He is so young, but he's done a good job down there in the Far Below, all things considered. I'm sure he'll make a reappearance.'

Brightling sighed, and put her head in her hands. 'No. I'm afraid he won't.'

'Did she tell you how it happened?'

'Poison.'

Garron Grinn shook his head. Rangle had never seen the Administrator look even mildly surprised. The world was an open book to him, one he had read too many times. But now his eyes were wide and unblinking, and he sat hunched over in his chair, hands drooping at his side.

They were on the balcony of the White Rooms. Rangle spent little time out there; the prospect was not remotely as commanding as that from the See House. But she hadn't wanted to stay indoors, tonight. Perhaps she felt the breeze would just blow everything away.

'Tactician Bardon was poisoned in his bed,' Garron Grinn said to no one. 'Tactician Bardon was poisoned in his bed.' He shook his head, and finally made eye contact with Rangle. 'How?'

'He always brings a little beaker of water up with him. Someone slipped something inside it.' She started to cough, a cacophony even worse than usual. It always seemed to happen in times like this, when she didn't know what to do.

'And so it happened here, in Memory Hall. Under the noses of everyone.' Garron Grinn was regaining his composure; Rangle could hear a new clarity in his voice. 'How could that be?'

Rangle sighed, and her chest burned. 'It's impossible to say. The Watchers are trying to find out.'

'Did she mention any suspects? They must have someone in mind. They always have someone in mind.'

'She didn't say.'

'Well, who has access to that room? There are the servants.'

Rangle shook her head. 'Amyllia is convinced it was none of them.'

'Hmm. Well, she may be right. I don't know her reasoning.'

238

'Careful now, Garron Grinn, when you speak about the Tactician.'

The Administrator nodded, but didn't seem to listen. 'So if not a servant, that leaves the Watchers themselves. Any guests the boy might have had – his parents, though that would be beyond reason, anyone can see they dote on him, and his position is the only thing saving them from poverty. Then, of course, there's us – well, it wasn't me, and it wasn't you.'

'Correct.'

Garron Grinn's eyes widened suddenly, and he raised a finger aloft. 'And of course, this comes just after the apparent suicide of Strategist Kane. In this very same building.'

Rangle nodded. 'I had thought of that. Brightling has, too.'

'Let us hypothesize that Kane did not leap to his death, but that someone encouraged him in his fall. That would mean that someone is killing the members of the Cabinet, before a Selection. That has happened before.'

'The Lonely Strategist.'

'He killed off the whole Cabinet, thinking it would impress the Machinery so much, it would Select no Tacticians, and pick him to rule alone. And it worked, until he ended up with a knife in his belly. Maybe someone is trying it again, but they think it will work this time. Maybe they think they will hold onto their power.'

'That would require several mad leaps of logic.'

'Someone who kills Cabinet members in the very centre of the Centre is probably not a million miles off mad. Oh, and skilled, of course. A mad, skilled, ambitious murderer. Quite formidable.'

Garron Grinn raised his eyebrows. 'That doesn't leave many options.'

He seemed to be on the verge of saying something else, something that Rangle suspected was very, very, dangerous. But the Administrator just shrugged, and closed his eyes.

In the dead night, after Garron Grinn had disappeared, Rangle sat alone where she always sat alone, doing what she had always done: staring at a book.

She reached out, and stroked the pages, that red hair, that white mask. *Where have you gone?* She would perhaps never return, this thing of terrible beauty, this green-eyed question mark. *What are you?*

As she stared at the page, a thought slowly hardened in her mind. It had been there for some time, taunting her, but she had ignored it. She hadn't wanted to face up to it. It might be nothing, for a start. But if it was something, she did not want to believe it.

Watchers. Servants. Families and friends.

She looked again at that face, the white skin, so close to perfection on the page, yet so far from the true beauty of the person.

They are not the only people to have visited Memory Hall of late.

Chapter Twenty-three

The crowd was a monstrous thing.

Brandione had seen mobs before, heaving battlefields filled with men. But this was different. It was strangely silent, and spread out like a plague, assaulting the Primary Hill. All the people were dressed alike, garbed in crude likenesses of the Operator's great cloak. The richer subjects wore sweeping robes of black silk embroidered with gold and silver visages, while the poor wore rough-hewn sacks on which agonised faces had been crudely painted. The difference was not important; what mattered was that they were all here, filing inside the Circus for the Selection of the Tacticians of the Overland. All of them carried torches, burning in the night like so many fireflies and glowing on the marble sides of the great building.

Brandione entered at the Western Gate, squashed in behind a group of children. One of them, a girl of about seven, gave him a stern look.

'Where is your cloak?'

The General smiled, and pointed to one of the upper levels. A great flag hung there, depicting a silver half-moon crown. 'That is my cloak.'

The girl flushed. 'I am sorry, sir. I didn't know you were with … them.'

'Don't worry.'

Brandione pushed his way through to a flight of stone steps, and saw he was at the side of the pit. There was no stage there, now. The sand-covered surface was open, exposing the entrance to the Portal, from which flames would pour and the Operator would emerge with the names of the new Tacticians. There had not been such a gathering for four years, since Bardon was Selected. Brandione remembered the sense of anticipation, the excitement in the air as the members of the mob hoped against hope that the Machinery would recognise their innate genius. The flames had burst forth from the Portal, a cold fire that spread through the pit in an instant and vanished as quickly. No one had seen the Operator, though some claimed to have spied a flash of the cloak amid the flames. When they were gone, a scroll lay on the ground, on which the name of the boy was scrawled. The Announcer had scooped it up, and the Watchers had vanished across the Overland, searching out the new Tactician of the South.

The crowd then had been far smaller and its excitement had been noticeably dimmer. Today, however, the Overland would receive a whole new set of Tacticians.

'General!'

Tactician Canning had appeared at Brandione's side, surrounded by a retinue of guards, their armour black and painted with sneering white faces. The onlookers cringed when they saw the silver half-moon crown, but turned away in disdain when they realised which Tactician the crown belonged to.

'Tactician.' Brandione bowed quickly.

'You seem tired, General. Have you been working too hard?'

Brandione hesitated, wondering if the Tactician knew of his recent assignment with the Watchers. It was not something the General wanted to talk about, particularly with the Tactician of Expansion, his nominal superior, even if he was a weak creature like Canning. 'I have been doing my duty, Tactician.'

'Good. As have we all.' Canning turned from the General and eyed the great flight of steps that led up to the Tacticians' viewing platform, below the half-moon flag. 'Why do we always have to sit at the bloody top?'

A guard behind him sniggered. *They'd never laugh at Brightling.* 'Shall we go up, Tactician?'

Canning sighed, and nodded.

It took them almost thirty minutes to climb to the viewing platform, Brandione following behind the lumbering Tactician. The crowds grew thinner as they went: the higher the level, the more honoured the spectator. Eventually, the only people the General saw were merchants and great landowners, their cloaks inlaid with diamonds and gold. The crowds below faded into a black cloud.

A golden gate was pulled open by a squad of guards on the approach of Canning and his group. As they walked through, Brandione was certain he heard laughter.

The Tacticians sat on silver thrones, each inlaid with the title of its occupant. The thrones were spread along a wooden platform, a sturdy structure of varnished wood. The entire Circus was visible from this point, and it was not even the highest part of the great stadium: there was another level just above and behind, on which sat an empty seat, wreathed in purple veils.

'I wonder who will sit there next?' Canning asked, directing the question at no one in particular.

'The Machinery knows.'

Canning's chair was in the centre of the platform, next to Brightling. She gazed down at the Circus with unalloyed fascination, the torches of the crowd below reflected in her eyeglasses. Her dress was woven from a material Brandione did not recognise, a shimmering red and orange burst of flame that seemed to dance like one of the torches. To Brightling's left sat Grotius, asleep in his chair with a tankard of wine gripped in his paw. At the other side of Canning's chair was Rangle, absorbed by some book as usual.

To the left of Grotius was an empty chair.

'Where is Tactician Bardon?'

Canning shrugged.

The Expansion Tactician took his position next to Brightling and signalled to Brandione to join him. The General squeezed in beside the throne, sitting cross-legged on the floor and casting an uneasy glance at Brightling. They had not spoken since his failed mission to locate Katrina Paprissi.

'Here he comes,' said Canning.

The crowd fell silent. A man had emerged from the side of the Circus. He was a huge being, wider even than Grotius, but his shape spoke of muscle, not fat. Robes of blood red and sun gold were stretched across his frame, flowing behind him and at his feet; a silken hat of similar hues sat atop his skull. Brandione could just make out the man's beard, an extraordinary outcrop of black bristles like some creature's defence mechanism.

This was the Announcer, whose job it was to retrieve the names of the new Tacticians when the flames died away. He lumbered forward until he came to a black marble plinth that had been erected at the edge of the Portal. He climbed it in a surprisingly graceful movement, then stood and gazed out over the crowd, his robes billowing behind him ferociously.

'Have you been to a Selection before, Brandione?' Canning was staring down at the General.

'Only Bardon's, Tactician.'

'So you weren't there on that glorious day fourteen years ago, when the Machinery saw fit to Select a whelk salesman?'

Brandione smiled. 'No, Tactician.'

Canning nodded. 'It was a strange day. Utterly unexpected but … consequential, unfortunately. I lost a great deal, that day. I'm quite sure of one thing, though; it won't pick me again!'

Brandione inwardly agreed. 'What will you do, Tactician?'

Canning seemed to think that over for a moment. 'I'll tell you what I'd like to do. I'd like to go back to my stall and sell my fish, like none of this ever happened.'

'Go back to your old life.'

Canning gave a wan smile. 'You can never go back. But it's the only thing I'm good at, I'm afraid.'

A bell rang from the marble plinth. The Announcer raised his arms into the air, and bowed to the crowd. It was almost time for the arrival of the Operator.

'Who Selects him?' Brandione asked.

'The Announcer? A good question.' Canning leaned down, whispering to Brandione conspiratorially. 'He is Selected by the Cabinet, in theory, and by Brightling in reality. That one is called Doriano, I believe, or is it Dariano? He was probably a Watcher. I don't know.' He fell silent for a moment, as if he was chewing over some new thought. 'I used to wonder how the Operator did it.'

'What, my lord?'

'How he gets out there without us seeing him. I've never seen him, anyway, though I've heard some claim they have.'

'And you don't wonder any more?'

'Oh, now I don't bother. We will never understand him. How he operates, as it were.' He chuckled.

Brandione turned back to the Circus. The Announcer reached a hand into the plinth, and the bell rang out again, loud and clear. A gasp issued from the crowd.

'It rings twice more,' Canning sighed.

The Announcer looked theatrically at the mob, then placed his hand once more into the plinth. Another bell rang.

'I am almost done,' Canning smiled. 'It will not Select me again. It cannot.'

'The Machinery knows,' said Brightling. It was the first time she had spoken.

'The Machinery knows,' echoed all the Tacticians.

The bell rang again.

All fell silent.

And nothing happened.

The Announcer climbed from the plinth and stared down into the Portal. He appeared to lean forward and take something from the ground.

'What is the matter?' Brightling glanced at the other Tacticians, and signalled to a Watcher below the platform, who sent word down the line. At the bottom of the pit, a Watcher ran forward to the Announcer. He quickly turned and ran back, passing something up the chain.

A murmur ran through the crowd as Brightling climbed from her throne and took a piece of parchment from the last Watcher in the line. She strode back to the viewing platform. There was a flicker of anxiety in the cool eyes, Brandione noticed.

'What has happened, Tactician?' asked Canning.

'The Announcer found the list. Here it is.' She held up the paper.

'There was no flame, Amyllia,' said Canning.

'And? Who are the new Tacticians?' That was from Grotius. He had abandoned his chair and was now peering at Brightling with trepidation. Rangle, too, was on her feet, her book discarded.

Brightling thrust the paper into the lap of the Tactician of the North. At first Grotius seemed confused. But soon his eyes widened, and he started to tremble.

'It has Selected no one.'

Chapter Twenty-four

There were only two doors left.

Katrina weighed her options: the black door, from behind which came the sound of rain; and the blue door, which masked a hum of conversation. *The only way up is going forward,* went an old Watcher saying. It always comforted her, somehow.

There was something about the chattering that came from behind the blue door that unsettled the Watcher. The babble was constant, and shot through with something.

These are the voices of pain, said the old part.

We should not enter that room.

That left the black door. She pressed her ear against the frame. The rain pounded steadily down, rhythmic and hollow as a drum. She steeled herself, took a deep breath, and pushed through.

A long, wood-panelled corridor stretched ahead. Three chandeliers drooped from the ceiling, and a thick carpet yielded beneath her feet. Portraits stared down from the walls, covered in generations of dust. There was incense in the air, a rich fragrance that hinted at some distant land. An image was painted on the walls at recurring intervals, a picture the size of a hand. It was a skeleton sitting on a rock. He rested his bony chin on his clenched fist; behind him a black night sky was broken by streaks of lightning.

That was the Paprissi Shield, and this was Paprissi House.

The corridor was as it had been in the olden days, before Alexander disappeared. *I have been here before. I have been in this exact moment.*

This was the night Alexander disappeared.

Katrina inched forward, her footfalls silent on the thick carpet, just as they had been on that evening fifteen years before. A side corridor broke away to her left, at the end of which sat her grandmother, asleep in her rocking chair, a mass of white lace and silver satin, like an old doll. Katrina halted, wondering if she should approach the woman, but quickly dismissed the notion. *This is not real.*

The door to the Great Hall was before her, a scarred hunk of wood, black with the centuries like a rotten tree, engraved with the Paprissi shield.

She pushed it open a crack and peered inside.

'Play, play, playing, like the little child you are,' the Operator said, rapping the arm of his chair with his fingers. She could not make out his face; he was turned away from her, his head hidden behind hunched shoulders. His gown fell over the grey stones like oil on water. The faces in the patterns came alive, then faded again, over and over.

There was a pattering of rain on the windows.

Katrina turned away. She looked back out into the corridor, to find it had disappeared, replaced with a black fog that crackled with a grey light.

She turned back to the room. The Operator stood, and the memories of a six-year-old girl crystallised before her mind's eye.

Not again.

As the Operator lifted Alexander on to the window ledge, Katrina rushed into the room. The Operator began to turn.

She looked down, and found she held marbles in her hand.

'What are you doing here?' the creature asked.

Katrina came to an abrupt halt. The thing standing before her was not the Operator, but a puppet, its body and limbs formed of interwoven wooden sticks held together by black string. The face was a painted ball, but seemed able to cycle through emotions, as if some invisible artist was constantly revising it. At one moment, the eyes were wide and white, the mouth a smiling twist of ragged red; in the next, black pinpoints stared out at her above a cruel sneer.

'Who are you?'

This was not the voice of the Operator, but something else, something old and indefinable, something that reeked of an ancient time.

'I am Katrina Paprissi. That is my brother.'

The creature looked at the windowsill.

'Your brother? It cannot be. There are no brothers here. No sisters, either, nor mothers or fathers or cousins, though there may have been at one time. We do not go in for that kind of thing. Not any more.'

The puppet stood away from the windowsill, and clattered over to the black chair, where it collapsed into a heap of wood and string.

'Operator,' Katrina began. The creature flinched. 'Operator, where did he go? The boy you were playing with.'

The painted ball spun in Katrina's direction.

'You saw.'

It pointed to the window.

'That is where he went.'

250

Katrina hesitated for half a heartbeat, then ran across the hall and leaned over the edge. The rain fell in perfect grey waves, the design once again of some clumsy hand. Eventually, she could make out something in the ground. It was the blue door from the hallway. Even from the windowsill, Katrina could make out a hum of voices.

She leapt.

Chapter Twenty-five

Brightling had placed Aranfal at a distance, and it was a cold place to be.

She had looked into him, that night on the balcony, and found him wanting. Nothing could be hidden from her, even without her mask, even when she stared into the soul of a Watcher as accomplished as he was.

I do not believe Brandione is guilty, so I am guilty too.

There was nothing overt in his exile. But he had been exiled nonetheless. He was no longer sent to lead the most difficult interrogations. Young Watchers did not consult him or seek his advice. Brightling no longer called him to her rooms; there were no knocks on the door from Aleah, who looked at him now with scorn when their paths crossed.

He still lived in the See House, but he was on the outside.

There was one saving grace, however. Brightling did not comprehend the extent of his suspicions. She thought he was merely *wrong*: that his worst crime was doubting her. She had not realised where his suspicions had begun to lead him. If she had even the slightest inkling, he would not be walking around the See House, showing Squatstout the Hall of Masks.

'Incredible,' the little man breathed. 'Just where do they come from?'

Aranfal pointed to the middle of the hall. In the centre of the floor was a black hole, just large enough for a man to squeeze into, though it was covered with bars that could only be opened by someone underneath.

'When the doors to the hall are locked, no one can get in,' Aranfal whispered. He found it unusual to speak in this place, which was like a library to him. 'That is when the Operator comes, and leaves us his creations.'

'Hmm.' Squatstout lifted a mask from the wall. It was a dog, its mouth a red smear. 'Perhaps my brother does *not* make them all. Perhaps he has help, in the Old Place.'

'The Old Place?'

'I am sorry: the Underland.' He placed the mask carefully back in its spot, but continued to examine it. 'These are beautiful things, and I have no doubt they work most well … but you know, yes, the more I look at them, the less I see of him in them. They are his idea, though. He has put the maker to work. Oh yes.'

Squatstout's gaze fell upon one of the images painted on the wall. It was a small painting, separate from the others, and showed a very simple mask, a pale, white image of a woman's face.

'Ah,' Squatstout whispered, walking up to the picture. 'Here we are, Aranfal. This is an image of one he made with his own hand: the very first he ever made. Do you recognise it?'

Aranfal went to Squatstout's side and studied the mask. 'Some Watchers have masks of humans,' he said. 'Some prefer them to the animal. It's not to my taste.'

'This mask belongs to no Watcher. If ever you meet the owner of this mask, you should run away. Oh, but before you do, tell her I would dearly love to speak with her!'

Squatstout laughed, and turned away from the painting. 'How do you choose who gets which mask?'

Aranfal shrugged. 'Each Watcher chooses their own, when they become an Apprentice. Some people see great significance in it, but I'm not so sure. They're just masks.'

'Just masks? Just masks that see into a person's heart, Watcher Aranfal. Just masks that strip away the armour of the soul itself!'

'But they are all the same.'

Squatstout nodded, though he did not look convinced. 'Well, be that as it may. You chose a raven. Why did you choose a raven?'

Aranfal turned his gaze to the walls, to all the images of masks that were painted there, ten thousand years before. He thought of the Operator standing here, bringing it all to life with the powers at his fingertips. *They are not just masks.*

'I chose a raven …' He clicked his tongue, as if to knock the words out from his mouth. 'I don't know why I chose it. Perhaps it chose me. It … well, the story is not a glorious one.'

'Please, do tell me.'

Aranfal chuckled. 'It fell on my head. I came in here with Brightling – this is a long time ago, now – and I was staring up there, on the wall.' He pointed at a shelf of masks. 'And then it just fell on top of me. I still don't know where it came from. There was nothing above me.'

'Perhaps it flew to you.' Squatstout grinned, exposing his teeth. 'And Brightling?' He was suddenly by Aranfal's side, gripping the Watcher's elbow in a pudgy little hand. 'I wonder, what is her mask?'

'It is a strange one. I've only seen it once, and no one else has ever seen it, or not since she became the Tactician, anyway.

Maybe Katrina has seen it. Brightling doesn't really need a mask, to see inside you.'

'Please … tell me what it is. I love to hear descriptions, you know. Please tell me about this beautiful mask, please tell me.'

His eyes were wide and gleamed with a dark spark.

'It is very unusual,' Aranfal said in a whisper, glancing into the corners. 'It is … a person.'

'You said that others have masks like this.'

'Yes, but this one is strange.'

Squatstout sucked in a sharp breath. 'You mean it is like this mask?' He pointed a finger to the white mask that was painted on the wall.

'No. It is … it changes. The mask seems to change the more you look at it. Once I thought it was a woman, with cheekbones so sharp you could cut yourself. But then, when I held it to the light, it was a man. He had such a cruel face. I have never seen a mask like it before.'

'Exquisite craftsmanship, this mask.'

'Greater than any other. But there's more. It is dark. I mean, it is *really* dark, as black as anything I have seen before, blacker than the Bowels. It is almost like an absence of light—'

Squatstout tightened his grip. 'Do you mean that? An absence of light? Do you mean … is there a kind of nothingness in this mask?'

Yes. 'That is it. A nothingness.'

Squatstout released Aranfal and stared into space, shaking his head furiously. 'Incredible, incredible. How did he do it? He must have kept a piece, from after the first war, or more likely the second. Unbelievable.'

'What wars?'

'What wars? What wars? *The* wars. From before memory. From before the Throne of Oak.'

'You are not making sense.'

Squatstout laughed. 'No, you do not understand what I'm saying. That doesn't mean I'm not making sense.' He nodded. 'So, he gave her this mask, this mask he made from his own hand. He must think very highly of her.' He flicked his eyes at Aranfal. 'My friend. You have been good to me, very good, so much better a host than I ever could have hoped for. But I fear I must take my leave of you, tonight. The One is not here. I was wrong.'

No!

'Squatstout, please. Stay a while longer. We're getting somewhere.'

'No, no. I fear the One is beyond our reach. There is nothing more that can be done.'

He doesn't understand. He doesn't understand about Brightling.

Squatstout turned to leave the Hall of Masks.

'Again, Aranfal, let me give you my thanks—'

'Squatstout, wait. I … have a theory. Please listen to me.'

Squatstout's eyes widened, and he gave a sharp nod. He was grinning widely.

'It's about Brightling. I'm not sure, you understand. But I think we should perhaps consider her … we should think about the things she has done …'

'Done? Done? What has she done?'

If Brightling had set Aleah or some other minor Watcher to follow him, then Aranfal's next words would be his death sentence. But it was time to get it out in the open. Squatstout would know what to do.

Aranfal beckoned Squatstout closer, and hissed into his ear.

'There has been something strange, lately. With the Tactician.'

'She seems a strange person.'

'Yes, well. I can't believe I'm saying this.'

'Please, please, continue.'

Aranfal sighed. He felt like Aran Fal again, stumbling through the world like an idiot. 'She has been making strange accusations, Squatstout, and they cannot be true. She has said things about Brandione that I do not believe, and I don't think she believes them either. I think she's trying to hide things.'

He looked up into the shadows. *Just say it. Squatstout will know what to do.*

'Squatstout, what if Brightling is like Arkus? Or worse – what if she is the One, and she is preparing Ruin?'

Squatstout pushed Aranfal away, and to the Watcher's great surprise, started to laugh.

It was a strange sound, a clattering cackle that bounced off the walls of the Hall of Masks. It weighed upon Aranfal, pressing at the sides of his skull like a vice.

'You are a *fool*,' Squatstout said between laughs, his voice changed into something sharp and cruel. 'You stand before me, a watching weakling, staring into corners because you cannot face the light!'

He raised a hand, and Aranfal fell to his knees.

'All this time I have been watching you, but truly watching. Watching all of you, all of you servants of Jandell. And the truth has become clear to me, oh yes. Don't you see what has happened? It is happening just as it was said at the birth of the Machinery. Ruin is coming!'

'We can stop her, Squatstout—'

'Stop her! You do not know anything. Brightling has murdered no one.'

Squatstout grabbed Aranfal by the scruff of his cloak and hauled him to his feet, dragging him to the wall. He pointed at the white mask, the white mask that stood alone.

'It is *the One*, Aranfal. The One has returned. Jandell thought he had won such a victory, but he failed. I have not come here to stop the One! I have come here to *throw myself at the feet of the One!* I have come to aid them!'

He nodded to himself, slowly.

'But now I see I was mistaken. The One needed no help from me. The One has already gone. I will return to my home. I have much to do there, oh yes.'

'We can stop it, Squatstout—'

When Squatstout spoke again it was not with his mouth, but a dead voice that echoed within Aranfal's head.

Stop the One? You may as well stop the movement of the planets. You may as well stop the birth of mountains or the death of stars. You cannot stop the One, and I would not want to.

Squatstout released Aranfal from the grasp of his powers and the Watcher fell to the floor.

'I am sorry,' said the creature in the hareskin cloak. 'You did not deserve this, Aranfal. You have been good to me, oh yes. But you are a servant of Jandell, like your ancestors. Even now, Jandell hides himself from the truth.'

As Aranfal stared up at Squatstout, standing before the white mask with his arms in the air and a terrible smile on his face, it seemed as if the wall behind was taking on a life of its own. The masks began to grin at him, and the white mask filled with a power that was not of the Overland; the eyes burned with a green light as they looked down upon Squatstout.

He bowed to Aranfal, and was gone.

The Watcher sat in the darkness of the room for hours, studying the white mask. It was nothing more than a painting.

Chapter Twenty-six

The Garden of the Past was always in bloom, but nothing grew there.

The flowers of the Garden were not roses or tulips, but statues of marble and bronze: great Tacticians and Strategists, raised on plinths, sitting on thrones, broken and discarded on the edges of stone pathways. There were others, too: Generals of the Overland, who broke rebellions and pacified nations; Watcher-sanctioned playwrights and artists; architects, merchants, and some whose identities were lost to time.

Towering above them all, on a raised platform of black stone, was the Operator himself, his fingers pointing to the sky, his cloak flowing in waves around him, its faces twisted and grotesque. Some said he had built the Garden himself, a few centuries after the Gifting, when enough people had achieved sufficient success to warrant a commemorative statue. But no one knew for sure.

The Garden sat on the southern slope of Primary Hill, just a short walk downhill from the Circus and no more than two miles from Memory Hall. No noise could be heard here, even on state occasions when the Circus was crowded with every yahoo the Plateau had ever spat up. There was something disquieting about the Garden, and those staring eyes of stone. A whisper ran through the monuments.

Annara Rangle liked it here. She preferred to be alone, now that Darrah had gone.

She had found a spot underneath the Operator himself, nestled in the folds of his cloak. By her side was a half-drunk bottle of wine and a box of sweetmeats that Garron Grinn had given her. She chewed slowly, stopping only to throw more wine down her gullet. In her hands she held a book. *What would my hands do otherwise?* She didn't even know what it was about: the planning of an old city, to judge by the maps. She just stared at it, chewing, wishing for something new, *something different, something to happen, something to take me away. I am too old, it was hard back there, it was so hard, I could not stop it …*

These thoughts were not her own. Where had they come from? They sounded like *her*, that green-eyed creature who stole away one night, never to return. *By the Machinery, I need Darrah back. I am losing my mind, and replacing it with someone else's.*

And then Shirkra was there, as if she had never left.

'He loves to build statues to himself. How can you people stand him?'

Her green eyes stared out from behind the white mask, the mask so close to her true face, but somehow different, somehow colder, *yes, the mask, the mask is so deceiving, she wears it not to conceal but to see what others have concealed, you know that it is so.*

The Tactician stood and walked to Shirkra, who was leaning against a Middle Period General and pointing a thin finger up at the Operator. She came close to embracing the woman. But that would have been … *I cannot embrace this thing, it is too cold, too cold.*

'You are in my thoughts,' the Tactician said, as if it was the most natural thing in the world to say. 'They aren't my thoughts any more. They are *our* thoughts.'

Ha ha ha ha ha ha.

'Look at it, look at it, look at it.' Shirkra stepped forward, still pointing upward. 'Did he build this himself? It looks like he did, yes, who else would flatter him so, such a glorious man, a glorious thing, ha ha ha. Oh, yes, he made this.'

She whipped off her mask in one movement, suffocating Rangle with those eyes, *these eyes, so hard and soft at once, yes ...*

'He is good with his hands, my brother. Don't you think so?'

Rangle nodded. 'So good, yes, so good.'

'He made this for me, long ago,' Shirkra held the mask aloft. 'He told me, "Sister, this will help you see true." And so it has, it has. It was the first of the Great Masks, you know, and the last remaining, hmm, the very last one. The ones his soldiers wear, they are just imitations, oh yes, he churns them out, oh yes, in his workshop in the Old Place.'

She turned back to the statue. 'He made such wonderful things. That chair, the black chair, he made that. The musical instruments of all the Old Ones, hmm, he made them. Did you know that?'

She did not wait for Rangle to respond.

'His is a great talent. But he did not make his own cloak, before you ask. Oh, no, that was made for him by the ... well, it was a punishment, wasn't it, hmm? It was a reminder.' She sighed. 'I shouldn't talk about it any more.'

Suddenly her shoulders tightened, and her head fell forward, as if she planned to charge the statue.

'And his greatest creation of all ...' She spat on the ground. 'That thing you all love ...' She spat again. 'He should not have been greedy, when he made the Machinery.' She spat, three times in a row. 'That is what will destroy it, in the end.'

She turned back to Rangle. She did not speak, but a voice made its way into the Tactician's mind.

I will show you what it was like, once. Would you like that?

Yes.

The past is a cold and a hard place.

Yes.

We will go?

Yes.

And then the statue of the Operator fell, smashing into thousands of shards and scattering through the Garden.

'Jandell, you will die.'

And Shirkra spat again, and it burned a void into the earth, and the two women fell inside.

Are we in the Underland?

We are not.

Then what is this?

The world. But an old world. From many eras past.

They were on a mountaintop, and the Operator stood before them. Rangle had seen that face in too many statues and paintings not to recognise it immediately. Yet he was so different. His hair was long and black, his face unlined, his skin a healthy pink, not the pallor of today. He wore a loose, white robe; the body underneath was hard, muscled, so unlike the thin, wasting creature she was used to seeing. He held something in his hand. She could not make it out, but it was small and flickering. A flame?

The Operator is so young.

No. He is older than almost all of creation, even here, even here. His appearance is not a reflection of his age, but of his mind. Here he feels strong, healthy, happy, oh yes, though it won't last, no. Not considering the things he would do. Now he is sick, and sad, and ill, and it is from his own guilt, oh yes. For what he did to us all.

The Operator looked straight at them, and Rangle quailed before his gaze. Soon she realized that he was not looking at them at all, but *through* them.

And then a woman appeared, walking through them as if they were made of nothing but air.

How is this possible?

Possible? Why should it not be possible?

Why can't they see us?

Because we are not here, no, we are not here at all. This is just a memory.

Oh yes, a memory, hmm. We are all memories.

Oh yes.

The person before them was Shirkra. At first glance she was the same as the creature Rangle knew. Her red hair fell to her shoulders in curls, and her green eyes sparkled with an inner flame. She even wore the same green dress, curling around her little white feet. Funny, Rangle had never noticed that before; Shirkra walked barefoot.

But there were some differences. This Shirkra seemed harder. *So powerful, so strong.* She radiated a kind of coiled threat, ready to snatch out your eye.

'You are bored,' said Jandell.

'Of course, of course,' said this version of Shirkra. 'How could I not be? You have made the world boring.'

'No. It is the future. And all of us created it, together. That is why it will work, this time.'

This Shirkra walked to the Operator's side. She took his hand in hers, and together they turned and looked out from the mountainside. Rangle joined them. There was a city in the valley below, vast and golden, spires of glass aflame in the burning sun and domed palaces casting shadows on wide boulevards of marble. It was similar to some parts of the Centre, but on a different scale entirely, expanding far away to the horizon.

'I cannot live like this, Jandell. I must go insane, oh yes. Or I must die. Yes, death. I will die.'

Jandell seemed to ignore her. He raised his hand, the one that glowed with a flickering thing.

'I have made you something.'

Shirkra spun towards him, clapping her hands and bouncing on her feet.

'I love presents from you!'

Rangle flicked a glance at the real Shirkra. There was a tear on her cheek.

What is this I am witnessing?

Jandell smiled, indulgent, patient. He opened his hand and the fire grew, burning with a strange, green light that gave no warmth. It kept growing until they were all of them within the flame, though it was more like being underwater, a place where everything slowed to a crawl and the noise of the world came to them in dull murmurs and groans.

And then the cold flame was gone, and Jandell held in his hand a white mask.

Shirkra reached for it, but the Operator held it back.

'This is a powerful thing,' he said. 'I made it when I was sorrowful; I took a piece of the Old Place, and I poured my hurt inside it. Do you understand?'

Shirkra nodded and attempted to snatch the mask again, but still Jandell held it away from her.

'This mask is not made to conceal, but to reveal,' he said. 'When you wear it, all things will open to you, unseen paths and hidden thoughts. But they may not come as you expect, and the angle may change and warp. You will not know if what you see is the truth, or a trick of the imagination. Such is my perspective, when my sorrow overwhelms me.'

He sighed, and handed the mask to Shirkra. But now she seemed reluctant to take it.

'This does not sound like a good thing, my brother, oh no, it does not,' she said. 'For my imagination is powerful, and could warp me in so many ways.'

Jandell nodded. 'You will grow used to the mask, and the mask to you. I do not give this to you to torment you, but to help you. Do you understand? I love what you are, but I must help you see the truth of our existence.'

Shirkra nodded. She took the mask from the Operator, who smiled as she raised it before her, delicately held in her thin fingers.

'You are the Chaos of the morning Shirkra,' whispered the Operator, 'and the Chaos of night. You are the torrent and the gale.'

Shirkra turned to him and smiled; her teeth were jagged, like a beast. The fingers of her hands seemed to grow narrower, until they were claws, long and curled. *A feral creature, a creature of Chaos, oh yes, oh yes.*

'Thank you, my brother.'

And she put on the mask, and began to cry.

They were somewhere else, though Rangle could not remember moving.

It was a throne room, but not one the Tactician had ever seen in the Plateau. This was a hall of glass and oak, bathed in glaring sunlight. The heat was intense; Rangle could feel it, though she knew she was not truly there. She had never been to the Wite, or even those bleached little habitations that straddled its border, but she had heard tales of it.

Is that where I am?

No, my dear, it is not where we are.

The people in the hall did not seem to feel the heat. There were hundreds of them, clothed in black gowns and clustered around circular tables, drinking from silver cups and gossiping to one another. Fawning servants replenished their drinks and brought them platters of delicacies. The diners were of all shapes and sizes and skin colours; it brought to mind an audience in the Circus.

At the front of the hall was an oak tree, an ancient and sturdy thing that reached to the top of the glass ceiling and through into the sunlight. At its base was a gnarled chair that seemed to grow from the oak. A man sat there, alone, drinking from a silver cup and plucking fruit from a plate of food that was balanced on his knee. He was old, older even than Rangle, but he glowed with a health she had never known, even in her younger days. His skin was amber, and his smile revealed teeth of a brilliant white. He chuckled and shook his head as he gazed out at the hall, at his subjects. He wore the same black gown as the rest, but on his head was a crown of silver.

It was a full-moon crown.

Is he a Strategist?

No.

A bell rang from somewhere, loud and clear, and the people fell silent.

The old man stood up.

'I have some good news for you all,' he said. His voice had a deep and warming tone, and his words carried throughout the hall.

266

The people looked at him expectantly. One called, 'What is it, Emperor?'

Emperor. An old word. Some in the Plateau took that title, but they all fell before us.

All emperors fall, child. Oh yes.

The old man smiled at them, an indulgent grandfather.

'My day here is done.'

Silence.

'It is time for a new Emperor to take the Oak,' he went on. 'Forty years is long enough. Besides, our friends need to look at a different face in the Cabinet meetings. They are older even than me, and they need some diversity every now and again.'

'We are indeed much older than you,' spoke a familiar voice, 'but diversity? No. We would have you rule for a thousand years.'

Jandell – the Operator – stood at the back of the hall, some way behind the Emperor's throne. He was leaning against a wooden pillar, his arms folded, a benevolent smile on his youthful face. The people here seemed pleased to see him; a smattering of applause broke around the hall on his appearance.

So different from our own world, where he is feared beyond measure.

That is what he prefers, these days.

Jandell strolled up to the Emperor, and they embraced like old friends. He turned his gaze upon the crowd, who watched him expectantly.

What is this place? Who are these people?

The past. All dead now, dust in the ground, ashes on the air.

'The Conclave will be held before the end of the moon,' Jandell said. Like the Emperor's, his voice was calming and quiet, but it still filled the hall. 'Go back to your people and

267

gather their thoughts. We in the Old Place look forward to your decision.'

He sighed.

'Many of you – all of you, in fact – are too young to remember the last Conclave. If you have any questions, remember I am always open to you.'

'As am I,' said the abdicating Emperor.

Jandell summoned a servant and took a glass, which he raised into the air.

'To the Emperor, may his days be filled with merriment, and to the Empire, may it last until the end of the world.'

The people in the hall leapt to their feet, and repeated Jandell's toast. As they took their seats they fell into murmured conversation.

These people are the leaders of society, correct?

Correct.

If this was the Overland, they would all be wondering if they will be Selected.

Here, it is the same. But the system is different. They believe they have more power over the future. Let us see how it works out for them, ha ha.

'Where will you go?'

Silence fell. Jandell searched for the source of the voice, before he found Shirkra, standing at the very back of the hall, at the open doorway. She was wearing her mask, and the green eyes seethed beneath.

'What do you mean?' asked Jandell.

'Not you, brother. Him.' She pointed at the Emperor. 'Where will you go?'

The Emperor was undisturbed by Shirkra's sudden appearance. He folded himself into his throne, and smiled. 'Home. To the coast. And I will say or think no more about politics.'

He sighed with exaggerated pleasure, and the people laughed. But they were afraid. Rangle could smell it.

Shirkra jabbed her finger at the Emperor. 'You are a liar.'

Jandell placed himself between Shirkra and the Emperor. 'Leave this place, Shirkra. We can discuss your concerns later, with the others.'

'Others? The others feel as I do, Jandell.'

'No.'

'They do. They always have. But you have been blinded by your creation. Your society.' She waved a hand at the people at the tables, who stared at her now with undisguised fear.

She pointed at her mask.

'This is the mask that reveals. And I have seen such things with it, Jandell.' She turned to the Emperor. 'He would take himself away from here, oh yes he would, but his ambition would overwhelm him – it put him in this chair in the first place, did it not, hmm?'

The Emperor smiled.

He is not afraid of you.

Oh, he was.

'And when he is on the coast, looking out at the beautiful sea, hmm, the twinkling waters, do you really think he will watch quietly, while another undoes all the things that he created? Do you think he will look on with happiness as you sit beside another ruler, Jandell, as you unite his memories with your own? No, not this one, no. I wear the mask that reveals, and I can see into his heart, and it is a treacherous thing.'

Jandell left the throne and walked to Shirkra. He took her hand in his own, and stared into the depths of the mask.

'I warned you about this gift, Shirkra. You are not seeing the truth.'

The moment has arrived, Rangle. The moment that set everything in motion. A moment born in Chaos.

'I see the truth, I see the truth, I see the truth …'

Her voice grew louder, until it filled the hall.

'I see the truth!'

Shirkra snapped her hand forward, and knocked her brother to the ground.

He did not expect it, you see, Rangle. He never sees danger coming, oh no, not Jandell. He believes in himself too much.

And all of them just watched her, all of them, even Jandell, as she grew from a woman into a flame, a pillar of green fire that burned with ice. Those closest to her fell instantly, their cries mingling with her own, driving her to a new frenzy. In the middle of the fire she stood, eyes blazing at the Emperor. She raised a hand and spat a word that Rangle could not understand, and the great tree at the front of the hall, the oak of the Emperor's throne, was uprooted and felled. It came down with a groan, and the Emperor was crushed by it.

Amid this she stood, Shirkra, the Mother of Chaos, and with a flicker of a raised finger, she sent her flame to meet the tree, and turned the Great Hall into an inferno. Rangle knew she was safe from the fire, but she still covered her eyes, as if she was in that flame herself, with those souls that Shirkra was burning.

When it was over, they stood in a field of ash, a blackened stump all that remained of the throne.

Jandell was on his knees. 'You have started a war.'

'Yes. You must choose your side.'

The Operator stood, and sighed.

'There is no choice.'

He embraced his sister amid the ashes.

Shirkra was broken.

Rangle found herself on a hill, lofty enough to remind her of the Primary Hill itself. But there was no Circus here. There was nothing at all in this place. The ground was blackened and charred, with thin tendrils of smoke rising from the blasted earth, as if a great conflagration had recently been smothered. The Tactician could make out the twisted remains of trees amid a layer of ash. Buildings had once stood in this desolate place. She could see their foundations, warped and crushed.

What kind of battle took place here?

The sun was rising in the east, casting a melted orange glow across the wasteland. At first Rangle thought she was alone, and wondered if she had gone to the future, instead of the past, to the final days of the world. But then she heard a sound, a low moan, hanging on the dusty air.

It was Jandell.

He was sitting on a heap of stones. His head hung low, and he touched his forehead with the tips of his fingers, and he wept.

At his feet was Operator Shirkra. Her green robes were torn into rags. Her face was pristine as ever – the mask was nowhere to be seen – but blood gleamed on her neck, her chest and her arms.

So these creatures bleed.

Jandell leaned down, and swept her into his arms. His appearance had changed; he was much closer now to the creature she knew, his pale face lined and worn and only a few strands of hair clinging to his skull. He picked Shirkra up with little difficulty, and his tears fell on her skin.

He was whispering something, over and over. Rangle had to come close to hear it, though of course he did not notice her.

'I should allow you to die,' he was saying. 'I should allow you to die.'

He should have allowed me to die.

271

The real Shirkra was at Rangle's side.

Jandell lifted the corpse above his head. He whispered something else, but Rangle could not hear any of it. He then lowered Shirkra and placed his open palm on her forehead, before he put her back in the dirt.

Then Jandell sat beside his sister, and crossed his legs. Time changed, rushing through its cycles at a new speed. The sun fell from the sky like a rock, and stars splashed into a black ocean, before they leapt away again as the burning orange star returned. On this went, over and over, as the smoke rose from the hill and Jandell kept a vigil by his sister's side.

Until she awoke.

It did not happen gradually. At one moment, Shirkra lay prone and lifeless. In the next she was on her feet, and staring at her brother with fury. She panted like a beast, sending clouds of vapour into the air. Her hands were claws – literally claws – curled and poised by her sides. She seemed on the verge of speaking, searching for the right word.

'Traitor.'

Jandell did not respond. He did not react in any way, but remained seated, staring at the ground.

'You destroyed them!' Shirkra cried. 'How could … you killed them! Oh yes, I saw it! You murdered our *family*!'

'No. You live, and Squatstout, and the Duet, and the younger ones.'

Jandell stood, and brushed the dust from his cloak. Rangle was suddenly aware of that terrible garment, with its contorted faces wailing silently from within whatever prison held them.

'What is that … what is that cloak?' Shirkra asked, momentarily seeming to forget her anger. She reached out, touched it, and recoiled. 'The Queen made this for you. I can sense it. What is it? Hmm? Why do you wear such a ... strange ... who are these ... these people ...?'

'They are my punishment.'

Shirkra pointed a claw at him, and for a moment it seemed as if she would tear out his eyes. Instead she backed away. 'Yes. Oh, yes. You needed her help, hmm. You would never have accomplished ... this ...'

Shirkra turned and pointed to a spot in the centre of the hill, and Rangle saw it for the first time: the Portal to the Machinery, a blackened hole that glowed red with flame. So this was the Primary Hill.

'Is that where you put—'

And Jandell had her by the throat.

'I have suffered you to live,' he said. His voice was a growl, as animal as Shirkra's claws. 'You and some of the others. Almost *all* of the others. Do not make me regret my decision, sister.'

There was fear in Shirkra's eyes, but still she managed to speak, sputtering out words like a woman who wanted to die.

'Only with the help of the Queen ...'

Jandell threw his sister to the ground, and she crumpled like a doll.

'The Queen is with me still, Shirkra. We have come to an arrangement.'

He pointed a finger to another part of the hill. Rangle saw that the ash there was swirling in strange patterns, like some isolated storm had taken hold. The Tactician thought she could see faces there, in the dirt, like those of the Operator's cloak. It stopped moving, and for just a moment it seemed that three women stood where once the ash had been, three giants wearing spiked crowns, staring back at her. But they were gone in an instant, and the dust blew away into nothing.

'I understand,' Shirkra whispered.

Jandell nodded. 'You have until the dark to leave the continent forever.'

Shirkra looked up at him, her eyes wide, and seemed on the verge of speaking. But she thought better of it, and turned her focus to the ground.

'I do not care where you go,' Jandell continued, turning his back on her. 'I should destroy you, after all the … after everything you have done. But Chaos is your nature. Go and find a new one.'

For a moment the sky seemed to darken, and when Rangle looked again, Operator Jandell had gone.

Shirkra sat in the ashes for a long while, weeping into the dirt. Eventually she stood and staggered towards the smoking pit, falling to her knees at its edge. She held her head in her hands and wept afresh. It seemed as if she would never stop, that she would remain here until nightfall, and Jandell would return and cast her into the fire.

Until she saw it.

There, at the other side of the pit, half buried in ash, was the white mask, staring at its owner with wide-eyed fascination.

Shirkra ceased weeping. She leapt to her feet and ran around the pit, skipping like a child. She seized her mask from amid the grime and held it in her arms – *embraced* it – like a long-lost child.

'You have returned to me, oh yes,' she said. 'I thought he had thrown you down there, to burn. But you have returned to me!'

She put the mask on and sighed with pleasure. Rangle suddenly became aware of the real Shirkra, at her side; she turned to find the Operator clutching her hands over her heart and grinning madly.

A wind picked up with a pained groan. The Shirkra of the past looked up in the air, green eyes shining under the porcelain.

'I *see* you,' she said. 'You are *here*!'

There was a moment of silence, in which the wind itself ceased to blow.

And then came a voice that Rangle would never forget, a harsh and cruel thing, like all the winters of childhood. It spoke with a feminine tone, but unrestricted by the trappings of male and female as understood by mere animals like the Tactician. Rangle cringed before it.

Yes.

'You live!'

Yes.

Shirkra seemed to hesitate, her eyes flickering. She fell to her knees and bowed her head.

'I will serve you,' she whispered. 'Tell me what I should do.'

The wind picked up force, howling madly.

We will wait until the time comes, and we will bring Ruin.

Shirkra raised her hands in the air, and roared into the storm.

Chapter Twenty-seven

Iron gates had been erected around Memory Hall.

Brandione could see them from where he sat, on the east side of the Cabinet Room. The spiked fence had been Tactician Brightling's first response to the panic that arose in the wake of the non-Selection. It was a safety measure, she said.

Things had deteriorated swiftly since the non-Selection. Illegal presses had whirred into action, their locations unknown. Brandione had seen a pamphlet claiming that the Operator had proclaimed himself Strategist. Another asserted that Brightling had formed her own army. Throngs of people had gathered in the Centre, hoping to find some source of leadership there. Instead they found the gates.

Brandione turned back to the Cabinet Room. The Tacticians of the Overland – they remained in office, it was assumed – were a sorry sight. This was the first time they had met since the events of the Circus. Canning was slumped over his throne on the lower level, rubbing his forehead and staring at the ground. Grotius was horizontal on a velvet divan on the north side, gnawing on a corncob and staring at the ceiling with watery eyes. Rangle was burrowing into a book and occasionally muttering to herself; she had seemed even more distant than usual, of late. Brightling sat in her chair by Canning's side, as still as the Operator statue in the Strategist's Throne.

The spell was broken by a crash as Tactician Rangle's book fell from her hand onto the floor below.

'But what does it all *mean*?' cried Grotius. He sat up on his divan as swiftly as his massive frame would allow, threw his cob on the floor, and answered his own question. 'It means the Machinery has abandoned us!'

Brandione glanced at Canning. The Expansion Tactician sat very still in his great chair, staring imperviously ahead.

Grotius writhed on his divan, his head darting around like an obese lizard's. He grasped a servant by the wrist.

'Get me a bird!' He turned back to the room until his swivelling eyes settled upon the figure of the Tactician for the West. 'What do you think, Rangle? Have you read about such a thing in your books?' A dark look fell across his flabby face. 'What are the consequences for one's digestion of all this?'

Rangle looked up suddenly. She seemed to think something over, as if on the brink of asking a question, before shaking her head.

'I do not know. Ruin is coming. Ha ha!'

She turned back to the floor, her book forgotten. The others watched her for a heartbeat, and then seemed to forget she even existed.

Grotius turned in Brightling's direction.

'Where is Bardon, by the Machinery? He is needed—'

'He is still indisposed, and will be for some time.'

All eyes focused on the Watching Tactician, who rapped her fingers on the arms of her chair. She smiled, and the room went very still.

'Stability,' she whispered. 'We must have stability.'

The Tacticians and their assistants leant forward in their chairs expectantly.

'Stability of what kind?'

It was the first time Canning had spoken. Brightling gave him a brief glance, then rose from her chair and walked to the Strategist's Throne. She reached out and touched the marble face of the Operator, before turning back to her fellow Tacticians.

'At times like these, an empty space appears. It *will* be filled. Something will take our place, whether we allow it to or not.'

A murmur went through the room.

'What will this thing be?' asked Grotius.

'Oh, who knows?' Brightling replied. 'Perhaps a powerful king, like Northern Blown' – the room gasped – 'or perhaps an oligarchy, like in the old West' – the room whined – 'or perhaps even an emperor, a title that so many have claimed' – the room moaned.

'What about the Strategist?' asked Canning.

Brightling turned on him. 'What do you mean? There is no Strategist.'

'No, not yet,' said Canning. 'But there will be another Selection soon, is that not so? We should wait and see what it throws up.'

'Ah, you are thinking too much of this damned Prophecy, Canning.'

Canning shrugged. 'It is the 10,000th year.'

'Ruin is coming,' Rangle said.

Brightling fell silent. She seemed uncertain, hesitant. Brandione felt a hollowness in the pit of his stomach.

'But the Strategist hasn't been Selected yet,' cried Grotius. 'Anything can happen in that time! We need to think about what happens now!'

All eyes turned to the Tactician of the North.

'What do you suggest, Grotius?' Brightling's composure was returning.

Grotius stood and stamped a foot on the ground.

'Strength!' *Stamp*. 'Power!' *Stamp*. 'Authority!' *Stamp*.

Brightling nodded. Canning and Rangle fell into their own little worlds.

'I will secure the loyalty of the Watchers,' Brightling said. 'We will wait for the judgment of the Machinery, Prophecy or no. Until that time, we will form a ruling council.'

Brandione sighed. He had noticed many times on the battlefield that the most decisive person was often allowed to make the decisions.

Brandione and Tactician Canning left the Cabinet Room immediately after the meeting. Canning had taken one of the guest apartments, immediately below the Strategist's quarters. They sat there now, around an ancient wooden table in a golden dining hall, drinking wine by candlelight.

'You should set off for the Fortress early in the morning,' the General said. 'There are many people on the roads these days, with the Selections and all.'

Canning nodded his assent. 'I did not ever expect to go back there.' There were dark circles around his eyes, and his pate gleamed with sweat. 'Things look different now, don't they?'

'Yes, Tactician. The same, but different.'

'Quite so.'

Canning poured them more wine, and leaned back in his chair.

'It is strange,' he sighed. 'How reliant we have become on an external object to guide us on the path to greatness.'

Brandione cast his eye at the door. This type of talk could be construed as Doubting.

'I wonder if it was always this way,' Canning continued. 'Back in the days of Arandel, do you think they fretted over the Selections, as we do? Back when the city was a few mud huts gathered around the walls of the Circus? They probably did. There is always something to worry about.'

'What do you think will happen now then, Tactician?'

Canning laughed. 'Tactician! I suppose I still am. Terrible! Ah, what now? Well, we will have one ruler.' Canning shrugged. 'Whether this spells Ruin, as they say, I do not know. But the Strategist, whoever it is, will rule alone. Another Lonely Strategist.'

'It is a strange title.'

'Hmm, and it all ended so badly before.' The Tactician fell silent for a moment. 'I say it again: Kane did not seem to me like the type of man who would jump off a balcony.'

'No,' Brandione agreed. 'He did not.'

Chapter Twenty-eight

Katrina fell into a bed.

The Watcher felt a surge of familiarity: this was her old bedroom in Paprissi House. But something was wrong: the dimensions were out of sync with her memories. She shook the feeling away. *This is the Underland.*

The room was far larger than she remembered. It was unfinished, like all the chambers of this place; the ceiling faded into shadow and the floor stretched into nothing, vanishing off in the distance in a haze.

There was a painting on the wall: the Eastern Peripheral Sea, all rocks and grey water and squalling birds. She remembered this image well from her early childhood. But down here, it was huge, like a tapestry from Memory Hall. The dolls that lined the shelves were beasts, their limbs like tree trunks. A spinning top in the corner was like a war machine. A painting of her family leered down at her: mother, father, sister and brother smiling at the doorway of a great house.

Katrina crawled to the side of the bed, where a ladder led down to the floor. She swung her legs over and descended. Even the cold flagstones felt different to the touch: insubstantial and transitory.

Voices came from beyond a door at the end of her bedroom, a door that did not belong in Paprissi House and from behind which emanated a sickly yellow glow.

Katrina gently pushed it open, and peered around the corner.

The people were strapped in with iron chains.

There were hundreds of them, sitting in grey rags in high wooden chairs. Row upon row stretched away from her to the end of the room, where there was a gaping black hole. No light came from its depths. Dozens of shelves lined the room, filled with rusted silver scalpels and jars of herbs. A stench of sweat hung over everything, like a shroud.

She looked to the black door, half expecting the Operator to be there. *Surely he knows I'm here.* But there was nothing.

Katrina stepped inside and shifted along the nearest row. The people were in varying conditions of health. Some stared ahead, motionless, while others chewed and spat, clenching their fists and kicking at the chains. Others babbled streams of gibberish. None of them seemed to notice Katrina. She walked past an elderly man with matted grey hair, who gnawed repetitively at his red hands. A pale, middle-aged man chattered incessantly: noticing her, he stuck out a black tongue and waggled it around.

The young Watcher stopped abruptly. *There is something about these people.* They were all of them men, for a start. But there was something more.

She leaned into the man beside her, and she knew what it was.

Every one of them is Alexander, at different stages of life.

The young Watcher stepped back. Strangely, she was calm. This was simply another example of the strange work of the architect of the Underland, whose creations were too ridiculous to be unsettling.

Just then, above the cacophony of the Alexanders, came a cough that Katrina knew well.

The Watcher backtracked along the row, searching out the source of the sound. It came again, this time from the vicinity of the black door at the other end of the hallway. Katrina crept towards it. All around her the Alexanders leered and babbled.

'Katrina.'

The word struck like a bolt.

'I am over here.'

It had come from somewhere to her left. She moved forward.

'Katrina.' Closer now. She went on. 'Katrina, I am over here.'

Eventually she came to the end of the row.

'Where are you, Alexander?' Her voice was perhaps a little loud; she was afraid the maddening chatter would drown out her words. 'I can't see you.'

'Over here.'

He was strapped in like the others, wearing the same grey rags. But there was a difference: this one was the same age as the boy who had been taken fifteen years before. His cheeks were flushed pink, and his black hair fell in curls around his forehead. But she did not embrace him; there was something that kept her away. It was not really him. She knew it, in her bones. *Instinct.*

I will play the game.

'Alexander!' Katrina ran to her brother's side. 'How can I release you?'

'You cannot.' He was still smiling. 'No one can leave here. Don't make me.'

Katrina looked around the room, at the rows of Alexanders. 'What are these, brother?'

'They were created by the Operator. He thinks I know something terrible, and that I'm keeping it a secret from him. That's why he took me here.' Alexander giggled. 'But it didn't work, because I don't know anything he doesn't know himself. He didn't believe me, though. So he made more of me. He thought one of the others would tell him.'

'How did he do it?'

Alexander shrugged. 'It was one of the Operator's special tricks. I don't know. Things work different down here. But it's not just him. The whole *place* is different, and there's not much use in trying to understand it. Sometimes it might want to show you things, other times it wants to throw you off course.'

Katrina nodded. *Is this the voice of the Operator, or of the Underland itself?*

'Why are they all different ages?'

'I told you,' the boy spat. 'Things are different here.' He fell into silence.

Katrina smiled, and looked to the black door. It was the only way out of this room, she was sure. But would the Underland show her the way, or would it prefer to throw her off course?

'Sister, please stay.'

The Watcher turned back to this imitation of her brother. He, too, was focused on the black door.

'If you stay here, we could talk of the past, and all the times we had. It would be lovely for me. You could free me, and we could go back, together. We could reclaim the house.'

What do you want, creature? Do you even know?

'Do you remember the day he took me, sister? When he stole me from you and mother and father? We hate him, don't we? We hate him, for what he did to us.'

'No.'

Alexander seemed taken aback. 'But he ruined us.' The creature seemed angry now. *What are you?*

'I mean, Alexander, that I do not remember the day.' She leaned into the impostor's face. 'You were taken at night.'

As Katrina marched towards the black door, all the Alexanders screamed her name, one louder than the others.

Chapter Twenty-nine

Shirkra never left Rangle. Not any more.

It seemed impossible that she even *could*. There were times, it was true, when the Tactician looked up from her studies to find that the Operator was not there: not physically, at any rate. Sometimes Shirkra could not be seen when the Tactician was forced to meet the rest of the Cabinet, or pretend to carry out business for Garron Grinn. But it hardly seemed to matter. Because there now was no longer a Rangle, and there was no longer a Shirkra. There was only one thing, one mind, and it had possessed the Tactician almost completely.

There were still occasions when she felt like herself. She would go to her study, or to the See House library, and take down a book, tearing through it with her old enthusiasm. But then another voice would come. *These are lies … Jandell wrote this, you can tell, it is so boring … How can this be so? Have you ever thought about that, hmm, my Rangle? How can this even be as it is written?*

Once, when she felt normal, she had summoned Darrah. She wanted to see her again, to lie beside her as if everything was just the same. But Darrah did not come. Before Rangle's servant could reach Darrah's lodgings, another messenger caught up with him, and sent him back to Memory Hall. Rangle had dispatched the second messenger as well, or so she believed. She couldn't tell any more. She never knew which of the voices spoke loudest.

'You killed the Strategist. And Bardon, too.'

There was no need for Rangle to say it. It was simply something that she knew, and Shirkra was fully aware of her knowledge. But a part of her – the old part of her – felt a need to articulate it.

Shirkra was sitting on a high, hard-backed chair in the reception room, her hands intertwined upon her lap. She was not wearing her mask. She rarely wore it in Rangle's company any more. It was deep night, and candlelight sparkled in her green eyes.

The Operator did not speak, but gave one curt nod.

'Why did you do it?'

Shirkra sighed. She unfolded her hands and scratched the sides of the chair.

I do not know. I only do what I am told.

'I do not understand.'

Shirkra stood and walked to Rangle, who lay on an ancient sofa. The Operator spoke in a hushed tone as she walked, as if spies could be listening to her every word, now that her words were dancing around outside the confines of Rangle's withered skull.

'There is a Promise, oh yes. You call it a Prophecy.'

'Ruin will come with the One.'

'Yes. It is old, that Promise. I know who spoke those words for the first time, and I know who will bring Ruin. I have been working for the One, all these long years. Jandell thinks he destroyed the One, and that therefore Ruin cannot

287

come. That is why he fails to understand recent events. But the One lives, and I work in the service of the One.'

'The voice that spoke to you, on the Primary Hill. That is the One.'

'Yes. The One will be Selected, and bring Ruin. The One holds such power, Rangle, even in a weakened state. I am compelled to serve. I have been told to kill. I must kill, for the One. That is what the One wishes.'

She was standing directly above Rangle, and leant towards her so that their noses almost touched.

'Do you follow me, you clever Tactician?'

'I do. But I cannot understand these murders. I know that the Strategist had to die, to begin the Selection. But why the boy?'

Shirkra's shoulders were trembling.

I did not want to do that, Rangle. I am not always cruel, you know, not always, oh no. But he did not feel fear, which is the worst of all things, truly it is. No, he just slipped away. She told me to do it.

She?

The One. She told me to kill him. She told me to kill them all. She wants to test me. She wants to make sure I am still cruel, and hard, after all these years.

Shirkra looked directly into Rangle's eyes, and placed a hand on the old woman's knee.

She wants to remove the powerful ones, anyone who could threaten her after she returns to full power. And she wishes to hurt Jandell. Always, she wishes to hurt Jandell.

Rangle bowed her head.

All of the Tacticians, she said. They must die, so they cannot threaten her.

I understand, Operator Shirkra.

I have enjoyed my time with you.

Rangle sighed, and smiled at the Operator.

Shirkra reached out a pale hand, touched the Tactician lightly on the forehead, and Annara Rangle was gone.

Chapter Thirty

'What do you mean, a museum?'

Brandione shifted under Brightling's gaze. He had managed to avoid a private meeting with the Watching Tactician since his journey to the Far Below, but there was only so long one could hide from the most powerful person on the Plateau.

They were once again on the upper balcony of the See House. It was late at night, but the Centre was overhung with a stifling heat. Insects chirruped nearby, a steady, rhythmic beat.

'There was a museum there,' he replied, his voice as steady as he could manage. 'It was filled with books, old ones from before the Machinery.'

Brightling cocked her head to the side and gave Brandione a withering look.

'This is the museum above an inn?' The Tactician was at her imperious best: her white hair was tied back tightly by an ivory pin, and she wore a close black dress studded with blood-red rubies.

Brandione heard laughter from the shadows of the room beyond.

'Yes, madam.'

'I spoke to my servants earlier,' Brightling continued. 'They say you were in there for some time. Then when you came out, you told them this story about a bar and a museum.'

'It was not a story.'

'Very well.' Brightling leaned forward. 'None of it matters, anyway. What matters is my young Watcher, who is still *missing*. There was no sign of her anywhere in this place, no?'

'No, Tactician.'

Brightling thumped a small, bejewelled fist into a cupped hand. 'You should have come to me about this earlier, General.'

'I am sorry, madam,' he lied. 'I meant to. Indeed I would have, but with the events of the Selection, it went out of my mind.' *You are blabbering like a schoolboy.* 'Anyway, I don't have any information that your Watchers haven't already told you.' Murmurs again, beyond. 'I don't know what happened to Katrina.'

Brightling stood from the table so abruptly that it gave Brandione a jolt. 'It's too warm out here. Let's move inside.'

The General followed the Tactician through the balcony doors. Candles had now been lit in the room beyond, and there was no sign of whoever had been laughing. They went through a small black door into a kind of study. The room lacked the sumptuous décor of the rest of Brightling's apartments; it was a drab brown, from the wooden floorboards to the wilting wallpaper. A long table ran its length, covered in parchments and quills. Brightling sat down on a hard wooden chair, and indicated to Brandione to take another.

'I thought I would be rid of this,' the Tactician said, waving a hand at the piles of papers before her. 'But no. It continues.'

'You do not seem unhappy, Tactician. I cannot imagine you, without work.'

Brightling smiled. 'Nor can I. I have always been like this: even as a child. My father was a merchant, out in the West. He earned a great deal of money, selling timber and things to the wealthy of the Plateau. He did that so I would not have to work. But I did not listen. Do you know why I work so hard, General?'

'Because you were Selected to do so.'

Brightling shook her head. 'No. That is true, but it is not the reason. I do all this because I am afraid.'

The General was surprised by both the confession and her candour. 'What scares you?'

There was a moment of silence. 'Change,' Brightling said eventually. 'I am afraid of change, and what it might mean for our beautiful Overland.'

The Tactician seemed to scrutinise the General, as if wondering whether to continue in this vein.

'But change is everywhere. So I try to manage it. The trade routes: we secured the resources and ideas of distant lands, while at the same time protecting our people from corruption. Not even I know where the stuff comes from. Did you know that? Only Jaco knew, and his men, and they are all gone.'

She sighed.

'The Operator speaks to me, sometimes, in the night. He thought the trade routes would be good for our people. His people. But then ... well, the unfortunate events of recent times, the goings on with the Machinery, began after Jaco returned from a voyage. And so the Operator thinks they are related.'

'Goings on with the Machinery?'

She studied him for a moment, and then smiled. 'It doesn't matter, General. The point is this: Jandell attempted to control

292

change. He put an end to our trade routes. But you cannot stop it, Charls. I know there will come a day when others sail. Not even the Operator will be able to control it. That scares me.'

Brandione nodded.

'From the trade we took the skill of using gunpowder; I managed that, so only the armies of the Overland could control it, under your excellent command.' She gave him a slight nod. 'And now we rule the Plateau. But as we learned this from abroad, this means there are others who control the same powers, and have mastered them more thoroughly than we have. We may have to face them, one day.'

She took a sip of wine, running a finger along the rim of the glass.

'And ah, how can I forget: the press.' She lifted one of the documents and held it before him between the tips of two fingers, as if it was toxic. 'A grand idea, indeed; now the people can read more and increase their learning, no matter how humble their station in life. The Machinery would approve.'

What makes you think you know what the Machinery would approve of, Tactician?

'And so I managed it; I print what the people need to know. But we've already seen what happens when others get their hands on a press, haven't we?' She tossed away the pamphlet before Brandione could read it. 'Through all this, General, I did not worry. Do you know why?'

'Because we have the Machinery.'

'Correct. We have the Machinery. It is the only constant. But all these things that have occurred. The Prophecy. The non-Selection. There is something wrong, even with the Machinery itself. And that, General, is why I am afraid.'

She looked at him, then, and for a moment she seemed afraid.

'What if it breaks?' she asked. 'What if it really is about to Select someone who will bring Ruin?'

'I do not know.'

'We will have to do something, General. You and I, and the other leaders, whether Selected or not. We will have to assume control. Perhaps *you* will have to take control.'

Brightling's eyes gleamed as she stared at him, scrutinised him.

'Perhaps you will be Selected, Charls.'

She seemed capable of anything in that moment, of crawling into his soul and digging through its contents. But then she seemed to shake herself, and laughed.

'General, it is late, and I have kept you too long.' She indicated to the door. 'I must thank you for your service to me. You have been loyal and true. I wish you luck in your remaining time in Memory Hall. I assume you will return to the military full time, when the Strategist is Selected?'

'I believe so, madam.'

'Good. It is right to have a place.'

Brandione stood, bowed to Tactician Brightling, and left the See House as quickly as he could.

Chapter Thirty-one

Katrina was in a kitchen.

A spluttering candle cast a dull glow on silver knives and golden plates that were strewn across a rough oaken table. Katrina was sitting on a high-backed wooden chair. Her white rags were gone. No, that was wrong. They had not gone. They had changed colour. The rags were now a dark purple, falling in waves to her feet.

A hunk of bread sat before her on a gold-leafed plate. Suddenly realising her hunger, Katrina grasped it and tore it in half. She recoiled as a host of maggots fell from the festering loaf to the floor. The Watcher leapt to her feet as the creatures inched their way across the kitchen. They reached a closed door, pushing their way through the cracks.

Katrina followed the unwholesome trail and approached the door. *What would Tactician Brightling make of me now, pursuing a family of maggots?*

Katrina listened. She could make out male voices beyond, the cadences of a heated conversation. The words seemed distant, and muffled by another sound: a creaking whine, like the movements of a rusted chain.

Steeling herself, she pushed through.

It was a throne room.

Walls stretched away into nothingness. The ceiling vanished into a black pit of a sky, pitching and rolling like a western storm. The floor below her was formed of cold flagstones, but they yielded to the touch. Each of the stones was painted with that recurring motif of the Underland: the black chair of the Operator.

In the centre of the room was the chair itself. It was far larger than she remembered from the night Alexander was taken. Here, it was a monstrous thing, as tall as five men. It was a simple construct, unadorned, carved from some black tree in some dark realm. Katrina felt herself weaken as she looked upon it.

The throne was occupied.

The Operator, like his chair, was stretched out of all proportion, a giant in a cloak of fire and shifting faces, his bald head gleaming in the strange half-light of the throne room. Insects surrounded him. Cockroaches and lice the size of Katrina's arms swarmed between the legs of the chair. The maggots from the bread inched their way to him. When they reached the black throne, they swelled into creatures the size of dogs.

Before the Operator was another chair, smaller and formed of gold. A boy sat there, held down by silver chains, which creaked as he moved. He was dressed as Katrina remembered from the day of his disappearance, but his clothing now hung from his body in rags. He seemed thinner: there was a look in his eye that made her avert her gaze.

He had not aged in fifteen years.

'What did it tell you, Alexander?' asked the Operator. His voice was deep, booming through the hall like cannon fire.

'It told me the truth. Ruin will come with the One. The One lives.'

Katrina crept forward, hiding in the shadows. She was sure this was the true Alexander, though she could not say why. *Instinct.*

The Operator laughed, a cold bark. 'This same old game.' His smile exposed a line of brown and broken teeth.

'I have told you all I know, Operator.'

'Ruin will come with the One,' the Operator said. 'Ruin will come with the One.' The giant leaned forward in his black throne. 'The One is dead. But in the Overland, some believe lies like yours. And so they murder Strategists and Tacticians, hmm? They hope to be like the Lonely Strategist! They are fools.'

Katrina fell back against the wall.

'That is sad, Operator,' said Alexander.

'Yes, it is sad. Yet something is ... something is happening, to the Machinery. It spoke to you, all those years ago. And it has made strange utterings since, in tongues that even I cannot understand.'

'Ruin will come with the One.'

The giant Operator leaned back in his chair, covering his pale face with his hands. Alexander stared directly at Katrina and their eyes met. He did not seem surprised to find her there, in the deepest recesses of the Underland. He smiled, and she smiled back.

With the slightest of nods, Alexander indicated in the direction Katrina had come from. The Watcher turned, to find the door to the kitchen was gone.

She was looking upon a beach. It was formed of black sand, its dark shoreline stretching so far into the distance that she could not see what lay at its end. The left side of the beach was dominated by a line of enormous dark dunes, as formidable as the walls of Northern Blown. To the right was the sea itself, its waters dark and unyielding. The horizon was a bowl of roiling black sky, at the heart of which sat a blood-red disc of a sun, an orb that seemed to radiate coldness.

Katrina turned back to the room.

'Operator, I must go,' said Alexander. 'It is almost time.'

The boy lifted his arm, revealing that the silver chain was broken. He ran to the end of the room, through the door and onto the beach, laughing as he went.

Katrina flicked her gaze to the Operator, who stood dumbfounded, the chain in his hand.

'No!' he roared.

The Watcher turned on her heel and ran after her brother.

Chapter Thirty-two

It was the early hours of the morning, and all was silence in the Fortress of Expansion.

Almost all.

'I never should have been here.'

Tactician Canning was slumped back in a leather chair, a glass of Redbarrel balanced on his knee. He had been like this lately, mumbling and gazing into corners.

'It won't work … never …'

Sometimes, in his darker moments, the General wondered about the Machinery, when he saw a man like this placed in such an exalted position. Canning would never have made it in the army. When they put down the West … soft men would not have done well there at all. That was a place for hardness: a place for true believers.

What, then, are you?

'Things will work themselves out.'

Brandione spun in his chair to look at Canning. The Tactician was now asleep, bubbles of saliva on his lips. How could he have spoken?

There was a knock at the door.

'Come.'

Canning's servant entered, bowing and scraping as he approached the General. He glanced up at the Tactician and rubbed his hands together.

'Ah. I see the Tactician is indisposed at present. Ah …'

'What is it?' Brandione was in no mood for this.

The servant cringed at the General and held out a piece of paper. 'An announcement from Tactician Brightling, sir. It came from the presses today, and I thought that Tactician Canning would be interested.'

Brandione took the paper from the servant's hand.

'This decree has been issued through the presses of the See House,' it read. 'Following the events of the day of Tactician Selection, the Overland finds itself threatened with heightened exposure to the illegal activities of the Doubters.'

Brandione looked at the servant, and at Canning, who was snoring quietly. *What has she done?*

'As such, the See House has enacted a state of curfew. None may leave their homes until midday tomorrow, when the Strategist will be Selected.'

Brandione crunched the paper into his fist. Something cold stirred in his stomach.

What is Brightling doing?

'How many of these have been printed?'

'Hundreds of thousands, sir, millions, I don't know. They're all over the city and the countryside. Brightling's got horses riding north, south, and west, faster than you can imagine. My wife, she works near Sellers' Square, she says the presses have been going day and night since the non-Selection.'

'The Watchers? Where are they?'

'Oh, we're quite safe, sir. They're all over the city … they're in the streets, on the roofs. Some say they're even down in the sewers, watching everything that's going on …'

The General read the proclamation again. Since his fool's errand to the Far Below, he had wondered about Brightling. He was not an idiot. She was toying with him, somehow. He could feel it. *But why?*

'Where is Tactician Brightling?

The servant seemed bemused. 'The Tactician? Normally, sir, I would think the See House, but not now. They're all of them staying at Memory Hall. She wants them together. That's what I heard, anyway.'

'Fine. I am going there. I'll find out what she thinks she's up to.'

'General, there is a curfew.'

'The Watchers can stop me, if they wish.'

Greatgift was empty, and the General rode freely through the night.

He would have preferred a crowd, in some ways. Only once did he catch a glimpse of life; just north of Banktown, on the roof of a stone mansion, sat a Watcher, looking at the General through a bear mask. But the Watcher did not speak, and Brandione whipped his horse forward.

When he came to Sellers' Square he saw that the door of the Printing Hall was open, issuing a yellow light. Noise came from within: the incessant grinding of the presses. Occasionally a Watcher would emerge, cloak wrapped tightly around a great swathe of papers, and disappear down an alley.

Brandione pushed on. Greatgift opened before him, grand and desolate. He stopped for a moment to take it in: was this the street where thousands had thronged for the funeral of Strategist Kane? It was as if all the life had been sucked from the very heart of the Overland.

He eventually came to the Western Gate of Memory Hall. A female Watcher stood on guard, leaning against the red marble and staring at Brandione through the slits in her mask. It seemed to be a cat.

'General Brandione.'

The General climbed down from his horse, and handed the reins to the Watcher.

'A quiet night.'

'Necessarily so. One does not know who could be abroad, these days. Though there is a curfew. Didn't you know?'

The General ignored her. 'Watcher, on what floor could I find the Tactician?'

'Madam Brightling? She is not here, I am afraid.'

'I thought all the Tacticians were here.'

'The rest are here. She will return soon, I am sure. You may wait inside.'

Brandione nodded and made to enter.

'General?'

'Yes?'

'Be careful tonight. There is something strange on the air.' She looked up at the sky, then her head snapped back and she flashed a savage grin at Brandione.

The General entered the People's Level of Memory Hall.

'Did you go to the Selection, sir? Or the non-Selection, I suppose we should call it?'

'Yes.'

'Was it good, sir?'

'Good?'

'Yes, sir, was it good, sir?'

'It was … it was nothing. Nothing happened.'

'Oh. Oh yes, I was told that.'

Bandles had located Brandione as soon as the General had entered Memory Hall. The little servant could sense when someone had entered his realm, like the world's strangest spider in the world's richest web.

They were standing before the Unknown Portrait, one of the more unusual works in the People's Level. It showed a youngish, black man, no older than forty, standing on the balcony of a great tower. In his left hand he held a full-moon crown, and in his right a piece of parchment. He was clothed in Strategist Purple, but it was torn and bloodied. The Unknown Portrait was well regarded among those who understood these things, because it had a way of tricking the viewer. At one angle, it seemed to be daytime; at another, night. From one perspective, the man seemed to smile; but at others, tears gleamed on his cheeks.

The man in the portrait and the artist who painted it were both unknown – hence the name of the work – but it had been established that it came from the Early Period. This fact, combined with the crown and the purple robes, led many to believe that it was the Lonely Strategist himself who stared out from the frame, in the days before he was butchered in his bed.

'General, you know, I've always thought that … never mind.'

'What is it?'

'Well …' Bandles shuffled on his feet. 'He looks like you, you know.'

Brandione cast another glance at the Lonely Strategist, or whoever it was. He sighed, and turned back to the servant.

'Is there still no sign of her?'

'Of her?'

'Brightling.'

'Oh, *her*. No, sir. No sign of her.'

Brandione looked around the hall, as if expecting Brightling to appear from behind a statue.

'But there are other Tacticians here, sir, if you are bored of my conversation and wish to engage with those at a higher level of station and intelligence.' Bandles said these words with no hint of self-pity. He had a deep and unshakeable faith in the genius of his superiors, and placed Brandione among their number.

Well, I suppose it couldn't hurt. Maybe they know something I don't, about this curfew and whatever else Brightling's up to.

'Very well, Bandles. Where are they?'

'Tactician Rangle always takes the White Rooms, General. The lord Grotius is in the Selection Suite.'

Chapter Thirty-three

Annara Rangle was dead, though no one could tell.

She went about her daily routine as normal. Avoiding detection was hardly difficult. All she had to do was sit in a study with a book, or play at a game of cards. Nobody knew what had become of her, not her servants, not the other Tacticians of the Overland, and not Garron Grinn.

But a new spirit danced within her.

The One is coming. The same words, over and over. *The One is coming.*

On the last day Garron Grinn came to see her. It was as if he knew this was the end.

'You have changed. I can see it. Is it because of the Selection?'

The creature in Rangle's body suddenly came to life. 'Selection?' it asked, in a passable imitation of the old Tactician.

'I suppose I mean the non-Selection.'

The Tactician laughed. 'There has been no Selection. Not yet. But there will be, soon. Oh yes, oh yes.'

Garron Grinn squinted. 'Tactician, are you all right? I don't understand what you mean.'

'We will make all of you understand.'

Garron Grinn stood. 'Madam, I came here to talk to you of the West. We must still take responsibility for it, you know. I have been up to my eyeballs, I can tell you, and no one will listen to me. The Watchers do not respect my authority. Not that they ever did.'

'You have no authority, oh no. None at all.'

The Administrator nodded. 'That is only the truth, madam. But they will still listen to *you*. I am sure of it.' He lowered his voice, his glance darting into the corners. 'You still rule in Watchfold. And who knows where you might be, after the Selection?'

At that Rangle laughed, and Garron Grinn stepped away, taken aback by the ferocity of it. The Tactician leapt to her feet and raised her right hand, palm open and pointed towards the Administrator.

'There is only one who will be Selected, fool. Do you not understand that? For how many years have you known of the Promise? And still you cling to your hopes that it is not broken, and that it will save you.' She went to the table and lifted a plate, then hurled it against a far wall, where it shattered into a dozen pieces. She pointed at the mess. 'That is now the *Machinery*.' And in an act that was more shocking still to Garron Grinn, Annara Rangle, Tactician of the West, spat on the floor.

The Administrator was a man of long experience, and there was not much in the world that surprised him. But now his eyes were wide, and his jaw hung slack.

'Tactician, you cannot be yourself. I wonder if I could—'

'You should leave. Immediately.'

Garron Grinn nodded.

'Good night, Tactician. I hope that you … feel well, soon.'

He walked to the door.

'Wait, you,' growled Rangle, before Garron Grinn could cross the threshold.

He turned to her, apprehensive.

'Are there any other Tacticians here?'

'Only Grotius, madam. He is staying in the Selection Suite, I believe.'

'Send him to me.'

The Administrator seemed unsure of this idea. 'He will not be happy to be disturbed, my lady. You know what he is like.'

'I said to send him to me, *idiot*.' She growled the words, and Garron Grinn looked at her with astonishment. 'This is no dream, fool,' she continued. 'I am not what you remember, and soon all the world will know about it, oh yes. Now *send Grotius to me*.'

Garron Grinn almost tripped as he fled from the room.

An hour passed, but still Grotius did not come.

She waited for him, watching a candle as it sputtered to its death. Eventually she stood, and left the White Rooms. She knew where Grotius would be.

She took the stairs of Memory Hall two at a time, skipping with a kind of childlike glee, until she found herself at an oak door. She tried the handle and was pleased to find it open. She stormed through a series of small rooms, each of them linked to the next by heavy gates, which had all thankfully been raised. *Some kind of defensive measure? Jandell, you do confuse me.*

Eventually she came out into a large hall, a place of clay and marble. A fire roared in a corner. Grotius sat in the centre of this room, at a table. He was slumped back in a chair, regarding her drunkenly. He wore a bloodied apron and held in his paws a jug of wine. Some kind of black sauce was smeared across his jowls, and sweat cascaded from his forehead.

'What do you want, you bitch?' He did not sound angry; perhaps this was just the way he and Rangle spoke to one another, in the days when there was a Rangle. His voice was heavy, his speech slurred. *What a glorious thing you made, Jandell, to Select such creatures as this to rule over your people.*

'I want to play a game,' Rangle said, approaching the table. 'All I have ever wanted to do is play games, oh yes. But Jandell stopped all that. Well, soon he will be gone forever, and the games will start again. Won't they? Hmm? Tell me they will.'

Grotius raised his eyebrows so high they seemed ready to leap from his fat head. 'What ... *by the Machinery* ... are you fucking talking about, you crazy fucking western whore?'

Rangle flashed him a savage smile, and he stood up from the table, backing away. He was beginning to realise that something was very wrong indeed.

'Your eyes are red,' said Grotius. 'Are you sick?'

'Oh, I am very well.' She scanned the room. 'But we still must play our game, Grotius. There must be a board of that game ...'

'Progress.'

Rangle clicked her fingers together. 'That's it! That's the one Jandell loves! Go and get it for me, like a good creature.'

Grotius disappeared into a corner, and then returned with a Progress board.

'Set it up, set it up. On the table.'

Grotius did as he was told. He was trembling, fearful. *Good.*

'Now take off that horrible apron,' she said.

He did as he was told. He wore a golden gown underneath: a Tactician's gown, like her own.

308

Rangle touched Grotius on the back of his head. He stood bold upright for a moment, and then slouched forward. She caught him and lowered him into the chair, as if he weighed no more than a small child. She went to the door in the corner and unlocked it, before returning to Grotius. She lifted a chair and placed it at the side, before she herself took a position at the opposite end of the table.

'We are expecting a third player,' she whispered. 'The Mother of Chaos herself. We must take her turns, while we wait.'

Grotius awoke. His eyes were now red, too. *Good.* He nodded, and they started to play their game.

'Oh,' whispered Rangle. 'I almost forgot. Take this, and place it somewhere within your gown.'

She slid a narrow blade across the table.

Chapter Thirty-four

The Tacticians were playing Progress.

Brandione had first gone to the White Rooms. There had been no sign of Rangle there, but a noise from above had drawn him to the Selection Suite, where Grotius stayed. This apartment was a honeycomb that led to a hall of red clay and black marble. There were no windows: the only light came from a large fireplace that was sunk into the wall. The hall had a suffocating atmosphere. There was a wooden door against one of the walls; it led to a balcony, Brandione knew, but was firmly closed. There was nothing to interrupt the monotony of the red and black: no paintings on the walls, no statues in the corners.

The focal point of the room was a smooth, red marble table, at either end of which sat Tacticians Grotius and Rangle. They were halfway through their game, from the look of the tiles. They stared at the squares with an odd sense of detachment.

'Tactician Rangle, Tactician Grotius.'

Brandione eased forward into the room, but neither Tactician acknowledged him. Rangle lifted a red Expansion tile and slid it into an eastern space. Brandione had not learned the latest iteration of the game, but unless the rules had changed, he could see the move placed Rangle in a powerful position. But the Tactician did not smile. She did nothing.

The General halted just before the table, standing over Grotius' shoulder. The obese Tactician clicked his tongue against his teeth three times in quick succession, then moved a white Watching tile into a western space. The General saw immediately that this was a bad move; it overextended his forces and exposed his eastern flank, where Rangle had placed her Expansion tile. She had strategically grouped her white tiles, while Grotius' were in a thin line from East to West, and therefore vulnerable.

'Tactician Grotius, you should have strengthened the West with Watching tiles,' Brandione whispered. 'She has moved into an Expansion footing there; you will fall. Do you have any Operator cards?'

Grotius did not respond: he just kept staring at the board. Tactician Rangle was motionless, too, though it was now her turn.

Brandione noticed then that the board had been set out for three players, with a host of black tiles of both Expansion and Watching grouped together in a menacing cluster. These were positioned in the northeast, just two spaces from Tactician Rangle's Expansion tiles. The General realised now why Grotius had moved his Watching tile to the West: he must be in alliance with this third player, who was protecting him from the North. But where was this other competitor?

'To the South, now, South,' Grotius whispered.

Rangle lifted one of the black Expansion tiles and moved it southwards. Brandione's confusion deepened. Were they playing together as this third person? There could be no other explanation. The move itself was strange; there was no

311

presence in the South of the board, and shifting the tile exposed both Rangle's forces in the West and Grotius' in the East.

'That was good,' said Rangle.

'A good move,' Grotius agreed.

'No,' Brandione interrupted. He felt light-headed. 'That move didn't make sense for either of you. It would only make sense if you had moved it on someone else's behalf. Now your East is exposed to Tactician Rangle, my lord Grotius. Your West is vulnerable, Tactician Rangle.'

The Tacticians looked at him for the first time. As they stared at the General, he saw that the eyes of both Tacticians held a red tinge, which seemed to expand and deepen until the pupils themselves disappeared, like stones in pools of blood. A balcony door swung open with a bang, and a gust of wind scattered the Progress tiles across the table. The Tacticians did not seem to notice.

'That was a good game,' said Rangle.

'Yes,' Grotius agreed.

A woman was in the room, now, sitting at the table in the empty chair, a white mask lying by her side. She was beautiful, her face as pale as a doll's, her hair a mass of red ringlets, her eyes green. He had seen her before, in a book in a museum in the Far Below. She smiled at the General: he wanted to run to her, to hold her, to feel the ringlets of hair in his fingers, and to stare into those eyes.

But he could not move.

'And then it happened,' she said, in a voice from a melody.

The Tacticians got to their feet, and each withdrew thin daggers from the depths of their gowns. Grotius walked around the table to Rangle's side. She smiled up at him and placed a hand gently on his elbow, before pulling back the dagger and thrusting it into his great gut. He did not resist, but simply grinned at the General, his gown turning as red as his eyes.

Brandione still could not move.

Rangle placed the blade carefully on the table, and blood dripped onto the Progress board. She turned to smile at Brandione as Grotius spun on his heel and tore out her throat with his dagger. She still smiled as she fell to the ground, her gore forming a pool on the black marble floor.

All the while, the woman in the green dress clapped and laughed.

Grotius staggered backwards, using the table for support and giggling as he lifted Rangle's blade. Ignoring the blood that poured from his ample frame, he turned his back on Brandione and hurled the knife through the open door and out onto the ground below. He spun back on Brandione and lobbed his own knife toward the General, where it landed at the younger man's feet. Then he fell forward, collapsing onto the corpse of Tactician Rangle.

'Why?' the General asked. 'Why are you doing this?'

The woman ignored this. 'Where are the other Tacticians?' she asked.

Brandione did not respond. Suddenly she was before him, the green eyes boring into his own.

'Where are the other Tacticians?'

'Far away from here. You cannot harm them.'

The green woman laughed. 'I will find them, in the end. It matters not.'

'Why are you doing this?' Realisation dawned. 'You murdered the Strategist.'

She giggled. 'I have not murdered anyone. I am just a weapon. My name is Shirkra. You have not heard of me?'

'No.'

'Everyone will, soon.' Shirkra sighed, and padded across the room, to stand by the balcony door.

'Why did you kill them?'

Shirkra laughed. 'Because Mother told me to. Everyone must obey their mother.'

There was a noise from the stairwell. Shirkra looked up in shock, as the door burst open to reveal Squatstout, running as fast as his little legs would carry him.

'*You*,' he said, when he saw Shirkra. 'I knew it was you. I have sensed you. Is it true that … does she live?'

Shirkra moved towards him, reaching out a hand. But she seemed to think better of it and turned to the balcony and fled the room. Squatstout said something in a strange tongue and followed her, disappearing into the night.

Brandione bent down to retrieve Grotius' blade. That was how they found him, standing above the corpses of the Tactician of the West and the Tactician of the North, a red dagger in his hand.

'Arrest the murderer.'

His last thought, as the Watchers fell upon him, was that the voice belonged to Tactician Brightling.

Chapter Thirty-five

'I didn't want this to happen, sir. I really didn't. I just wish you hadn't of been such a traitor to the Machinery.'

The blood had hardened on Brandione's face where they had beaten him. That had come as a surprise. He had assumed the Watchers would have more elegant forms of torture than kicking him around a dreary cell in the Bowels of the See House.

'Why'd you do it, General Brandione? All those Tacticians! I've never heard the like of it. Three of them! My word. And the Strategist!'

Farringer. Of all people to be with him, now, as he approached the end: Farringer.

'Did you think it would pick you, eh? Cause you killed them all? That's a strange thought, sir, a strange thought.'

The little man was leaning against the bars of Brandione's cage, looking triumphant. He was dressed in regal flummery, a golden doublet shining through his black cloak, an open silver helmet on his head. His garb contrasted starkly with the dirty rags that Brandione wore. Farringer seemed to relish the reversal in their stations.

'What about Canning, General? That's what I've been wondering about. You had him right there, in the palm of your hand. You were alone with him all the time. Why didn't you do him first? And oh, the poor boy. Brightling's told everyone about what you did to him. At least you poisoned him. At least he didn't die afraid.'

Brandione sat up in his cage, wincing. They were on a carriage, slowly being dragged forward by two of the sorriest horses Brandione had ever seen. The sun was high in the sky. *The South*.

'Farringer,' he said in a papery voice, 'where are we?'

'Where are we? Where do you think we are, sir? We are going where all Doubters go. They wanted you to have a military escort, before you were handed over to the gaoler. So I volunteered. Don't get any ideas, though. It's not just old Farringer here. There's more muscle, in the front.'

'No. Please, Farringer. There has been a terrible mistake.'

'They told me you'd say that, the Watchers.'

Brandione winced. 'When is the Selection? Has it happened yet?'

But before Farringer could respond, the General passed out against the bars of his cage.

'Where'd they catch you then, eh? Where'd they catch you?'

Brandione's eyes were wedged shut. He touched them with his fingers: sand. He was caked in it.

'You'll need water for that.'

And he had it, whether he wanted it or not, soaking the crown of his head and pouring down his face. He did not protest. On the contrary, he stuck out his tongue. When he had had his fill, and when the sand had been dispersed, he found he could open his eyes.

He was on a wooden cart, being dragged forward by a mangy horse, its progress barely discernible. The miserable beast uttered an occasional snort as it protested against the lashes of the driver – a silent, hunched figure clothed in black, his head hidden under a hood.

He was no longer in a cage, but it didn't matter. There was no escape, now. Sun. Sand. A burning heat. *This can only be one place.* The Wite.

The sand stretched away into the horizon, shifting endlessly in the scorching winds. The General felt a wave of panic. How long had he been asleep? Farringer was gone. He must have handed him over to these people.

Who is the Strategist, now?

But it did not matter, in the end. Not where he was going.

Brandione pulled himself up into a sitting position, wincing at the effort. There were four others on the cart. Three old men sat at the front, just behind the driver. They looked like they were together, wearing similar patrician robes and pulling at similar white beards: bureaucrats, most likely. They stared at their feet, morose. Brandione wondered how such men had ended up here. He wondered how he had, too.

Beside him was a woman: the giver of the water. She was old, too, but livelier than the men. She smiled at him, a toothy expression somewhere between a grin and a grimace. Curls of grey hair fell around her forehead, and she wore a battered red gown, punctured by holes that exposed cords of coarse wool wrapped around her sturdy legs.

'You were asleep for a long time,' she beamed. 'I poured some water down your neck, but I didn't think that would be enough. They didn't leave us with any food. Just the water.'

Brandione pushed himself up on his elbows. 'Thank you.'

The woman chuckled. 'You shouldn't be thanking anyone that keeps you alive: not where we're going, anyway. It might've been better to die.' She coughed. 'But we'd be best to just accept our fate.'

Brandione took another mouthful of water, slurping it down greedily. He could feel the pain in his throat begin to ease.

'Where are we going?'

The woman narrowed her eyes. 'You really don't know?' She laughed again. 'Good for you. I won't disabuse you of your ignorance. Anyhow.' She looked out to the rolling dunes and smiled. Brandione saw that she had the pale skin of a northerner, but it was weathered, red and raw.

'So where'd they catch you, then?' she asked.

'There's been a mistake. I'm not a Doubter.'

'Oh. I see.' The woman smiled at him.

They fell into silence. The only sounds were the wind on the sand, the creak of the wheels, the crack of the whip and the snorts of the horse.

A handful of low, wooden buildings had emerged on the horizon. There was something strange about this place; Brandione could feel it, weighing upon him.

'There's no point in worrying about it, my boy. We're in the Prison, now. We can't get away. No one has ever got away from the Prison, not once in ten thousand years.'

'There is only a driver here,' Brandione whispered. 'There are five of us – we could overpower him. I could do it myself. There are no guards!'

The woman threw back her head and laughed, a bark that echoed across the dunes.

The old men at the front looked up: Brandione caught a glimpse of frightened, watery eyes.

'Did you ever hear of anyone escaping from the Prison of the Doubters, my boy?'

Before long, they were in the midst of the buildings – low, wooden structures divided into clusters. Further along the road Brandione could just make out another batch, in the centre of which stood a squat stone tower. The tower was a dark thing, rippling with power in the sun. It reminded him of the See House, and he turned his gaze away from it.

The driver stopped at the fifth building along. It had nothing to distinguish it from the others they had passed. The windows were all shuttered, and no noise came from within.

'We must be here,' said the old woman.

She stood, brushed herself down, and climbed onto the sand. Brandione followed closely behind and the old men shuffled along in his wake. The door of the shack swung open, as if the sand had permitted them entry.

The old woman and the men went inside. Brandione followed, taking a last look at the departing cart before the door swung closed behind him.

The interior was almost as sparse as the desert: a wooden table in the centre of the room, with no chairs. A solitary candle had burned down to a stub. Along the walls were five wooden platforms, which Brandione took for their beds. His fellow prisoners spread out among them, and Brandione took the last remaining spot, next to the old woman.

The woman looked to the ground. For the first time, the General noticed that every surface was coated in fine sand, which swarmed across the floor, making patterns on the stone. He thought he could make out shapes there: faces, like those that danced across the Operator's cloak. But then the candle spluttered out.

'Goodnight,' said the woman. Brandione heard her turn over on her side.

The scream came, and then one was gone.

Brandione leapt to his feet; he had barely been asleep. He fell back against the wall, waving his arms before him to meet whatever had attacked them. Two of the other men were on their feet, too: one stood by the table in the centre of the room, his face covered by his arms. The other was also against a wall, staring forward. His breath came in sharp gasps.

The old woman was still lying on her bench. She looked serene.

'What happened?' Brandione asked.

The woman hardly looked at him. She brushed a strand of grey hair from her eye.

'There's no point in being afraid. Whatever will come will come.'

Brandione looked around the room. There was no blood, no body, and no sign that anyone had entered or exited the room. But there were now only four of them: two old men, the old woman, and himself.

It was only then that he saw the new candle on the table. It had been lit.

'You should keep your eyes closed,' the old woman said.

The sand was swirling on the floor, though there was no draft to move it.

It happened twice more: just the same way.

'Are we being executed? What is doing this to us?'

'I told you. It's best not to worry. Here, take this.'

She handed him a pinch of a red herb. He ate it, and fell into a black sleep.

He awoke to visions. Once, he thought three women sat before him. They were identical, and wore gowns that swirled like the sand in a storm. The sand fell from them, like a storm on the beach, cascading into the air until all three of them disappeared.

The old woman looked at him with a face full of sorrow. He told her about the dream.

When he next awoke Brandione was alone. Another new candle had appeared on the table.

He sat up on the wooden bench. The effects of the red herb were wearing off, and he felt light-headed. Where was the old woman?

His thoughts turned to the woman in the green dress. Who was she? Would she kill again? No one could stop her, now. Not even Brightling. *Maybe the new Strategist will be able to stop her. But maybe she* is *the new Strategist.*

He noticed movement on the ground. It was the sand. It was strange, that stuff, moving in patterns and shapes as if drawing pictures or spelling out words. He wondered if the red herb was still affecting him. Getting off the bench, he got down on his knees and scooped up some of the fine powder. It continued moving in his hand.

He dropped the sand back on the floor and watched as it merged together once again. As he stared, he was amused at the thought that faces were appearing there, swirling faces with curious eyes and open mouths. They were the women he had seen earlier, dark, imperious and beautiful. As they grew in clarity, he wondered at their glory: this could be no trick of the light, surely.

And then he was gone.

Chapter Thirty-six

The beach was cold.

The sand was black, and the sun was red. *Things never work the same down here.*

Katrina walked and walked, but the black dunes never changed. Even the waves of the ocean were repetitive, crashing methodically against the shore with no hint of nature.

On she went, along the beach, a dark sandpit that melted beneath her feet, billowing and flowing madly like the Operator's cloak. She grew frustrated. Occasionally she called out for Alexander, but her voice was muffled, and there was never any response: just the sound of the waves.

Eventually, something changed. Far ahead, below the line of dunes, she saw a spot on the horizon. Time seemed to hasten: the waves themselves crashed at a faster pace, and the sun seemed to leap up in the sky, as if it had been yanked forward on a chain.

Finally, Katrina reached the spot. It was a pile of brown and yellow rags, gathered in a heap below one of the black dunes.

'Alexander?' she asked.

The head of an old man leered out from the rags.

'How do you know Alexander?'

Katrina recognised the weary, leathery face before her, though she had not seen it for fifteen years.

'Amile. Is it you, or another nightmare?' But she already knew the answer.

'Everything real is created, somewhere along the line,' Amile said. The voice was his, but the words were not.

'It's strange to see you,' Katrina said. 'I haven't seen your face since Alexander was taken.'

'Alexander? How do you know Alexander?'

What is this? 'You know how, Amile. I am his sister, Katrina.'

Amile snorted. 'Alexander had no sister. Just a cuckoo in the nest.'

'The disappearance was not my fault, Amile.' Katrina knew this was not truly her old tutor, but she could not control herself. 'I couldn't have stopped the Operator. I tried to tell Brightling and the rest of them, but they didn't believe me. They thought I was lying.'

'Try,' Amile spat. 'Always try. Try, try, try, lie, lie, lie.'

Katrina turned from Amile, and continued along the beach. *I must resist these apparitions.* She wondered what Brightling would do in this situation. *She never would have found herself here. She would have arrested Shirkra, not followed her into madness.*

Another spot had appeared in the distance. A piece of furniture became slowly visible: a rocking chair, holding a woman Katrina recognised immediately.

'Grandmother.'

The old woman was as she had been on the night of the disappearance, a ball of satin and grey hair. A pair of watery eyes peaked out from beneath the material.

'Finally, you are here,' the old woman said. 'I thought you would never come.'

Katrina turned, staring along the beach. There was another dot on the horizon.

'Who is up there? What else is there to throw at me?'

Her grandmother ignored the question. 'You should not have come here. You should have stayed where you belong. But it is too late now.'

The Watcher turned back to the old woman. 'And where do I belong? Paprissi House? It is gone, grandmother. The See House? I'll never make a Watcher. Maybe I belong down here.'

'No,' grandmother said. The voice flickered briefly. 'There was peace, for a time. And now you are here, to ruin it. He will not be happy.'

'The Operator.'

Grandmother nodded.

'What are you, and that thing that looks like Amile?' She pointed along the beach. 'Did the Underland create you to torture me?'

The old woman shrugged. 'Who knows? How can you ask me what I am? Do you know what *you* are? Perhaps I am real, and you were created by the Underland.' She laughed, a rasp as dry as the black sand of the beach. 'Or maybe we both are. Maybe we all are! That would be a jape, wouldn't it?'

'It knows I am here, and has sent you all to punish me.'

The old woman shrugged. 'It might like having you here. It might think these nice images from home are just what you need. Or maybe it doesn't even know of your existence. It is very important, you know.'

Is there any use in talking to this thing? Am I learning anything?

I must try.

'You said the Operator doesn't belong down here. Does Shirkra belong down here?'

The creature in the satin shuffled around.

'Where did you hear that name?'

Katrina hesitated. 'The Operator told me about her,' she lied.

'The *Operator* told you about Shirkra? I find that hard to believe.'

'It is true.'

'You are a liar.'

'Who are you? You, and the rest of them – who are you, really?'

The grandmother creature smiled. 'Sparks of a dream, I suppose. Never mind.' Her expression hardened again. 'Is Shirkra here, among us?'

This is a waste of time. Katrina walked away from this false image of her grandmother, and carried on along the beach. She turned once, to find that no one was there.

The next dot on the horizon grew clearer in fitful jumps, until Katrina could just make out another person, waiting for her in the black sand. This one sat behind an ornate oak dressing table, its legs buried into the sand. She was female, with tangled knots of chestnut hair falling around her thin frame. Her face was lined and worn, though not old, and she was dressed in an intricate blue nightgown. She was a rich woman: her fingers were studded with golden rings, and she wore a silver necklace.

'Mother.'

The woman did not respond. Her eyes were glass balls that stared unblinkingly ahead.

'Can you hear me?' The Underland's artist had excelled himself this time. This was her mother, from the shape of her face to her slightly rigid posture.

Katrina stood in the same spot for a long time, wondering what to do. Brightling would not approve of any sentimentality over a figment of the Underland. But that did not matter now. The Watcher reached forward, and touched her mother's face.

For the briefest of moment the woman's eyes sparked into life; she looked at Katrina, confused, before smiling. But the moment vanished as soon as it had come. A wind whipped across the woman's face, which shifted like the sand on the beach. Dust flew into the air, taking the identity of Katrina's mother with it. The sand disappeared into the ocean, and Katrina was alone.

'They never last down here.'

Alexander was by her side.

'Where have you been?'

Alexander shrugged. 'Don't know. It doesn't matter anyway. It's all too late.'

'What?'

The boy looked out into the sand dunes. 'The Selection is upon us. The One has come, and will bring Ruin.'

'No. We can still stop it.'

Alexander smiled at her. 'No. No one could ever have stopped it. It was fate.'

'There is no such thing.'

'There is. It seemed to go away for a while, but now it's back.'

'I don't understand.' She took his hand in hers. 'Alexander, where is the Machinery? We must try to fix it. Do you understand me?'

Alexander pointed to the dunes. 'I think it was up there, once.'

'*Was?* Where has it gone?'

'It has fled, from the One. Not even Jandell can find it now. But it doesn't matter. It will not be able to hide from the One. Not for long.'

Katrina ran, then, in the direction of the dunes, where her brother had pointed. She did not know why. But she kept running, scrambling up the black slopes until she reached the top and stared down at the scene below.

Black sand, black sand, stretching on forever. There were dots in the distance: more creatures from her past. She did not want to meet them.

'I told you. It is gone.' Alexander had reappeared at her side. 'The Selection is over. But the One has come, and the Machinery will give her such powers, that none can prevent the coming of Ruin.'

'It cannot be. There must still be time.'

'No. There is no more time. In a way, Jandell was right. I did not tell him everything I knew.'

'What do you mean?'

'The One has returned. But I *know* who the One is. I only ever told father. He didn't believe me. He would never believe me.'

And then a new voice came.

'It is time. The powers of the Machinery are here, in the wind. It is breaking, and they have been released. I can feel them. It is time for the One to take them.'

Katrina turned to find Shirkra at her other side. The Operator was not wearing her mask.

'I have done such terrible things, such terrible things!' Shirkra cried. 'You must believe my devotion now! You must!'

Katrina staggered backwards.

'What are you talking about, Shirkra?'

Six thrones reared up from the sand, beautiful in the dark light of the beach. All of the Cabinet were there, with the Strategist in the centre. Kane, Rangle, Grotius and Bardon sat with their heads slumped forward. Blood fell from their lips, forming pools in the sand at their feet.

'What is this?' Katrina moved forward hesitantly. Canning and Brightling sat in the thrones at the very right. Their eyes were open, and they stared ahead. There was no blood upon them.

'Death,' said Shirkra. 'I have brought death, even to one that I loved. But two of the Tacticians yet live. Do you want me to find them now? Or should I wait?'

'Shirkra, you are mad. I don't want you to kill anyone.'

'But you already have. You already have. I was ever your weapon.'

Another voice spoke, then, through Katrina's mouth: an old voice that she knew well. A voice that had always been a part of her.

'You have done well, my child.'

Shirkra fell to her knees.

'You have cared for me, all these years.' Katrina felt herself move forward. Against her will, she reached out a hand and touched Shirkra's head. 'Everything you have done, you have done for me. You have brought your Chaos to Jandell's world. You have removed threats to our power. You have sewn disorder among our enemies. You will be rewarded.'

Who are you? asked the younger side of Katrina Paprissi. It was not yet dead, but it had grown weak, so very weak.

Alexander was at her side, his hand in hers.

'That's why it came to me, you see. It told me the One had returned, and it told me who it was. It thought I could stop you. I told father, but he wouldn't listen. But I wouldn't tell the Operator, no matter how much he tried. I wouldn't want him to hurt you. Did I do the right thing, sister?'

She smiled at her brother, though the smile was not her own.

Who are you? the younger part asked again, though now it was fading quickly, floating away like sand on the wind.

I am your guide. I am your friend and companion.
I am Mother.
I am the One.
I will bring Ruin.

Chapter Thirty-seven

Aranfal had a bird's-eye view of the end of the world.

Most citizens thought the Strategist's chair was the highest point in the Circus. They were wrong. It was certainly the most elevated spot that one could reach with any degree of safety. But there were other places, far above the throng. The Watcher could now be found on one such spot, a block of marble that protruded from the base of an Operator statue. This one depicted Jandell – if that was truly his name – at his most sorrowful, his head resting in his hands and his shoulders slumped. To Aranfal, the Operator seemed miserable in every representation.

Not that he was any better. He had spoken to no one since Squatstout had left.

It was cool up here, at the base of the statue. The wind howled at him, pecking at his cloak. It made a welcome change for this son of the North; to a child of the Centre, like Katrina Paprissi, it would probably have been unbearably cold.

Katrina Paprissi. The name made him shiver. All the threads in this tapestry could be drawn back to her. He could feel it. *What have you done, you fucking brat?*

The Selection was upon them. *Ruin will come with the One.* Well, if it was coming, they would find out today. And it seemed that all the world had come to view the party. He had never seen the Circus so crowded. In the distance he could make out the Tacticians' dais, where she sat, the star of the West who cast her cold light across the world: Brightling. Aranfal felt a sense of trepidation when he looked upon her. They said she had arrested Brandione; she had caught him in the act of killing two more Tacticians. But Aranfal did not believe it. Squatstout had laughed at him, when he revealed his suspicions. He hoped the little man was right.

The Watcher chastised himself for these maudlin thoughts and turned his attention to the centre of the Circus. The Announcer was standing on his plinth by the Portal, awaiting the flame and the piece of parchment that would reveal the identity of the new Strategist. The second Lonely Strategist in history. *I'd better get down there, in case it's me.* He smiled. *That would show Aleah.*

But something was wrong, down below. He could sense it in the body language of the Announcer, as he climbed down from the plinth and hunched over that black hole in all his finery. He could feel a tremble in the crowd.

It should have happened by now.

Tactician Brightling left her spot on the dais and descended the steps to stand at the Announcer's side. Something spoke to Aranfal, and he never would know if it came from his own mind, or from another place.

Go to her.

He moved quickly. Something told him to avoid the steps, and so he scaled the walls of the Circus like a spider.

And then the flames came.

He stopped where he was, halfway up the building, and craned his head around. The fire spewed from the Portal like it had always done, but something about it was different; it burned with a strange intensity, a fierce, elemental power. The Announcer and Brightling fled before it, the Tactician towards the steps, back to the dais.

The flames died, and a woman stood before the Portal. No: she stood *on* the Portal. The entrance to the Underland had closed. She was instantly familiar: the pale skin, the black hair, the rags. But now the rags were Strategist purple, and the eyes burned with the same colour.

By her side, from nowhere, another woman had appeared. She wore a green dress and a white mask, the one that Squatstout had shown Aranfal in a painting in the Hall of Masks. This mask was more powerful than any Aranfal had seen. It seemed to shift as he looked upon it, like it was another face: a second skin.

Katrina Paprissi raised her hands to the air, and the crowd surged forward. She flicked a finger, and at the southern side of the stadium, a statue of Jandell crumbled to dust. She shouted something, and the other statues fell, collapsing into the Circus in mounds of marble, crushing dozens of the Strategist's new subjects.

Aranfal knew, then. He saw clearly, for the first time, what he had always sensed in the Watcher.

Ruin will come with Katrina Paprissi.

He found Brightling standing on a broken segment of Jandell's head.

She was by the eastern entrance. Thousands of citizens poured through, streaming forward to their new Strategist. There was something inhuman in the way they moved, like insects crawling over a rotting carcass. They clambered over one another, ignoring the bodies at their feet, their eyes burning.

Brightling stood alone, a circle of calm. Aranfal climbed the rubble and took a position to her right, where he had stood so many times before.

'What is happening?'

At first he wondered if she had heard him. Eventually, however, she turned to him, and broke into a mirthless grin.

'Don't you know?' she asked, her voice hoarse. 'We have a new Strategist.' She pointed ahead.

'Katrina Paprissi.'

'No,' came a new voice.

Aranfal and Brightling turned as one. The voice came from a doorway in the Circus wall, where a figure stood, his face hidden behind a hood.

'It is you,' Brightling whispered.

Aranfal looked from the Tactician to the new arrival. Once again, he felt the weight of his ignorance. 'I don't understand,' he said.

The figure lifted a hand and beckoned them forward. The door closed behind them, and a torch burst into life high upon the wall, though no one was there to light it.

The figure removed his hood.

'That creature may have once been Katrina Paprissi, but she is Katrina Paprissi no more.'

'Operator,' Aranfal said, and fell to his knees.

'Stand,' said the old man. 'There is no time. We must move quickly, before she knows we are here.'

The voice was strong, youthful, so at odds with the ancient creature that stood before them.

'Amyllia, I have failed you all,' the Operator said. He reached out and stroked the Tactician's face with the side of a bony hand. Aranfal was shocked to see her eyes moisten. 'I have sat in the darkness for so long, and could not tell truth from fantasy. Do you understand?'

Brightling nodded. It seemed like she was about to speak, but the Operator silenced her with a gesture.

'It is true,' the Operator said. 'The Machinery is breaking, though it is not truly broken yet, I feel. It has Selected *her*; I should have seen this from the start. But I thought I had killed her. What a fool! Who else could bring Ruin but her? And now, look at what she has wrought. She has used Shirkra as her tool. She has set about killing her rivals, and thrown us all into disorder. That has always been her way, since the beginning of everything, and still I failed to see her.'

The Operator sighed, and stared at the stone floor.

'There is so much I do not know. I do not know where she has been hiding. I do not know if any allies remain that can help us.'

He looked up.

'But I know someone who does. Someone who watches everything.'

No. He cannot mean …

'Operator,' Aranfal said, 'if you mean Squatstout, I am afraid he has been with me for some time, but now he has gone.'

The Operator smiled at Aranfal, a thing of such glowing warmth that the Watcher felt all his fear slide away. 'I know where he is gone. He will be expecting us.'

He turned to the Tactician.

'Amyllia, you are not safe here. The Strategist will come for you, now, and Canning. Do you remember I told you once about my toy, far in the North?'

Brightling nodded. The Operator put his arm around her, and whispered something into her ear. She nodded again, and the Operator smiled, before turning to Aranfal.

'Do you know my name then, Aranfal?'

Aranfal nodded. 'You are Jandell.'

'I am. Jandell the Bleak, Jandell the Wise, Jandell the Fool.' The Operator laughed, though there was no humour to it. 'I will see you before long, Brightling.'

The Operator turned to Aranfal. 'As for you, Watcher – you must stay here.'

Aranfal bowed, though he was uneasy. 'Watcher, this new Strategist—'

'We will need someone here to watch things for us,' said Jandell. 'Free Canning, if you can. She won't kill him right away. Not now. She'll savour it. Try to blunt the edges of whatever cruelties she has in store, her and Shirkra. We will see you again, I hope.'

Aranfal bowed again.

'Operator, I will stay, but please—'

'You have a question.'

'Yes.'

'You wonder who is your new Strategist, if not Katrina Paprissi.'

'Yes.'

The Operator seemed to think about his answer, or whether he should answer at all. But he quickly gave in, and nodded.

'She is my mother.'

Chapter Thirty-eight

Brandione stood before the tower.

He had seen this place when he had first arrived in the Prison. It had been in the distance then, standing out like a wounded thumb amid the low, wooden buildings that housed the prisoners. It looked different now, its yellow, blasted walls giving off something of a regal air. A blackened hole served as a door, and the wind howled through it.

The sun was rising on the horizon, casting its merciless heat across the battered desert.

He studied his surroundings. A narrow path led from the tower to the wooden buildings where he had been kept, then on out into the Wite itself. He was sure he could walk that path without being stopped. But that was no escape. The Machinery knew where the next town was – probably as far away from here as possible.

The General turned back to the tower. He had no choice. All other directions led to death.

He entered, and was immersed in blackness so complete that the contrast with the desert outside hurt his eyes. Feeling his way around, he established that he was at the end of a narrow corridor, which led away to the right.

'Come,' said a female voice, somewhere up ahead.

Brandione hesitated. But there was nothing else for it. Slowly, he crept along the corridor. As he went, he noticed the emergence of a cold light, like a reflection on water. It did not so much give him hope as increase his sense of dread. Eventually he felt a wall before him. The dull light came from a door to his left, glowing from chinks and holes in the surface.

'Come,' the voice said again. It was behind the door.

Brandione entered, immediately covering his eyes with an arm. It was so bright in here that he briefly wondered if he had returned to the desert. But when he was able to look again, he saw that he was wrong.

The room before him was as large as the People's Level of Memory Hall. Brandione wondered how it could possibly fit within the dimensions of the small tower he had seen from the desert: perhaps some trick of the light. Five long, narrow windows divided the back wall of the room, and the sun poured through them. There was no glass in these windows, thank the Machinery: they were merely holes in the wall, like the door to the tower itself.

It seemed as if no one had been here for a very long time. Every surface was covered in dust, fine sand of the kind he had seen dancing around in his cell. It swirled around the floor, driven by some manic breeze he could neither feel nor hear.

He walked into the room and the heat struck him like a wall. The clay burned through his leather shoes, as if they were nothing more than thin sandals.

He walked the length and breadth of the room, a process that took some considerable time. He stared into the corners, and scoured the ceiling. But there was nothing.

Eventually his gaze fell on three mounds of sand, which had gathered before the central window, at the back of the hall. *Strange. I did not notice these before.* He approached them, and reached a hand out to search inside. But something about that sand frightened him, and he withdrew. Eventually he grew tired of searching. *I am either in a nightmare, or someone is playing a trick on me.* He did not relish either possibility, and decided to leave, turning his back upon the mounds and walking back to the door, hoping as he went that the voice would not return.

'Do not leave,' came the voice, dashing his hopes.

Brandione turned back to the room.

'Are you hiding in the sand?'

There was a pause. 'No.'

'There is nowhere else you could be. Unless you are in another room, and throwing your voice here. I've seen magicians do that, in the market.'

Another pause. 'I am not a market magician.'

Brandione stepped forward. 'I've never heard of a market magician who lived in a tower in a prison in the middle of the desert, that's for sure.'

'I am not a market magician.'

Brandione was about to speak again, but his attention was suddenly diverted.

'How are you doing that?'

The mounds were changing. The dust piles melted away, swirling into strange shapes, like the sand he had seen on the cell floor. *No. That's wrong. It's not melting away. It's becoming something else.*

Three women sat before him, born of the sand.

They were identical in every way. Their bodies were long, somehow stretched and contorted to three times the size of a normal person. Their features were in constant flux, flowing like the sand in the wind, so that he only caught glimpses of dark eyes and red mouths. Lengthy grey robes fell from their thin frames, swathing them entirely, and on their heads they wore spiked crowns of glass. They were three aspects of the same being: one creature that sat on three grey thrones of swirling dust.

'I am not a market magician,' the three women said with one voice.

The General stepped forward, his fists clenched. 'Who are you?'

The women – no, the *woman* – laughed. 'I have had different names. More recently, people have called me the Dust Queen.'

A young man appeared at the Queen's side, from nowhere. He looked like something from a court painting of the Early Period. He was black, his hair woven into tight braids and interwoven with colourful cloth, and he wore a short, velvet jacket over a flowery white shirt, which was stuffed tightly into dark hempen trousers.

'Is this him, madam?'

The Dust Queen swirled into sand, and surrounded Brandione. It seemed to move *through* him; all his memories were coated with it, and all of his being was infested. He did not try to resist. There was no resisting her.

The Dust Queen reformed, and the three faces beamed at Brandione.

'I have waited for you for ten thousand years,' she said. 'You are the Last Doubter.'

'I am not a Doubter.'

'You are the Last Doubter. You are a soldier, and a scholar. You are a man of many parts.'

She swirled into dust, and vanished through the windows.

'Come, General,' said the man with a smile. 'Come and see what the Queen has for you. She has prepared it now for ten millennia, and she is *so happy* to finally be able to use it.'

'Who are you?'

'Oh, me? I am the Queen's courtier. She made me, long ago, to be her companion and while away the long centuries until you came. My name is Wayward.'

He bowed deeply, then walked to the General and took his arm, guiding him to the window. They climbed through onto a balcony, where the Dust Queen had reformed.

'My army,' the Queen said. 'My army, for you to command.'

The people stretched away for miles, hundreds of thousands upon hundreds of thousands, right to the horizon. They were as pale as the Dust Queen herself: from what Brandione could tell, they were formed of sand, too, swathed in yellow cloaks. Each wore a glass helmet and carried a glass spear, and each stared up at the Dust Queen with dead eyes. There were men, women, and children: a vast army of the desert.

'Hail!' they cried as one, as the Dust Queen raised her arms. 'Hail!'

'They are calling to you, my General!' the Dust Queen cried. 'Are you pleased with them?'

The General nodded. He did not know what else to do.

Wayward leaned into him, and whispered in his ear.

'General, honestly. This is going to be *such fun*!'

Chapter Thirty-nine

She awoke in flame in the Circus.

What Circus? What land? The old land. Back! It is done!

She drank in the scene. A throng, ready to play.

Alone, but surrounded with these people.

She looked. To her side, one daughter: Shirkra, unmasked.

I knew you would be here, at the beginning of the end. You have done well.

She felt, and saw. Robes – rags – purple rags.

Mourning. This is no time to mourn.

She laughed. It was finally over.

I will bring Ruin.

Chapter Forty

Tactician Brightling sat on the Bony Shore, her mask in her hand.

She never used this thing. Not if she could help it. It had too much power; it made her skin crawl to look at it, and it had been made for her. But now, she was glad of it. It made her feel safe.

It had the features of a woman, in this moment, her own features, framed around open eyes and a wide mouth. But when she turned it in the sun, or when a shadow fell upon it, it seemed to change its very essence, becoming something else; a man, a child, sometimes even an animal. No other mask did this.

It had been many years now, since the Operator had given it to her. He had made this one himself, he had told her. He had made it for her, from a substance that was not of the Overland or the Underland. It stared up at her, utterly black, like a void. She despaired, when she looked upon it. The Operator called it a Mask of Absence, and she knew what he had meant. To look upon it was to lose one's sense of self; it sucked at the viewer, like a leech. She had only used it occasionally, when she was an active Watcher. She had seen into the souls of her subjects with such a terrible clarity that she felt as if she were taking them over, scraping out their very being and devouring it.

And so she never used it, unless she was forced to. Perhaps it helped explain why she had grown into the Watcher that she was. She had never relied on her mask, as so many others did. She had grown to rely on herself.

And what are you now? A Watcher?

She turned, and looked at the great fortress behind her. Northern Blown. This was where it had all started, the madness of recent times. *No. It started long before that. It started ten thousand years ago, though the Operator did not believe it.*

She had been tempted to stay in there, within the castle, when she had first come here. But she decided against it. There was no telling who lived in there, and what side they were on. That being said, she had seen nobody else on the road to the North, though she had kept herself well hidden. The country was empty, and it seemed that no one had been sent to find her. She felt somewhat offended by that.

This, then, is how it ends. These could be your last moments on the Overland, and you're spending them in this place. She thought of Charls Brandione, in the Prison of the Doubters. *He must be dead, by now.* She thought of all the others she had humiliated, and crushed, and undermined. She thought of Timmon Canning. She had made him into what he was. She had taken his spirit from him, over the years. It had been easy.

But one thought dominated. The image of a girl, in rags.

You failed her. You must have failed her. It is your fault. No matter what the Operator says, it is all your fault.

She looked at the mask again, and came to a decision. *When this is done, I'll make it right. For everyone. I'll make it right.*

And then she saw it, on the water.

The ship was narrow, sleek, and entirely black, from its prow to its sails. Standing on the deck was a figure she knew better than any other.

She stood, and waded out into the water, to join the Operator on his vessel.

Chapter Forty-one

'What time will it begin tonight, Samyel?'

'Soon, mother. You need to get ready.'

'Oh, I'm not interested in that stuff, my petal. That's grim stuff.'

'You shouldn't say things like that, mother.'

'Ha! Why not? Will you report me to Lord Squatstout, my petal, will you my love?'

'Mother!'

She shrugged and laughed, but soon collapsed into a coughing fit. She had grown worse; Samyel was sure of it.

'Mother,' he said, placing his hand on her hunched shoulders. 'Are you well?'

'Ha! Yes my lamb, yes!'

She stood from the kitchen table, supporting her chubby frame with a stick and wincing. 'Well, you've only got a couple of minutes to get there, Samyel. Off you go.'

Samyel nodded and leapt up from the table, almost hitting his head on the low ceiling of their hovel. He grabbed a ragged brown cloak from the doorway and launched himself outside, turning to wave to his mother as he went.

It was a grey day, as usual. The sky was a granite slab, the rain its grim debris. Unnamed Street, where the family lived, was really no more than a dirt track in this weather, flanked on each side by hunched little wooden houses, from the doors of which came cruel smells. Most of the population had already gone to the Choosing, so the street was empty. The boy would almost have preferred to have the inhabitants there, despite their strange and unsavoury ways.

Samyel stared at the road ahead and whistled through his teeth; he had not climbed in weeks. From here, the city wound upwards through the miserable shacks of the Lower Third. The Habitation was built on a rock that protruded through the centre of the island like a ragged bone, divided into sections that were called Thirds, though there were five of them. It was difficult to climb, each Third reachable only by scrabbling along the steep, sheer road. Samyel was well used to this journey, however, and while he did not relish the effort, it was not long until he reached the Middle Third, where the rich people lived. An old woman with leathery skin poked her face out from the window of a golden palace and glared down at him, shooing him along.

The crowds grew thicker as he got higher. *It might have begun already*. Not that it mattered. He had seen eight Choosings, now, and could remember at least three of them. The first bits were boring: just ceremony. The really important part came at the end. He was sure he would be there in time for that.

At last, after thirty or forty minutes of climbing, he reached the top of the rock. The Higher Third was a pulsating throng, a crowd of sweaty excitement, of varying ages and types, from Lower Children like himself to Middler merchants in sealskin cloaks and Administrators in silver chains. This was literally the peak of Habitation existence. Samyel immersed himself in the multitude, threading his way through the legs of older islanders to reach the front of the crowd. A man behind cuffed the back of his head. Samyel didn't know why, and didn't care, either.

Ahead of him, perhaps fifteen paces away, was the edge of the cliff. Torches had been erected at equal intervals among the crowd, casting an orange glow onto the faces of the onlookers. Far below, Samyel could hear the crashing of the waves of the Endless Ocean, and felt himself shake with anticipation.

'Sammy!'

He turned to see his sister, Ellyssa. At thirteen, she was five years older than him, so was tall enough to watch the Choosing from three rows back. Others were jostling around in front of her, jockeying for a better position, but she ignored them. She was the image of her brother, with her red curls and pasty skin.

'Where's mama?' she asked.

'She's got the cough again,' Samyel shouted back. 'Where are the Unchosen?'

'The Guards haven't come out yet. Wait, there they are now!'

Sammy turned to see the Guards in front of him. He shivered; he did not like these people. No one knew who they were, but it was said they were picked at birth. They were covered from head to foot in chainmail that clanked as they moved, overhung with short, dark green cloaks. On their heads they wore wide-brimmed hats. Their faces were covered by metallic masks with long, beak-like noses. They held long pikes in their hands, twice as tall as a man. They were like monstrous hybrids of men and birds.

'Bring them out,' called one of the Guards. His beak was gold, and he spoke just like Sammy's headmaster Luvus. *Could it be him?* It was possible.

There was a cave, just below the very peak of the rock, where the road came to an end. The Guards filed up to it one after the other, walking stiffly, before disappearing into the dark. After a few moments they returned, each dragging along a man or woman. These were the Unchosen. Their faces were downcast in misery, their bodies clothed in filthy brown rags. They were all of them broken creatures, who had to be physically pulled to the edge of the cliff by the Guards.

Sammy spat at them as they passed, but he could not reach. Perhaps next year.

'So, no one was Chosen this time,' said his sister. 'All Unchosen again.'

'No one's ever Chosen,' said Samyel. 'No one's ever good enough.'

'All bow for Lord Squatstout,' called a Guard.

The crowd fell to its knees as the saviour of their land, the Lord of the Habitation, emerged.

He was, as his name implied, a small creature, round and tough. As ever, he wore his coarse hareskin shawl, the sign that he was a man of the people. He was nothing of the sort, despite his appearance. He was the Autocrat, he had told them: the last of his kind; the only survivor of a group of higher beings.

Lord Squatstout walked to the cliff's edge and faced the crowd, his back to the Guards and the Unchosen. He closed his eyes and bowed his head. As if in response, the rain intensified, forming great grey curtains across the lightning-scorched sky while thunder beat a constant drum. The populace were soaked through, but that could not dampen their enthusiasm. Even the water falling from the dark sky seemed to avoid Squatstout; perhaps it held him in the same awe as his subjects did.

'These are the Unchosen,' he said, his voice booming among them. 'Ten thousand years ago, I came to this place, and I heard the Voice.'

The people murmured together: 'All hail the Voice.'

'I heard the Voice, at the top of this rock,' Squatstout continued. Everyone knew these words by heart. 'The Voice is a mighty thing, but it must have a body of its own.'

'A body of its own,' the people said.

Squatstout waved a hand at the Unchosen. 'The Voice saw fit to test these people, but none of them were found worthy. And so they are Unchosen, and we must wash our hands of their shame.'

'Wash our hands of their shame,' they said.

Lord Squatstout raised his arms to the sky.

'Let them fall.'

The Guards raised their pikes into the air in a single, sweeping motion.

The people cheered.

The Guards turned to face the Unchosen.

The people laughed.

The Unchosen screamed.

After it was done, and the Unchosen had disappeared, a guttural, grinding noise rumbled from the populace, like the movements of some machine.

'Sammy!' Elyssa was at his side. 'What's that?'

Samyel, still smiling, tore his eyes from Lord Squatstout. 'I see nothing,' he said.

'Out there. There's something on the water.'

Samyel looked to sea.

'It's too dark—'

There came a crack of lightning, and he saw it, cast in searing blue light. There was indeed something on the water, like a bloated, black cousin of one of the fishing ships they used in the Lower Third.

'It is a floating house, Elyssa.' Samyel said.

'It is,' said Elyssa.

It was coming for the island.

Acknowledgements

I had the idea for *The Machinery* in 2008, and since then it's been through too many drafts to count. I've spent endless mornings staring at a computer screen and chewing over the plot, killing off characters and obsessing over every sentence. I could have kept redrafting for another seven years, so I hope you enjoyed this version.

I'd like to say a huge thanks to Harper *Voyager* UK, particularly Natasha Bardon, who was the first person to give *The Machinery* a chance, and Rachel Winterbottom, who edited it with great skill, patience and understanding. Thanks also to my brilliant agent, Ed Wilson of Johnson & Alcock, who has been an amazing guide through the publishing world.

My friend Eamonn Bell read this book in its early incarnations, and steered me away from some of my more insane ideas. I am also massively grateful to Celine Kelly, whose advice has been invaluable throughout.

My parents, Marie and Ronnie, have encouraged me in everything I've done since I was a child. They have built up and underpinned my confidence right from my earliest poems about witches and ghosts, and this wouldn't have happened without them.

Most of all, I would like to thank my wife, Sarah. She has shouldered more than her fair share of family duties while I wrestled with this book, and has always been there with an encouraging word when I needed it.

Finally, thanks to you for reading *The Machinery*! Please do leave a review somewhere, and I hope you will join me again for Book Two, *The Strategist*.